Sword Of Trust

Winds of Change Series

This book is dedicated to my father—a man who gave me a wonderful role model to find a husband—and to my mother, a woman who found strength when trials came her way. I count myself blessed.

Sword of Trust
Winds of Change

Published by Wakefield Press

ISBN: 978-1-955080-00-2
E-Version ISBN: 978-1-955080-01-9

All Scripture is taken from the King James Version of the Bible.

This book is a work of fiction. Names, characters, places, incidents, and dialogues are either products of the author's imagination or used fictitiously. Any resemblance to actual people, organizations, and/or events is purely coincidental and is unintentional by the author.

Edited by:
Louise Gouge https://louisemgougeauthor.blogspot.com/

Cover Design by:
Kim Killion Cover Design of The Killion Group, Inc.
www.TheKillionGroupInc.com

Acknowledgements

Books are the efforts of so many people and this book is no exception. I always want to give God the glory first and foremost as He gave me the desire in my heart to write and the story to put on paper. He is my Rock and my Comfort.

I want to thank my wonderful husband who was the first person to encourage me to write a book. He always encourages me and believes in me. Thank you, Joe. I love you always and forever!

I'd like to thank Kathleen L. Maher who once again saw this story as all my stories in its raw and unpolished form and fell in love with it. She has walked every step of this road with me, critiquing Sword of Trust. Her insight has been invaluable and her friendship irreplaceable. I'm so thankful God put us together. My life is richer because of it. Thank you, dear friend. You'll never know the impact you've made.

A HUGE thank you to my English friend, Joanne. You have been a godsend. When I couldn't find answers to my questions you were always there to respond and put me back on track, looked things up and discussed problems I encountered. I just cannot say thank you enough for keeping my history straight! God bless you!

Thank you to the ladies of my street team who help me get the word out about my new books. You ladies are amazing!

A special thank you to my beta readers, Jessica Alvarado, Lynda Edwards, Amber Ludwig, and Connie Ruggles. Your eagle eyes for errors are a huge blessing.

Thank you to Louise Gouge, my amazing editor. I so appreciate you!

Lastly, as always, I want to thank my family who stood by me, cheered me on, and believed in me. You'll never know how much that means to me.

Endorsements

Be transported to the age of knights, castles, kings and lords with this action-packed and page-turning romance. Bryce Warwick is back, and he steals the stage with twice the conflict, twice the intrigue, and twice the chemistry of his younger brother Royce. Debbie Lynne Costello's skill with plot twists and unforgettable characters will enchant you and inspire you with an uplifting tale well told. Whether you're a faithful fan or new, you will fall in love anew with this fresh message of trust against all odds. –Award Winning Author **Kathleen L. Maher**

Debbie Lynne Costello writes about medieval times in a way that makes them feel contemporary. Her characters leap off the pages and embed themselves in your mind and heart so that you care about what happens to them! –**Connie R.,** Reader, Reviewer, Beta Reader

A broken trust is a difficult thing to mend.
What an incredible treat to read! I found myself setting it aside for a few moments just to gather my thoughts - and perhaps because I was a little worried about how some of the characters were going to survive to tell the tale. The author has a masterful way of drawing you into the story, so much so, that you most certainly champion some of these unforgettable characters over others. –**Betti Mace,** Avid Reader, Reviewer

Beautiful prose immersed me in the story from the start, transporting me to another time and place. I loved the blend of romance, humor, and adventure, giving me a new favorite book by this author! –**Lynda Edwards**, Reader, Reviewer, Beta Reader

I love the authentic feel of Debbie Lynne's Winds of Change Series. The characters are vibrant, the scenery lush, and the vernacular enjoyable. 'Tis no small task to bring to life a forgotten era. I am anxiously awaiting with great anticipation of another! –**Amber Ludwig,** writer and editor at The Grammar Princess.

My heart raced in rhythm to the horse's hooves as they dashed in and out of danger. Debbie held me captive 'til the very end of this medieval novel where mistrust abides with every clang of a sword. –**Jessy D'Alvarado,** Reader, Reviewer, Beta Reader

Debbie Lynne Costello has populated her story with wonderful, believable characters and a plot that had me boning up on my British history! Costello keeps her readers on the edge of their seats as we watch the border fractions and the cutthroat actions common during that time period. I love it when an author writes in such a way that I feel connected to their characters and I did here. Even secondary characters. And pets, one a very unusual one, but you'll have to read the book to find out how unusual. Well done! Highly recommended. –**Susan Snodgrass,** Avid Reader and Reviewer

Complete with all the medieval details, charm and wonderfully strong characters, this book has it all. Secrets, betrayal, forgiveness and trust… It's a book you want to read to the end, but yet, never want it to end! –**Sunnie Reviews**

Glossary

Aboot – about
Aftermete – part of the day that follows the noon meal.
Anon – Soon
Atilliator – someone who makes bows, arrows, and other archery equipment
Bailey – an open area inside the castle complex that contained the domestic and other necessary buildings of castle life. An inner bailey was laid in an area inside the main castle and its safety, while the outer bailey was outside the main castle defenses, making it more vulnerable should there be an attack.
Bailiff – someone who oversaw buildings and lands of the manor. They collected rents as well as fines and kept records of money
Bloodlust – strong desire to kill
Bolt hole – a hidden door in a castle used for escape
Burgh – village under the protection of a castle
Caitiff – wicked man
Chemise – long, loose undergarment for women
Curtain Wall – a fortified wall around the castle
Dais – raised platform
Dearling – endearing term such as darling
Demesne – part of the estate of the lord of the manor for his own use and support and often subleased
Destrier – warhorse
Dinna – do not
Fash – worry
Fortnight – 14 days
Grammercy – thank you
Great Hall – multi-purpose room where meals were taken, guests received, business conducted, and even used as sleeping quarters when needed
Gyngerbrede – Honey and Ginger flavored sweets

Hauberk – long tunic made of chain mail used for protection
Hoodwinked – deceived or duped
Hosen – men's woolen pants
Ken – know
Kent – knew
Keep – fortified tower in the castle
Laird – Scottish word for lord
Larder – a large room used for storing food prior to use
Lying in – period of confinement during pregnancy
Mantle – a lush cloak that would be fastened in front by a large brooch, buckle, or pin
Master-at-Arms – the man responsible for the training of soldiers at a specific castle
Melee – medieval battle
Mews – housing for falcons and hawks
Milaird – Scottish version of milord or my lord
No' – not
Numptie – idiot
Oot – out
Pater – father
Plait – a braid or plait of hair
Prithee – please
Reiving – the act of rustling, stealing, and plundering
Reivers – cattle-rustlers, plundering
Sennight – 7 days
Solar – private sitting room often found above the main floor and used by family and close friends. Solars could be connected to bedrooms.
Squire – shield-bearer or armour-bearer to the knight. Squires are promoted from the rank of page at about the age of thirteen or fourteen, they were then trained further in knightly pursuits. The squire was a candidate for the honor of knighthood and learned from the knight he served by performing any tasks that the knight might require.
Steward – a servant who oversaw the lord's household and estate

Surcoat – cloth dress that covers an underdress. Surcoats were also made of leather and worn over armor during heraldry. They might display the coat of arms.

Tae – to

Trencher – trenchers were used to serve and eat food, much like modern day plates. Stale loaves of bread (or stale crusts of bread) were used to soak up food and eat it. Leftover pieces from trenchers were often given to the dogs or distributed to the poor as alms.

Troth – promise

Tunic – the medieval equivalent of a shirt. A tunic was usually longer and looser than a modern shirt.

Villein – a tenant who paid dues and/or services to his lord in return for land

Ward – another word for bailey

Wimple – headdress

Yer – your

Yestereve – refers to last evening

Yesternight – refers to last night

Chapter 1

Cumberland, England
January 1399

A black crow flew out from the green leaves of a tree branch as Deirdre Mackenzie passed by. It was a bad omen. But it was too late to turn back now. Besides, the most dangerous part was behind them. She and the young men from the *burgh,* as well as Walter, a man in middle age, managed to slip over to the wretched English land and gather eight cows without a dog even lifting its head, let alone sending an alarm out to farmers—or worse, knights on watch duty.

She attempted to shrug off the ill feeling the bird brought, but instead a shudder racked her body, a confirmation she'd made a grave error in her choice to come out this night. The clouds parted and a bright moon threw its light onto their path.

"Nay," she whispered under her breath. She'd made no mistake.

She let out a sigh in an attempt to release the tension knotting the muscles in her neck. Gilbert, a round-faced lad who had the misfortune of growing very little facial hair, steered his horse into the woods to bring a wayward cow back to the herd.

The chill in the air bit through her *mantle, tunic,* and hose. She shivered. Patrik had offered his heavier mantle, but she'd refused. Though the tallest in the group, he had no meat on his bones with which to keep warm. He needed his mantle more.

The cow that Gilbert guided back to the herd lowed, protesting its compliance and breaking the silence of the night. The urge to shush the animal remained on the tip of her tongue, and she almost laughed at the absurdity. If only there were more noises in the woods to hide the cracking branches and rustling leaves—sounds that echoed through the evening air announcing their whereabouts should anyone happen upon them. Fear of her uncle's anger and what he would do should he discover she'd left the safety of her village swept through her. But the risk was worth the reward. For the winter had proven a lean one and the people of the burgh would have meat to fill their bellies, and milk to share with their children.

Another tremor quaked over her body even as she thought on good things.

Guilt! That's what afflicted her—guilt and fear—guilt for not listening to her uncle when he said that she was never to leave the village. Should he discover she'd gone to the Englishman's land at night… she didn't want to think about that right now.

Uncle seemed more protective of her and concerned for her identity of late. He made sure that Mairi, the sweet woman she lived with, and she had food to eat and clothes to wear. But the man liked people to obey him—and she had not.

He never missed an advantageous opportunity. No, and as she got older, she realized he was like her father and all men of power who did not care whom they trampled if they were to gain wealth and allegiances.

Why could she not have been born a man?

If she'd been born a man, life would be much easier. Men never had to seek permission or an escort. Their minds were their own, as well as their bodies. Deirdre wanted two things. To see that the tenants ate well through the final winter months and to exact revenge on the Englishman for what he'd taken from her. And tonight she planned to have both of those.

The last time the village men had gone *reiving*, they were nearly caught. The time before that, they'd come back empty handed, for other *reivers* from nearby villages had raided the same farm and burned the crops and house to the ground. Though she'd not gone with them, she'd heard tales of how tongues of fire had licked the sky, and smoke billowed into the air for miles. So this night she'd insisted on going and making sure they'd returned with the spoils of her enemy.

She shrugged off the failures of the past and reminded herself they'd brought eight cows home with them this time. She gazed triumphantly at the young calf she'd insisted on bringing, much to the men's displeasure. It was adorable, with a shaggy white lock of hair atop its brown head, and she couldn't bear to leave him behind, though he might slow their escape. No sooner had her victory settled over her, than the calf stumbled and went down. Deirdre jumped from her horse and ran to it, only to have it right itself and scramble ahead.

When they'd arrived on the Englishman's land and she'd seen the mother nursing its calf, she made sure it was one they rounded up. The milk would be appreciated by the mothers with bairns. And she'd not leave the calf to starve as much as the others wished she would.

Walter, the oldest in the group, rode on the right side of the cattle along with Fionn. He sent a warning glance at her and scolded in a low tone. "Git back on your horse, lass."

She opened her mouth to explain herself and quickly shut it. They rode in silence for fear their voices would carry on the night wind. She'd not risk giving them away.

Walter had made it plain that he didn't agree with the raid even though he'd lost not only cattle but also had his fields burned by English marauders. He'd argued that the night was no good for plundering and believed it no place for a woman, especially her uncle's niece. But she and her renegade band had already been well on their way when the old knight, who'd given up his sword for a plow, realized they were gone and followed after them. His harping would not persuade them to turn back. The other three men closer to her age had welcomed her expertise. She was a better shot with a bow and more accurate with the toss of a knife than the three of them, and well they knew it.

Walter grudgingly gave in. Whether because he wanted to be the one returning with the much-needed meat, or whether he wished to ensure that no harm came to her, she couldn't be sure. She hoped the latter but probably both played a part. She cared deeply for Walter. Beneath his gruff exterior lurked a kind man who looked after her.

But he'd been angry with her since they started out. And now that the clouds had blown off and the moonlight shone down brightly upon them, easily giving them away should someone come along, his argument echoed in her mind.

"*'Tis a guid night tae plunder the Englishmen. There is no moonlight. We will be safe,*" she'd told him.

"*'Tis a full moon. The clouds can blow off, and then there be no cover for us.*"

She'd looked up into the dark sky. "*You bring up empty arguments, Walter. The clouds cover the sky as far as the eye can see.*"

"*You put each of our lives in danger.*" Walter's bushy eyebrows drew down into a deep *V*.

"*I have forced no one tae come.*"

"*You rally young lads who follow you blindly.*" Walter had spat.

Shaking off the thoughts, she twisted her horse's mane around her hand and swung onto its back. By the time she'd put herself aright on Storm, her palfrey, the calf had settled in beside his mother and walked along with the rest of the herd.

They crossed over onto Scottish land before Deirdre allowed herself to relax. Though the terrain looked much the same, being off English soil gave her peace.

She let out a sigh and glanced over at Walter, giving him a smile. "We made it."

"We are not home yet, lass." Walter spoke in that low, even tone that raised the hair on her arms.

"Ach! But we are on Scottish soil."

"Keep your voice down. Do you want to announce us to the whole countryside?"

Deirdre frowned, the joy she felt only moments earlier snatched like a bug before a frog.

She'd no sooner dropped her shoulders to sulk when a shrill whistle split the air and a horse and rider crashed from the woods and into their path.

Deirdre sucked in a startled breath and exhaled in a scream. "Run!"

Gilbert dug his heels into his horse, sending it barreling into the woods. Patrik lingered on the other side of the intruder. Relief swept over Deirdre as Patrik finally spurred his mount on. The white horse, like a phantom glimmering through the trees, disappeared as the shadows swallowed it and its rider.

Walter pulled his sword and moved his mount in front of her.

"Go! I will follow shortly." He threw the words over his shoulder without taking his eyes off his adversary.

Fionn, the youngest and certainly not yet a man, broke to his right and Deirdre followed, but before they could get more than a few paces, three more men crashed through. Deirdre pressed her leg into Storm's right side as she pulled the reins to the left. The surprise of the enemy sent her mare whirling away from the other riders. If she could only make it to the cover of the trees, she'd have a chance of escape. Her chances were better if she could get lost amongst the trees and dead underbrush.

A rider drove his horse between her and freedom. Storm startled, turning abruptly. Deirdre fought to stay on her mount but with no saddle, she slid off the animal's sleek back and onto the ground.

Her hood fell off. She snatched it back on her head and tucked her short red hair inside before rising from the ground. She reached out for Storm's reins before the horse attempted to bolt.

One of the men seized the leather leads and leveled his sword on her, the tip pressing at the bottom of her neck. "I would not move if I were you, lad."

Deirdre froze. English! She stole a quick glance from the corner of her eye as Fionn, still on his horse, pulled his sword from its scabbard at his side. But his inexperience made him too slow. Before he could raise his weapon, the enemy's blade swung in an arc and across Fionn's neck. Even with only the moon's light, Deirdre could see the blood spurting from his wound.

"No!" she screamed. She turned to him but was stopped by the blade's pressure at her own throat. She watched helplessly as Fionn toppled to the ground, lifeless. *Cursed English!* Another life stolen by the enemy—another friend gone.

A pricking lump rose in her throat, and she swallowed it. Crying would not help them right now.

Walter continued to fight, his sword clanging as steel met steel. There remained little hope now with four against one, unless Patrik and Gilbert circled around. But she doubted they would.

The plan had been to head back to her uncle's *demesne* should they encounter trouble. After the slaughter she'd witnessed nearly two years ago, she'd decided it would be each man for himself should they get caught.

She'd never mastered a sword, but she was quite proficient with her knife. She moved her hand to the knife at her side. The pressure of the sword's tip pressed deeper into her skin. A pricking sensation released a warm trickle down her neck and into her woolen tunic.

The knave pressing his sword against her called out to Walter. "Lay down your sword, or I'll run the boy through."

The clinking of blades rang out even as Walter spoke. "Let the lad go and I will surrender."

"You are not in a position to bargain with us. Do you want his blood on your hands?" the reprobate asked.

Walter continued to ward off blows and push his opponent back, clearly the better swordsman. "How do I *ken* you will no' kill us both?"

The man battling Walter let out a snicker. "You will have to take your chances."

Walter's blade sliced into the man's sword arm, and he let out a grunt as he tossed the hilt to his other hand.

The Englishman holding her at sword-point yelled out. "Drop your weapon now or the boy dies."

Walter stopped in mid-swing. His head jerked around, and he locked eyes with her. She knew as well as he did that the strike he'd been about to make would have killed his opponent.

He dropped the sword and it tumbled to the ground with a resounding thud.

The man moved his sword from her neck in a directive motion. "Throw your knife to the ground."

†††

Bryce Warwick, Lord of Rosen Craig, had his fill of the reivers on his borderland. His father had fought this battle his whole life as lord. However, Bryce had no intention of spending his life squelching one uprising after another. Atop his new and unruly chestnut, Tempest, he maneuvered through the trees and the fast-approaching darkness, attempting to see any movement of the men who'd raided several of his tenant farms. The still, evening air carried the hoot of an owl and the lonesome howl of a single wolf announcing the impending long night.

He'd always known he'd inherit this problem from his father. He just never dreamed it would come so soon. He should have had another twenty years without this responsibility. It was one thing to be sent out by his father to deal with the reiving, but quite another to have the responsibility to stop the thievery and establish some sort of peace in a recalcitrant land where no sort of law or order prevailed. It seemed impossible. And if not for love of his people, he would consider it a waste of time.

With a king he no longer knew or trusted with his people's best interests, Bryce was well aware that he'd get no help from the throne. Scotland and England had both given up on the borderland and left them to a life of lawlessness. Pillaging, cattle rustling, burning of houses, even kidnapping and murder were not uncommon. It would now be up to him to bring his region under control.

The raiding had more than doubled in the short time since his father died. The unexpected death had sent Rosen Craig into a change of hands and was surely what had given reivers their boldness. They tested the eldest son of Henry Warwick.

That was why he'd sent word to his younger brother, Royce, and wished to meet with him soon. They needed to discuss the brief tenure that Royce had overseen the demesne. One never knew what sparks could start a blaze. He never would have thought that Clarice could have caused the deaths of his father and mother, and almost his own.

In fairness, even when his father lived, he'd dealt with the repercussions of the never-ending Scottish-English wars. The people had grown tired of seeing all their hard work go up in smoke as they watched their crops burn to the ground. They were weary of the two countries' border skirmishes, so some chose not to replant their fields and took up trades instead. In many areas along the border, the land lay barren as a wasteland. But he'd not have that on his land. He'd protect what was his.

His father tried to protect their people and land by stationing knights up along the border. And it had worked—for a while. The presence of Rosen Craig's knights safeguarding the countryside had dissuaded some of the villainous behavior. But ever since Bryce had taken his father's position as lord of Rosen Craig, there had been a steady stream of ever increasing reivers flowing over onto his land.

Bryce leaned forward on Tempest as he peered through the tree-covered twilight, hoping to hear or catch sight of the troublesome men they searched for.

Distant shouts broke through the quiet of the night. He pulled his mount to a stop and cocked his head in an attempt to determine the direction.

Then he heard a scream.

Chapter 2

Bryce darest not call out lest he spoil the element of surprise.
He approached the source of the sound with the stealth of a
wolf, the fine hairs on his neck bristling with caution.

The scream had sounded like a child, perchance a girl.
Heaven above, he could only pray for no repeat of what
Royce had dealt with during the last border uprising. Though
his younger brother had seemed to have found peace with the
killing and *bloodlust* that had taken place under his
command, he had confessed to Bryce that his guilt had nearly
torn him apart inside and kept him from Brithwin, the woman
he married.

The sun had long disappeared beyond the horizon, but
the night clouds cleared, leaving the moon's light as his
guide aiding him while he searched for his men. Tree
branches slapped his face and tugged at his tunic. Tempest
swung his large muscular body around a tree encircled in
thick underbrush, bringing them upon a path.

He wished he had Wolfhound with him to tell him if
they were downwind or up. Wolfhound was a young dog, but
she was smart. Royce and Brithwin had gifted him the animal
when their hound Thor had sired a litter. He'd chosen the
little red female because she stood off by herself and looked
lonely, much like him. He'd named her Wolfhound so she
had no name she must live up to. Nothing but what she
was—a wolfhound.

Not able to see the path clearly enough to tell if there
were fresh hoofprints, Bryce decided to follow to the right
and see if it would bring him to his men.

He spurred Tempest down the path. The horse's hooves
dug into the ground, throwing clods of dirt into the air. As he
rounded a bend, he caught sight of riders a stone's throw up
the trail and tensed as he eased back on the reins, slowing his
mount's steps until he could make out faces.

They certainly weren't concerned about being seen. They sat out in a wide area where the path split and the moon shone brightly down on them. Two sat on horseback side by side under a tree between the *Y* of the two paths while four others on the ground appeared to be arguing.

Bryce stopped Tempest as he tried to ascertain what was amiss. He recognized Geoffrey's voice—always the voice of reason, along with Finley, a fairly new knight in his service.

He moved forward, wondering who had screamed, what the problem was, and whether they'd found any reivers. As the thought went through his mind, his eyes snapped up to the two men sitting on their mounts under the tree.

The one most certainly was not a man but a boy. They'd brought no *squire* with them, so his men had managed to capture at least two of the thieves.

One of the men who'd been arguing with Geoffrey strutted over to the two on horseback. Geoffrey pulled his sword from his scabbard, sending Bryce's eyes searching for the threat, but what he saw made his heart stop. The boy and man sitting on horseback had ropes about their necks.

He dug his heels into the animal's sides with so much force that Tempest nearly reared.

As Tempest's hoofbeats neared Finley, he swung around to face Bryce. "Who goes there?" The knight pulled his sword.

But Bryce didn't answer, and his horse galloped past and toward the two about to be hanged.

Instead, he removed his own sword from its scabbard. "Halt!" He yelled to the knight ready to send the horses on their way.

But the words came out too late. As they left his lips, the man who'd been arguing with Geoffrey brought a hand down on each of the horses' backsides as he let out a yell. The animals shot from beneath their riders. And the two figures, a man and a boy, swung from their neck by ropes.

†††

Deirdre closed her eyes as her horse darted forward and the rope cut into her neck. This was it. She would die and so would Walter. Fionn already lay in a pool of blood, and it was all her fault for encouraging the men to go on this raid. Aye, they all had been eager to raid the English, except for Walter. If it hadn't been for her, they'd have turned back at Walter's bidding. How could something she'd meant for good turn so bad? Did God want her people to starve?

Aye, God took everyone she cared about from her. Today He would take Walter and Fionn. Guilt bit at her conscience. If only God would take her and spare their lives.

Instead of dangling from the tree, convulsing as the rope choked out her breath, and right before she'd lost consciousness, she hit the ground. Pain shot through her hip and head as she struck the dirt. She lay there grappling for her senses and allowing the coolness of the ground to ease the ache in her body. She thought to lie there and not move in hopes her enemy would think her dead. But as she tried to take in a small amount of air, none would come. Panic laced through her body—she would suffocate. No quick death where she was here one moment and gone the next.

Her hands remained tied behind her back. She rolled to her side and gasped for air, but still none came. Lord have mercy on her. Would she lie here and die a slow and agonizing death? Perhaps it was her punishment for leading her friends to theirs.

She glanced up to see the bottom of Walter's boots dangling above her. Her heart clenched. Walter hadn't even wanted to come. In a blink, the man who always looked after her crumpled to the ground with his legs twisted in an unusual position and the rope still around his neck. His eyes remained closed, and he didn't move. She wished she would die so quickly. But that was not to be her fate. Instead, the rope had done its damage, constricted her breathing, and she would die a much slower death.

Everything around her disappeared as she struggled to force a breath into her body. An icy panic raced through her. She deserved to die. She'd caused two men's deaths—friends. Then why couldn't she stop her desperate attempt to sit up and squeeze air into her lungs? Dizzy and weak, she collapsed back to the ground as blackness overtook her.

She awakened to strong yet gentle hands lifting her to a sitting position. The next thing she knew the rope was off her neck and her hands were free. Heaving, she grasped her throat, knowing it wouldn't help.

A little air reached her lungs. And then a little more, giving her hope and easing the panic that had filled her moments earlier. Breaths continued filling her lungs until finally she could not only breathe, but she could think. Maybe she wouldn't die.

Now that her mind worked, she was thankful that even in her fall the hood had stayed on this time. She didn't want to think about what would happen to her should they discover she was not a lad.

The conversation around her came into focus. Walter still lay beside her crumpled. The words she heard came from behind her, but it wasn't a conversation at all. The man who'd apparently untied her hands squatted to the side and leaned into her vision.

"How do you feel?" The man's concerned eyes locked onto hers.

She had enough wits about her to lower her voice slightly to sound like a lad in his adolescence. "You *dinna* need *tae fash* yourself *aboot* me, Englishman."

"Watch your tongue laddie." A man standing in front of her spoke. "You're talking to our lord."

Deirdre looked at the man who had spoken. At least they believed her ruse. She reached forward for signs of life in Walter. The English *laird* had cut her rope through before Walter's. It felt like hours, but surely no more than a moment had passed—surely not enough time to make a difference in her life and his death. Had the extra weight of his body broken his neck? A tremor racked her body. Her heart fell into her stomach. Aye, her friend was dead.

Apparently assured she was fine, the laird stood. "I am Bryce Warwick, Lord of Rosen Craig, and these cows you have stolen belong to me." His gruff response told her the compassion she'd seen in his eyes had disappeared.

Deirdre shrugged, and a stabbing pain shot through her shoulder and into her neck. "We heard the animals lowing and came tae see. They were wandering on Scots' soil. We only rounded them up tae bring home. Better tae be in our safety than at the mercy of wolves."

Lord Warwick snorted. "You expect me to believe that? Fortunate you are that I didn't let my men finish the job they started."

Deirdre's heart skipped a beat, and she twisted around to see Fionn as she stood. Shoving aside the pain, she straightened her body to her full five and a half feet. "Am I, Englishman? I wish you had. I would rather have died with me friends than be captured by the likes of you."

She turned and took a step toward Fionn.

"Where do you think you are going?" A big oaf stepped in her way.

Instead of answering, she stepped around him and scurried to Fionn. She knew he was dead. He hadn't moved since he was struck, but she knelt beside him anyway and leaned forward to listen for breath and see if his chest moved. Footfalls stopped behind her, but she didn't bother to turn around. Let him stand there and see what his sword had done. Fionn was merely a boy in a man's body, so young was he, and now his death darkened her soul.

She swiped at a tear that streaked down her cheek. It wasn't supposed to happen like this. They were supposed to be celebrated as heroes with plenty of meat for food and stories of how they took revenge on their enemy. They were to be the talk of the burgh for sennights.

A sob escaped, and she quickly turned away. No man would cry over a friend's death in front of others. She coughed to cover her mistake as she stood.

She lifted her chin and spat on the good-for-nothing in front of her. "You will pay for their deaths, Englishman."

The words had barely left her mouth when the back of his hand slammed into her cheek and knocked her to the ground beside Fionn.

Dazed, she sat up. A warm trail of what could only be blood trickled down her cheek and onto her lips. The metallic taste confirmed her thoughts.

"Roger Guernon!" Laird Warwick roared.

The knight turned around. "Sir?"

"What are you doing?"

"The demon spat on me, milord, and threatened us."

"Do not lay a hand on him."

"Aye, milord." The man growled his reply.

"Were there any others?"

"Aye, milord."

"How many and where did they go?" The laird seemed more irritated at the man than interested in his answer.

"Two I think went north."

"Did Hugh and Ranald pursue them?" The laird asked.

"Nay, we separated earlier to cover more ground with the encroaching darkness."

"'Twas a good choice." The laird seemed to be trying to make a decision. He turned to her. "What is your name, and from where do you hail?"

Returning to her feet, she pushed back her shoulders and lifted her chin as she'd seen so many young boys do to make themselves look taller. "Gavin." She wanted to look anywhere but into this man's face for fear he'd see the lie in her eyes, but she met his golden-brown eyes with a solid, unwavering gaze. She would not look weak to this English laird.

†††

If Bryce weren't so angry, he'd have laughed at the way she tossed her shoulders back and lifted her chin. Did the little thief really think he'd believe she was a boy? 'Twas impossible to miss her femininity. He couldn't really see her face hidden in the hood, only a slight scar on her neck, and though boy's clothes covered her body, her walk could not deny what she truly was.

Roger stepped forward. "Milord, we caught these no goods with hands soiled. We should hang him now. These Scots have caused us more trouble than they are worth."

"I told you before we left, we would avoid bloodshed if possible." Bryce could hardly believe what he heard. Roger wasn't one of his kinder knights, but he ought to know to obey his lord when he'd given an order.

"Aye, milord. But the lad nears manhood. If he reives at such a young age, he will be a menace in a few years. I say we hang him and leave him as a warning to the others who dare to come onto Warwick land."

Bryce thought to remind him they were no longer on Warwick land, but was too stunned that he believed *Gavin* was a lad.

"Enough blood has been spilt. 'Tis late. Perchance Hugh and Ranald are back to Rosen Craig with the rest of their party." Ranald was a skilled swordsman and Bryce's *master-at-arms*. Hugh, on the other hand, was good about details in battles. He was also the one man in his keep that had women nearly swooning over him.

Bryce contemplated what to do with the two bodies. Darkness was upon them, and he needed to get the cows back to safety. They didn't have the tools to dig graves for the men, and if he left their bodies where they were, by morning they would be gone—ending up a meal for one or more of the wild animals in the forest.

"Geoffrey, Roger, throw the bodies onto a horse and secure them. The animal should find its way back home." He hated to give up a horse, but he'd not leave their bodies exposed to hungry beasts and he'd not take the time to bury them this night.

A grunt came from Roger.

Bryce turned to the "lad." *Gavin, indeed.* "You'll ride with me."

"I will no' touch an Englishman. I would walk first." She folded her arms in front of her and once again squared her shoulders.

Tired after a day of practicing on the field with his men before coming out searching for reivers, Bryce was not in the mood for arguing with the little wench.

"I think not." He picked her up, and she stiffened. He half expected her to kick and pound his chest, but she didn't. He walked over to Tempest, tossed Gavin on, and swung up behind her.

If he thought she was stiff before—she held true to her promise that she would not touch him.

"Keep yourselves alert. We don't know how many more could be out there." He knew he didn't have to tell them. Vigilance kept them alive. But warning them was habit and something they tolerated of him.

Several "ayes" came from behind him.

They rode in silence until they reached Rosen Craig land.

He supposed the woman in front of him could have passed for a boy not quite coming into manhood. She was thin, but when he picked her up, he detected curves that her tunic hid, along with the faint hint of roses. Aye, she was all woman. If he'd had any doubts at all, he could now put them to rest.

Leaning forward, he tried to see the color of her hair, but she'd tucked it under her hood.

"'Twas not smart to be reiving on such a clear night," he whispered.

Her rigid body tightened more, which he'd not thought possible. Perhaps it was because he'd touched her when he'd attempted to see her hair.

"'Twas no' clear when we left." She kept her head pointing forward.

"Aye, but any *man* knows you do not tempt fate when it comes to the clouds."

She gasped.

He smiled to himself. "What was your *troth* to the men, *Gavin,* to get them to follow you on this ill-fated pursuit?"

"Me? I am but a lad. I hold no influence over anyone."

"Nay, you deceive me," he whispered in her ear. "You hold sway over your men. I have but to determine how."

Bryce had finished talking—angry that she continued to try to *hoodwink* him. He would get to the bottom of her lies. He'd fallen for another woman's lies, and it cost his parents their lives and nearly his own. This woman hid something more than her femininity, and he would not rest until he found out what.

Chapter 3

Exhaustion soaked into Deirdre's body like rain into freshly turned earth. She remained occupied with more than a little guilt over Fionn's and Walter's deaths. But she must stay strong and not let the enemy wear her down.

They continued moving slowly, steering the cattle from whence they'd just come. The hoot of a distant owl pierced the damp evening air. She wrapped her arms around herself to stave off the chill threatening to send a shiver through her body. The urge to lean back into the warmth of her captor was but a fleeting thought. Ordinarily she loved the damp smell of evening after the dew had fallen, but the chill in the wet air offered no comfort tonight. Nay, it reminded her of the forewarning she'd tried to shrug off earlier.

Attempts to keep the hope alive for rescue slowly died with each acre they crossed. She knew deep down that Patrik and Gilbert wouldn't bring help. Even if they planned to tell her uncle, they would first wait outside his tower walls in hope of her return. By the time they would admit to themselves she wasn't coming back, they'd have to work up the courage to confess to her uncle the whole sordid story, and by then her enemy would have her securely behind his castle walls. And that was *if* they had the courage.

As her captors drew her closer to what would be her prison, Deirdre's stomach knotted. This was the enemy who'd more than once attacked their village unprovoked.

"What do you plan tae do with me? I would have rather you just let me die back in the woods with my friends."

"Let me remind you, *Gavin,* you do not have a choice in the matter. You were caught stealing my cows." Lord Warwick sounded half amused and half annoyed.

"If you plan to torture me, I can save you the trouble. You will no' get anything *oot* of me, so you might as well kill me now." Lord have mercy on her. When they discovered she was a girl... She wished they'd have let her hang.

They broke through the copse of trees into an open field that she imagined was a beautiful green with the rain they'd had. The castle walls stood as a silhouette against the moonlit sky in the distance. She drew in a deep breath to keep her fear at bay.

"I do not torture my prisoners, so put your mind to rest. Although I am not sure as to what to do with you. You and your fellow reivers have caused my people much trouble. You must be made an example." Lord Warwick pressed his heels into his horse's side, encouraging the animal to pick up speed.

"You speak as though we were unprovoked."

"You were, but it matters not. You take what is not yours to take."

Deirdre clenched her back teeth. "You took what was mine!"

Behind her, Deirdre almost thought she felt him flinch. Was he remembering all the Scottish lives put to the sword two years ago? The hatred welled up within her, sending her stomach into a knot. Perhaps she would get a chance to return the favor to him. She should be glad she was captured, for it would give her a chance to repay an eye for an eye.

"And what would that be that I have taken of yours, *Gavin?*"

Suddenly the fire inside her extinguished as she remembered the Ian she used to know. The sweet young man who always smiled. He'd never been the same after that night. He'd changed—and sometimes that change scared her. She dropped her head and whispered under her breath, fully knowing he wouldn't hear. "My best friend." But she'd not say it for his ears. She'd not tell this *numptie* anything. She'd never tell him how the lucky ones were the ones who died. They didn't live with the guilt of surviving. Ian had changed so much after that fateful day. He was like another man. One she didn't know but still cared for. But she couldn't give up on him. She wouldn't walk away. She tried to help him find his way back. The laird would never understand, for his heart was made from ice.

She was thankful that they now approached the outer *bailey*, for the laird didn't have time to demand an answer from her.

"Who goes there?" A knight called from the gatehouse.

"'Tis your lord. Open the gate." He leaned forward whispering for her ears only. "We have visitors."

The iron gate groaned its compliance as it disappeared into the stone wall. "Visitors are not forced against their will, English."

A deep rumble bubbled up from the man behind her, and he let out an amused chuckle. "'Twasn't you I spoke of, laddie, but the cows. They get my protection for the night."

And who would give her protection from the English animals? Deirdre let out a most unladylike snort. Her mother would have been appalled, had she'd heard her. Could she hate this man any more than she already did? She'd thought she couldn't, but the bitterness that welled up within her at his remark told her otherwise.

They entered the outer bailey and the laird's men brought the cattle in with them. They guided the cows that would have been sweet revenge and food for her people to the far side of the bailey. The laird nudged his horse through another gate and into the inner ward.

The grounds were quiet now, but she imagined during the day it was bustling with activity. Torches burned around the inner *ward*, giving light to those going about their business. Laird Warwick pulled his horse to a stop and in one fluid movement dismounted without so much as touching her.

He reached up to help her down from his *destrier*. She'd never take help from the man responsible for the murder of her people. The hurt in her heart overrode the fear in her body. She understood a little more how Ian must have felt as he walked away from the massacre with no injuries when so many of his friends died, for she wished with all her being that she could take Fionn's or Walter's place.

She slid off the other side of his horse.

The animal sidestepped, hitting her with his immense body and knocking her to the ground. She shoved the animal's leg to keep it from stepping on her, but the horse merely swayed.

Scrambling to her feet, she huffed. The torch-lit wall caught her attention and brought her back to the gravity of her situation. There was no escaping this stone structure. Not that she would have a place to go if she did manage to find a way out.

She'd envisioned her uncle disowning her and taking her away from the old widow and marrying her off to some wretched old friend of his when he discovered that two of his men had died because of her. She shivered and tried to tell herself he had been good to her and Mairi. But she'd seen his wrath when subjects did not obey. Would he forget she was his niece? She shivered again. Aye, and what choice would she have in the situation? She had no place to go, no one to take her in, for no one would defy her uncle.

"Gavin! Are you deaf, boy?" The laird gazed down on Deirdre from the front of the horse. "Come with me, *Gavin*. I must take care of my horse."

Deirdre eyed the man. "Do you have some sort of a problem with my name?"

He raised an eyebrow. "None at all. I might even name a son that someday, should I have one." He wrapped his large palm around the horse's reins and walked away.

Deirdre narrowed her eyes. No problem, indeed. There was some reason he said her name with…with, well, she wasn't really sure what. But in the short time she'd spent with him, he never once said her name without emphasis on it.

He stopped several feet away. "'Twas not an option if you followed me." His gaze shifted to beyond her. "Get your mount and bring her with you. She'll need a good rub down and food for the night."

Deirdre had to tell herself not to turn around and run to Storm. She hadn't realized they'd brought her horse. But why wouldn't they? Storm was a fine-looking grey-dappled mare. She turned around. Her anticipation of seeing Storm dissolved as quickly as a chip of ice on a hot coal. It was Fionn's horse, not Storm.

Everything had happened so quickly she'd not noticed what happened to their mounts. It was hard to know where her loyal horse was this night. She hoped the animal would find her way home. She grasped the reins of Fionn's mount and gave the mare a quick pat on the neck, wondering how long she would be a prisoner of the English.

"Do I need to drag you along with that horse?" The laird had stopped again and stared at her.

Nay, he would not be as kind to her as he was to this horse. She moved toward him, and the mare followed without prompting. Aye, Fionn's horse would be fed and taken care of this night.

They reached the stable and Deirdre glanced around for a stable hand. He was tending another's horse. She waited for the laird to call to him. But instead, he walked over to a shelf on the wall and tossed a cloth to her and returned to his horse and removed the saddle, carefully setting it over a short wall.

He glanced up at her. "Do you not know how to care for your horse, *laddie*?"

There it was again! "I most certainly do. I am in disbelief that you care for your own. I expected you tae beckon your stable hand."

He didn't lift his head to answer but reached for his cloth and began rubbing his black where the saddle had lain. "I care for my own. 'Tis loyal to me and I am to him. I see to his needs."

She raised her brow. For some reason she wanted to provoke the man. "Aye, I can understand. Only an animal would be loyal tae you."

He let out a growl. It pleased her that she had irritated him but at the same time the anger burning in his eyes terrified her.

"Watch your words. If you were a—" His words trailed off.

She'd started rubbing down the mare but paused. "If I were a what?" Why did she provoke the man?

He continued to glare at her. "Take care of your horse. It needs your attention."

She wanted to argue. She wanted to tell him what she really thought of him, but no young boy would stand up to a laird. Nay. She'd have to bide her time. And she had no doubt the time would come when she could tell him what she really thought of him.

†††

Bryce was so angry he'd liked to have throttled the little shrew. Loyalty was something one had to earn, and even then, one never knew how loyal a person truly was. Deceit was an art in some people. They were so good at it that they could appear loyal.

He rubbed Tempest so roughly that the horse stepped away and eyed him. Bryce drew in a deep breath, patted the stallion's neck and went back to caring for the animal.

What was he to do with the woman? He couldn't put her in the dungeon. Not after hearing Brithwin tell of the time she'd spent down there while Royce recovered from injuries. Heavens, if Royce's wife had been down there much longer than she had been, he wondered if she would have survived.

Gavin may be a reiver in men's clothing, but underneath that façade was a woman. He peeked over his horse to see if he could discern her features, but she kept the hood up over her head, shielding her face and hair.

Bryce let out a sigh and as he did, Tempest cocked his

rear leg resting the edge of his hoof on the ground and dropped his hip as he lowered his head. Bryce grinned as he continued to rub the beast down. His horse knew his moods better than anyone. "What do I do with the woman?" He whispered into the horse's ear as he massaged its neck.

Walking around to the other side, he waited for Gavin to lift her head. He could hear her whispering softly to the mare and wondered what secrets she told her horse. Tempest knew more about him than any person. When he was frustrated or needed to think, he climbed on his horse and went for a ride, many times talking to the beast just to get the frustrations off his chest.

He wondered if this woman was the same with the way she now spoke quietly to her horse. He wished the horse could talk so he could find out her secrets.

"Are you finished?"

She stepped around the front of the animal. "I am."

"Come with me."

"What will you do with my horse?"

"Your horse? You mean *my* horse. Consider it payment for all the aggravation you have caused me this day."

"But she is mine!" The little shrew dared to raise her voice at him before she remembered she was feigning to be a boy.

He turned away and walked out of the stables expecting her to follow. Michael nearly ran into him as he rounded the stable door.

Michael Iannetta had come to Rosen Craig at Bryce's request. He'd only been the new lord for a few sennights when he'd bade his friend to come. They'd served together as squires and even as knights early on. A bond had formed over the years that distance and duty could not break.

So when Bryce needed someone he could trust, he sent for Michael.

Michael stopped abruptly. "Do I hear cows?"

Bryce grinned and slapped Michael on the back as they

walked toward the keep. "Aye, you do. We caught reivers with eight of our cows. I brought them here and left them in the outer bailey for safe keeping this night."

"Did you catch any of the reivers?" Michael cocked his head in expectation.

Bryce stopped. He'd assumed the little wench would obey and follow him out, but he had forgotten about her when he'd seen Michael. Bryce swung around. "Gavin!"

Michael raised his brow. "Gavin?"

"Aye, one of the reivers."

"And you left him alone?"

"Nay, 'twas an oversight."

"Surely you jest."

"I have much on my mind, Gavin being one small fraction of my problems."

"Why is he a problem?"

"I know not where to put the lad." Bryce was curious to know if Michael would see what he saw.

"Put him in the dungeon. Any reiver should be glad to receive such punishment. Lucky he is that you did not kill him where you found him."

"Gavin! Do not make me come get you."

Michael narrowed his near black eyes that matched his black hair. "Why are you not overly concerned the little thief hasn't attempted escape?"

"I just walked away. Gavin is still there. And Hugh is inside as well."

As if to confirm his words, the woman stepped out from the stable and walked toward them.

It didn't take long before Michael let out a low whistle. "Aye, I see the problem. Nay, the dungeon is not an option."

Bryce chuckled. His friend didn't let him down. "How could she think her disguise would fool anyone?"

Michael stroked his beard. "She doesn't know that you are privy to her trickery?"

"I have played along with her little game. Until I know it

will not benefit me, anyway."

She stopped when she was several lengths away and lifted her chin.

"How old are you, boy?" Michael threw out the question.

"I am thirteen." She folded her arms in front of her and then seemed to think better of it, dropping them to her side.

"You're a scrawny thing for thirteen. Don't they feed you?" Michael goaded.

She narrowed her eyes but made no response. Instead, she turned to Bryce. "Do I sleep in your dungeon tonight?"

"You will know when I'm ready—" A call from one of the night watchmen cut him off.

"A rider."

It wasn't Hugh, because he'd been in the stable, or Ranald, because he approached him. His men had made it back to the keep before he had. It wasn't like the watchmen to announce every approach.

"Stay here." Bryce ordered Gavin, then turned to Ranald. "Watch him until I return."

He and Michael walked from the inner to the outer bailey.

"Close the gate." Bryce called out to close the gate between the two baileys.

He and Michael made their way to the gate leading outside.

"Who is it?" Bryce asked when they were within ear shot.

"Looks like a horse with a body…or two, milord," the watchman called down.

"Open the portcullis and bring it in."

The iron groaned as the men cranked open the gate, raising it into the upper wall where it disappeared.

"Seems to be just a horse and two dead men, milord," he yelled down to Bryce.

"Get the horse in and close the gate."

Bryce waited with his friend for the animal to be let in.

He groaned when he saw the horse. The very one they had tried to send on its way back to its master.

"I take it you know these men?" Michael grinned.

"Aye. They are two of the reivers. I had not wanted to deal with their bodies and hoped the beast would return from whence it came."

He had to admit he was a bit relieved that it wasn't some ploy by the lass's accomplices to rescue her. He wanted no more blood split this night. He glanced over his shoulder to see Gavin standing at the inner gate, hands holding onto the iron as she eagerly watched the horse and its burden.

When the outside gate closed, the watchman opened the inner gate. Gavin released her hold and stepped back.

The little wench waited until the gate rose high enough to slip beneath it and then bolted to the horse. The palfrey stopped in front of her.

She stroked the dapple grey's neck. "What a guid lassie you are."

It was at that moment that Bryce realized this was her horse, not the one in the stable. He'd assumed the other was because 'twas the one she'd sat upon when he cut her from the hangman's noose. But the beast had been too big for her. If he'd not had so many things on his mind, he'd have noticed that. This little mare looked more her size. And it certainly was a loyal creature. It wouldn't leave her. It followed them, lugging two full-grown men even though they'd tried to send the little mare the other way.

Gavin walked to the side of the animal where her fellow reivers were draped over the mare. A half-gasp, half-cry fell from her lips.

Bryce wasted no time getting to the woman. Seeing her friends dead must have been too much for her. He feared the lass might swoon before he could reach her.

He clasped her arm and tugged her away from the horse and the corpses.

She jerked her arm free and ran back. "Nay, he breathes."

Bryce had seen how the mind played tricks on a person when they were on the battlefield. And hadn't the lass just experienced something equally as gruesome? Bryce grasped both shoulders and again tugged her away from the horse and bodies.

"Nay," she cried with a tremor in her voice. "He's alive."

Chapter 4

Deirdre's knees nearly buckled beneath her. Walter was alive. She pulled away from the English laird and ran to Walter. "Speak to me, Walter."

"Take...care...Gavin." Walter forced out the words, but never lifted his head.

She turned to her enemy. "You have tae help him." She half expected one of the barbarians to take their sword and finish him off.

The laird yelled to a couple of his men, who came running from behind them. They untied Walter.

"Careful with him, Hugh," the laird said.

"Where do we take him, milord?" the man named Hugh asked.

A pause spanned as they lifted Walter from Storm's back.

"Take him to the keep's north tower where we had the old candlemaker's workshop. One of you stand guard."

"Aye, milord."

"Michael, send for Millicent." Michael headed for the keep before the laird had finished his words.

"Is Millicent your healer?" Deirdre asked.

"Aye," the laird replied.

"I must go with my friend." Deirdre knew she was but a prisoner and had no right to demand, but she had nothing to lose by saying it. "I have helped on the battlefield with injuries. I can assist." She added as an afterthought so they would not think it odd. She held her breath as the laird stared at her.

She resisted the urge to pull the hood forward a little more. The moon and torches lit the bailey like day, and she did not want him to see the anguish she felt inside.

"I will escort you." The answer came with no hint of emotion on his face or in his voice. Mayhap she should be relieved that she'd not angered him by her demand. But she was angry at him and wanted him to lash out at her so she could rail back at him.

*Oh, Walter. . .*The unfairness of it all. She had to wonder if God even cared about the Scottish people. A coldness set in her heart as her thoughts manifested in her soul.

"Gavin!" The laird jarred her out of her dark thoughts. "Come." He stomped up the steps.

She followed behind. She wasn't sure how much time she'd spent outside brooding when the laird had gained her attention, but by the time they'd made it up the flight of stone stairs and into the tower room, Walter was on a bed and a woman fussed about him.

The laird held her back and looked to the woman. "Do you need help, Millicent?"

The white-haired old woman crouched over Walter, lifting his hands, poking and prodding him. "Nay, milord." She shuffled over to the laird and gave Deirdre a thorough examination from her head to her toes that left Deirdre feeling her ruse had been exposed.

"Can he see his friend?" The laird tilted his head toward Deirdre.

The healer raised her brows. "Aye, milord."

Once free of the Laird's restraint, she hurried to Walter's side. She lifted her friend's hand and squeezed, but he didn't return her grip.

"Walter," she whispered. "It's Deirdre. You will get well, do you hear me?"

He smiled. "Aye, I hear you." His eyes slowly shut.

She clutched his hand and lowered her voice. "I am so sorry, Walter. 'Tis my stubbornness that has gotten us intae this predicament. I will figure a way oot, even if I must bargain with the rotter."

Millicent and the Laird Warwick whispered near the door. She strained to hear. *"Can't move...dying...matter of time."* The laird nodded his head in response to the woman's words. His eyes locked on to hers. 'Twas not true. Walter couldn't die. But the pity she saw in the laird's eyes told her he believed otherwise.

She didn't want the Englishman's pity. He was the reason that Walter lay on his deathbed. She'd pay him back for Walter, for Ian, and for every Scot who fell to the sword of the Warwicks.

"Deir— Gavin." Walter opened his eyes, and he gazed at her.

She squeezed his hand and leaned down to hear his forced words. "Aye, Walter."

His breathing was shallow, and she wanted to take deep breaths for him. "'Tis not your fault. Fionn, Patrik, and Gilbert would have come with or without you. They'd made up their minds—foolish boys wanting tae be men." His words were slow, faint and raspy.

Tears welled in her eyes. She swallowed and willed them away, but a rogue tear rolled down her cheek. "But you came because of me. Tae keep me safe. 'Tis my fault you are here."

"Nay, lass. I would have followed your friends tae keep them safe even if you had not come."

"Oh, Walter. I dinna believe you." She brought his hand up to her lips and kissed it. "Do you want a priest? They canno' deny you."

"Nay, 'tis too late for this dark soul."

"I will pray for you. You are a guid man with a guid heart."

"Dinna fash yourself aboot me." His eyes grew serious. "Beware of who you trust. I have tried tae keep you safe." He seemed to gulp his air. The words came out in a whisper and faded. His eyes grew wide, and his chest slowed its rise and fall.

She drew in a deep breath willing him to do the same. "Dinna go. I need you, Walter. Dinna leave me," she whispered in his ear.

She thought she saw a slight shake of his head, but her eyes must have deceived her. Walter's eyes closed, and she waited for them to open, to confirm he'd fight—that he'd not die. She looked to his chest, but it didn't move.

She turned to the healer. "Help him. He is no' breathing." Panic invaded her body.

"There is nothing to do for him. The rope has done its job."

She swallowed down the lump burning in her throat. Tears pricked the back of her eyes. She wanted to scream. To say *no*, this couldn't happen. But instead, she gave a nod.

The laird glanced around the circular room. There was not much here—a bed, chair, and a small table. His gaze turned back to her. "We will leave you with your friend to say good-bye." The healer went out, and then he left and closed the thick wooden door behind him.

†††

Bryce dropped the thick board across the door, securing the woman from escaping, and then turned to walk away. He'd have to have the body removed. Muffled sobs slipped from behind the door. He stopped. His heart twisted.

Why should he care for her loss? The wench tried to deceive him much like Clarice had. He had to remind himself that not all women were like his former betrothed. His mother and Brithwin were proof of that. But this one, she was born of the same spirit as Clarice. Her deceit was proof of that. She not only stole from him, she had no remorse. And she pretended to be someone she was not. Just like Clarice.

Aye, Clarice had taught him a valuable lesson. One he would not forget. He headed down the stairs and came upon Millicent waiting at the bottom.

She gave a slight incline of her head. "Milord."

"What is it, Millicent?" Ever since she and her husband had snuck him out, wounded, through the bolt hole, and cared for him until he regained his strength, his relationship with them had changed. The couple had grown dear to him, and he treated them as such.

"Did I hear you correctly? He?" She raised her gaze up toward the room in which they'd left Gavin.

Bryce nodded. "Aye. That is what you heard."

"You do not believe that is a boy up there do you, milord?"

Bryce couldn't help but grin. "Nay. I see through her ruse. I do not want her to know that until I am sure it isn't something I can use."

Millicent nodded. "'Tis good to know. You had me worried for a moment, milord."

"Do not worry for me, dear lady. I still can tell a woman when I see one."

Her eyes warmed when he said *dear lady*. Millicent was dear to him. Perhaps like a grandmother. Not a bit of guile in her but only his best interests.

"Go to bed, Millicent. I am sure that Neil is waiting for you."

She touched his sleeve. "Thank you, Bryce. You need to get some sleep yourself."

"I will. As soon as I talk with my men."

Bryce headed to the hall and found Michael and several other men sitting near the fire. He leaned against the large stone hearth.

"Guernon, since you are the reason I have two dead men on my grounds, I want you to bury them."

Guernon grunted.

Bryce pushed away from the stone fireplace and began to pace in front of it. "Take three other men at daybreak and go to the border and bury them on Scottish soil."

"Why should they get the decency of a burial? They were thieving on your land. I could dump them beyond Rosen Craig."

"Nay, you will bury them. I did no' want bloodshed if possible. 'Twas made clear when we left. Lucky you are that

I am not giving you punishment for your lack of judgement."

He folded his arms in front of him. "They had drawn their swords."

"'Twas not much more than a boy whom you killed today. 'Tis sure I am that you could have disarmed him without killing him." He thought to add that he wanted to kill a woman, also, but chose not to.

Bryce stopped his pacing and turned to the other men. "Any other news?"

"There are rumors that Rothburg is striking up a deal with Richard," Michael answered.

"No good can come from that alliance, but 'tis no surprise. Richard has not made it a secret he favors the man." Bryce reached down to pat Wolfhound's head, which had come to stand beside him. "The king pushes his nobles beyond reason."

Geoffrey leaned forward and clasped his hands. "Our king thinks rather highly of himself and not as the Lord's servant."

"'Tis true. But what does one do when they no longer trust their king? This desire for revenge by the Appellants and their constituents burns within our king. I fear even though he has beheaded the Earl of Arundel, exiled Beauchamp, and arrested the Duke of Gloucester, his own uncle, his hunger for vengeance has not been sated. Aye, he cannot seem to let the past go. He has his favorites, and if you are not one of those—well, then one must beware." Bryce patted his chest and Wolfhound stretched her legs up, resting them on his shoulders. He scratched the coarse hair on her neck, and she melted in his hands. "We need to keep an eye on Rothburg. He hatches some plan, of that I am sure."

"Aye. The peace is gone, and well the king knows it. His subjects are not happy with his choices," Michael added.

"Nay, and with all the Scots reiving, it reminds us we must be alert and not forget the mistakes of Otterburn."

Wolfhound tried to lick Bryce, and he turned his head, saving himself from a wet kiss. "We fight battles both from within and outside our land."

They all became sullen remembering when the Lord Appellants were running the country in '88 and the Scots had won a great victory at Otterburn.

There seemed no good answer for England since many believed it was God who put a man on the throne. But Richard made many a mistake. He cared for himself and not his people. He had his favorites, and Bryce was not one of them. The only good thing the king had done of late was to marry the French princess and give England peace with France.

Bryce wished the king had married a Scot. For then perhaps he'd have peace at Rosen Craig.

Geoffrey stood abruptly. "You don't suppose that Rothburg is once again disputing parts of your land?"

Bryce snapped his fingers, and Wolfhound jumped down. He turned to Geoffrey. "'Tis possible. My father did say that Rothburg again contested the settlement of the property even after Edmond's father was stripped of Rosen Craig for being a traitor. Before Edmond lost Rosen Craig, there had been much contention between Edmond's father and Rothburg over property settlements. When my father received Rosen Craig, we thought that had died—but we learned anon we were wrong."

"Do you suppose he does this now because he thinks you weak? Rosen Craig has had three lords in less than two years," Michael questioned.

"'Tis very possible, milord." Geoffrey nodded. "And with the problems at the border, what better time to strike? The land has been contested for all of Rothburg's life. He may tire of waiting and plan to take things in his own hands."

Bryce threaded his fingers through his hair. "Aye, the borderland of Rosen Craig is in a precarious position with the threats from the Scots in the north, Rothburg to the east, and even perchance the king to the south."

The room grew quiet with Bryce's last words. The men sat staring into the fire. Bryce knew there would be a skirmish at best. Only, from what direction should he expect it? By the rood! He had inherited an angry beehive.

Guernon stood. Bryce could see fire in the man's eyes.

"I'll find some men to bury the dead." Roger scowled.

Bryce had forgotten about his prisoner up in the tower room. He'd have to find something to do with her. He couldn't put her in the dungeon. He supposed he could leave her locked where she was.

His thoughts fled when the door swung open, and Hugh stepped into the hall. "Milord, there is a Scotsman demanding to see you in the outer bailey."

Chapter 5

Deirdre pulled the small knife from her boot and strode across the room to check the door. It was secured from the outside. She knew it would be. Returning to the other side of the room, she pulled the small table next to the chair, and then sat down. She laid the knife on the table. Walter was gone. Fionn was gone. She wished she could have taken one of their places. At least Gilbert and Patrik had gotten away.

There was no fire, only a torch to throw light into the darkness and not much heat, leaving the room cold. She shivered as she threw off her hood and picked up her blade. Why hadn't they searched her for weapons? Such careless men, the English. A Scot would never forget to check their enemy for a weapon—especially one who was brought into their domain.

Ah, well, it was to her advantage. She ran the edge of the steel over her finger to test for sharpness. A thin line of blood appeared. She smiled and raised the knife to her neck.

She'd been careless as well. From the day her father had nearly found her, she had lived her life as a boy, keeping her hair short and dressing as a young lad. The people in the village where she lived with Mairi, the old widow, knew the truth, but they kept her secret and protected her.

She'd gotten comfortable of late and hadn't shorn her hair. Taking a deep breath, she grasped a handful of red curls and sliced through the hair. She laid the few inches of curls on the table and reached up to grasp another lock and cut it off. She fought back the tears that wanted to invade. It had never bothered her before when it was cut. After all it was only hair. It would grow back. And she'd left it longer than she should. But she could hear her mother's words when she combed her hair as a young child. *You have bonnie hair, Deirdre. There is none that compares to yours. Dinna cut it, my dear. 'Tis your crowning glory.*

A tear slipped down her cheek. Out of all the things she remembered, why did she have to remember that? "'Tis sorry I am, Mama." She whispered. "'Tis for my safety. I ken you understand." She'd enjoyed having hair touch her shoulders—to feel like a woman. She grabbed another handful of curls and sliced through them, longing for the day she'd never have to cut it again.

When she'd finished, she picked up the short, thick curls and went over to Walter, pushing them into his boot. They'd bury her hair with Walter and never be the wiser.

She slid the knife into her belt and hid it within the pleats. 'Twould be easier to get to should she need it. Pulling the hood back onto her head, she waited for her enemy to return.

She didn't have to wait long—barely having sat down when the clicking of heels on the flagstone steps reached her ears. She braced herself, wondering what she faced. 'Twas in her power to do this. If she could be separated from her mother, she could get through anything.

The clunking of wood from outside the room could only be the removal of the heavy wooden board which kept her captive. She waited. The door slowly creaked open.

The laird stepped in with two other men, and they walked over to Walter.

Deirdre stood abruptly. "What are you aboot?"

"He needs burying." The laird answered so matter-of-factly she almost felt foolish.

"No' on English soil. I will no' have his body desecrated." She didn't bother to keep the anger from her voice.

The laird paused mid-stride and turned to her. His face as cold and unfeeling as a block of ice pulled from winter water.

"Be thankful he gets a burial at all, *Gavin*." His words were harsh. "I owe him nothing." He paused. "I owe you nothing."

They lifted Walter's body and carried him out the door. The board slammed back into place on the outside of her door. She ran to it and checked, even though she'd heard the wood slat fall. Pressing her ear against the crack of the door she listened.

She didn't move so as not to give herself away.

"Why didn't you tell Gavin someone had come for the bodies?" one of the men asked.

Someone had come for the bodies? How did they know where to come? And who came? She wanted to run back to the window and look out, but her desire to hear the laird's reply was greater. She'd given up when footfalls retreated away from the door. As she turned to go to the window, the laird answered. Pressing her ear back against the crack, she held her breath so no sound would obstruct her hearing his fading voice.

"...As I said. I owe him nothing."

That statement was correct. The laird owed her nothing, so why did he keep her alive? He had to want something from her. Information? A bargaining chip? He could never know how valuable she was. She rushed over to the window and gazed toward the gate. When she saw the white horse with the single black leg standing by the wall of torches, she knew it was Patrik who'd come. He must have followed them.

This could be her one chance to escape. She wasn't sure how she could do it, but sitting in the tower room did not bode to end well. The English laird had proven with all the bloodshed that he hated her people.

They carried Walter and Fionn toward Patrik. The gate remained raised. If she hurried, maybe she could sneak out the gate while they were tying the bodies onto the horse. Surely that kind of activity would garner the guards' attention on this cool evening rather than gazing out at motionless land.

Glancing down from the window, she determined that

she was only two or three floors up. If she hung from the window's ledge, her jump would only be one and a half or two levels up. Small brush grew at the base of the tower that might cushion her fall—although she doubted it would help much. Seeking encouragement, she reminded herself that she had jumped from trees when she was young. Freedom was within her grasp. She had nothing to lose, for she knew not what kind of torture she faced.

Before she could change her mind and before Patrik could leave, Deirdre climbed up into the window and let herself down, dangling from the window as her hands fought to hold on.

As she clung to the stone ledge, she realized she'd made a grave error. Stones protruded from the tower. She'd have to push herself away as she let go in order to avoid hitting them on the way down. The ache in her fingers weakened her hold on the ledge. Struggling to hold on, she attempted to get a better grip. Instead of a better hold, the stone slipped from her fingers before she could push away.

Having enough sense about her, she gritted her teeth so she'd not scream. Little did she realize she'd not need to worry about that, for the next moment a searing pain shot through her head and everything went black.

†††

Bryce walked with the men as they strode toward the Scot waiting to bring his dead home.

Guernon grinned. "It saves me from wasting time riding to the border and burying these reivers in the morn."

Bryce gave him a frown. Guernon shrugged. When they'd reached the man claiming his friends, Bryce stopped while they tied the bodies onto the extra horse the man had brought.

He was barely a man. It seemed Gavin had brought all boys with her, other than the one she called Walter.

"Here are your dead. You save me from having to bury them." Bryce spoke to the young man.

He gave a quick nod. "Is this all you have?"

Bryce took his measure. "Were you one of the reivers who raided my land?"

The boy lifted his head. "I would be a fool tae answer that."

Bryce narrowed his eyes. "Aye, you would. I would have the right to do the same to you."

The lad swallowed hard but didn't back down. "You have no one else?"

Now Bryce was annoyed. "I give you two dead bodies, and you want more? I have no more to give unless you would like me to add you to the count."

The lad stepped back. "N-nay. I will take my dead home."

"'Tis a good idea. Count yourself lucky I let you. You are young, and I admire your courage coming here. But let this be a warning to you and those who raid my lands. I will not tolerate reiving." Bryce left no doubt he'd brook no more thievery.

He left the boy standing there, waiting for his men to finish tying the dead to the horse. Bryce glanced up at the castle tower window to see if Gavin watched. She did not. It irritated him that he did not know the woman's name.

Pursing his lips, he let out a shrill whistle. Wolfhound came immediately to his side and fell in beside him. The dog had been exercising by running all over the bailey. Bryce strode toward his keep, ready to turn in for the night. There was much to do in the morning.

The weight of the problems that plagued his keep at times overwhelmed him. He couldn't help but wonder how his brother, Royce, fared down at Hawkwood. He might have to make a trip to see him.

He sighed as he neared the steps. The wench was a burden to him. He should have sent her away. But to let a reiver go with no punishment would only encourage others to do the same. Nay, as much as he disliked the position he was in, he could not let her go unpunished.

He reached the steps, and Wolfhound ran off. Bryce whistled for her to come back, but she continued on and stopped at the tower. He started up the steps and yelled to her. "'Twill be cold out here tonight. You had best come now if you want a fire to warm you."

She didn't come. He shook his head and pulled the door open. Wolfhound let out a sorrowful howl. Bryce froze. The dog only made that sound when... He turned around and ran down the stairs and toward the tower base.

Had the lad coming to retrieve his friends only been a ploy? Had they snuck men in while he and the others talked and tied the bodies?

He slowed as his eyes fell upon a crumpled body. Wolfhound nudged it with her nose. His mind raced.

He turned the body over to see the face.

He groaned when he realized it was his prisoner. He leaned down and put his head to her chest. Her heart still beat, with the shallow rise and fall of her chest pressed against the side of his face.

Egad, the woman lay on the ground unconscious more than on her feet since he met her. He scooped her up into his arms and made his way back to the steps with Wolfhound at his side.

He called out to one of his men to open the door. The knight lunged up the steps three at a time, his boots clicking with each step, and held the door before Bryce made it to the top.

Michael emerged from the hall as the two entered the keep. "What is this?" His friend hurried over to him.

"My prisoner. She obviously tried to escape and nearly fell to her death."

Michael stroked his beard and then grinned. "She must not like your hospitality."

Bryce needed to find Nog, the white-haired cook, and Millicent, and have them ready the basket room, a small room off the kitchen. It was used as an overflow and they didn't keep much in there except empty baskets. Nog could keep an eye on Gavin when Millicent wasn't there. And there were no windows for the daft woman to jump out of. He handed Gavin to Michael. A squeal and then some chattering followed before Michael's pet squirrel, Alex, freed himself from between Gavin and Michael and peeked his head out of Michael's tunic.

"Sorry, Alex. Bryce didn't mean to squish you."

Bryce gave him an annoyed look and headed to find Nog.

Michael kept on talking to his squirrel. "Don't take it personally, little knight. If you are going to get stuck between something, what better than me and a nice soft woman?"

That made Bryce grin. He talked to the animal like it understood him.

A few minutes later, Bryce had tracked down the cook and sent her to get the small room cleaned up and a bed put together.

Nog's tanned wrinkled face suddenly went white. "Milord." The woman's voice warbled. "Are you bleeding?"

Bryce glanced down at his shirt. It was saturated in blood. "Nay, Nog. 'Tis the prisoner's blood. Get Millicent now! Send her to the basket room."

Bryce returned to Michael, who had moved again into the *great hall* and sat on a chair with his head leaned back, eyes closed, and Gavin still in his arms.

"The lass bleeds. She is injured." Bryce rushed over, unhappy with himself that he had missed that.

Michael stood to his feet and looked down. "And bad from the looks of it."

Bryce didn't have to look far to find out what caused her wound. The hilt of a knife protruded from beneath her belt. He carefully lifted her tunic to assess the severity of her injury. He couldn't tell if it had disemboweled her.

"Leave the knife where it is. Pulling it out may cause her

bleeding to quicken," he told Michael. "Come."

Her hood had fallen back, revealing a mass of vibrant red hair. A large knot protruded from her forehead. Cuts and deep scratches on her face trickled blood down her cheek.

If she survived, the poor woman would be in much pain. She looked so small and frail. He should be relieved she was the one crumpled on the ground and not one of his men, but a small knot began to form in the pit of his stomach.

When they reached the basket room, Millicent helped Nog, while two of his knights carried in the frame of a wooden bed that he recognized from the sick room. Within minutes, Millicent instructed Michael to put the lass down on the readied bed.

With a flick of her hands, she sent them on their way. Bryce crossed his arms as Michael, Nog, and the other two knights went out. "I will be staying."

"'Tis not proper, milord," she replied.

"I am not leaving."

She huffed and lifted the tunic right above where the knife entered.

"Think you that it hit something important?" He leaned closer to get a better look.

She clucked her tongue. "'Tis hard to tell. 'Tis close. I can only try to stop the bleeding and pray she does not catch the fever." She looked up at Bryce. "If you must stay, milord, make yourself useful. Go fetch some water."

Bryce didn't have to be asked twice. He was out the door and had returned before she'd finished crushing the stonecrop leaves. She moistened the leaves in the small bowl of water he'd brought, then used a cloth dipped in the leaf water on her wound where the knife still protruded. He knelt down. He knew what the stonecrop would do. The memory remained fresh in his mind when Millicent had fought to keep him alive. It would relieve some of the pain should she wake.

Millicent waited a moment allowing the stonecrop to do its work. Handing Bryce a clean cloth, she nodded to him.

"When I pull the knife out, I want you to apply pressure to the wound. 'Tis a good thing you did not remove the knife. She has already lost much blood."

With a quick flick of her arm, the knife came out. Blood gushed from the hole. Bryce pressed down on the wound with his cloth. Blood seeped into the white cloth widening the circle of deep red until it became more crimson than white.

"She's going to bleed to death," Bryce called to Millicent, who had walked away to retrieve her basket from near the door.

"She may." The healer shuffled back with basket in hand, setting it on the table.

Bryce had no warm feelings for Gavin, but he didn't want her to die, especially under his watch. At least that was what he kept telling himself. But there was something about this woman that drew him to her.

Memories flooded back of Clarice falling to her death and breathing her last breath at his feet. The woman had conspired with his uncle against him and his family. Her surprise to see him alive had caused her to lose her balance and plunge to her death. He closed his eyes and shook his head. Perhaps God's judgement had fallen on both women.

Millicent dug through her basket and pulled out a jar of salve. Setting it aside, she continued to dig until she pulled a needle with a long thread attached.

"Remove the cloth and hold both pieces of skin together so I can stitch her closed."

Bryce nodded and did as she told him. If anyone could save the lass, it was Millicent. After his uncle had killed his parents and left him for dead, Millicent and her husband had discovered him hanging onto life while they prepared him and his parents for burial. They killed a deer and put it in the box in place of his body. Sneaking him out through the bolt hole, they did not return to Rosen Craig but took him away and cared for him until he became strong enough to return.

His thoughts were jarred back to the present as Millicent's needle pierced the soft white flesh. The healer took each stitch with great care so as to not leave an ugly scar, something she'd not be as concerned about if on him or one of his warriors. When she had finished her stitches, she tied a knot and then spread the salve over the newly sewn skin.

"How long before we know if she will live?"

She shrugged. "Her injuries are substantial. Only God knows. If the knife missed her organs, she could die from her head injury or the fever."

"Do the cuts on her face need stitches?"

"Nay. They will heal and never be seen."

The woman who called herself Gavin appeared battered. It was true. No one but God knew if she would survive.

"How did this happen?" Only now that Millicent had done all she could did she take time to ask.

Bryce winced. "She tried to escape by jumping from the lower tower window. The knife must have been in her belt and stabbed her on impact."

"And the head wound?" She gently prodded the knot.

"She could have hit her head on the stone coming down, or when she hit the ground. Either way her head took a fierce hit."

She didn't look so small and frail when he'd first cut her down from the tree. Heavens! If she lived, the woman experienced a day that would bring her nightmares for ages to come. Surely that was punishment enough.

Millicent looked over every inch of Gavin and found a bad ankle and broken arm to add to her injuries. "Why do you dress as a man and do a man's job?" she whispered. "Such a beautiful face." She ran the back of her hand over Gavin's cheek. "I venture to say you will have a beautiful name to go along with it."

Bryce found himself not only wanting to know her name but to feel the soft skin on the girl's pallid face as he stared down at the woman lying on the bed. He shook the desire off. The lass probably wouldn't live.

Chapter 6

A thousand soldiers marching couldn't liken to the pounding in Deirdre's head. The room remained dark when she opened her eyes. Daring not to move her head for fear the pain would become more than she could stand, she closed her eyes and listened for sounds around her, but there were none.

She fell back asleep, and when she woke again, it was to humming. The light, though not terribly bright, sent a stabbing pain through her head. With a moan, she instantly shut her eyes. "Where am I?" The words came out a dry whisper.

The person stopped humming and appeared at her side, grasping Deirdre's hand. She cracked her eyes to see who had come to her aid—an old woman. Her white hair peeked out from beneath a brown cap and framed wrinkled, bronze skin that reminded her of a raisin. But it was her smile that went all the way to her pale blue eyes that caught Deirdre's attention. The old woman held so much compassion that she found herself immediately liking her.

"So pleased to see you are awake, dearie. How do you feel?" She started lifting Deirdre's *chemise*.

Deirdre frowned and held the fabric down. She didn't recognize the chemise she wore. "'Tis fine I am. *Grammercy* for asking." Even as she spoke, her eyes sought out her own clothing. She spotted them folded on the end of the bed.

The woman clucked her tongue. "I am Millicent, the healer here. And you are at Rosen Craig. You gave us quite a start. I feared you would not wake up."

A bolt of lightning shot through Deirdre's veins, draining her of the little strength she had. How could she be at her enemy's domain? She had so many questions. "What happened to me?" The last thing she recalled was... She wasn't sure what the last thing she remembered was.

The woman shrugged. "I was called to see to you. I was

not with you when you arrived."

"I understand." She nodded her head and quickly stopped. That little movement sent shards of color piercing behind her eyes with blinding pain.

Millicent appeared with a goblet and pressed it to her lips. The cool water trickled down her parched throat. She gulped the liquid with her eyes closed until the woman pulled it back.

"Take your time, lass." She brought it back to her lips.

This time she drank slowly, sating her thirst. "Grammercy," she told the woman when she'd finished. Her mind searched for answers on why she was here.

"I must let milord know you have awoken."

Before Deirdre could protest, the woman scurried out of the room.

She needed to get out of her enemy's house before the woman came back with him. Tightening her stomach muscles to sit up, she let out a low cry and fell back to the bed. Mercy. What had happened to her? A quick lift of her chemise gave her the answer she sought—stitches in her belly. Lifting her hand with thoughts to probe the wound, she let out another whimper and pulled up her sleeve to find her arm splinted.

What had these people done to her? The need to get out of the bed nearly overwhelmed her. She pulled down the chemise and with clenched teeth forced herself up and swung her feet to the floor. Stretching her good arm toward the end of the bed, she grasped her clothes.

Gingerly, she removed the splint on her arm and shimmied out of her chemise. Pressing through a wall of pain, she managed to get her own garments on, thankful for the wide sleeves of her tunic. But before she could stand, the door opened.

"I would not do that if I were you." She recognized the man standing before her as her enemy.

He tossed a handful of red curls onto the table. "I

thought you might be missing this." He glared at her.

The memories came flooding back. Fionn. Walter. Her attempt to escape. She glared back at him. "What do you want from me?"

The man actually smiled. "'Tisn't what I want from you, *Gavin*, 'tis what am I going to do with you."

She lifted her chin defiantly and shrugged. Even that action caused her pain but not enough to stay the surge of terror that shot through her veins. "I care no' what you do with me, *Englishman*." She hoped he could not see the terror that filled her.

He came and stood in front of her. He was no small man. Not even for a Scot. She tilted her head back to see him. She'd like to have stood, but she feared should she try to stand, she might find herself on the floor.

"What is your name—your real name, *lass*?"

She hesitated, weighing the consequences of her answer. "Deirdre."

"Deirdre who?"

She'd hoped her given name would be enough but knew it would not. What she did know was giving her uncle's last name, which she'd been going by, would not do her well. The Kincaids hated the people of Rosen Craig. And she could not give her true last name, for if her father ever found her…she held back the shudder that threatened her body.

"I am waiting. You try my patience." He glared at her.

"Maxwell. Deirdre Maxwell." She held her breath hoping he'd believe her lie.

"Why were you feigning to be a man?"

"Do you really need tae ask me that, Englishman?"

He frowned. "You are impertinent. Remember, Deirdre, you are the one who came to my land and stole from me. I have the right to…" The man paused and seemed to scrutinize her.

She pushed her shoulders back and lifted her chin. She hated that she could not stand in front of him and show him she did not fear him.

But you do fear him, a small voice whispered within.

"…the right to punish you. You need to turn from your ways."

The scoff came out before she had time to stop it. He raised a single brow, his gaze challenging her.

She wished the tremors within her would cease as she gazed into the eyes of this English blackguard. She could only hope that if he'd meant to seriously harm her, he would not have gone to the trouble of stitching her up. The thought gave her courage. "I did nothing you dinna deserve. You are a murderer!"

The man never flinched. He continued to stare her down, but the fire in his eyes gave her pause. Then a slow smile played at the corners of his lips. "You are hiding something from me, Deirdre, or do you prefer *Gavin*? I would know what you keep from me."

She gave him another shrug of her shoulders, suddenly not feeling so sure of herself. He may want to keep her alive for other reasons, ones just as horrifying as torture. "I ken no' what you speak of. The only thing I have hid from you is that I am no' a man."

"Aye, you are no man. 'Twas foolish of you to think I would believe that ruse. Nay, you hide more. I see it in your eyes."

She fought the shiver that threatened to overtake her. He only guessed. He could not know. She'd not even told him from where she hailed. "You see a woman who is in the hands of her enemy. 'Tis all."

"Where do you come from? Who do you thieve for?" It was as though he had read her thoughts.

"I told you. We found the cows." Her lies continued to compound. Did it count against her more than once should she repeat the same lie?

A knock sounded on the door, but before he could answer, it opened and a young boy of about nine or ten stuck his head in the room. His gaze skimmed over the laird and landed on her. He didn't say anything, and his eyes never wavered from her. He slid through the cracked door and gave her a bow. "Good *aftermete*, milady."

"Lucas." Laird of Rosen Craig's voice was stern, stopping the boy from continuing into the room.

The boy answered without taking his gaze off Deirdre. "Aye, milord?"

"What is needed of me?"

The boy didn't withdraw at the laird's gruff response.

"I-I don't recall milord." Lucas smiled but still didn't give the laird his attention. "She is beautiful, is she not? No wonder you disappeared."

Laird Warwick scowled. "I will speak with you when I am done here. You may leave."

"But milord, your brother told me to always respect a lady. 'Twould not be right if I left you alone in here with her." He came over and sat on the chair and smiled up at her. "I will protect milady's honor."

Deirdre would have liked to wrap her arms around Lucas. What a sweet boy. It was obvious that the laird's brother was more of a gentleman than this overgrown oaf if he taught this young lad his manners.

†††

Bryce could have strangled the boy. Lucas was smitten with the young woman. The lad's eyes had gone all soft as soon as they fell on Deirdre. He could see the boy would not want to return to Hawkwood and Royce as long as Deirdre remained at Rosen Craig.

Lucas was a good lad. He had begged Bryce's brother to stay at Rosen Craig on their last visit. Bryce had encouraged Royce to let the boy stay on and be his page for a few months.

With Brithwin's lying in and sickness, Royce might have been thankful to be temporarily relieved of the little imp. Lucas could be a real handful at times.

According to Royce, the boy had come a long way. He'd become tough out of necessity and his desire to live. Growing up an orphan would do that to a child. But now Lucas's home was with Royce and Brithwin, and the boy seemed quite happy.

"Lucas."

"Aye, milord."

"Look at me," Bryce demanded.

The boy tore his gaze off the woman.

"You may go wait outside of the room. Perhaps you will remember what you needed to tell me and why you barged in here."

"But, milord, you would not want to sully this lady's reputation."

"She does not need my help to do that, lad." He would not exactly call Deirdre a lady either. There were a lot of things that came to mind—thief, reiver, liar, *beautiful*— Bryce shook his head, not liking how that last word had invaded his thoughts.

Lucas didn't move. Bryce gave the boy a burning glare. There was a real struggle taking place inside the boy on whether he should champion the lass or obey his lord. Bryce could see it as easy as he could tell he was besotted with her.

"Go, before I decide to have you scrubbing the soot off the walls in the great hall."

Lucas pushed himself up slowly from the chair and looked back at Deirdre. "I will be right outside the door should you need me, milady."

Bryce gave him a glare that sent him out of the room. The boy was impertinent. He really should do something about that, but the fact that he truly attempted to champion the woman took some of the bite out of it.

He almost laughed. Lucas had done him a favor. If the woman wasn't afraid of him before, she surely should be now. The lad made him sound like he was anything but a man of honor. Before the door shut, Lucas gave a forlorn look at Deirdre. That did make Bryce smile.

When the door closed, his smile disappeared before he turned around. He moved closer to the woman.

Eyes greener than a newly budded leaf stared up at him. His breath hitched. Heaven above, the woman was beautiful—even her bruises and abrasions couldn't hide her exquisite features.

A riot of red curls newly released from the weight of her recently shorn hair made a halo around her face. "Did you truly believe cutting your hair would conceal you are a lass? Do you give yourself so little notice?" He picked up a lock of her hair and curled the softness around his finger. Her hair didn't even brush her shoulders. He wished he could see her with long red tresses reaching her waist.

He pushed away the unwelcome vision, angry with himself for feeling anything other than loathing. The woman seemed speechless. Didn't she know her own beauty? No woman with such delicate features could be unaware. How else did she get those men to come on a fool's mission?

The bandage that now lay on the bed beside her reminded Bryce of her injuries. "How are your arm and leg?"

Instead of answering, the daft woman merely blinked with an incredulous look on her face. Perhaps she'd hit her head harder than he'd realized. He dipped his head toward her arm and spoke slowly. "You broke your arm and sprained your ankle. Are you in a great deal of pain?"

Pounding on the door drew his attention away from her. "What is it?" he called.

Expecting to see Lucas, he was surprised to see Michael step into the room.

"There is news you will wish to hear." His gaze fell upon Deirdre. "I will be waiting in the great hall." He shut the door behind him as he exited.

What to do with the woman sitting on the bed? He did not wish to keep a guard on her at all times, but she made it quite clear she would do whatever it took to escape, even risking death.

Bryce walked to the door and turned to her, thinking to test her. "You will have to come with me. Can you walk?"

The fury in her eyes could not be missed. She pushed herself off the bed, never taking her gaze from him. He noticed that she shifted her weight immediately to her left leg. She took one step, the heat in her eyes turned to pain, and she nearly ended up on the floor. Had he not started her way as soon as he saw she favored the ankle, she would have crumpled to the ground. But he made it to her side just in time, sweeping her up into his arms and promptly placing her back on the bed.

"Nay, you cannot walk. I will send someone to sit with you."

"I dinna need a nursemaid." She continued to glare at him.

He raised his brow. So perhaps the bump on the head did not affect her mind. "I do not imagine you do. But I also will not take a chance on you attempting to escape again." He made it back to the door and grasped the handle. "I will send someone straight up."

He jerked the door open with enough force that Lucas came flying in with it.

The boy thought to duck his head. "I can sit with milady, sir."

Bryce let out a sigh. The boy was going to be no good to him with this infatuation. "Aye, you may sit with her until Nog comes. Then you are to bring her morning meal to her."

As soon as Bryce made it down to the great hall, he sent someone to find Nog to sit with Deirdre until he could figure out what in the name of St. Jude to do with the woman.

Bryce sat in his chair on the *dais*, Michael pulled up a seat across from him, and Geoffrey, Hugh, Roger, and Ranald filled the chairs around them.

The look on Michael's face told him the news was not good. "What report do you have?"

Michael took a deep breath. "John of Gaunt has died."

"Died? Are you sure?" Bryce questioned his good friend.

He nodded. "Aye, 'tis no rumor but the truth. The man has gone to meet his Maker."

Silence surrounded the men. Ranald made the sign of the cross. The hall had been bustling with activity a few hours earlier when the men had come in to break their fast. Now the only sounds came from beyond the buttery, in the kitchen.

Hugh leaned in on his forearms. "What think you this means?" Frown lines etched his brow.

"'Tis hard to say what lies in store for us. This so-called peace we have lived in has been fragile enough."

"Do you think this is bad then?" Ranald asked.

Bryce shook his head. Not really to answer Ranald's question but more to get control of all the thoughts running through his head.

"Richard and John have never been close, but John has always been loyal to Richard—even when his son, Henry was exiled. The man is, or I should say *was*, faithful to his king," Bryce explained.

"Aye, he was. But do you think he kept Richard in hand, or do you think he encouraged Richard in his dealings with his nobles?" Ranald threw the question out there, but Bryce was asking himself the same thing.

"I guess time will tell how John influenced his nephew." Bryce leaned back in his chair to think.

Hugh clenched his hands into fists and slammed them onto the table. "But it might be too late by then. Have they all forgotten the minions whom Richard awarded titles and land to? Or have they forgotten what he did to the Lord Appellants? Beheading one, stripping another of his title and lands, and we all know that he had his uncle killed—whether they can prove that of Gloucester or not, we know it to be true."

"Do not forget Bolingbroke's ten-year exile and

Mowbray's lifetime sentence. No nobility is safe under his rule." Roger added the words that every noble had felt the weight of.

"Nay, we do not forget. 'Tis why all the nobles stand ready to defend themselves against their king," Bryce said, thankful his men were so passionate about their lord.

"I say we rally the nobles and their knights and overthrow the king." Michael spoke emphatically.

"'Tis treason you speak of." Geoffrey finally spoke up.

"Our kings are put on their thrones by God." Bryce said it, though he struggled with the belief. He'd always been told it was true, but did God really put evil men in high places to rule over innocent people?

"Aye," Geoffrey agreed.

"'Tis a sad day when we cannot trust our king. He has broken our trust, and even though many years have passed, here we sit, asking ourselves can we believe in this man to rule us justly?" Michael leaned forward and rested his forearms on the table.

That spritely creature Michael kept as a pet jumped from his shoulder to the table and ran along the edge, stopping halfway down to pick up a small piece of bread that had been left over from the meal. The squirrel sat down with its long bushy tail curling at the tip. Hugh reached out to capture the small creature, but the animal evaded him. Roger brandished his blade as the squirrel scurried past. Michael laughed.

Out of harm's way, Michael's pet stopped to scold them, its chirpy chatter filling the room.

"Can you not control that vermin of yours, Michael? We eat at this table." Bryce huffed.

Michael grinned. "Alex merely offers his service to milord."

Bryce frowned. "And how is that?"

"He is cleaning up the tables for the kitchen servants. He wishes to be helpful." Michael tapped his fingers on the table, and Alex ran back and up his arm to rest on his shoulder with his prize food still in hand.

"By the rood, Michael. Can you not be serious for half an hour?" He and Michael were alike in so many ways but in others so different. Bryce knew he was way too staid, but the lighter side of him, the side that enjoyed life, the side that didn't feel like it had a cloud over him all the time was gone. It left the day he came home and learned he'd been betrayed. Michael sometimes irritated him with his lightheartedness. But that lightheartedness was the very reason they were good friends. Michael kept him from living in a dark and somber world all the time.

Michael shrugged. Bryce knew his friend wouldn't retaliate with words. He really didn't care that he got under Bryce's skin.

"Let me ponder this. Perchance I will ride to my brother's home and to some of the neighboring nobles and see what their thoughts are." Bryce needed time to think about this new development himself. Nothing was so urgent that he must act this day. He had to know what he wanted before he started approaching others.

"I think perchance we should bring Henry back and make him king." Michael's eyes sparkled with mischief.

"Lord have mercy!" Geoffrey hissed. "Do you wish to have us all hanged on the gallows?"

Chapter 7

A *sennight* had passed since the laird had been called from her room, and he hadn't been back to check on her. From what Lucas had told her, the nobles were quite upset with their king, and no one trusted Richard. Perhaps the laird would forget about his prisoner with all the encircling political pressures.

Suffering with only a limp now, Deirdre made her way around the small room, wishing for a window. A knock sounded on the door. She hurried back to the bed, wincing from the pain as she went. When she was settled, she bid them enter.

Lucas stepped in. "Good aftermete to you, milady." The boy gave a slight bow.

"Guid day tae you, Lucas. What brings you by?" She gave him a smile.

The boy brushed his slippered toe around on the stone floor. Hands clasped behind his back and head down, he fidgeted as she waited for his reply.

"I…I only thought to see if you would be needing something, milady."

The sheepishness in his voice made her smile.

"Well, grammercy very much but I canno' say as I need anything other than tae go home."

"Do you miss your home?" He lifted his head, curiosity gleaming in his eyes.

"Aye, I do. But I will no' be going there anytime soon. Your laird does no' seem in a hurry to deal with me."

"He is a busy man, our lord."

She supposed that was true, but the man had brought her to his keep. He would have to deal with her sooner or later. She'd prefer it be sooner, though what she wanted would matter not.

"How long have you been here, Lucas?"

"Not so very long. My home is at Hawkwood with milord Royce and milady Brithwin. I am here with milord's brother so he can teach me things." He leaned in toward her and gave a quick surveillance of the door. He lowered his voice. "But if you really wish to know why I am here, 'tis because milady has not been feeling well, and I have been annoying milord whiles he worries about his wife."

It would have taken great effort to keep the smile from her face. "Sure I am Laird Royce is missing you."

He grinned. "When he wants me to shine his armor."

"Do you ken how long you will remain here with the laird?"

"Nay, milady. But I am not in any hurry to go. You need a protector, and I will not leave you."

"Grammercy, kind sir." Deirdre's heart warmed. What a sweet young boy. 'Twas true he could get a wee bit annoying, but the lad had a good heart. "Your parents, do they work for your laird?"

"My parents are gone."

"Gone? Where did they go? Why did they not take you with them?" She supposed that since he was a page, it was not so uncommon to serve away from his parents.

The boy hesitated, his expression turning woeful. She almost wished she'd not asked him. She'd probably just reminded the lad of how he missed home and his parents. "You need no' answer that, Lucas."

He shook his head. "They died when I was a young boy."

Died? When he was a young boy? He was still young. Her heart ached for Lucas. Looking at him brought back all the fears and insecurities she'd lived with when she was his age. She wanted to put her arms around him and hug him. "Who took care of you?"

He pushed his shoulders back. "I took care of myself."

"But who fed you and gave you a place tae sleep?"

"I told you, I did." He puffed up.

"No one looked after you, cared for you? Surely you have other family." But sometimes other family was no better than a stranger—and in her case, perhaps worse.

"I did not need anyone." He lifted his chin, and she imagined he'd been teased in the past and had developed his hard exterior.

"Do you have any other family?"

"Nay, milady."

Deirdre wanted to weep for the bairn. At least she'd had the old woman who raised her to care for her. She gave in to the desire and pulled him into her arms and hugged him. Every child should know what it felt like to be hugged. Tears welled in her eyes. He hugged her back. She sniffed. He pushed away.

She blinked the tears away. "What is wrong, Lucas?"

He put his head down. "I do not like it when milady cries."

Smiling, she pulled him back into her arms and gave him another hug. "They are happy tears. I am pleased you are my protector."

He glanced up at her, uncertainty etched on his face. "Lady Brithwin always says her tears are happy tears."

"Does Lady Brithwin give you hugs?" She held her breath after asking him that question. She really didn't understand the relationship between his laird and Lucas but hoped that the laird's wife found Lucas as irresistible as she did. The last thing she wanted to do was to make the lad feel unwanted or unloved by his laird's wife.

"Aye, she does." He eased out of her arms and looked back down at the floor, this time to draw circles on the stone slabs with his toe. "But your hugs are much nicer, milady."

Deirdre smiled and changed the subject to help disperse the discomfort the conversation obviously caused the bairn. "What are your duties this day?"

"I will do milord's bidding—fetching the things he needs, serving milord, and cleaning his weapons."

"Do you like tae do those things?"

"I do, milady. One day I shall be the greatest knight England has known! I will protect my people and be good to them, same as milord." He quickly added, "as well as protect you."

Deirdre wanted to ask him which laird he spoke of but decided against it. The lad certainly couldn't be speaking of the Englishman who had imprisoned her. There was not an honorable bone in his body. And she doubted he'd ever done a sacrificial thing in his life.

As if her thoughts had conjured him up, the laird muttered a warning and then opened the door. The man had the manners of a boar. Had she been disrobing, she would not have had a chance to cover herself.

"Lucas, you may leave." The laird's gruff words seemed unnecessary.

"But it would not be proper, milord," Lucas protested.

"Lucas." The laird drew out his name with no less harshness in his voice.

"Aye, milord." He got up and slowly moved toward the door. "I shall be right outside your door milady, protecting your honor."

The laird looked heavenward as the door shut and whispered something under his breath.

She waited for him to speak as she sat on the edge of the bed. He seemed in no hurry as he stared at her. She crossed her arms protectively before her. She'd not let this man frighten her again. She'd always heard that the Englishmen were small weaklings who acted like women with their whining and sniveling. However, this man was not small, nor had she heard anything that resembled sniveling come from him. He seemed to know what he wanted. She thought about that comparison—it wasn't a very nice account of women, for the women she knew were strong and never let a complaint fall from their lips.

Aye, the laird was every bit as large as the highlanders,

and he could be intimidating. At the moment, she knew he attempted to be exactly that as he stood in front of her and stared at her with hands clasped behind his back.

He'd brushed his dark brown hair back away from his face, revealing level brows and golden-brown eyes. His face was shaven, and she had a sudden urge to reach out and feel his skin to see how smooth it was. Most of the men from her village had full beards as well as mustaches.

She wasn't sure if that made him look nicer or meaner. For without a beard his scowl was more evident. She sighed inwardly, tightened her crossed arms, and decided she'd not let the laird frighten her. The man had stood there long enough without speaking.

"What do you want from me?"

He lifted one eyebrow. "What makes you think I want something?"

"You have no' been in here for a sennight, and now you come in and stand before me saying no' a word. I demand you hand oot your judgement and punishment or free me. I will no' sit in here day after day and be compliant for you."

The bearish man actually laughed. She narrowed her eyes at him and stood. Realizing her mistake, she quickly allowed her leg to buckle beneath her and tumbled back onto the bed.

His laugh abruptly stopped as his gaze dropped to her ankle. "Your ankle still pains you."

He wasn't asking her a question. It was a statement. She inwardly smiled. If she hoped to escape, it was imperative he believe it impossible for her to stand on her leg. She leaned over and rubbed her limb to emphasis the pain, making sure to wince as she did it.

"I will send Millicent up to take a look at that leg again."

"Nay, 'tis no' necessary. I can take care of myself."

He frowned. "Something is wrong. You should be improving by now."

Shaking her head, she repeated herself. "Nay. I dinna

want your help. I will see tae it myself."

"Tell me, are you still in pain?" His eyes warmed to the color of dark honey with something that looked almost like compassion if she didn't know better. She stopped rubbing her leg. "'Tis improved."

The man was an enigma. If she didn't know better, she'd have thought he really cared. But if he had any concern at all, why did he keep her locked in the tiny room with not one window? And if he cared, why did the compassion melt away when she said her leg was better?

"Then you will answer me. What do you hide from me? I see the deception in your eyes."

†††

The woman had a stubborn streak in her that surpassed that of King Richard. Bryce frowned as he waited for a response from her. But instead of a response, she kept her folded arms before her and glared back at him. The wench not only had spirit, but she had courage. Bryce grudgingly admired that in her.

He didn't want to like or admire her. That complicated an already complex situation. He still hadn't figured out what to do with the woman. It might help if he knew what she kept from him and—he paused in his thoughts—if she didn't get more beautiful every time he saw her.

Lord have mercy on him, but in the past sennight the swelling had gone down in her face and the bruises had begun to fade, giving him a glimpse of her real beauty.

He continued to wait for her answer. Little did she know that her silence spoke volumes. It told him that she did keep something from him.

As he continued to stare down at her, he searched through his memory for a clue of what secret she kept. He thought back on some of her outbursts. She'd called him a murderer and said he'd taken what was hers. And then when he'd asked her what he'd taken of hers, she'd whispered so quietly he knew she didn't think he'd heard. But he had and it had bothered him more than he'd wanted to admit. Aye, he heard the pain in her words, *my best friend.*

There had been many a skirmish on the borderland, but how could she think he caused her best friend's death? He'd not ever drawn his sword on a woman. But if her best friend were not a woman, if he had caused this man's death, that would mean she was a part of the burgh that bordered his land toward the west and the people who had forever plagued Rosen Craig.

Kincaid's people had been a thorn for the Warwick family since the day they moved into Rosen Craig. That alone could cause the hatred he saw in the woman's eyes.

Her loathing for him was there for all to see. She didn't try to hide it. It was laughable, really. He'd done nothing wrong but catch her in the act of thievery.

The thought made him stop. Devil's ransom! Had the man she called Walter been her best friend? He was older than her, but she'd watched the man die. Perhaps he was her protector and she'd grown fond of him. No wonder she turned her anger and hatred on him. He'd seen the tears she fought when he'd left her in the tower room with Walter. A rogue tear had escaped, and she'd abruptly swiped it away. Aye, that would explain much.

His heart cinched tight, and he reminded himself that he'd caught her in the midst of a crime. There was no reason for him to feel guilty or be concerned with her loss. Walter had been caught in the act as well. They made their choices when they decided to reive from Rosen Craig land. Even the Bible tells of the consequences of sin.

Bryce broke the lingering silence. "I will allow you to rest." He spun on his heel and left the room, happy to put distance between them. He didn't like what the woman made him feel. Not only a thief, she was a Scot, his enemy, and worst of all, deception was her game. He'd managed to stay busy enough to avoid her for the past sennight with the death of John. He and his men had spent much time discussing the problem at hand. He wouldn't have gone in now if it weren't for the fact that he needed to decide what to do with the little wench.

Lucas slipped in the door as Bryce headed for the stairs.

His shoes clicking on the stone steps, Bryce hurried down to find Millicent before gathering his men for the trip to neighboring lords.

Walking into the great room, he found the healer resting in a chair by the hearth. "Precisely the lady I am in search of."

She turned to him and smiled. "Good day, milord. What do you wish from me?" She started to rise.

He put his hand up. "*Prithee*, remain seated."

The woman's cheeks turned bright red. Bryce sat in the chair across from her as she returned to sitting. "Are you feeling well, Millicent?" The dear lady looked exhausted.

She smiled and lowered her head. "I'm doing well for an old woman."

Bryce's heart warmed. "You are not old. You merely have years of wisdom. I worry for you. I want you to go home to Neil, and unless there is an unforeseen incident requiring your attention, I do not want to see you back here for at least a sennight."

He'd expected her to argue. She didn't. Instead, she held her smile. "Aye, milord. I could use a little rest."

He nodded as he stood, reaffirming his words. "I will see you no sooner than a sennight."

Now he needed to find someone to sit with Deirdre while he was gone. The woman caused him more trouble. He wished he'd sent her back when the lad had taken Walter's body. The truth niggled at him—if he truly wanted her gone, all he had to do was open her door.

He headed outdoors as Geoffrey and Michael strode toward the practice field with swords in hand. He let out a piercing whistle, and both men turned. Bryce called Geoffrey over and Michael gave him a frown. He knew what that frown was for. Michael and Geoffrey were forever in battle over who was the finest on the field. Geoffrey had over ten years on Michael and claimed his extra time and practice made him better, while Michael argued that those extra years took their toll on Geoffrey's body, therefore making Michael the better warrior. Truth be told, it depended on which man had the better day.

Geoffrey stopped in front of him. "Aye, milord?"

There were days that Bryce hated the formality with some of his men. Today was one of them. How many times had he told Geoffrey to call him Bryce? "How is Ella these days?"

Cocking his head and closing one eye as the sun shone down into his face, Geoffrey gave him a curious look. "Ella is doing well," he said slowly.

"And your children?"

"Doing fine as well. What is it you wish to ask me, Bryce?"

His friend knew him well. "I need someone to sit with Deirdre and would prefer not to put one of my warriors on her door." He'd been telling himself it was because he didn't want to use that manpower on a female thief, but there was a part of him that didn't like the idea that one of his knights would be spending so much time with her.

Geoffrey nodded. "Ella would be honored to come."

"She should not be too much trouble as she still is unable to walk." He gave him a sharp nod to assure him of his words. "We will be leaving as soon as we can gather our things." Bryce gazed toward the field where Michael had found another competitor.

"I will summon Ella, immediately." Geoffrey grinned.

"I will meet you at the stables within the hour."

Geoffrey turned to go but stopped mid-turn. "Where do we go?"

His mind still on the young woman in his castle and not where it needed to be, Bryce shook off the image of the enticing redhead. The sooner he did something with Deirdre, the sooner he could get his mind back where it belonged. "We go to ride the border lands and make our presence known."

By the time Michael rode up, Geoffrey, Hugh, and Finley were saddled with their packs, waiting.

Ella waved at Geoffrey as she made her way up the keep steps to sit with Deirdre. He gave a slight nod of his head.

The group moved out of both baileys and passed by the cows grazing outside the walls. Bryce continued to keep them close to the castle, lest more Scotsman come.

Michael rode up beside him, and Bryce braced himself.

"'Tis a funny thing what a woman can drive a man to do."

Bryce ignored him. Michael tried to rile him.

"Where is it we go, milord?" A hint of laughter tinged Michael's voice.

Closing his eyes and taking a breath in an attempt to not allow his friend to irritate him, Bryce let out a sigh. "You know we go to the borderland."

"Ahhh, aye." He dragged out the words. "I forgot. 'Tis so unusual for you to leave your keep to do the job that any of your men can do."

"True. However, we did just send two dead bodies a *fortnight* ago. I wish to see for myself how the border fares."

Michael chuckled. "And this trip has nothing to do with a beautiful lass held in your castle?"

"Nay." He would not let Michael get to him.

"'Tis just strange that you would choose now to leave Rosen Craig." Now the man didn't even try to disguise the humor in his voice.

"You are not the lord of Rosen Craig. I choose not to put my men in harm's way unnecessarily."

"And a good thing it is that I am not lord of Rosen Craig."

His blood heated as it flowed through Bryce's veins. He

turned to his friend. "You question my decision?"

A smile fixed upon his lips that appeared immovable by Bryce's tone. "Never would I challenge your decisions, milord."

They rode down the packed dirt road and cut off to the left and into the green grass. The click-clacking of hooves was soon muffled by the soft grass cushioning the sound. The silence was welcome, and just as the tension began to fade, Bryce knew Michael was about to send it soaring.

Michael wrapped his hand around the pommel, lifted slightly out of the saddle as he pushed against the stirrups, and settled back in. "'Tis glad I am the lass has not caught your interest."

Bryce kept his head forward and his eyes looking straight ahead. He needn't inquire, because Michael would not be able to refrain from explaining.

But a strange movement caught his attention and Bryce turned just in time to see Alex's tail slip out of Michael's *surcoat* and scamper up the horse's mane, balancing precariously between the large beast's ears.

"I be of a mind to get to know the little lass if she has no interest for you." A crooked smile played on his lips.

"You are not here to find a wife."

Michael nearly choked. "I did not say anything about a wife."

"You know as well as I that I cannot allow you to fraternize with the prisoners. But if you were to say you want to marry the lass—" Bryce held back the smile wanting to bud forth. "Weel, then, I might be willing to make an exception since we are such good friends, for it would get the lass out from under foot, and I would know you would keep her under control."

He loved to get the upper hand on his friend. Michael reached out and plucked his pet squirrel from his perch and stroked it, something that Bryce had noticed his friend often did when uncomfortable or excited.

"Perchance we could convince the lass to marry for her freedom."

Michael frowned. "You know that is not in my plans."

Bryce shrugged. "'Tis the only way, my friend."

By the time night fell, Bryce was happy to get off his horse and stretch out before a fire. He hoped to get a good night's sleep beneath the cloud-covered sky. For on the morrow, they would begin traversing some of the most lawless land in England.

Chapter 8

The knock on the door sent Deirdre scurrying back to her bed.

"Aye?"

The door cracked open, and a woman in her mid-thirties stuck her head in the door. "Good day, miss. I have come to keep you company." The woman pulled a chair in behind her. "I am Ella."

Deirdre eyed her warily. "Guid day tae you."

"I see you already have a chair in here. No harm done. Perhaps you will wish to sit on a chair instead of resting on the bed. I can help you move to a chair if you'd like." The dark-haired woman chattered cheerfully as though she'd known Deirdre a long time.

Did the woman talk because she was nervous, or did she prattle like this all the time? She didn't want to be locked in the room with a sprightly woman when she herself had nothing to be cheerful about. Unless the woman brought news of her release, which she heavily doubted since the woman appeared to be settling in.

"My friends call me Ella." She repeated herself and smiled, showing a mouth full of teeth.

"What do your enemies call you?" Deirdre forced herself to look the woman in the eye when she asked.

She thought the woman might bolt for the door when she quickly glanced behind her. Guilt twinged inside Deirdre, but she pushed it away, telling herself that she was a prisoner in her enemy's home. She wasn't in the best of moods. And rightfully so, she told herself.

"Well…well, I-I do not believe I have any enemies." Ella stuttered.

"Weel, I believe I am." With each word Deirdre spoke, she felt lower than the enemy who held her imprisoned. The woman was so cheerful, and truly Deirdre had no joy left.

She couldn't reach down inside herself and pull out even a hair's breadth of kindness.

Ella seemed to be searching Deirdre's soul, and it took everything Deirdre had not to squirm where she sat under the woman's perusal. After she seemed to have taken her measure, a smile spread over Ella's face.

"No, I do not believe you are. I am certain you and I could be friends. I know I am a wee bit older than you, but I do believe I like you."

Deirdre dropped her gaze to her hand rubbing the cloth over her broken arm. "I should no' have lashed oot at you. You are at the mercy of the men here in England as I am in Scotland."

"Milord is a fine lord," she said with so much conviction that Deirdre could almost believe her. "You could not find a finer man to run this keep."

That made Deirdre smile. "Weel now, if he's such a fine man, I do no' suppose you could convince him tae let me go home now, could you?"

Ella blushed. "I do not be thinking that milord would listen to the likes of me."

Deirdre nodded her head, and the motion caused her shortened hair to bounce. She reached up and touched it, wishing she'd not cut the locks now that the laird knew she was no boy. "Nay, I dinna suppose he would."

Silence lingered and Ella had found a fascination with a vein on her hand as she fingered it, causing it to move around. Deirdre couldn't think of anything to say to make up for her very unladylike behavior of moments earlier. She was sorry for her words. They hadn't seemed like they hurt the woman, but they certainly had made her uncomfortable. And quite honestly, she could use an ally.

Apologizing didn't come easy to her. She sat there in silence and ran through her mind the different ways she could tell Ella she was sorry. But the longer she delayed, the heavier her heart became. She'd always had a bad habit of lashing out when something frightened her. Truth be told, even when her uncle told her she'd never be able go home because of her father, she wasn't this scared. Her father was an important laird, owning properties in both the highlands and the lowlands. It wasn't wise to defy the man, her uncle said. But her mother had saved Deirdre from him and marriage to a man like him. She'd sent her away and then feigned Deirdre's kidnapping, her uncle said. God only knew if her father would blame her mother for her part in it. Her mother was never good with lies, her uncle said. He told her everyone knew how cruel her father was, but no one spoke those words out loud. They were only whispered behind closed doors.

She shook off the shiver of painful stories she'd heard since her youth, thankful her father didn't know where she was.

She took a deep breath, delaying her apology no longer and freeing her soul of the dark cloud. "'Tis sorry I am, Ella. My words were uncalled for, and my mother would give me a set down with very stern words were she here tae have witnessed my inexcusable behavior. I was no' raised tae be so uncivilized."

Ella's eyes warmed, and she reached forward and took Deirdre's hand. "You have been through much, dear lady. 'Tis hard to lose close friends. And to be surrounded by strangers..." Her voice trailed off, then she continued. "I take no offense to your words."

The woman's kindness shocked Deirdre. She'd always been told that the English were rude, weak, thoughtless people who were self-absorbed and cared little for others. Unlike her people who had bonds stronger than steel. This woman was more than gracious.

Even with her heavy heart, Deirdre smiled at the woman. She deserved kindness. "Why have you come tae sit with me?"

"That would be our lord's doing, miss. He asked my

husband, he did, to have me stay with you whilst he remained away."

That caught Deirdre's attention. "How long will I be privileged with your company?"

The woman patted her hand. "From what my husband tells me, he and the lord will be gone for nigh onto a sennight." She leaned back in the straight-back chair. "Can I get you anything, miss?"

The thought of food nearly made her belly rebel, but as Deirdre considered declining the offer, a plan started to materialize in her head. The laird would be gone a sennight? Aye, God made a way for her to escape. Perhaps He heard the cries of her heart, for she knew it couldn't be her prayers because she'd not lifted so much as a word up to Him. "I believe I could eat something, Ella. Grammercy." For without sustenance, she'd have no strength to escape.

Ella went to the open door that allowed light to flow in and called a servant, giving her orders to bring up some bread, cheese, and water. Deirdre had lots of questions for the woman. She dearly hoped she'd not get her in trouble when it was all said and done, but without the right information, she'd not stand a chance of freeing herself from this place.

Making a big ordeal of hopping from the bed to the chair only a few feet away, Deirdre hoped to cement in the woman's mind that she couldn't walk.

"Can I help you?" Ella hurried back from the door.

"Nay, I am aboot there." Deirdre collapsed into the chair a little harder than she'd planned and let out a gasp when pain shot up her back and down her leg. It really couldn't have been more perfect even though she'd not intended to fall so hard.

Ella, who'd been easing herself down in her own chair, jumped to her feet and again was at her side. "Oh, I see you have hurt yourself. I should have insisted on helping you. Milord will not be happy with me if you were to get injured again."

"Nay, nay, sit yourself down." She motioned with her hand. "I am guid. Give it a moment for the pain to pass."

The concern in Ella's eyes told her that the woman believed every bit of what she saw.

"So, let us not talk about me." Deirdre smiled, trying to put the woman at ease. "With no window in this room, I have no idea what goes on in your courtyard. But I have noticed there are days when there seems to be much activity outside."

Ella nodded. "Aye. Sundays are a bit quiet, many people taking their day of rest, but on Thursdays 'tis near mayhem out there."

Deirdre pretended to be mildly curious. "Oh? And why is that?"

"'Tis the day that many of the market venders come to sell their wares. 'Tis also the day that the kitchen pantry is refilled. And then many come to visit with others. 'Tis a bustling place of activity. And easy to lose a child or two. I would know." Ella laughed.

"Really?" Deirdre said the word with utter fascination. Aye, God surely was on her side.

†††

Bryce woke at sunrise. Sitting up, he gazed across a field scattered with gorse. The bright yellow flower seemed to glow as the orange rays from the morning sun broke through the cloud holes and onto the field. He breathed in the welcome musty scent of the ground. Pushing himself up, he continued to enjoy the beautiful picture painted in the sky. The birds chirped a cheerful melody while squirrels ruffling leaves carried on the morning breeze. Bryce strolled over, nudging Michael with his foot.

"Wake up, pretty boy."

Michael opened one eye, yawned, and then stretched. "'Tis lucky you are indeed that I am your friend. I am no one's pretty boy."

Michael stood combing his fingers through his unruly

hair, and Alex scampered up his leg to rest on his shoulder and groom his fluffy tail.

Bryce glanced between the two preening themselves and grinned. "Aye, as you say, my friend."

Michael was a handsome man, and he had broken many a woman's heart without trying. No broken nose, no sword scars—nay, his scars went deep, but they could not be seen.

Bryce supposed that was why he did not like the idea of Michael around Deirdre. What woman didn't fall for the man? Bryce shook off his thoughts. "Break your fast, men. We have much ground to cover this day."

The men rolled up their blankets, secured them to their mounts, and quickly sipped on weak ale and ate bread.

Bryce climbed on his horse and the men did the same. They rode along in silence for no reason other than it was early morning. They'd gone about a mile when Bryce heard the sounds of children playing.

They moved out of the thick trees and into the open space and sunshine. Bryce scanned the area to see where the squeals came from. A creek, with no more than a thumb's depth meandered through the field and back into the trees. The children played on the wooded edge, heads down and entertained by something they saw.

Bryce urged his mount forward. The children all popped their heads up in unison as he and his men approached. They all seemed too terrified to run. Bryce reached into his satchel. All eyes followed his movement except for one little boy whose spell seemed to break, and he disappeared into the woods.

"Would you like some sweets?" Bryce asked the half dozen children still standing there.

None spoke—that was, until the youngest in the group put out her hand. "I like sweets."

He moved his horse closer and leaned down to drop a piece of *gyngerbrede* into the child's hand. The others quickly put their hands out, and Bryce promptly dropped a piece in each of their hands. They eagerly ate their sweets.

Bryce nodded to the oldest boy in the group, who'd not seen more than eight years, he was sure. "Good aftermete to you."

"Guid day," he responded.

"What brings you much joy in the stream this early morning?"

"'Tis nothing." He eyed Bryce carefully.

"Perhaps you would like another gyngerbrede?" Bryce asked and five dirty little hands shot out. He dropped another piece on each palm.

But before they could get them to their mouths, a woman came screaming from the forest. "Dinna put those in *yer* mouths. He be tryin' to poison ye, tae be sure."

She snatched the small sugary piece from one of the children's hand and threw it at Bryce.

He caught the piece with little effort and popped them in his mouth. The woman looked to be about forty years, with tawny brown hair in disarray.

"If you be waiting for me to drop dead, you have a long wait," Bryce shot back.

One of the other children looked down at the sweet in his hand and quickly stuck it in his mouth. The others seeing the boy's courage did the same.

"Spit those oot. Do ye want tae be laid in yer grave this evening?" the woman yelled at the children.

"'Tis not poison, ma'am." Bryce attempted to sooth her fears.

"Dinna tell me ye were jist being kind tae the bairns. They must be poison."

The young girl who'd had her gyngerbrede snatched from her hand began to cry, asking for more.

Before Bryce could respond the woods came alive with men and swords. "Protect yourself, but do not harm them if possible."

They had the advantage, for he and his men were all on

their destriers. As they fought off their attackers, the clanging of metal resonated through the woods. The men they fought were not trained as well as his men, and before long they had tired. One by one Bryce and his men confiscated their swords till they all stood helpless.

Bryce looked back at his men and their horses—all appeared unscathed. He glanced over the small group of Scots around them and saw little blood. "We did not come here to battle with you. We have come in peace."

One of the men spat on the ground near Bryce's horse.

"Nay Englishman comes in peace. Did ye come tae entice oor wee ones with yer sweets so ye could take them as yer slaves?"

Bryce crossed his hands on the pommel and leaned forward. "Now, if we came to harm or steal, would we have disarmed you with nary a cut?"

"Be sensible, man," Michael spoke up.

"Then what ye be doin' up this far?" The man locked eyes with him.

"Keeping the peace and protecting our lands from reivers," Bryce answered in no uncertain tone.

"We no' be reivers." The spokesman for the Scots folded his arms in front of him. "We toil on oor own land. If what ye say be true, then ye be different than the others."

"What others?" Bryce cocked his head with interest.

"The ones coming up tae take what is oors."

It was hard to know if the man spoke of Englishmen or Scots. For when it came to reiving, some didn't care from whom they stole. It wasn't unheard of to have a Scot reive a fellow Scot.

As Bryce's men returned the weapons to their owners, Bryce hoped they'd not turn on them again. He didn't want to shed blood, but he would not keep his men from protecting themselves.

To his relief the men all sheathed their swords.

"I will not tolerate reiving from my people or yours. I

wish for peace on this border."

"Weel, then ye needs tae be speakin' with yer people."

"My people do not reive. I see to their needs," Bryce shot back. He detested the insinuation.

The man shrugged. "If it no' be you, then it be another Englishman. They are all the same."

The other Scots laughed.

Bryce wanted to know if they knew Deirdre. "Do you know a lass who goes by Deirdre Maxwell? Red curly hair, about yea tall." He held his hand out above the ground.

The laughing stopped abruptly. "We ken no Deirdre. As tae the red curly hair, look around ye. Ye have jist described half of us Scots. If ye no' be needing anything else, we have work tae see tae."

All but the man speaking turned and headed back from where they came. He seemed to be waiting for Bryce's reply.

"Aye. If you hear of anyone who knows Deirdre, send them to Bryce Warwick."

He wasn't sure, but right before the man turned, Bryce thought he saw a glimmer of fear in the man's eyes.

Chapter 9

Deirdre pretended to sleep and waited for Ella to leave for the night. Needing to know what kind of security they kept on her, she laid in wait for what seemed an eternity. If she hoped to free herself from this place, she had to do it before the laird returned. Once he returned, she knew he'd be ready to mete out her punishment. Heaven above, he may never release her from her prison.

After all was quiet, she sat up in her bed, letting her feet dangle off the side, and didn't move. She waited for any sounds. Nothing. The floor cooled her already chilled feet as she pushed herself up to stand. She waited, straining for sounds that would alert her to someone roaming around the castle. Again, nothing. Tiptoeing to the door, she placed her hand on the handle and lingered. When no sounds came through the door, she gently pulled.

The heavy wooden slab didn't budge. She squared her feet, and this time braced her left hand against the wall next to the door and pulled, hoping the force wouldn't cause too much pain in her broken arm. The door let out a noisy crack in the silent air. Deirdre's heart plummeted, sending her blood surging through her body. The hair pricking on the back of her neck told her someone lay on the floor outside her prison even before he spoke.

"Who goes there?" The voice was strong, unlike someone who'd only this moment woke.

She pushed the door shut, thankful closing the door didn't cause it to creak like opening it had, and nearly ran back to her bed. Throwing the cover over her body, she lay down and waited for the guard to come in.

Several minutes passed before the door opened, sending a glow from a torch clutched in the knight's hand that filled the room with light. She closed her eyes and breathed heavily, hoping he'd think her asleep.

Muffled whispers filled the small room, letting her know more than one person had entered. Her guard must have called for someone to bring the torch. Footfalls sounded all around the room as she could only imagine they tried to find someone hiding. With so little furnishings, the room should have required nothing more than sticking their heads in to see no one was hiding. The one holding the torch came and stood over her bed. Even with her eyes closed she could see the light through her eyelids and feel the heat radiating against her skin.

"She sleeps." The man spoke to the other with no concern of her slumbering. Another set of footfalls moved toward her bed.

To pretend she still slept would only make them suspicious, for the man had spoken loud enough to wake a deaf person.

The only thing she could think to do she loathed. She opened her eyes slowly. The two men stood next to her bed, staring down on her, the one man holding the torch above her.

Deirdre let out a shriek with all of her being. She'd never been one for screeching and didn't care to be around women who had a propensity to do so. But she imagined that most English gentlewomen would scream if they woke to two men leaning over them. So scream she did.

The man holding the torch nearly dropped the thing on her as he fumbled to keep it in his hand. The other kept telling her to *shh*, batting his hands downward in a manner that she supposed he thought would quiet her, which she decided would make an Englishwoman yell all the more. So she did.

Before she could think of what to do next, her room filled with men of all sizes. The two who had been searching her room began speaking at the same time, endeavoring to outspeak the other as they attempted to rationalize why they were in her room at night.

Deirdre decided to help. "These—these beasts were leaning over my bed when I opened my eyes." She pulled her cover up to her chin and gave a shudder before turning to them. "What were you in here for? To attack me whilst I slept?" It was best to put them on the defensive. She most certainly didn't need them accusing her of trying to escape.

"I thought someone entered your room, miss." The one knight apologized. "'Tis sorry I am to have frightened you."

Deirdre tightened the cover under her chin and tried to act as upset as possible.

"You 'ave gone and scared the lass immeasurably. She will possibly 'ave white hair in the morn. Leave her be, Ulric. A dream must 'ave woken you, no' a noise."

Ulric argued, "A soldier is not a heavy sleeper if he wishes to remain above the grass. 'Twas not a dream, 'twas the door."

The men who'd come in the room wanted to go back to bed and pushed Ulric's protests aside.

One of the other men stepped forward. He gave the slightest of bows. "Ranald, at your service. Sorry we have troubled you, lass. Prithee, return to your sleep."

Deirdre gave a slight nod and pulled the covers up over her mouth to hide the smile.

If she had been the least bit tired before, she was wide awake now. After her audience left, she lay on the bed reflecting how severely her ankle pained her. She doubted she could escape. She'd have to wait. And if she must do it under the laird's watch, so be it.

†††

Bryce looked on Rosen Craig. He was weary after a sennight of sleeping outdoors and eating bread, cheese, and dried meat. He determined he'd gotten soft. At the moment he didn't care. He just wanted to eat a meal cooked by Nog and sleep in his own bed. And as much as he loathed to admit it, he wanted to see how Deirdre fared. When he had left, the lass could hardly walk.

Why did the woman plague him so? Throughout the trip, she was never far from his thoughts. After seeing to his horse, Bryce made his way into the keep and to the great hall, knowing the evening meal would be finished.

He took his place on the dais, and his men joined him. He stretched his legs out under the table. The scent of cinnamon and nutmeg tickled his senses. His mouth nearly watered thinking of the meat that Nog had made. There was nothing better than a well-spiced piece of meat. And he had no doubt the cook had made sure there was some left should he return this night.

He was not disappointed. Nog herself carried in two *trenchers* followed by three more serving wenches with trenchers. She placed one before him and the other before Michael.

"'Tis good to have you back, milord." Nog gave him a smile lacking several teeth. "I saved the best for you."

Bryce smiled. It was good to be home. "'Tis thanks I give you, Nog. My men and I were tired of each other's cooking. The food looks wonderful."

Nog rolled her eyes heavenward. "Aye, I know what your cooking consists of. 'Tis the truth, I'd be wanting me own cooking too if I had to eat what the likes of you five cooked for a sennight."

After the meal, Bryce slipped away and knocked on the door where Deirdre recovered. More than concern for her health drew him there. He waited for Ella to answer. He couldn't shake the feeling that the lass was not honest in all things. But those green eyes that tried to hide the fear the first time he confronted her, wooed him to the door.

The door cracked, and Ella's sweet smile was the first thing he saw.

"Good eventide, milord." Ella cracked the door more. 'Tis good to have you back."

Bryce returned her smile. "Aye, but not as happy to see me as your husband."

She blushed. "Nay, milord."

Bryce looked over the top of Ella's head, looking for Deirdre. "How is the lass faring? Have her arm and ankle healed?"

"Come." She swung the door open. "See for yourself." She walked over to an empty chair. Across from it he could see Deirdre's back and the cropped red hair dancing on her shoulders.

Bryce moved to stand across from the two chairs where Ella had taken a seat and Deirdre sat. "How are you feeling, Deirdre?"

Her arm remained wrapped, her legs were tucked beneath her in the chair, and the bruises had faded to a slight green hue. The swelling was nearly gone. She was beautiful. His admiration dissolved when she lifted her eyes and gave him a cold, hard stare.

"'Tis none of yer concern, *milaird*. I am tae live, if 'tis what you came tae see."

Bryce half-heartedly attempted to hold back a grin. This beauty intrigued him long before she was beautiful. He supposed from the moment he laid eyes on her dressed as a boy, trying to conceal her identity. If he could put it to rights in his head, he'd have to say it was her courage that drew him.

"Aye, 'tis the truth you shall live. I believe you are too contrary to do anything else."

She scoffed. "Have ye given me any other reason, milaird? I be locked in a room with light only from a fire. I ken know one. I can barely walk, my arm still pains me, and now I am bestowed the wonderful gift of explaining myself to my enemy. What better day could I ask for?"

Bryce chuckled. "'Tis glad I am that you enjoy my company, lass. You will be most fortunate in seeing more of me."

"What is it you want? I have no money, I have no belongings, and I have no important information tae give you for my freedom."

"I wish for you to be honest with me."

"I have been."

"Nay, you have not. The cows did not wander onto Scottish land."

She shrugged. "'Tis of no concern now. You have your beasts."

"True. But I wish to hear the truth come from your lips."

"Truth? You want truth? I will tell you truth. You and your rich fellow Englishmen come north and try tae steal from my poor clansman. You murder withoot cause. You are vile." She spat the words out.

"I cannot speak for all Englishmen because I know some are wicked men. But I do know my people, and we do not reive your land or your people. 'Tis not tolerated." Bryce couldn't believe the anger in this woman. She carried with her much hatred.

Ella nodded her head. "Milord has never allowed such behavior from his people."

Deirdre looked at Ella as though she wanted to believe the woman. But when her gaze returned to Bryce, anger burned within. She locked eyes with him but spoke to Ella.

"'Tis sorry I am tae tell you this, Ella, but I ken that no' tae be the truth." Her eyes full of fury and hurt seared into Bryce. "I ken the laird of Rosen Craig came tae our land and pillaged the village and murdered many of oor men. I ken. I was there."

Bryce was sure that Deirdre knew what she'd just done. For she turned away with pinched lips. He said nothing, waiting to see if she would continue. She didn't. Aye, she'd told him who she was and confirmed his suspicions. But she also caused more problems. If her people were the Scots whom Royce and his men had engaged in a skirmish over a year ago, then she was not who she claimed. She was a Kincaid.

And he wouldn't tell her that he lay near death during

that time. Nay, he'd not tell her that Royce came back to be the lord of Rosen Craig when his parents were murdered. For Royce had battled those demons already, and he'd not heap those coals on his head.

"You do not know the truth, lass. My men were not unprovoked."

She sniffed and turned her head away as though the sight of him was more than she could stand. "So you say. Who am I tae disagree? I am in no place tae argue with the laird of Rosen Craig."

A knock sounded on the door before he could respond, and he was happy for it. He wanted out of the room and away from the redheaded lass with the sharp tongue. What had ever provoked him to come in and check on her? He made it to the door in three long strides and yanked it open.

Michael stood before him. "There is more news. We need to speak."

Bryce gave a quick nod of his head and turned back to Ella and Deirdre. "I must go, but we will finish this conversation later." Glad for the reprieve, Bryce ducked out the door.

The two men headed for the flagstone steps, quickly making their way down.

"What is the news, Michael?"

"You are not going to like it," his friend answered.

"You did not take me from the lass's room to tell me that."

They reached the bottom of the steps and headed toward the great hall and the chairs before the hearth.

"Richard has exiled Henry permanently and has confiscated John's lands," Michael explained.

Bryce nearly fell into the chair. "Confiscated the lands? Exiled Henry permanently? Saints alive! What does our king think he is doing? Does he believe his subjects will stand by passively and wait for his greed to overtake us all?"

Chapter 10

Deirdre's ankle was nearly healed, for she only had occasional twinges of pain. Surely its healing was a sign from God of His mercy on her.

It was a second chance for her to escape. She remained awake for hours, working through each problem as she formulated her flight. In the morn she would begin to implement her plan, but even with that decision made, sleep still evaded her. The night wore on and exhaustion finally took over, and she closed her eyes, giving in to sleep.

The next thing she knew a knock on the door awakened her. Deirdre opened her eyes and rolled to her side, facing the door.

Ella peeked in. "Good morn, Deirdre."

The room remained dark with no torch. Only a sliver of light filtered into the room behind Ella, highlighting her form. Deirdre wasn't sure how long she'd stayed awake working through her plan, but it wasn't until she'd heard people moving around in the kitchen that she finally closed her eyes and surrendered to sleep.

Morning had come too soon. "Come in, Ella."

Ella sashayed into the room with a small loaf of bread, a piece of cheese, and enough energy for both of them. "I have not wanted to trouble you with questions, but the servants are abuzz with what happened to you the other night. I have been defending your honor, miss."

Deirdre smiled at the memory. At the time she did not find much humor though. "You mean the men standing over my bed trying tae scare me unto death?"

"Aye." Ella chuckled. "I have heard you may have taken several years off their lives with your scream."

"Serves them right." Deirdre harrumphed.

Swinging her feet off the bed and sitting up, Deirdre smiled at Ella. "Grammercy for the food and defending my honor."

"'Tis good for you to fill your belly. 'Twill help you keep your strength up." Ella set the food on the table and helped Deirdre sit in the chair, then sliced the cheese and warm bread. "As to your honor, I am a good judge of character and well I know you were an innocent party. Men! Barging into your room whilst you slept. They act like animals. 'Tis glad I am that you were not harmed."

The heavenly aroma of fresh bread before her made Deirdre's stomach growl. "Grammercy for this." She waved her hand over the food. "And for believing in me."

"'Tis nothing you would not have done for me."

"Do you really believe that, Ella?" Deirdre's heart warmed.

"Aye, I do."

"Have you eaten? Would you like to break your fast with me?"

Ella smiled. "Geoffrey likes to break his fast with me before he starts his day."

Deirdre fumbled with the bread as she thought how to change the subject and ask for the supplies she'd need for her escape. "'Twas quite chilly last eve. Sleep evaded me for most of the night." She kept her voice casual as though talking of nothing of importance. It truly had gotten cold, with no hearth and fire to keep the chill at bay.

"You poor dear. I will find you another cover to help keep you warm. Sure I am that milord has more around this chilly keep. Is there anything else you'd be needing?" Ella asked with sincerity sparkling in her eyes.

"I do not wish tae cause you any trouble. You have been very kind tae me." She hoped she would not cause the dear woman any problems with her laird.

"'Twill be no trouble, miss."

"I could use a needle and thread. My blade went through my clothes."

"I can bring you both items. It will be my pleasure." The

woman bent over the bed, pulling the woolen blanket up taut on the mattress. "How is your wound doing, miss?" She asked over her shoulder.

"Prithee call me Deirdre. I am afraid it pains me enough that I will not be doing anything where I must exert myself. Most movements are painful." She gave Ella a pained look. "I dinna believe the laird will be letting me oot tae do much anyway."

Ella returned her smile. "Our lord is a good and fair man."

Deirdre certainly wasn't going to disagree with the woman because she'd been so kind. Yet she couldn't agree either. She'd been brought up her whole life to hate the English. Ella wasn't anything like she'd been told her enemy was. The woman must be an exception to that rule. "I am thankful, however that I have no fever for that is guid."

"Aye, that is good, indeed," Ella chirped cheerfully.

The two chatted, but the day crept by. If it had gone by any slower, it would have seemed to have been a sennight. Ella filled every bit of silence with chatter, leaving Deirdre with no time to work on her plan of escape.

But to her benefit, later that day, Lucas came by to see if she needed anything. Ella slipped out to gather the things Deirdre had asked for, bringing her one step closer to leaving. Not really wanting to take advantage of the boy's kindness but needing his assistance, she asked him for some torches to help keep the chill off at night. And she would also put the light from those torches to good use as she sewed together her garment.

Truth be told, she missed daylight. It had become hard living day and night inside a room with no window. She longed to see the sunshine and feel the rays warm her face. Never had she thought she'd miss such things as her shadow on the ground or the way the sun's light bounced off a river, making it glimmer like a thousand diamonds dancing on the water's surface. The burning desire to feel the breeze rustle her hair or to smell the damp soil as she rode through the woods kept her focused on her goal.

Ella returned with the needle and thread, as well as a tan colored woven blanket. She apologized for the holes and large brown stain on it. Deirdre thought it perfect for what she needed and thanked Ella for fetching it for her. The holes and stain would only make her look like a poor *villein* and aid in her escape.

If Ella told the truth and her laird was a guid man, he'd not harm her should she get caught. At least that is what she kept telling herself to keep her courage from faltering. Taking a deep breath, she lifted her chin. She'd let no Englishman put the fear of death in her. Nay, the Scottish people would not have it. They were a proud people, and she'd not shame them.

As evening approached, she encouraged Ella and Lucas both to leave for the night by yawning and saying she was near exhaustion. Lucas however did not take the hint. The lad just sat and smiled at her. To her relief when Ella took her leave, she ushered the boy out in front of her, pulling the door shut behind.

With the two of them out of the room, Deirdre slumped back on the bed, glad for the silence and time alone. She needed to get to work on her disguise. The good Lord had given her a second chance. She must finish her cape so she could escape before the laird returned.

Gathering up the things Ella brought, Deirdre started to work. Her dagger was gone. They'd not given it back to her after her little mishap. She lifted the woven fabric to her teeth to start a small tear and attempted to rip the fabric, sending a scorching pain of fire up her broken arm.

Remembering from her childhood when lasses stepped on their gowns and put an unwanted hole in them, she placed her foot next to where she wanted to split the fabric. Pulling with her good hand, she felt the fabric gave way and began to separate. With great care, she tore out the pieces she needed to fashion a long cape with a hood.

The method she had to use for tearing the fabric ended up very time consuming. She reminded herself that time was all she had, but then corrected her thoughts that she needed to be on her way. For fortune had shone on her, and the laird once again was called away on business. This time she didn't know how long.

By the time she'd gotten the pieces torn like she'd wanted them, she was tired. Folding the fabric up, she stuck it under the thin mattress lest someone should come in and see. She then climbed into bed, knowing she had gotten that much closer to leaving her enemies' home forever. Dare she hope that God would allow her to go home to Scotland?

†††

Bryce sat in front of the great hall hearth at Hawkwood across from his brother's wife, Brithwin. She sat snuggled up next to Royce, who had his arm draped over her shoulder. Amidst the country's turmoil, his brother looked so relaxed and at peace.

After Michael had given his report, they'd gotten a few hours of sleep and then left Rosen Craig, coming straight away to his brother's keep.

Michael sat to the right of Bryce with his capricious squirrel on his shoulder that looked like he searched for food in Michael's hair.

"Michael, are you hiding nuts in your hair?" Brithwin had the same thought.

Royce laughed.

Michael's gaze shot to Bryce's brother. "Do not voice the words that are now forming in your mouth."

Royce shrugged. "I merely wondered if the creature knows what is in that head of yours better than us."

Listening to the banter back and forth between his brother and Michael did nothing for Bryce's mood. He and his entourage had pushed their horses to get to Hawkwood, not stopping to rest or eat. Much was amiss with King

Richard, and he wanted to speak privately with his brother and Michael. He must wait for Royce's wife to excuse herself for the night so they could talk of graver matters.

The evening grew late with light conversation. Bryce would have enjoyed the evening more had he not been weighed down with such a heavy burden.

"You said you had matters of the king to speak with me?" Royce asked.

Glancing toward Brithwin, Bryce made his apologies. "I thought to wait until your wife took her leave."

"Brithwin can remain. I keep no secrets from her." Royce's admission took Bryce by surprise. His brother had told him he loved his wife, but even their father, who nearly worshiped the ground their mother walked on, didn't allow her to sit in on important political conversations.

"'Tis fine, Royce. I have had a busy day and would like to retire for the evening." She leaned over and kissed Royce, not seeming to notice or be bothered by her audience. She stood and gave a slight curtsey. "Good eventide, gentlemen."

Royce's gaze followed her until she had ascended the stairs and then he turned his attention on Bryce. "This must be important for you to come with much haste."

"Aye, 'tis. This morn we received word that Richard has rescinded the ten-year banishment of Henry Bolingbroke and made it a lifetime exile." Bryce gave his brother the ominous news. And waited for him to process it.

"Life banishment? What does he gain by this? With Gaunt dead…" Royce's words faded as realization took over.

"Aye, Royce. You are seeing the truth of it. Richard craved John of Gaunt's money. Why, with John's money, Richard could support his extravagant lifestyle as well as help finance his crusades to Ireland." Bryce shoved his fingers through his hair as the true gravity of the situation seemed to only exacerbate with time.

"Nay, he cannot take John's estate. 'Tis not lawful," Royce argued.

Bryce sneered. "You should know by now, brother, that Richard believes he is above the law. He makes his own rules to live by. He has made Henry's exile for life so he can confiscate all of John's land. For Richard cannot claim them with Henry here."

Royce leaned forward, resting his forearms on his knees. "Nay, he has no right to claim the lands with or without Henry here. Henry is the king's cousin, for saints' sake."

Michael pulled Alex off his shoulder and stroked the squirrel's back. "Which brings us to another question. Did John die of natural causes, or was his death hastened by Richard?"

Bryce nodded his head in agreement. "That thought has battled in my head since I learned the news. 'Tis hard to believe our king would stoop to such a thing, but when I think of what he has already done…his punishment of the Appellants, giving his favorites lands and titles that were not rightfully theirs, and now stealing what is justly Henry's, 'tis much easier to believe he could kill his uncle."

Royce's gaze stayed on Bryce. "If Richard will turn on Gaunt and Henry, from one of England's most powerful noble families, what will keep him from turning on you or me? No man's property is safe."

"Richard is arrogant. Thinks he that his nobles will sit by whilst he oversteps his authority?" Michael continued to pet Alex, and the little squirrel closed its eyes, oblivious to the tension in the room.

"Aye, he is. But the man must have lost his mind to banish Henry and confiscate his lands. Surely Richard knows he pushes Henry and even his nobles too far by taking this derisible action." Bryce shook his head. The whole thing made his head pound. Could things get any worse?

What were they going to do? Their king had to be stopped before he stripped each and every noble of his position and put his favorite pawns in their places. Richard had proved himself untrustworthy before when he took his revenge out on the Appellants, but now…now he committed treason against his own people.

Silence had fallen upon the room as all three of the men stared into the flames. Saints above, what were they to do? No man wanted to speak the words, but something had to be done about their king. He no longer had England's best interests at heart. The only interest Richard had was his own. That was not the kind of king England needed and certainly not the kind of king Bryce needed with the trouble he had on the border.

The talk had left all of them solemn and at a loss for words. Bryce had always tried to be faithful to his king. The man had tried his father over the last ten years as well himself, seemingly siding with Rothburg at times over the ownership of Rosen Craig. The king knew he had no real grounds. But then Richard had no rights to John of Gaunt's land either. There comes a point when a man must stand up for what he knows is right regardless of whether it goes against his king.

There had always been hope in Bryce that Richard would gain his senses and mature as he ruled England. But it seemed that Richard remained the spoiled little child who always had to have things his way. His experiences hadn't made him any less selfish or any more honorable. The king proved that when he punished the Appellants without a second thought.

Well, that was not true. Richard had given it a second thought, all right. He'd dwelled on it for ten years and never forgave them. Instead, he sought revenge.

Ack! What to do? He hadn't voiced his thoughts to the others yet, but Bryce's only conclusion would be considered treasonous by those loyal to the king.

Chapter 11

Bryce sat across from his brother in Royce's *solar*. Like so many evenings since he'd been there, Brithwin sat next to Royce, snuggled up like a little puppy drinking in the attention of its master. The smiles and special looks they gave one another made Bryce's heart twist. He preferred not to notice or care. He detested the fact that he felt jealous of what his brother had.

He loved his brother and wanted him to be happy, but the yearning Bryce felt within made him angry at himself. Royce deserved to be happy. Bryce didn't suppose he deserved much of anything. Nothing would come easy for him. Nay, he supposed his soul was blacker than most out there. For he was the reason his parents had died at his betrothed's hand. And what woman would want a man like that? Someone like Clarice. Certainly not one like Royce's wife.

Brithwin had not only outer beauty, but her faithfulness to her husband showed in almost everything she did and exposed her inner beauty as well. 'Twas obvious the love that filled her for Royce. He was happy for his brother. He loved Royce. But this ache in his chest wouldn't leave, though he wanted it gone...gone forever.

Clarice's betrayal would forever be a reminder and a warning to him. The hurt of caring had left him weak. He wouldn't make that mistake again. There was too much at stake in his sphere of influence to let soft emotions distract and weaken him.

Yet, when he looked at his brother, he did not see a weak man. Nay, quite the opposite. And the peace he saw in Royce was like nothing he'd ever perceived in his brother before. If only a woman could do that for him.

Royce glanced up and caught Bryce gaping at them. His brother smiled. "Brithwin and I have been talking. 'Twould do you good to bring *Pater* back with you to Rosen Craig."

"I need not a priest, brother." Bryce's retort came out a little sharper than he'd planned.

"Nay, 'tis not a priest you need. Of that I will agree. My father-in-law is not just a priest. He is just a man who seeks God's will and fulfillment. The man wishes to return with you, and Brithwin has agreed as long as he is at Hawkwood by the time of the wee one's birth."

Bryce frowned. "Why does the man wish to leave?"

Brithwin pushed her head off Royce's shoulder and sat up, leaving her hand on his leg. "The truth is my father would like to go back and see some of the people he met during his brief stay there."

Bryce nodded. "I understand. I myself missed the people of Rosen Craig when I was being cared for by Millicent. If that is what you and he wish, I will be pleased to accommodate you."

"When will you leave then?" Royce asked.

"Early on the morrow. I have many more places to stop and give the news to. I want to know who is with us and who stands against us." Bryce unfolded his legs and stretched them out before him, glancing around at the white-washed walls covered with colorful tapestries.

"Will you go to Rothburg?"

"Nay. You know as well as I that the blackguard would use that as an opportunity against me. I know where the man stands. He is a friend of Richard. As long as the king continues to do favors for Rothburg, the man will not be swayed from his loyalty to the king."

Royce nodded and pulled Brithwin back to his side. "Aye, 'tis the truth. And the man could cause us much trouble should he catch wind of what changes we plan for our country."

"I will stay clear of him. Saints truth, Royce, I never thought I would be speaking words against our king. I've always believed God put our kings on their thrones. Who are we to remove them?"

"Then why the change now?"

Bryce shrugged. "One might say that God and I aren't on speaking terms. I do not think God cares much of what I do these days. But you, my brother, I am surprised that you would go against God's king. You with your religion." He hoped he didn't sound as condescending as it sounded to his ears.

Royce smiled. Not an ounce of irritation showed in his eyes. "I do not consider myself a religious man. Just a forgiven man. 'Tis true that God ordained many a king and leader, but there is a verse in Hosea that says, *They have set up kings, but not by me; they have made princes, and I knew it not; of silver and gold have they made idols that they may be cut off.*

"That scripture tells me that not all kings are given their authority through God. Some are from man. Richard has been given his chance to serve as king. He has taken his position of authority and misused it. It is time for us to call him to accountability. We have more than ourselves to look after, we have our families and our people."

Bryce leaned forward. "And that is the reason that I chose to oppose my king. I do not wish for the people of Rosen Craig to ever have to worry about an unfair lord. If Richard were to appoint one of his minions, 'tis hard to say how evenhanded they would be."

By the time Bryce had gotten to bed that night he couldn't sleep. He'd have liked to have gotten up, gathered his men and headed out. But with Pater coming along, he'd not drag the old man from his bed. Instead, he tossed and turned until the sun peeked through the trees and cast a dim light into his room.

When the chirp of birds floated through the windows, Bryce swung his feet to the floor. Glad the night had ended, he slipped on his breeches and linen shirt before securing them with his belt. Swiftly scooping up his boots, he balanced as he slipped on the leather footwear. He pushed his arms through the sleeve holes of his doublet, snatched up his sword and dagger, securing them on his belt, and threw his tunic over his arm.

He left the room buttoning his doublet as he headed down to the great hall. To his pleasure, when he arrived, Pater already sat at the dais finishing his meal.

"Ah, good morn to you, milord." Pater nodded as Bryce briskly stepped up.

"'Tis a good day to travel." Bryce sat down, and a servant appeared at his side setting a trencher of cheese and dried fruit before him. "Has Royce broken his fast this morn?"

"I have not yet seen him." Pater grinned. "Perhaps he is up burrowing in with his lovely wife."

"I take exception to that." Royce bellowed from the flagstone steps. The twinkle in his eyes proved he was all bluster. "I met with the steward and bailiff whilst I delayed filling my belly with food, waiting for you to wake. I had begun to fear that you would sleep your day away, brother, and I would miss breaking my fast whilst I waited on you." He laughed.

Bryce couldn't keep back the grin. "Then come and eat with us now, for I must leave soon."

"Aye, 'tis time, indeed." Royce nodded to the servant to bring his food before dropping down onto the high-back wooden chair. "I am sad to see you go, brother. Your stay was too short."

"There is nothing to be done for it, Royce. I have many keeps to visit and many lords to speak with. And my own keep, though left in capable hands, will have a list of things I must attend to upon my return." Bryce let out a weary sigh.

Michael walked into the room and made his way over to the table. "'Tis the truth, I should have remained at Rosen Craig." He slapped Bryce on the shoulder, stopping by his friend. "Then you would have had no concerns whilst you were gone."

"You are too humble. I am not sure how you live with yourself." Sarcasm laced Bryce's words.

Michael moved away but not before he stole a cherry from Bryce's plate. He plopped down on the chair next to Pater. Alex popped his head out from Michael's shirt, and the squirrel took the small piece of fruit from his hand.

"It can be a bit much at times. If only more men were like me." Michael gave Bryce a smirk.

Pater choked. Michael banged his hand on the man's back. "I hope you are not coming down with something, Pater." Michael grinned,

"I am fine." Pater's words came out barely over a whisper as he continued to cough. "But you, my son, may want to confess your sin of vanity."

Michael shrugged. "I speak only the truth, Pater. There is no vanity in me." He kept his eyes on his pet, running his hand down Alex's back and tail.

"I see 'tis a good thing I come to Rosen Craig. Perhaps you are the reason the Lord leads me there, Michael." A twinkle glimmered in Pater's eye as his voice strengthened.

Michael let out a loud chortle, causing Alex to scamper up his arm and rest on his shoulder. "Aye, Pater. You will have your hands full with me." He paused and glanced across the table. "And Bryce."

"Do not bring me into this, my friend. You have brought Pater's wrath on you all by yourself. I want nothing to do with it."

Michael continued with his good-natured antics through the meal. When they'd finished breaking their fast, Bryce said his goodbyes and headed out to the horses that had been readied for them.

He and his men spent the next sennight riding to meet with the other lords, informing them of Henry's banishment and Richard's confiscation of the land of England's most powerful family.

The neighboring lords stood with him and his brother, appalled that their king would overstep his role as ruler.

All were concerned that if Richard could do such a thing to Henry, there would be nothing standing in his way of seizing their land and giving it to his favorites or even using it to support his lavish lifestyle and his wars. And then there was the unspoken question—did John of Gaunt die of natural causes?

The constant drain on his nobles for more taxes had already put a strain on the relationships between king and nobles, but Richard played a whole new game with this move.

If the nobles waited too long in this battle of wits that the king played, they would soon find themselves checkmated.

†††

Deirdre tried on the plain tan cape and hat that she'd finished late in the night. It had taken her nigh a sennight to finish the garment. Many nights Ella stayed late because her husband was not at home. Other nights she'd wake up with the fabric and needle in her hand and only a few stitches made. But she had finished, and the old blanket given to her by Ella had worked well. She prayed she could accomplish what she'd set out to do and that God would lead her. Because surely, He did not wish for her to stay in England.

A knock sounded on the door, sending her into a burst of movement as she scurried to the bed to hide the cape before the person entered.

She'd done exactly that as the heavy door creaked open and Ella stuck her head in. Deirdre tried to look casual, having nearly dived onto the bed and now lay sprawled across it. No doubt she looked a fright.

Ella rushed in the room. "Are you sick, Deirdre? You look flushed."

Deirdre shook her head. "I am fine."

Ella made her way to the bedside and placed the back of her hand across Deirdre's forehead. There was no making an excuse because none came to mind. And she most certainly couldn't tell her the flush wasn't from fever but from fear of being caught.

"Are you sure?" Her brow furrowed as she looked intently at Deirdre.

"Aye, 'tis nothing wrong with me." Other than the anxiety inside her. There would be one chance for her to escape. If she failed this time, there would be no second opportunity with the way they watched her now.

"Are you cold?"

Without thinking, Deirdre answered. "Aye, just a wee bit."

Ella glanced around. "Where is the blanket I brought to you?"

Panic ripped through Deirdre as she glimpsed her freedom disappearing. "'Tis here." She nodded to her cover and grasped an edge of her new cape from beneath her blanket, hoping she'd not pull out a newly stitched seam, and showed Ella the fabric.

"Oh my, dearie, if you are chilled with all those covers, I fear you must be getting sick." Worry etched Ella's words.

Deirdre shook her head to reinforce her words. "Nay, I am feeling well."

"If you are sure." She hesitated before continuing. "I must go and attend to a family of boys who have lost their mother."

Her heart clenched as she thought of the children. She knew what it was like to grow up without a mother.

Aye, she knew very well the loneliness, the ache that went so deep it made her insides hurt, the fear of being alone, the longing to have someone love her. Aye, she knew all those feelings, for they had never left her.

"Go care for the family. They need you more than I." She sat up. "Who will guard me?"

Ella winced and her gaze went to her hands as she stood next to the bed. "Since you are unable to walk, Sir Ranald, who is overseeing things whilst our lord is gone, said you do not need a *keeper*. I hope you do not get lonely in here by yourself. I could have one of my daughters come."

"Nay." She hoped her quick response didn't offend the kind lady or cause her suspicion. "I have much tae think aboot, and I am still a wee bit tired."

Ella's eyes warmed. "You get some rest. I will put in a good word for you when the lord returns. It should be any day now."

"Grammercy." Deirdre replied. Guilt filled her being. She could only hope that she would not get this gentle lady into any trouble. She would pray for Ella.

She decided to do just that when Ella left.

The door closed and Deirdre bowed her head. She didn't really know what to say. She'd never been good at fancy prayers. And she'd not prayed much. It was hard to know what to say to God when she didn't understand why her life had turned out like it had.

Lord. She hesitated. Not expecting to hear from Him, but hoping to feel something, she continued. *Please watch over Ella and keep her from harm when it is discovered that I have left. Amen.* She felt nothing and reminded herself why she'd quit praying.

With any luck Ella and God were on better terms than her relationship with Him. Deirdre thought back over her childhood and determined she wasn't an overly bad child. She'd tried to do the right thing growing up.

God didn't hear her when her mother had sent her away secretly, or when she just wanted someone to love and care for her. He didn't hear her when she missed her mother and cried herself to sleep at night. Nay, God didn't hear her.

Chapter 12

Deirdre stayed on her bed until the sounds of the outdoor activity appeared to be at its peak. Fluffing the covers up over a couple of baskets that had been thrown in the corner, she did her best to make it look like she slept in the bed. Then an inspiration hit her, and she bustled over to the table where the laird had tossed her hair. She gathered it up and with much care, placed the auburn locks on the pillow, so anyone peeking in from the door would think she'd covered her head with the blanket and her hair spilt out.

With that taken care of, she pulled her hair back and wrapped some of the thread around it several times, before tying it in a knot. Then she pulled the cape from beneath the covers, careful not to disturb her artwork, and put the cloak on, drawing the hat up over her head.

Her insides quaked. And try as she may to quell the trembling within her, she couldn't. She pulled her hand out of the cape and reached for the door handle. Her unsteady hand clasped the cool iron, sending an icy omen through her body. Drawing in a steadying breath, she wrapped her fingers around it and pulled just enough to crack the door.

Her room remained cool with only a torch for heat, yet beads of perspiration trickled down her back. She could do this. She *must* do this. Wasn't this what she'd been striving for since she'd been brought here? What worse could happen to her? They were already going to charge her with stealing their cows.

She sucked in a deep breath, lowered her head, and slipped out the door. If she could get past the kitchen without notice, she was sure to make it to the door that led to the outside and freedom.

Chatter and laughter floated on the air, along with the smell of fresh bread as she neared the kitchen. Deirdre suddenly realized she was famished but pushed the thought aside, concentrating on the task at hand. With any luck the women in the kitchen would be busy and not notice her.

She rushed past the kitchen door and didn't glance in. For some reason it felt safer not to look. She thought she'd made it when she heard a yell from one of the kitchen maids.

"You there!" the woman yelled.

Deirdre stopped, but didn't turn around. She wanted to run to the door, but her common sense told her to wait.

"Go fetch me some firewood, boy. And be quick about it," the woman said.

Deirdre nodded but didn't turn around.

The woman mumbled something about boys these days. When her voice faded, Deirdre hurried toward her chance at freedom. As she put her hand up to open the door, it flew open, squashing her between its wood and the wall.

Two very tall knights dressed in *hauberks* entered. Her heart pounded so loudly she knew she'd just given herself away. But the men didn't seem to notice or perhaps care that they'd just shoved her into a wall.

She kept her head down so they couldn't see her face. Thankful her clothes beneath the cloak were that of a young lad, Deirdre hoped that the men wouldn't look past her attire. Slipping around the door and through the opening, she made it outside.

The sun felt blessedly warm on her skin. She squinted in the light to ease the discomfort. At best, the room she'd spent the last sennights in had always seemed like early dusk. How she had missed the open air. She missed the breeze on her skin that now cooled away the perspiration that had trickled down her back. But most of all, she missed the heat of the sun's rays on her face.

She allowed herself only a moment to enjoy her freedom before the gravity of her situation pressed back down around her. She quickly dropped her head to hide her face as she waited to see if anyone recognized her.

The inner ward bustled with activity. She dared to look

up and see what her next move would be. Her first objective was to fade in with the other people in the bailey. With determination in her step, she made her way to the largest group of villagers heading for the portcullis carrying food, cloth, and different items they had purchased.

Just as she stepped into the crowd, she thought she heard her name. A bolt of icy fear ripped through her. She only heard things, she told herself. The wind had called out to her. Her mind played tricks. No one here knew her, and only a handful knew her name. Fear of being caught caused her to hear things, she supposed. The crowd shuffled along, and Deirdre merged in, becoming one with them, all the while keeping her head down as the group buzzed with chatter and made its way well beyond the outer gate.

With each step she gained a wee bit more confidence. Each step brought her closer to freedom. Each step brought her closer to home.

It suddenly felt odd. These people were going about their daily activity with not much worry other than a broken plow that needed fixing or what they were going to cook for the nooning meal. And here she stood amidst them all fleeing for her life.

When the villeins began to disperse, each going their own way, Deirdre took it as a sign she should make her way to the woods and cover. As she stepped into the canopy of the trees, the warmth of the sun she'd been enjoying fled. A damp, ominous chill enveloped her.

It meant nothing, she told herself as she hurried on. She needed to stay away from the path they'd taken when they brought her to Rosen Craig, certain they would expect her to go back the same way she'd come.

Thankfully, Deirdre had spent a good deal of her life outside and in the woods. She'd learned how to hunt, fish, and navigate as well as any man on her uncle's land. She could best most of them with a bow and arrow as well as the toss of a knife. Finding her way home would not be difficult.

However, finding food might prove another issue altogether, as she had no bow or knife with which to hunt. As long as she had enough strength to get home she didn't care if she had to go hungry.

Her feet slowed and then faltered. Home? She really had no home. When her uncle discovered she'd been the reason that at least two men had died, one being very important to him as the eyes and ears of their village—when he learned she was the reason he'd lost horses… She tried to swallow, but her throat had gone dry. And when he learned she'd been taken by the enemy—oh mercy! She couldn't return to her uncle's estate. He'd never believe she hadn't been ravished by the English. She wouldn't even be lucky enough to be married off to one of his wretched old friends. No, she wouldn't be good enough for them now in his eyes.

Dread built up from her stomach until bile filled her throat. Where would she go if not back to her uncle's home? Perhaps she could convince him—plead with him to believe her. She could be a scullery maid. Nay, he'd not trust her words. She could return to Mairi, for the old widow would never turn her away. But that would be the first place her uncle would look for her. She wouldn't be able to hide long there. And she cared too much for Mairi to have her feel the wrath of her uncle's fury. There was Ian, but Ian was such a troubled soul, he might not welcome her, and even if he did, she wasn't sure she could marry him. Her thoughts ran to and fro, making no sense.

Silence filled the forest, even the birds had stopped chirping. Her gaze shot around, looking for a place to hide. That was when she heard the snap of a twig and a thud. To her right was a decaying fallen tree. She rushed over to it and found the ground hollowed out beneath it where an animal had made a small den. Cautiously, she slid down into the hole and waited.

It wasn't long before Lucas stumbled into the opening where she'd been standing. "Milady!" He called out to her at nearly a yell.

She sat still, hoping he'd give up and go back. How had he found her? Perhaps she did hear someone call her name back at the laird's castle. "Go home," she whispered to herself.

"Milady, I know you have escaped." He started running in the direction she had fully intended on taking.

She let out a sigh. She'd have to go a different way and hope she wouldn't run into him or any of Rosen Craig's men. She started to rise when Lucas came crashing back through the trees. She ducked down, afraid to slide back into the hole for fear he'd hear her.

The boy looked as angry as a dog whose bone had been taken from him.

Lucas stomped past her, not looking her way but muttering as he went. His arms swung back and forth, and he bent forward as though leaning into the wind.

When Deirdre couldn't hear Lucas plodding through the brush and trees, she pushed herself up using the old fallen tree.

Hurrying now to get as much distance between her and Rosen Craig, Deirdre stopped thinking about where she'd go and what she'd do. Right now, all she wanted was to return to Scottish soil.

She walked as quickly as her ankle would allow her. Her chest ached, her ankle and arm ached. But she kept moving toward her beloved Scotland. Before too much longer she'd need to start searching for a place to spend the night. The air would be cold and wild animals would be looking for food. With no weapon for protection, she'd be wise to find herself a tree where wolves wouldn't find her easy prey.

But instead of looking for a place to spend the night, Deirdre kept pushing herself forward. She had to get as far away from her enemy as possible. The fear drove her on. But as the sun threatened to remove its light, Deirdre decided it was time to stop.

She found a tall old elm tree and tried to pull herself up with her one arm, but to no avail. She glanced around, looking for a tree with lower branches. A stone's throw away stood just what she sought. With a slower gait due to her long walk, she made it to the smaller elm and managed to pull herself up onto the lowest branch. Looking above her, she found a nice spot where several branches intertwined. It took the last bit of strength within her, but Deirdre managed to heft herself up onto the branches and settle in for the night.

Not much time had passed before she realized the position she was in would not work. With both of her feet dangling down over the branch, her sprained ankle and leg began to throb. It hadn't troubled her much for nigh onto a sennight, but the running on uneven ground and twisting her ankle over and over must have taken its toll.

It took a lot of maneuvering and even more concentration to arrange herself so she could prop her aching leg above her body. Letting out a sigh, she sank back onto the cluster of branches that gave slightly under her weight and looked up into the sky and thanked the Lord for her freedom.

It felt wonderful to be outdoors and staring up at the heavens. For the moment, she had no worries. She was cradled in the arms of the tree, wrapped in the heat of her cape as drowsiness crept in. Soon sleep overtook her.

†††

The crashing of branches, thunder of hooves, and the scream of a child woke her from her slumber. Deirdre nearly tumbled out of the tree, for she'd forgotten she'd obtained her freedom.

Beneath her cape her heart thudded against her chest. She strained to hear beyond the horse and frantic child, but for naught. If she shimmied down the tree, she could easily find herself in the hands of her enemies and back at Rosen Craig before the night's end.

The rumbling of hooves grew closer as did the cry for the horse to halt. The animal ignored the bairn giving it orders. Deirdre fought within herself for what she should do. The animal came in her direction. If she came down from the tree, she could possibly stop the fleeing horse and rescue the child. But it could be at the expense of her freedom. Though the child obviously attempted to stop the animal now, he must be running from someone to have been on a horse as darkness fell.

The fact that the child had a horse at his disposal meant that he was privileged and not a villein, for few could afford a horse to ride—that was, unless he stole the horse, and then someone would surely be looking for him.

Deirdre knew she was either about to surrender to her enemy or find herself in the hands of someone worse, but she had to help the bairn being chased. Just as her feet hit the ground, a terrifying scream pierced the night air, followed by a disheartening thud—and then only the sounds of hoofbeats.

The last rays sent just enough sunlight amongst the barren trees for her to be able to make her way through to where she hoped to find the child. The childless horse crashed through the bushes ahead of her and into a clearing where it slowed.

She paid little attention to the animal other than to note it was a destrier. Not the kind of horse she expected to see a bairn on.

Scanning the area before her as she hurried, she searched the ground. There was no way of knowing exactly where the horse had lost his rider. She stopped and strained to hear a sound, but heard nothing other than a distant owl and the evening sounds of the rustling leaves.

She half-ran, half-limped, ignoring that her leg pained her. She had hoped in a day or two she would be as good as before her fall. But the strenuous activity of the day had set her back. Her arm was taking more time than she'd expected, as well. With luck, a few more sennights and she would be done with the wretched wooden contraption.

The trees grew denser, making it harder for her to see as

the light of the moon didn't penetrate the branches as well. She slowed to a fast walk, knowing that time was of the essence.

She'd nearly tripped over the child before she saw him. And lucky she was that she did, or she'd have plummeted down a steep embankment. The horse had probably reared in order to keep itself on solid ground.

Lowering herself down to the young boy, she rolled him over and gasped. "Lucas." He didn't answer. A black substance trickled down his forehead. She touched her finger to it and brought the warm sticky substance to her nose. The metallic odor confirmed her fears—blood.

If the lad lived, she would need to get him help. She put her head to his chest and felt the rise and fall of his breathing and heard the beating of his heart. She felt his arms and legs, searching for broken bones, of which she found none. Her heart ached for the lad. It was because of her that he lay on the ground lifeless in front of her.

With deft fingers she probed his head, noting a rising knot. He needed help, and he needed it now. Scotland was too far. But to get him help in England meant she risked losing her freedom.

Chapter 13

It was early morning when Bryce returned to Rosen Craig. He was weary for they'd ridden through the night and not had a good night's sleep for many days. Tonight, he would sleep in his own bed.

When they'd begun their journey, he'd worried about Pater's stamina, but the man proved to be in excellent shape and never slowed them down one whit.

With his party riding in from the west, the outline of Rosen Craig against the rising golden sun welcomed him home. He stopped on a small rise to drink in the sight—pink clouds made the backdrop for his home. They had been gone over a sennight, but it felt like a fortnight. An unexpected sadness filled him as he thought of his role now. Most men rejoiced in being master of their own demesne.

But what it had cost him to be lord of Rosen Craig came at too high a price. What he'd give to be just a knight in his father's service.

Michael rode up next to him on his destrier. Bryce steeled himself for his friend's humor. Instead, a hand came down on his shoulder.

"It will get better, my friend. The pain may never go away, but it will lessen."

"What, do you read minds now?" Bryce almost expected an affirmative answer.

"Nay, I see the hurt you experience. As I said, it will get better. Give it time. Let us go home and find a warm meal." Michael nudged his horse forward, breaking the invisible barrier keeping Bryce on the small rise.

Returning home didn't go as Bryce had expected. When they entered the bailey, he rode into nothing short of utter chaos. It seemed half the village stood in his courtyard.

Bryce reined around the people milling about, talking and shouting. Ranald strode with determination toward the crowd. Digging his heels into his mount, Bryce headed for the stables. One of the young hands hurried out to meet him and Bryce threw him his reins as he dismounted.

His gaze met Ranald's as his man in charge reached the crowd. By the looks of Ranald, he'd been summoned from the practice field. The sun's rays glistened on his skin, and he still held his sword in hand. The crowd gave Ranald a wide berth as he stormed into the group.

Bryce picked up his pace and pushed his way into the throng of villeins. It only took one man realizing that it was his lord pushing his way through. "Milord!"

The people parted as though he were the king himself. He couldn't help but notice how many eyes went to the ground. Meeting Ranald in the middle, his heart nearly gave way.

Surrounded by people, Lucas lay draped over and tied to a horse—his horse. Not Bryce's personal mount but one he used when Tempest was injured or needed a rest.

His gut knotted with hot fury. The boy looked to be dead. What would he tell Royce? He pushed aside the people who blocked his way to the boy. What would he tell Brithwin? They entrusted this boy's welfare in his hands, and he had let them down.

Reaching out, his fingers brushed the boy's pale cheeks. A fleeting glimpse of hope emerged when the skin remained warm. He wasn't dead—yet. Ranald flew to his side and untied Lucas while Bryce leaned his head down to the boy's chest.

"He still lives." Relief spilled from Bryce's lips. "Call for Millicent." Bryce spoke the words to no one in particular, but Ranald was halfway to the keep when Bryce carefully pulled Lucas from the destrier's back.

The people started to disperse as Bryce turned to take the boy into the castle. "No one leaves. I wish to speak to each of you when I return."

Finley came up behind him. "What would you have me

do, milord?"

"See no one leaves until I can speak with each one." Bryce sometimes tired of the young knight who never seemed to be able to see things that needed to be done. He was young, and because of that Bryce had tried to be tolerant of his lack of leadership. Perhaps he would be man enough to keep the people from sneaking away. Bryce would get to the bottom of what happened to Lucas and nothing would stop him.

When he'd pushed through the doors, Lucas's arms and legs dangled. It was as though there was no life left in him.

Ranald met him at the bottom of the flagstone steps. "The healer is up in the sickroom waiting for you." He moved back and allowed Bryce to pass.

Taking the steps two at a time, he reached the top and turned toward the room where Millicent awaited. When Bryce gently put Lucas on the bed and stepped back, he saw the gash and large lump on his temple. Lord have mercy on the person who had done this, because he would show them none.

He stomped to the door and paused without looking back at Millicent. "When the boy awakens, summon me." He had to believe the child would live, for he couldn't bear any more death in his home.

He didn't wait for her answer. He didn't need to. She would do as he requested. Now the anger that boiled through his veins continued to rise as he strode out to the waiting villeins.

He stopped before them. "Who can tell me what happened to this boy?"

It seemed everyone wanted to be the bearer of the bad news. Bryce raised his hands to quiet the crowd as each one attempted to outspeak the other.

A hush fell over them.

"Now, can someone tell me what happened to the child?" Bryce's gaze fell to Finley as he stepped forward.

"I believe I can help, milord. From what the people tell me they saw Lucas following a man into the woods. However, some claim it was nothing more than a boy."

"And Lucas was well when he entered the woods?" Bryce quizzed.

"It would seem so, milord." Finley nodded.

"How did he end up tied to the horse?" Bryce directed his question to the man who'd just spoken, hoping the man could answer the question.

The knight shrugged.

"'Tis not an answer. I expect you to speak."

Bryce had not only embarrassed the knight, but the fire that flashed through Finley's eyes told that he'd angered the man, too.

"I dinna ask, milord," Finley spat out.

Turning back to the crowd, Bryce looked over them. "Who found the boy?"

The way no one met his eye, but several moved forward let him know the anger brewing inside had shown through. Three men and two women stepped toward him but none of them spoke.

He looked at the man nearest him. "What is your name?"

"Peter, sir."

"What did you see, Peter?"

"I see'd someone run into the woods away from the lad strapped to the horse."

"Do you know who that person might be, Peter?" Bryce tried to calm his voice. Getting angry wouldn't help these people.

"Nay, milord. I had never seen the lad that I could remember."

"Can you remember anything about him?" Bryce pushed for more answers.

"Nay, milord." The eagerness to tell the bad news had seemed to have fled.

"How do you know it was a lad if you didn't see him

well enough to remember anything?"

"He-he was too small to be a full-grown man."

"Aye, he was scrawny if he be a man." The other villein piped up.

Bryce stepped forward and the man shriveled back. He didn't care if he frightened them. "If you two grown men saw a scrawny boy run into the woods, what kept you from bringing him to me so I could get answers?"

Both men dropped their gazes to the ground. Bryce looked to the woman whom he thought might flee. "Do you have anything to add?"

Eyes wide, she shook her head.

He clenched his back teeth. How could they let this person slip away? Bryce turned to Finley. "See if you can find out anything else." He growled out the order and spun on his heel to head back to the keep.

He glanced to his left as he stormed back into the keep. At the sight of Ella, he remembered Deirdre and almost let out a moan. He'd forgotten about her. And by the look on Ella's face, he would wish he'd not been reminded, for Ella seemed beside herself. The little wench must be keeping the poor woman busy.

Happy to avoid Deirdre and all the unwelcome feelings she stirred within him, Bryce made his way up the steps and back to Lucas.

Millicent didn't look like she'd done much at all for the boy, other than clean up the cut on the side of his head. The healer didn't glance up from where she stood next to the bed feeling the boy's arms.

"Appears to have no broken bones." She seemed to speak the words to herself.

"He still sleeps?" Bryce asked.

"Aye, the hit on his head is not good. As ye know, the longer he remains asleep, the less chance he will awaken."

Bryce was well aware of that. Millicent had had that same worry when she and her husband had taken him away and saved his life. She'd told him she'd worried he would never wake.

Standing at the boy's side, Bryce removed from Lucas's wrist the wide tan cloth belt that had bound him to the horse. He'd been in such a hurry to get Lucas to Millicent he'd not finished untying the binds before rushing him up to the sickroom.

As he wrapped the tie around his own hand, a light knock sounded on the door.

"Enter."

Ella entered the room with Ranald on her heels.

"Milord." Ranald's gaze went to the bed where Lucas lay lifeless. "The boy?"

"We know nothing more than there appears to be no broken bones. He still sleeps." He continued wrapping the belt-like tie around his hand. "Is there news on who did this?"

"Nay, I have heard no more on it, but Finley is still questioning the people who have not managed to sneak off."

He had too much on his mind to worry over Finley's lack of knightly skills, but the news still grated on his nerves.

Glancing to Ella and then back to Ranald, Bryce knew his master-at-arms was not just paying a visit to the boy and he couldn't imagine why he had Ella with him. The woman looked like she may swoon. "You wish to say something?"

Ranald stepped forward. "Aye. The Scottish lass is missing. She seems to have escaped."

"Escaped?" Bryce drew out the word as he took in the two people before him and now understood why Ella stood next to Ranald.

"Aye. She is nowhere to be found. Though I do have people looking for her now as we speak." Ranald stood tall and looked Bryce in the eye as he gave him the news. One of the reasons his father had chosen the man for the position— he never gave an excuse, but always took action. "I relieved Ella from keeping watch over her because I believed her unable to walk without assistance. I should have seen through the woman's ruse."

Ella, however, could not take her eyes from Bryce's boots.

"Ella."

She lifted her head to meet his gaze. Tears pooled in her eyes. "Aye, milord." Her voice quivered.

"Carry on, Ranald. Come to me immediately should you find the lass," Bryce instructed.

Ranald gave a quick nod and spun on his heel and disappeared from the room, pulling the door shut behind him. Ella flinched, as the door clicked shut behind her.

He'd had Ranald leave because he could see the woman was near tears. He'd thought to alleviate some of those fears by removing one of the two men towering over her in the room. But by the way the woman's *wimple* quivered on her head, he'd only made the matter worse.

No man he knew liked to see a woman cry, and he was no exception. He always felt awkward and inept at calming the woman's fears or sorrow. Having Ranald leave the room just proved how little he knew about the whole subject.

"Come here, Ella."

The plump, middle-aged woman shuffled to stand before him. "'Tis sorry I am, milord for letting you down."

"You did no such thing, Ella."

"But I should have known the woman could walk. 'Twas I who led Sir Ranald to believe Deirdre could not escape."

"Do not blame yourself. For most people in your position would have thought the same thing. I too believed the woman lame. 'Tis hard to say how long she played this game."

Ella swiped at a tear that had fallen. "Thank you, mil—" Her gaze fell on to the binding he had enfolded around the knuckles of his hand.

Did she think he would hit her? Surely not. Bryce had never given her nor anyone else a reason to believe such a thing.

The color drained from her face as though a plug had been pulled. "Wh-where did you get that?" A strangled whisper escaped as she pointed to the tan material encasing his hand.

†††

Deirdre knew she'd taken a risk by returning Lucas to Rosen Craig, but her conscience wouldn't allow her to take him all the way to Scotland, especially when she didn't really have a safe place to go herself. And leaving him where she'd found him was not a choice.

She had done what she thought best, and truly it had turned out better than she'd hoped. For that morn when she'd come back to the edge of the woods she'd escaped into and gained her freedom just the day before, she saw several villeins milling around the area.

Double checking Lucas's bindings to be sure he did not fall from the horse, she'd led the animal and his precious cargo out into the opening. The destrier had already caused the boy injury by running like a fool. She didn't dare leave the creature on its own to find his way back to his master— whoever that was.

Instead, she'd taken his reins that now were much shorter since he'd broken them in his flight and tied them to a tree branch. The poor horse had deep cuts on his side, which most likely sent him into his fury to escape the pain. Lucas must have dropped the reins and the horse probably stepped on them, snapping them like thread as he ran out of control.

Cupping her hands around her mouth, she'd yelled as loud as her lungs allowed and then hurried back into the cover of the trees. There she'd watched, hiding behind a tree until she witnessed two men hurrying toward Lucas. It was only then, when she'd known the boy would be taken care of, that she fled into the safety of the forest and back toward Scotland.

Her ankle pained her again as she'd twisted and

retwisted it, trying to put as much distance between her and Rosen Craig before they sent out a search party for her. Truth be told, one might already be searching for her. For they'd most likely noticed her missing yestereve. She could walk right into her captives as she headed north toward her home country.

But if she did, her conscience would be clear. At least as clear as it could be. For she knew the reason the boy had been in the woods was that he'd discovered her escape. She didn't think he had come to bring her back. Nay, if that had been the way of it, he'd have brought along help. He'd probably come to try to convince her to return or possibly assist her in her escape. She'd never know now, because she did not plan on returning or getting caught.

She dearly hoped Lucas would recover from his injuries, and she sent up a prayer that his injuries would not take his life. 'Twas hard to trust and have the faith because not many of her prayers were answered. If they were, she would be with her mother, and her father would be a good man.

She would have liked to have gotten Lucas back and kept his mount, for if she had a horse, she could return to Scotland before the laird and his men found her. She certainly didn't want to add horse thievery to the list of wrongs that was held against her.

Perhaps since he had his cows back and had buried two of her friends, he would forget about her. The man loathed her. 'Twas as though he couldn't stand the sight of her. She lifted her head, a wee bit indignant over the thought. If he didn't chase her down, he would never see her again.

With her ankle paining her as it did, she wasn't sure how long it would take her to get off Rosen Craig land, again. And if they did come after her, she wouldn't be hard to catch up with. Determination sparked within her. She would not get captured and returned to Rosen Craig.

In a fluid motion, she reached down as she hurried along and snatched a long thick dead branch from the ground to aid her in walking. Jabbing the stick into the ground, she expelled her anger with each step.

Why did it bother her that Bryce Warwick could barely stand the sight of her? She'd lived as a boy for so many years that most of the village saw her that way, she was certain. The boys she lived with showed no real interest in her other than her hunting skills. So why would she care if her enemy didn't see her as attractive?

She touched her cropped hair, which barely reached her shoulders, and suddenly felt very ugly. Once again, her mother's words flooded back, this time with guilt. *You have bonnie hair, Deirdre. There is none that compares to yours. Dinna cut it, my dear. 'Tis your crowning glory.*

No wonder the laird could not stand the sight of her. Slamming the pointed end of the branch into the ground with more force than she intended, she sighed as it groaned with a crack. Why did she care? Getting home was all that mattered.

Maybe that was what troubled her. She didn't have a home to go to anymore. Truly, she didn't know where she would go other than returning to her home soil of Scotland.

Tears burned her eyes. She tired of playing the adolescent boy who shot an arrow straighter and threw a knife with more accuracy than the other boys. The art of being a woman had slipped her by as she honed the skills of men. And what good did it do her now?

The only man who would want her now was one who married her because of her father or her uncle. One who was old and either never could find a woman who would marry him while he was young or who had been through several wives, sending them all to their graves.

She let out a whimper that ended in an angry scream. She didn't care if the whole world heard her. Every emotion inside her, she hated. The hurt, the anger, the fear, the shame, she wanted them all gone. Why did her life have to be so complicated? Why couldn't she have been born to a villein couple somewhere who tilled the ground for a living?

The beatings she feared her mother had received when she returned to her father without Deirdre would never have happened if she'd not been born. The death of Walter and Fionn—all her fault. A sob escaped her, and she collapsed to the ground, the grief within her stealing her strength.

The tears wouldn't stop. She was alone. There was no one who cared, no one to rescue her, and no one to love her. When she'd spent all the tears she had, blessed sleep took over.

Chapter 14

Bryce thought he might have to catch the woman in front of him when she swooned. He reached out and steadied Ella. "Are you feeling ill?"

The trembling beneath his fingers made him want to call Geoffrey or perhaps Millicent. But when she lifted her eyes and he met her gaze, he knew it was fear that had taken over her.

"Mi-milord." She stammered.

"What is it, Ella?" Bryce continued to steady her with his hand.

"It-it w-was m-my d-doing."

Bryce frowned, trying to understand what she implied, and instantly wished he hadn't, for her trembling grew to almost convulsions. "All will be well. There is no need to trouble yourself so."

"B-but you do not understand. It was Deirdre, and I gave her the means to escape."

Anger boiled in Bryce's blood when he'd finally gotten the story out of Ella, learning she'd supplied Deirdre with a blanket and needle and thread, the same blanket that the binding had been made from—stain and all. There was no question who had bound Lucas to the horse. His anger was not toward Ella, but Deirdre. She was not only responsible for Lucas's condition—she took advantage of a sweet lady.

He'd not made it out of the keep when Ranald met him with news that one of the villeins remembered something about the person fleeing. He had a slight limp. Ranald's confirmation that Deirdre was responsible for Lucas's injury only added to the turmoil going on inside him. He was angry at himself for putting off her punishment, angry at her for what she did to Lucas, and angry at God for allowing it to happen to the boy.

It didn't take long before they were mounted up and ready to ride. Bryce looked at his men. There were only four of them, but how many men did one need to retrieve a limping, weaponless wench? He nudged his destrier forward. Michael moved in to ride beside him, and Roger Guernon and Finley fell in behind.

Finley would not have been his first choice, but Geoffrey needed to comfort Ella. Pairing Finley up with Roger might not be a bad idea. Guernon at least had no problem making decisions. The man worked hard, rarely questioned Bryce, and took initiative, although he could at times be impetuous.

Michael interrupted his thoughts. "Where is that mind of yours wandering to?"

Bryce turned his head to answer Michael but lost sight of what he was about to say when Alex poked his nose out of Michael's tunic. "Can you go nowhere without that thing?"

Since Michael's arrival, there had been ongoing sparring about his newly acquired pet.

Michael grinned. "I do not bring him with me. He chooses to come."

Bryce let out a harrumph and shook his head.

"What? You do not believe me, Bryce?" Michael's tone held humor in it.

"Nay, I do not."

"Alex does not take kindly to being left behind. Although truth be told, he has never been left."

Bryce drew his brow down, wondering if Michael had been hit in the head and addled since they'd served together.

"I know what you think, Bryce. But *you* should try to stop a squirrel that is set on going. 'Tis not an easy task if you do not wish to harm the animal. If you do not believe me, try catching a squirrel the next time you see one."

That made Bryce laugh. "You mean to tell me that Alex has made you his surrogate mother?"

Now it was Michael's turn to frown. "Aye, laugh if you want. But the ladies like him. Gains me much attention."

"We shall see how much your wife likes it when you marry, and she must share her bed with the creature." Bryce kicked his heels into Tempest, sending the horse into a trot as they headed out the gate.

"You are just jealous." Michael grumbled as he spurred his horse on to catch up.

"I think not." Bryce threw over his shoulder before sending his destrier into a full gallop once through the portcullis.

Michael perhaps would have been better suited as a lawyer, for the man would argue anything and not quit. Bryce found it best to make it impossible for him to continue the conversation.

He needed to keep his mind on the situation at hand, and that was pursuing a certain little wench. Torn between flogging her and letting her explain herself in hopes that there was an explanation, he pressed on.

What would he do with her when he found her? He'd spent more time avoiding her since he captured her sennights ago. He didn't like what she stirred within him. Her deceit was much like Clarice's, and he could not fall into another trap.

At least this woman didn't try to hide the fact she hated him. He had to give her credit for that. There was no deceit there. His heart told him Deirdre and Clarice were as far apart as the east from the west, but he could no longer trust his heart, it had cost him too much.

Following the path that led down to the village, Bryce slowed and took in the people milling around, going about their daily activities. But instead of turning into the village as they neared, he veered to the left and into the open field that bordered the woods where they were told Deirdre had disappeared.

He glanced back at the village, realizing how close the houses were to the woods and wondered why the woman would risk bringing the boy halfway into the open field, putting her life in jeopardy when she could have fled, and no one would have been the wiser.

And why hadn't the lass taken the horse? The animal was much more valuable than a cow.

Bryce shook his head as he passed the spot he imagined she'd left Lucas. He didn't like the fact that he questioned what she did.

He wanted to not care, to not have any feelings about what needed to be done with her.

Michael, who sometimes seemed like his personal mind reader, once again broke into his thoughts. "Did the stable master speak with you about the grey that brought Lucas in?"

Bryce didn't bother to look at Michael, but kept his eyes scanning the area ahead and around them as they entered the tree line. "Nay. I did not see him. Did the wench injure the horse, too?"

That would certainly explain why she didn't take the animal. He was probably lame and of no use to her.

"Nay, I doubt she did. The stable master seems to think that an arrow sliced his belly. Lucky for you it did not puncture the animal but left a long laceration where the arrow grazed his side."

Bryce rubbed the side of his face that had more than stubble on it after many days out. "The woman is too small to be able to pull a bowstring back, let alone come close enough to hit a moving target."

"Not to mention that her arm is broke, and to our knowledge she did not have a weapon when she left. I do not think she could hide a bow." Michael chuckled.

"She hid her red hair and broken arm." Bryce mumbled. "So we may be looking for another attacker besides the lass. Perhaps, she met up with them in the woods."

"Or perhaps the lass be innocent and tried to save the boy's life," Michael shot back.

"'Tis possible. Unlikely that she would risk her recapture in exchange for saving his life, but 'tis possible. I will give you that."

Michael let out a chortle. "You do not like what you feel for this woman."

"The only thing I feel is anger, and I want to see justice. Do not forget that I lived through the deception of a woman like Deirdre and lost my parents because I trusted her and did not question things I should have."

"Aye, I do not forget, my friend. But not every woman is like Clarice."

"'Tis true, but Deirdre has proven to be deceptive just as Clarice was. And 'tis obvious the wench has a great aversion for me and mine. I would be a fool to trust her."

"I say not that you should trust the woman, Bryce. I say only perhaps she is not as guilty as you make her out to be."

"I know not, but I intend to find out."

"I admire the woman." Michael spoke the words with enough conviction that Bryce looked at him.

"Surely you jest."

Michael grinned. "'Tis not many women who would do a man's work. She wanted justice and sought it herself. Most women are fragile creatures, but Deirdre..." Michael's voice drifted off.

"You have seen the woman less than I. What makes you believe she is different?" Bryce knew he should end the conversation. He didn't want to hear any words that might gainsay his thoughts.

"Think what she has been through. I know not a woman who would try to escape through a high window or who would go through those lengths to escape. Most would cry and plead to be released. But Deirdre did not."

Bryce didn't like one whit how Michael talked about the woman. But what bothered him most was it wasn't *that* Michael defended her but *why* he defended her. Bryce remained silent and decided it was time to end the conversation.

They had ridden hard for several hours when the forest

grew still. They maneuvered through the thick underbrush. It was common for the woodland animals to stop their chatter and business to keep their presence unknown, but something made the hair on Bryce's neck prickle.

He raised his hand and with his fist gave two quick jerks—the sign for silence, and they might approach danger. All eyes scanned the trees around them.

Bryce saw the movement of the rider before the arrow was released and kicked Tempest into a gallop. Had he not, the arrow that whizzed by his back very well could have hit its target.

At that moment, the woods came alive. Bryce drew his sword, determined to run down the owner of the arrow that nearly had him meeting his Maker. The man met his eyes and swung his horse around to flee. *The coward.* The man should fight him face to face.

The clashing of steel resounded through the trees. Not knowing how many men had ambushed them, Bryce could not leave his men to fight as he chased a coward. He would remember that face, and someday they would meet.

With a flick of the reins, Bryce sent Tempest toward the thick of battle. He never enjoyed battles like some men did. He was more like his father and sought peace. There were times when there was no other way for it. But today...today he welcomed the battle. Perhaps the anger that burned within him could be sated. And perhaps he could forget this turmoil that roiled in his belly every time he thought of the Scottish lass.

Michael fought two men, holding his shield up on his left side as he swung his sword on this right. Finley and Roger battled with three men, a fourth lay writhing on the ground.

Digging his spurs into his destrier, Bryce readied himself as he reached Michael's aid. The man to his friend's left turned and swung his sword at Bryce, swinging too soon and hitting only air, leaving an opening for Bryce.

Bryce swung his sword in an arc, coming down on the man's neck and shoulder. His opponent slumped in his saddle before tumbling to the ground. There was no time to think about how he felt about killing the man in the thick of battle.

"Behind you, Bryce!" Michael yelled moments before a blade sliced across Bryce's back.

The pain only helped his cause. Bryce swung around with a growl on his lips as he raised his sword. Metal met metal sending a clank that reverberated down into his arm as both swords were met with equal force. This man was every bit the warrior that he was.

Bryce grinned. Aye, he'd met his match, and when he looked into the ice-cold eyes of his opponent, he could see the same realization on the man.

The two swords hit over and over until Bryce could no longer hear the battle around him, so intent was he on his challenger. Sweat trickled down his brow and into his eyes. Even his hand had become moist. He tightened his grip on his sword—once his father's sword. The thought gave him strength as his adversary swung his sword in a downward cut. Bryce called on that strength and met it with a sideway blow, nearly knocking the blade from his rival's hand.

The man looked momentarily stunned but swung his horse around to give himself time to recoup. Bryce struck and his opponent parried. Bryce twisted his body as the next thrust nearly sliced through his torso. The knight smirked, knowing he'd nearly ended it there. Jerking on Tempest's reins, he swung the horse's rear quarters around, putting his enemy where he wanted him.

He thrust his blade forward in a downward arc. His foe's parry came up short. Bryce's blade met its mark, and his rival lost his balance and fell from his horse, his one foot caught in the stirrup as the horse ran from the battle.

Bryce swung around ready for the next challenger, only to see all three of his men sitting with interest on their mounts, watching.

"You did not think to come help?" Bryce growled.

Michael shrugged. "You looked to be having too much fun."

Bryce glanced back to where the destrier dragged the knight away from them. The horse and rider had stopped, and the man pulled himself back into his saddle.

"Do we go after him?" Finley asked.

Bryce looked at the men sprawled on the ground around them, blood seeping into the ground. The man who'd disappeared further into the woods would not stand a chance against them with his wound. It wouldn't take much with four of them to find him. They would go and bring the man back and learn who had sent them on this mission of death. There had been enough killing today.

But before he gave orders a scream rent the air. Just as the hairs on his neck told him they rode into an ambush, this time his heart told him the cry came from Deirdre.

Tempest knew what he wanted from him. Before he could dig his heels in, the destrier headed the direction of the cry at a full gallop.

Bryce lowered his head and torso close to Tempest's neck to avoid the branches slapping at his face. They tore recklessly through the trees along an old deer path. The pounding hooves of his men sounded close behind him. Broken limbs from the knight who'd escaped led Bryce down a path in the direction of the scream.

He really wasn't sure what made him look to the right as he came upon a bend in the trail, but something inside him told him, and when he did his heart squeezed.

Red hair splayed out of a hooded cape, crumpled at the bottom of a steep embankment. Rage mixed with fear—an emotion he didn't want to examine at the moment—shot through his chest and into his head. He pulled Tempest to an abrupt stop, sending the men behind him off the path.

"What is it?" Michael asked as Bryce turned his horse in the direction of the woman.

"Deirdre," Bryce yelled. "Go find him and bring him back alive. I have questions I want answered." He wasn't sure they'd heard all he said because all he could think about was getting to Deirdre and finding out if she was still alive.

He jumped from Tempest before the horse had come to a stop and ran to Deirdre. Her arms were bent upward on each side probably attempting to stop her fall. She wore the cape she'd made from the old blanket that Ella had given her—the same fabric that bound Lucas to his horse, he reminded himself.

He pushed the thought away, not ready to deal with the implications of that. If the lass lived, there would be plenty of time to find out the truth concerning Lucas.

With bended knee, he dropped down beside her, the cool damp earth seeping into his breeches. With as much care as picking up a delicate flower that had been trampled, he rolled her to her back.

The sight of her head flopping to the side, lifelessly, caused his gut to roil. He'd seen so much death today. *Just let her live so I can understand why I want to avoid her as much as I want to be with her.*

Lowering his head to her chest, he could see the shallow rise and fall of her boy's tunic before he heard the rhythmic beat of her heart.

A sense of relief washed over him, like a cool breeze after a hot day on the practice field. He raised her head onto his leg and brushed the dirt from her cheek with the back of his finger before wiping it off her forehead.

A knot had risen on her forehead much like the one Lucas had. He paused before pushing the thought away again and wiped the blood that trickled down her temple.

He would figure out what had happened—later. Right now, he needed to get Deirdre back to Rosen Craig for Millicent to look after.

He tucked a short red strand of wavy hair behind her ear and tried to remember what color her eyes were. Michael was right, she was a woman to be admired even if she did consider him her enemy.

Michael rode down the steep embankment, stopping his mount only feet away. "How bad is the lass?"

"She received a good knock on the head, which could be why she does not wake up. I need to get her to Millicent."

Michael reached up and stroked his squirrel, which had just popped his head out of his tunic. "The healer has been busy these last few sennights."

Bryce slid one arm under Deirdre's knees and the other behind her arms, gently picking her up as he stood. "Aye, that she has."

Head injuries sometimes were the worst because one never knew if they would die until they just quit breathing. At least with a wound or sickness, the person often showed signs of weakening.

"I can take her," Michael offered as Bryce walked to Tempest.

"Nay, she is my responsibility. I will see her safely to Rosen Craig."

Michael dismounted and met Bryce at his horse, taking Deirdre in his arms until Bryce mounted.

By the time Bryce was settled in his saddle and Michael had remounted his horse, Roger and Finley had returned without their prisoner.

"We lost his trail and did not want to leave you unprotected," Roger announced.

As they made their way through the woods, waves of unsteadiness wafted over him. He shook it off, focusing on getting Deirdre to his home and finding out how Lucas fared. Only after Lucas woke would he know the truth. Even though his gut told him one thing, his mind remembered the treachery of his past.

It wasn't until the outline of Rosen Craig could be seen in the distance that the fog he'd been fighting since he climbed back on Tempest began to assail him. The weakness seeped into his body threatening to overtake him.

Chapter 15

If Michael and Geoffrey hadn't hopped off their mounts and run to him when they entered the portcullis, Bryce was certain he and Deirdre would have both found themselves on the ground. One man on each side of him, the two friends kept him in his saddle and guided him through the outer bailey, across the inner bailey and to the steps that led up to the keep.

Guernon reached up and took Deirdre from him. Michael and Geoffrey supported Bryce as he dismounted out of his saddle. When his feet hit the ground, his legs buckled. He fought to get enough strength back in them to stand supported. His legs were as useless as a newborn babe.

By the time they made it up the steps and into the keep, Millicent had been summoned. Bryce glanced up to see Guernon stood at the top of the stairs, still holding the lass.

With her surcoat hiked up to prevent tripping, Millicent hurried as quickly as her old legs would take her. "Milord, looks like you could swoon."

Bryce attempted to put her at ease with a smile. "I will not swoon. Go up to my mother's room and tend to Deirdre."

Millicent crossed her arms and squared her shoulders. Bryce recognized that stance and almost groaned. He'd seen it before when she and Neil had found him near death and nursed him back to health.

"'Tis sorry I am to disobey you, milord. But I will be tending to you."

Bryce glanced back up the stairs to see that Guernon had taken Deirdre to the room. "Go, Millicent. Nog can see to my wound. The lass needs you more."

She squared her shoulders, and Bryce knew he was in for a fight unless he could get the advantage. The woman was as stubborn as they came. "'The lass is not my lord, nor does she have a demesne full of people relying on her. Too many good people need you, Bryce."

When she used his name, she was reminding him of what they'd been through. He insisted she call him Bryce when she had tended to him in her home. But at the moment, Deirdre was all he could think about. He squinted his eyes. Not so much to intimidate her but to keep the fog and darkness at bay. "Aye, 'tis true the people of Rosen Craig depend on me. 'Tis why I wish to live. But the longer we stand here and argue, the more blood I lose and the less chance I have of a quick recovery. Now if you wish for me to be seen to, then you go tend Deirdre and allow Nog to see to my wound. When you are finished, you may come approve Nog's work."

Her shoulders fell in defeat, and she let off a huff before she started up the stairs. Bryce sighed with relief. If she'd have held her ground much longer, Michael and Geoffrey would have had all his weight, and he'd have had no say in who tended him.

Once in his room, Michael stripped him of his shirt and tunic, and they helped him to his bed where he laid face down. Never had he been so relieved to be off his feet. The fog in his head thickened to a stormy black.

Bryce fought the darkness. "Michael, you surprise me. You did not voice your opinion with Millicent." He lifted his head and glanced at his friend, expecting a reply only to see worry etched in the wrinkles of his forehead.

"'Twas not my battle to fight."

Nog came in the room with a small basket of supplies and sat on the bed next to him. She pulled out a cloth and began wiping the blood from his back. "I need water."

Geoffrey went to the door and yelled out for water to be brought.

"'Tis why you should wear your armor when you go out milord. Tunics do not do much for stopping swords." Nog said the words with so much conviction that despite his struggle, he smiled.

"Find out how Lucas and Deirdre fare, Geoffrey." Bryce needed to know if the boy had improved. What would he tell Brithwin?

The water arrived and Nog cleaned the wound. His shirt and bedding were soaked with blood and the cook would need to see what she was doing. She dug in her basket. Bryce fought to stay awake, but darkness called.

"Help me sit him up."

Michael came over and helped Bryce sit up.

"Drink this water. You have lost much blood." Nog pushed the cup into his hands with as much authority as a lord.

"I do not want to sleep. I need to know how the boy and lass fare."

"'Tis water, milord. Drink."

Bryce hadn't realized how thirsty he was. He tipped his head back and let the glass of tepid water drain down his throat before he grimaced. "'Tis not water. 'Tis bitter."

"Oh, 'twas water, and wee bit of Valerian."

He lay back down on the bed too weak to care that his cook had disobeyed his orders and his healer had argued with him. He had to stay awake until Geoffrey returned with the news from the other two.

"I cannot wait for sleep to take him. He continues to bleed."

Bryce wasn't sure whether Nog spoke to Michael or to herself or for a forewarning to him. But the needle piercing his skin caused him to suck in his breath. The pain was good. It would keep him awake.

That was his last thought.

††††

Deirdre didn't want to open her eyes, and she wanted the gentle voice wooing her to open them to go away, for her head felt like someone was using it to thrash wheat on. But the persistent voice wouldn't quit. If only she could sink back into the soft black nothingness from whence she'd just come before the voice called to her.

Her eyes flickered open, but the movement allowed enough light to penetrate to send a stabbing pain through her skull.

"Nay, nay. Open your eyes, lass," the soothing voice enticed.

She wanted to obey, but the darkness called to her.

"Come back, Deirdre. Do not give in to sleep. You must fight it."

The voice knew her? It sounded worried. She didn't want the voice to worry. She fought to come back to the pain and the light.

"Come to me, Deirdre," the voice continued to coo.

She licked her cracked lips, but her mouth was so dry it didn't help. "The light," she croaked. "Hurts."

"Cover the window," the voice said.

Hot fear soared through her body. "Nay, not darkness." She rasped out. She didn't want to be locked in darkness again without feeling the sun's heat on her face.

"'Tis all good, lass. When the light does not hurt your eyes, we will uncover the window. Now open your eyes."

The fear fled. She was not locked in a room. This voice was kind, and there was a window in the room. Was she back at Mairi's on her uncle's land? She forced her eyes open. The sun streaming through the window filtered through an old blanket, leaving enough light for her to see yet ease the discomfort. An old woman with white hair stood by the window, arranging the blanket. She couldn't make out her features—but not Mairi.

The woman turned toward her. "'Tis good indeed to see you awake." Then turning back, she fidgeted once again with the fabric hanging on the window.

It wasn't the voice who had been wooing her to wake. She turned her head to the other side of her bed, searching for the person who owned the kind voice.

Her stomach somersaulted and sent heat through her

veins and up into her head. "You!" The word spewed forth with more strength than she had.

"Aye, 'tis me," the laird answered.

It was the kind voice that had wooed and encouraged her to come back to consciousness. She closed her eyes. She wanted to be any place but here. Not here. Not at Rosen Craig. Not with the laird. Not locked in a room with no li— She stopped her thought. There was light, and there was a window. A glimmer of hope emerged.

But as quickly as the hope arose, it evaporated. One of the men hurt in battle would be in the room they had nursed her back to health in before she'd escaped. Once he healed, they would move her there.

A hand slipped behind her shoulders and neck, forcing her up slightly. "Take a drink, lass. 'Tis too long you have gone without water."

The glass touched her lips, spilling cool liquid down her chin and onto her tunic. She gulped the water, enjoying the relief it gave her throat.

"Slow down." The laird spoke with the authority she was used to hearing.

She stiffened.

He softened his tone. "You do not want to choke, lass. There is no hurry."

Deirdre relaxed and followed his order, attempting to pull her memories together and to determine how she ended up back at Rosen Craig.

The pain in her ankle had slowed her progress getting back to Scotland. The first time she'd reinjured it, she had stepped in a hole while running, which caused her to turn her ankle. From then on, it seemed every small stone, stick, and hole made her ankle give way.

But she hadn't stopped. She couldn't. For she knew they would be looking for her. She lifted her gaze from the glass to Bryce. She'd been correct in that assumption.

She took one final gulp and leaned her head back. The

laird lowered her down and gently removed his arm from behind her shoulders before placing the glass on a small wooden table beside the bed. Closing her eyes to keep her focus, Deirdre went back to what had led up to her capture.

Her progress had been slowed due to her injury. She'd been tired and hungry, with no weapon for protection or to gather food. She sifted through the muddle in her mind.

The fighting…she'd heard the clang of swords not far from her. Why hadn't she fled in the opposite direction? Why had she stolen back to see who warred against each other? Because in her optimism, she'd hoped someone had come to rescue her. That someone had cared enough that she was missing to come find her. That someone was willing to fight for her.

She let out a huff and quickly opened her eyes to see the laird with raised brow. Nay, there was no one who cared enough to come save her from her enemy, but there was one who cared enough to come after her to see to her punishment.

The men who ambushed the laird of Rosen Craig and his men where not familiar to her. When she'd seen who battled and knew it was no savior, she should have fled, but still she watched. It was when she knew her enemy had won that she tried to slip away, but the escaping rider had pushed past her as he absconded, knocking her down the ravine she'd been following along.

She closed her eyes again, realizing her folly. What a fool she'd been. Fighting the tears that bit at the back of her eyes, she drew in a deep, shaky breath, hoping the blasted things would not fall. She could not appear weak.

With everything Deirdre had in her, she opened her eyes, let out her breath and spoke. "So, here we are again."

She really didn't know how she'd expected this enemy of hers to respond—certainly not as he did, for the man smiled at her. And not an arrogant smile, but a genuine smile. For some reason, that scared her. She'd have rather seen the haughty smile of a man who had beaten his opponent.

"Aye, here we are. And once again you have injured your ankle. 'Tis often that you hurt yourself?"

His words held no condemnation. She knew he'd only asked a question. But it made her angry. For she was anything but clumsy. Her years pretending to be a boy made her all the more sure-footed, always feeling she had to best the other boys and prove herself even though the whole village knew she was no lad.

It was a strange thing, the struggle she'd had within her the first few years as she'd given up her gowns for breeches. It was embarrassing at first—now she understood she'd felt shame from being different. Being so young, she struggled with being something she was not. She was a bairn—too young to understand. She supposed that was why she eventually determined to be as good as or better than the other boys. It took her mind off who she really was and why she was there.

"Only when I am running for my life." She narrowed her eyes as she spat the words out.

"As you have done for some time, now, eh?" His eyebrow was raised as though there was more behind his words. Yet he did not lash back with venom as she had just given him.

"Tae long." The words slipped out a whisper before she could stop them. She could only hope they didn't reveal too much.

"Aye, I suppose so." The kindness in his voice caused a small crack in the ice surrounding her heart.

"Must I wait several sennights for my punishment tae be met?" She was quite proud of herself. Even in asking about her punishment, her voice did not waiver but stayed strong. She supposed that making her wait for her sentence had been all part of the atonement she was to pay.

"There will be no punishment, lass. You have suffered enough at your own hand."

She stared at him, not sure to believe him. No

punishment? Dare she allow herself to experience the relief that begged to come? But then the rest of his words sank in, and the relief that wanted to flood her body dried up with the flames of anger that consumed her being.

"At my own hand? Perhaps you dinna notice that until I became your prisoner, I was in guid health."

The man actually had the decency to wince. "You are not my prisoner. You may leave when you wish, but I would suggest you choose to stay until, at the very least, you are healed."

It was strange what emotions could do, because until that moment Deirdre hadn't realized the amount of her discomfort. But suddenly every muscle in her body screamed out in pain as the fear and then anger subsided. She glanced down at her body covered in cuts and bruises—the broken arm rewrapped. If she'd not known better, she would have thought she had been in the thick of the battle she'd watched from afar.

Though she knew vanity was a sin, she raised her good hand to her face, searching for deep wounds that would leave her scarred and disfigured. Her cheek stung from a raw scrape but nothing deep. She almost heaved a sigh of relief when her thoughts leapt to the reason she ran through the forest—Lucas. Did he live?

But before she could ask, rapping sounded on the door, and the laird's voice boomed. "Come in, Michael."

She recognized the man with the smile on his face as the laird's close confidant. How did the laird know who knocked at the door? Determining it was in the rhythm of his knock, she kept her gaze on the man.

"Good day to you, Deirdre." Michael inclined his head, and what she could only describe as mischief twinkled in his eyes.

"I have had better, sir." Deirdre decided to wait to pass judgement on him.

"And so I would hope." He smiled at her, and then she

had no doubt it was mischief she saw dancing.

Michael turned to the laird. "And you, Bryce? I see you are up and moving around. How do you feel?"

"I am well. 'Twas only a scrape."

"A scrape that caused you to lose much blood." Michael shot her a quick glance before setting his eyes back on his friend. "You could have died from such a deep wound."

The laird shrugged. "'Twas not that bad, Michael."

"Oh, 'tis not true, my friend, and well you know."

"You exaggerate." The laird sounded irritated. "'Twas only a wound that many, yourself included, have experienced."

Deirdre watched in fascination as the two bickered back and forth.

The grin that could make an enemy like him or hate him, she supposed, spread across Michael's face. "Aye, that much is true. But 'tis hard for me to understand how you cannot fear death from a blade wound, yet swoon when the healer sticks a wee needle in you."

"I did not swoon, Michael." Annoyance filled the laird's voice.

Michael shrugged. "'I only repeat what the healer told me."

"Nog is not a healer." He paused before continuing his argument. "But even so, I did not."

"'Tis not the tale the cook tells. She speaks of you swooning with the first stitch of the needle."

Chapter 16

Bryce would have liked to meet Michael out on the practice field and prove his strength, but the wound in his back wouldn't allow it. After Nog had stitched him up, Bryce slept through that night and the following day and evening, only getting up when his food was brought to him. The loss of his life's blood had not only weakened him but had tired him as well.

On this day, though, after much rest, Bryce could feel his strength returning. He would be back to his men begging for mercy on the practice field within a few days.

Alex stuck his head out of his friend's tunic, and the sweetest "ooooh" followed a sucked in breath from Deirdre. Michael grinned and pulled the squirrel from his clothes and walked over to the bedside.

Deirdre reached out her hand but hesitated. "Will he bite?"

"Nay, Alex likes attention. Especially from the lasses." He winked at her, and Bryce's body temperature shot up.

"Mmmm, he's so soft." She ran her hand down the little squirrel's back and over its fluffy tail.

The pure pleasure in the lass's eyes left Bryce struggling with jealousy. He wasn't sure if he wished he could be the squirrel, enjoying Deirdre's sweet caresses through his hair or if it was Michael whom he envied, who now received the woman's adoration.

He didn't have time to think on it too long because a frantic knock sounded on the door. Before he could respond Lucas flew in the room. Bryce was about to reprimand the boy, expecting him to rush to Deirdre's bedside. But the lad's feet skidded to a halt as his eyes sought out Bryce.

"Milord."

"Lucas, what is the hurry?" Bryce said his words slowly to calm the child down. The boy had recovered quickly and bounced around Rosen Craig like he'd never been injured. He was happy for the boy. If only he had the same healing ability within his body.

"Sir Geoffrey sent me to fetch you." His eyes widened. "There is a messenger from the king waiting to speak to you." To his credit, the boy did remember where he was even in his excitement and turned to Deirdre. "Good day to you, milady."

Bryce didn't miss the look on the lass's face as she attempted to recover from what he could only guess was the news of the king's visit.

"Guid day tae you, Lucas."

Interest piqued on Deirdre's face. Bryce could not be certain if it was just curiosity or if she thought Bryce some important subject of Richard's. But that couldn't be any further from the truth.

The fact that it was a messenger who came was reassuring. It could easily have been guards to drag him to the king, where he would have to defend accusations of treason.

The flash of a memory shot through his mind like the glimpse of lightening—a shadow slinking out the door as he, Michael, Geoffrey, Hugh, Roger, and Ranald sat around discussing the plight of the nobility and their lands. He pushed it out of his mind and turned to Deirdre. "If you will excuse me."

He turned to leave. Michael raised his brows and moved to follow.

Deirdre's voice followed him out the door.

"Lucas. 'Tis glad I am you look well. 'Twas a guid surprise to see you bursting through the door."

Bryce grinned. Perhaps it wasn't the king who put amazement on the lass's face after all. Last she knew the lad looked near death, but his injuries were not as serious as first thought. And he for one was grateful. He did not want to have to do any explaining to his brother and certainly not to his brother's wife, Brithwin.

And why did he care what the lass thought? What was wrong with him, spending so much time thinking about the enemy? And that was what she was—and he needed to remind himself of that more often.

He might not keep her as a prisoner now that he knew the truth of what happened with Lucas. The woman had risked her freedom to bring the boy back to Rosen Craig and medical help. He had to reward her somehow and releasing her seemed fair—a life for a life, so to speak.

He could only hope she had learned her lesson about stealing from his land and his people. She'd lost a close friend and faced death because of it.

Lucas hurried beside him as he made his way down the stairs. "Milady looks good, does she not milord?"

Bryce looked heavenward and grunted. "She is not milady. She is a cow thief from a clan who has been no more than a thorn in my backside."

Lucas, with his much shorter legs, ran down the stairs as Bryce continued to take them two at a time. "But she is so beautiful, would not you agree, milord?"

Bryce ignored the boy as he descended the last step and turned toward the great hall.

Lucas skipped alongside him. "Do not you think she would make a nice bride? I would not mind waking up to that face every morn."

"Lucas! Go shovel out the horses' stalls." Bryce did not like where the boy's words were taking his mind. He did not need to be thinking about a woman like Deirdre. He was wiser now and would not trust this lass.

Bryce's long stride ate up the ground, and Lucas fell behind him.

"Milord, do I have to?" Lucas whined. "I want to hear what the king's man has to say."

Bryce stopped, and the boy ran into his backside. "'Tis not a conversation for a page's ears. Go, before I have you helping clean the chamber pots."

"Aye, milord." Lucas raced toward the large wooden doors that led to the courtyard.

Michael came from behind and fell in step with him as he turned to enter the great hall. "Do you worry?"

Bryce scanned the hall and laid eyes on the king's man, sitting near the kitchen, eating.

"'Twould be a lie if I said it is of no concern. We spoke words the king would find treasonous within these walls not long ago."

"Aye, those same thoughts came to my mind as well." Michael put his hand to his neck. "I have grown rather attached to me head."

"Do you ever take anything seriously, Michael?" Bryce shook his head, smiling. He'd not encourage the man, but his friend's insouciant attitude helped lift the dark cloud that had hung over him since Lucas flew into Deirdre's chamber.

They approached the king's man. He glanced up, shoved another bite of meat into his mouth, ran his sleeve across his lips, and stood.

Bryce nodded to the man.

"I'm Lord Warwick. You wish to speak with me?"

The king's messenger wiped his hand on his tunic, unbuckled a strap on the leather pouch he carried, and pulled out a letter sealed with the king's ring.

Bryce took the parchment from the messenger and broke the wax seal before scanning the document. When Bryce looked up from the paper the man still stared at him, probably hoping it was not bad news.

He nodded and refolded the letter. "Finish your meal, and I shall have a servant see to a place for you to rest this night."

The man held a hint of a smile. "Thank you, milord. 'Tis much appreciated."

Bryce spun on his heel and headed out of the great hall, his mind racing.

When they reached the doorway and stepped into the significant entry way, Michael turned to him.

"I would say by your response the news is not bad but since you show no emotions either way, tell me?"

Bryce tapped the edge of the folded letter on his hand. "We keep our heads...for now."

"So, it is good news." Michael smiled.

"We will soon see. The king comes for a visit."

Michael's smile fell from his face. "Here? The king comes here? Now? He has not come here for many years, not with his friend, Rothburg so close. 'Tis not good news, Bryce. 'Tis not good at all."

The king's impending arrival indeed was a surprise to him and not a welcome one either—not with the tension between the crown and his lords. Especially since he had gone out to the lords surrounding him and informed them of Richard's highhandedness. Nay, he doubted very much that anything good could come out of Richard's visit. "Nay, I suppose not."

"How would the king know of our..." Michael glanced around him and lowered his voice as they stepped outside. "Our talk of Henry?"

"'Tis a good question, my friend. I do not know."

"Do you think one of the lords you spoke to has turned on you?"

"I was careful where I stopped and with whom I spoke. I do not think any of the lords I met with would support Richard. They all know the man cannot be trusted." Bryce glanced over his shoulder in time to witness Roger slipping out the great hall door down near where the king's messenger sat. It triggered a memory of the shadow slinking from the room the night they had discussed their concerns about the king's rule—a discussion that some might interpret as treasonous.

"One never knows what will motivate a person to play both ends. If Richard offered favors..." Michael suggested.

"Aye, 'tis true, but as I said, I was careful. I did not approach anyone who I believed could be bought by Richard."

Michael let out a sigh. "Then we should have nothing to concern ourselves with the king coming."

Bryce snorted. "I did not say that. With the precipice this country sits on and the vulnerability of the throne, which Richard is well aware of, we can never be too sure what to expect out of the man. As you said yourself, do not forget the sins of Richard against the Lord Appellants. We would be fools if we did. We must keep our guards up and be ready to answer any question Richard throws our way."

"Aye. I will be ready."

†††

Deirdre searched the face of the woman who sat beside her bed for anything that might give away her thoughts on the king's messenger. She recognized the woman, Millicent, as the healer at Rosen Craig from her previous mishap. She'd not said a word while the laird and his friend were in the room interrogating her.

With a huff, Deirdre shut her eyes. Interrogate might be a bit strong. But she would not give him any allowance, for he did remain her enemy and was the cause of her friends' deaths.

A darkness surrounded her soul as the thought entered her mind—it was her own actions that had brought death to Walter and Fionn. She pushed away the thought that caused churning in her gut and focused on the laird.

He'd been the one calling to her to return from the nothingness that had held her. She wished he'd just left her in the blackness that numbed all pain. His voice had sounded so kind and so worried. It was difficult to put the kind voice with her enemy.

"How do you feel, lass?" the healer asked.

Deirdre's head pounded again. "'Tis fine I am."

"Awe, lass, do not lie to me. I have been a healer for

more years than you have been on this green earth the Lord created. Now, what pains you?" The healer pushed her old body up from the chair and placed wrinkled weathered hands on the bed.

Deirdre shrugged her shoulders. The slight movement sent a pain surging across her back and up her neck. "'Tis the truth."

The white-haired woman with kind, pale blue eyes met Deirdre's gaze. "Do you count me for a fool? No one takes a fall such as you did and feels no pain. Do I need to start pressing and prodding to see from where you flinch? Or perhaps bring me lord back in here to ask questions." Her brow shot up revealing more wrinkles in her weathered skin.

The woman was impossible to dislike or get angry with. Her eyes so full of concern softened her threatening words. Deirdre relented. "'Tis mostly my head—and perhaps a few aches and pains throughout my body."

"'Tis more of what I expected to hear." She shuffled away from the bed and over to a basket sitting on the table. She muttered something Deirdre couldn't make out as she dug through the basket. "And after that fall nothing else troubles you? No pain in your shoulder?"

"Perchance a wee bit." Deirdre rubbed the joint as she answered.

"Aye, I saw you wince when you shrugged." She continued to search in the basket, setting jars and herbs out on the table as she did.

"'Tis no' more than I have experienced before." The last thing Deirdre wanted was to come across as weak.

"That may be, lassie, but that is not what I asked you, now is it?" The woman stopped long enough to stare across the room at her.

Deirdre ducked her head, wishing she was alone in the room with her aching head and body.

Millicent shuffled back over to the bed and opened a jar. After dipping her finger in the oil, she rubbed it on Deirdre's temple and the base of her neck. She took the jar and shuffled back to the table, setting it down and picking up what looked to be garlic and an herb. "I shall return *anon*."

Deirdre closed her eyes as the scent of rose oil permeated her senses. She must have dozed because when she opened her eyes again, the healer had returned and carried a glass to her.

"Drink this." She pushed the vessel into Deirdre's hand.

Deirdre stuck it beneath her nose and inhaled. "What is it?"

"How is your head?" The healer ignored her question.

"'Tis better. The hammering is more like tapping now."

"'Tis good. Now drink." She nudged Deirdre's hand.

Deirdre smelled the concoction again and wrinkled her nose. "What is in it?"

Millicent scowled. "The most important things are willow bark, garlic, and frankincense. Now drink." With that she pushed the glass to Deirdre's lips.

Deirdre held her breath and gulped down the foul-smelling concoction.

Chapter 17

The bitterness lingered on Deirdre's tongue as she woke, but even the tapping in her head had subsided, and the stabbing pains in her body whenever she moved had softened to a mild ache.

Millicent was gone, as was her basket of herbs, oils, and potions. Deirdre sat up and cautiously swung her feet off the bed. Testing the amount of discomfort, she pushed on to her feet and surprisingly felt little pain.

Frowning at her lack of clothing, she stood in her chemise and glanced around the room for her gown. The golden fabric draped over the back of the chair caught her attention.

With a deep breath, she took a step and smiled. She wouldn't be bound to the room after all. And the laird did say she was not a prisoner, therefore she must be a guest, and guests could move freely about. Something she intended to do. She slipped into the dress, trying to protect her arm as she did.

Once at the door, she grasped the black iron handle and pulled, half expecting it not to budge. But the heavy wooden door swung easily on its hinges, and she stuck her head through the opening to survey her surroundings.

The corridor to her room was devoid of people, giving her the opportunity to slip out and make her way down the hallway to the stairs without being seen. Peering down into a large entryway, she leaned forward to get a better view as people hustled to and fro. With a good grip on the railing to keep herself from tumbling down should a sudden pain seize her, she carefully descended and stepped into the entryway.

"Escuse m', miss." A young woman with her hands full of rushes hurried past her into the great room.

Deirdre moved out of her way only to step into someone else's path.

"Pardon, miss." Another woman close to her age quickly darted around her. The woman hastened her way to the steps from whence Deirdre had just come.

A tall, thin man brushed by her in his hurry, never turning back to see whom he'd bumped. This was not the place to stand and watch. Hurrying a few strides toward the great hall, she again had to stop and allow someone with an armful to pass. When she made it to the hearth, she slid down onto one of the cloth-covered chairs to watch the commotion.

Never had she'd seen so much activity. People came and went, everyone seemingly attentive on their task at hand. Six women seated on the floor wove rushes into a large covering mat for the floor.

"Guid day tae you, Miss Deirdre. I am Finley." A tall, broad-shouldered young man with hair as red as hers stood before her.

"Guid day tae you." She recognized him as one of the knights who'd gone with Bryce. "Quite the commotion." She nodded to the bustling of activity.

"Aye. The king comes. We must have everything in best of shape." He snorted. "We would not want the king to know how we really live."

"You are from Scotland?"

He grinned. "How do you ken?"

"Your speech is no' that of an Englishman."

"Something I can be thankful for then, aye?"

She frowned. "You dinna like the English either?"

He hesitated. "I did no' say that." He took a quick glance around. "But I have Scottish blood, no' English."

"From where do you hail in Scotland?"

He shrugged. "Here and there. 'Tis sorry I am but I must return to my duties. I will look forward tae seeing you again."

He walked away. What a strange conversation. Why did he not wish to tell her from what clan or area he hailed? They were in England after all. It was not as though he must concern himself with rival clans.

She had too much on her mind to trouble herself with the odd man—things like what she would do next. She could try to get word to her mother, she supposed, but that would be at the risk of her father finding out where she stayed. Even her uncle, a hard man himself, claimed her father was a brutal man.

Memories of her father were muddled at best. What she did recall was the man was always busy. And she'd never seen her mother after that day—the day she left her with her uncle. She'd never said good-bye. Being a wee bairn when it happened, she only knew what her uncle told her.

Times like now her heart ached. She thought her mother loved her, but if she had, how could she never return? The same notion that always came to her mind to answer that question came to haunt her once again—*she's dead*. She didn't entertain the idea like she often did. Sometimes thinking she had died, perhaps trying to come back to her, suppressed the ache—but in her heart she knew no one had ever loved her.

Dare she even consider returning to her uncle? The man could be ruthless. She'd seen that firsthand from his subjects. He showed no mercy to them if they crossed him.

He'd never had children of his own, and though she did not live with him, he'd always treated her well. And he spoke so highly of her mother. It was obvious the man loved her. For whenever she would want to go see her mother, his concern for his sister's safety always deterred her. If her father ever found out that her mother had left her with her uncle for safe keeping, her uncle worried her father would punish her severely. In that respect he was a very good man. And he hid her away as a boy with Mairi, a woman who treated her well.

Part of her was happy that she couldn't remember her father. Perhaps he was so wicked her mind blotted him out. What she did remember was when he came looking for her, it was that day she became a boy.

To her young memory, not much time had passed between the first and last times she'd seen her father after being rescued by her uncle. He was angry and yelling, his face contorted in anger as she peeked around the corner of the manor balcony. A woman spotted her and scuttled away with her. A shiver ran through her veins. She never wanted to see that man again. The anger in his eyes frightened her still to this day.

And truth be told, that was probably why her mother never risked returning. No, she'd never be able to return to her mother or even risk getting word to her where she now resided. For if she did and her father discovered what she'd done, she feared for her mother's life.

That left her uncle. The question was would he blame her for the loss of his two men? She wanted to believe he wouldn't, but deep in her heart she knew he would. And though he'd never harmed her, she feared the wrath she'd seen meted out on his subjects.

A tear slipped from her eye and trailed down the side of her nose. She swiped it away. Could anyone be less loved than she?

††††

Bryce glared at the man standing in front of him as the bailey bustled around them. Whatever provoked him to allow this man to serve under him? The Scots he'd encountered were hard workers, but Finley had been a pain in his Achilles heel since he'd arrived. The man just would not take initiative to do anything. And now he stood before him complaining about his duty.

"Why do you wish to be taken off the duty of watching the lass?" Bryce growled out the words hoping to intimidate the young man.

"'Tis a waste of my time. Put a woman to watch her. I am a warrior, not a nursemaid," Finley shot back.

"So you tell me that this castle's safety is not your

concern?"

"'Tis and that is why I wish to be taken from this duty. I would do something important."

"Watching the lass is important. And she knows you are Scottish. You will put her mind to ease."

Finley shifted his weight to one side and folded his arms before him. "I shall see if any others would like to—"

"You will do no such thing," Bryce barked out. "You swore fealty to me, and you will follow orders, or you will find yourself another lord to serve."

The man had enough about him to duck his head. "Aye, milord. And what am I to watch for, sir?"

It took all of Bryce's patience not to roll his eyes. Had the man always been this way and he'd not noticed when he'd hired him? "The lass hails from the border area of Scotland where there is much unrest with my demesne. A people dwell there who do not care for the English. They burn our crops and reive our land, and she was caught stealing our cows. Need I elaborate?"

He blinked, opened his mouth, and then shut it. Bryce turned to leave.

"Ye wish me tae make sure she does not steal any cows?"

Bryce stopped mid-stride and turned. "Aye, Finley, cows and anything else that belongs to me and mine."

The young man nodded. Perhaps leaving Finley in charge of watching the lass wasn't his best idea. He shrugged the thought off. With the king coming, he needed capable men who could get a job done without asking twenty questions. Finley was where he needed to be.

He'd made it halfway to the stables when Michael joined him.

"What has you in such a huff, Bryce?"

"Remind me why I took Finley on?"

Michael chuckled. "What has the man done now?"

"You mean to tell me he actually does things?"

Michael put his hand on Bryce's shoulder as they continued. "If memory serves me, I advised against it. Told you he was Scottish and could be trouble. You said everyone deserves a chance, and he could be an asset with the border problems. Guess you should have listened to me."

"Aye, perchance I should have. But 'tis not trouble he brings. At least in the way you speak. He merely lacks initiative. And I have to say the man has little ambition."

"Could prove to be interesting when the king arrives, aye?"

Bryce opened his mouth to speak and stopped as a soft fluff of fur ran down Michael's arm and on to Bryce's shoulder. "Michael, I say naught to you about that squirrel, but he is not welcome on my shoulder."

Michael scooped up Alex and with great exaggeration choked back a laugh. "You have plenty to say about my li'l furry friend here. But I do not mind. Methinks you are jealous."

Bryce shook his head and grinned. "Methinks that Finley could use a mentor—one with a furry friend."

Michael really did choke then. "You would not do that to me."

"Oh, aye, I would. He needs someone who is sure of himself, motivated, and a bit arrogant. Cannot think of anyone better."

"So, what you are saying to me is you wish him to leave. I am certain he will not last more than a few days under my perusal."

"You are most likely right, and I do not have time to worry about such things now with Richard coming."

Wolfhound rounded the corner of the stables and trotted to Bryce's side. He reached down and scratched the dog's ears. "Where have you been, ole' girl?"

The wolfhound looked up, and Alex scolded the dog with its chatter. Wolfhound lunged and knocked Michael off balance and nearly to the ground. Alex jumped off and ran up the side of the stable. The dog gave chase.

Bryce laughed.

"Now you are in a good mood when your dog nearly puts me to the ground?" Michael scowled at him.

"It did brighten my mood, I will admit." Bryce grinned.

They stepped through the stable doors to see Gilbert, the stableman, at the end of the stable on his knees.

Bryce spoke loud enough for his voice to carry. "Is something amiss?"

The grey-haired man turned his head back toward them as they approached. "Something got the cat. She never came back, and all her kittens have died but this wee one." He held up a tiny grey and white kitten smaller than his palm. "She will not survive, I fear. I thought to put her out of her misery."

Bryce took the little creature, whose eyes had yet to open, into his hand, and she yawned, laid her head down, and snuggled into a little ball. Bryce's heart hiccupped. He couldn't let the man kill the thing, and he certainly didn't have time to take care of a kitten. If he made an issue over finding someone to care for it, he would never hear the end of it from Michael.

And then he smiled. The memory of a certain redheaded Scottish lass sucking in her breath and oooohing at the sight of Alex gave him an idea.

Chapter 18

"I shall see to the sprite. I need you to get the stable fit for a king." Bryce's disposition suddenly changed.

Gilbert quirked an eyebrow. "Ye be jesting me, sir?"

"Nay, 'tis the truth of it. King Richard comes through and will stay at Rosen Craig."

His eyes grew large. "The king hisself comes? And I will be keeping his royal horses? Oh, my." He looked back and forth and around the wooden structure.

"You will have at least a sennight to ready the place. Clean the stalls and arrange feed and tack in an orderly fashion. As the days draw near, you will need to have fresh bedding for his beasts." Bryce stroked the sleeping kitten as he spoke.

Michael followed Bryce out. "What plan you to do with the kitten?"

Bryce held the grin wanting to spread across his face. Nay, he'd not let Michael best him on this. "I have an idea. Gilbert needs to concern himself with the readying of the stalls, not an orphan kitten."

Out of the shadows of the stable, Wolfhound stood sentinel at the corner, and Alex sat on the edge of the roof chattering at him.

Michael snorted and stomped toward the two. "Can you not keep control of your beast?"

Bryce snickered. "Wolfhound, come."

The animal started toward him and gave a backward glance at his opponent before coming to Bryce's side. "Look what I have, girl." He could only hope the dog would have some maternal instincts and not harm the tiny creature.

Wolfhound nudged the kitten, flipping it up with her nose. Bryce held his breath, hoping she wouldn't open her mouth to make it a meal. Then she licked it. He smiled. "You will help care for it." And he whispered, "with a wee Scottish lass."

He left Michael trying to coax his pet down off the roof. "If ye do not get down here, I am going to leave you to your own demise. Ye may find yourself on the dinner table..." were the last words he heard from his friend as he strolled away with a grin.

Wolfhound kept her gaze on Bryce's hand holding the kitten as she pranced alongside of him, head tipped up and eyes alert.

Bryce went to the basket room off the kitchen where Deirdre had been kept when she'd foolishly injured herself attempting to escape. He swung the door open to find a few baskets stacked in the corner. He chose one big enough for the kitten to move around. Wolfhound sat at the door waiting.

Back in the kitchen he found Nog busy preparing the meal.

"Good aftermete, milord." Nog smiled, creating lines around her eyes on a dark, wrinkled face.

"Good aftermete. I need a cloth for the bottom of this basket." He held up what would be the kitten's new home.

"I believe the laundress brought some by earlier." She shuffled over to the corner where a bench sat and came back with just what he wanted.

"You have my thanks, Nog."

Her old eyes sparkled at his appreciation. She rose up on her toes and peered into the basket empty. Her brow crinkled.

"'Tis for this kitten. It lost its mother and littermates." He held out the kitten to show her. "Me needs you to get it some milk."

"'Twill have to be cow's milk." She rubbed the back of her fingers against the soft grey fur.

"'Tis fine. She needs nourishment. I have work to see to, so I will leave her in your capable hands until I return."

Before leaving, he placed the cotton cloth in the basket and gingerly deposited his new pet on it. Wolfhound settled next to the basket and propped her head on the edge.

He was heading toward the door, then stopped and turned. "The king will be our guest in a sennight. You will need to fix the meals appropriately." He took another step and stopped. "Bring in more help if you need, Nog."

He'd made it to the door when Nog's strangled voice stopped him.

"Milord, I have not cooked for a king. I do not know how to make all the fancy dishes the king will expect."

"You are a fine cook, Nog. I see no man who looks to be starving in Rosen Craig. You shall please the king." He turned to walk out.

"If ye'd marry, I would have a mistress to help me with such things, I would," Nog said under her breath.

Bryce knew she didn't mean for him to hear, and he chose to pretend he didn't. Nog was old, and cooking for a king was much to ask. Cooking for his knights was hard enough.

In the great hall, the women worked at weaving the rushes, removing and beating the wall hangings before rehanging them, washing the walls, and bringing in herbs to freshen the room. Did Nog not ask anyone why the castle bustled with activity? Bryce shook his head. Or perhaps she thought he would ask someone else to prepare the food.

Next on his list of tasks was to decide which rooms would best suit Richard and his attendants. Bryce found Ralf, the steward, arguing with Lucas in the manor house.

Ralf's calm composure seemed to be ruffled. "My lord, would you please tell Lucas I do not have time to worry about a Scottish...ruffian."

Lucas turned to Royce. "Milord, Milady is no ruffian. I only request that she be given her due."

Bryce raised a brow. "Given her due, you say? I do not think you would want that."

"But she is a lady. Surely, you can find it in you to give her a bigger room."

Bryce didn't bother correcting Lucas on "milady." He'd

given up on the boy's infatuation of Deirdre. "Did the lass request this?"

"Oh no, milord. I thought to surprise her." Lucas puffed his chest out, so proud of his idea.

"Ralf is right. He does not have time for this with the king coming—and we will not have empty rooms with his arrival. Now go make yourself of use in the *mews*. They need to be cleaned and gotten ready for King Richard's arrival."

Lucas's shoulders drooped. "Aye, milord." He pushed his slippered foot around on the floor like Bryce had seen so many other times when the boy had something on his mind. "'Tis my surprise. You cannot give it to her."

If there was not so much work to do for Richard's arrival, Bryce would have smiled at the lad's bravado, but he had no time for it this day. "Go, Lucas, before I find a job you do not like. As I said, there are no rooms to give away."

That seemed to satisfy the boy, and he ran out of the manor.

"Thank you, milord. The child is persistent, I shall give him that." Ralf let out a sigh. "What can I do for you, sir?"

"The king shall have my room to retire in. I would ready the other rooms as well as we do not know how many attendants he will bring. Have you thought about the entertainment whilst he is here?" He needn't ask the steward, for he was a man who always fulfilled his duties—but for peace of mind Bryce did.

"Aye, milord. Do we know how many days we shall be blessed by his presence?" Ralf's temples had greyed, something Bryce had only just noticed. Richard's presence would probably add a few more grey hairs to his steward.

"Nay, I fear not." But as soon as Richard found out whatever it was he hoped to find out, Bryce was sure he'd be on his way. He just hoped he did not find out the truth. "Plan for a sennight." And he would hope and pray for less.

"Aye." Ralf's weary voice told him his steward was as pleased about the visit as he was.

"Plan a hunt early on. We can use the meat for the feasts." He would keep the king busy to keep him from asking too many questions.

Bryce left the manor. Standing in the middle of the bailey, he gazed over his surroundings looking for things to ready for Richard's arrival.

Michael strutted toward him.

"I see you retrieved your squirrel." Bryce chuckled.

"Aye, he is not too fond of that hound of yours." Michael scratched behind the creature's tiny ears.

"The feeling is mutual, I believe."

"Has there been any more news of Richard?" Michael asked.

"News of his coming or news of his overstepping his position as king?"

"The latter."

"I have no doubt Richard makes this trip to see who is for and who is against him. He knows that many of his nobles are not pleased with him. I believe his stop here is to discover whether I will stand behind him as king or conspire against him. He does not trust his nobles anymore. He remembers when he lost the crown to the Appellants."

††††

Deirdre moved into the parlor to stay out of the madness going on around her. Everyone rushed around readying the manor house and grounds for the arrival of their precious king. She, on the other hand, was not overly impressed by anything English and especially His Royal Highness.

It was the clearing of his throat that brought her attention to the fact that someone stood in the room where she sat. Still a bit on edge staying in the enemy's domain, she startled and jumped up.

The laird had entered, and he stood before her holding a basket in his hand and smiling at her. She refrained from shaking off the shiver that wanted to course through her body. Why would her enemy be smiling at her? Perhaps he really didn't mean she was not a prisoner and was pleased with himself for finding her tucked away.

Her throat went dry. She glanced toward the opening asking herself if she could make it around him and escape.

"Good aftermete. You are a difficult person to find."

His smile remained, and she believed it sincere. He gave no indication of displeasure.

"Guid day, tae you. I thought tae sit in here and stay oot of the way of your servants. They are all vera busy." She was pleased she'd kept the tremor from her voice while her insides quaked.

"Aye. 'Tis not every day one receives the king into his home. For which I am thankful." His hair, the color of alder tree wood with its light and dark browns, framed his golden-brown face.

She decided he was handsome and immediately laughed inside at herself. What was she thinking? Her enemy's appearance most assuredly should not appeal to her.

"You dinna care for your king?" She'd heard about the turmoil within England. She was well aware of the trouble between nobles and their sovereign.

His brows, darker than his hair, shot upward, sending lines across his forehead. "Not my words, lass."

"But perchance an implication?" What had gotten into her? This was not her friend.

He chuckled and his brown eyes lightened as they caught the stream of light filtering in through the window. "You wish to trap me with my words?"

His tone was not accusing.

"Nay, I only ask." The ease of the conversation nearly unsettled her.

"'Tis the work it causes my people. There is much work to do around the manor and grounds when one does not have the king coming. So when it has to be fit for the king's stay, it is too much work." A squeak came from the basket he held, and he stuck his hand in it.

"You dinna like your people tae be overworked?" Her uncle did not seem to be troubled with that, nor her father, from what she'd been told of him.

She kept her gaze on the basket and the laird's hand that seemed to move methodically in a stroking manor.

"I have a favor to ask of you."

She lifted her eyes and met his. "Of me?" He would probably ask her to leave. He would not wish for her to be here when the king came. What nobleman would want a reiver in his home when his king arrived for a visit?

"Aye." He reached in the basket and pulled out a tiny grey fluff of fur, which was swallowed up in his large hand. "Would you look after this?"

Deirdre's heart melted, and she reached out as she stepped forward. "Ooooh…what an adorable kitten."

"It has no mother. Its eyes are not open yet. 'Tis very young. Nog put milk in a jar and a cloth to get it to eat. I do not know how long it had gone without food before we found it." He deposited the kitten in her outstretched hands.

"Does it have littermates?" She ran her finger around the silky fur of its face.

"Nay. 'Tis the only one to survive."

"Does it have a name?" Probably a silly question to ask a man who'd named his wolfhound, Wolfhound.

"I give you the honor of choosing the right name for her." He reached out and ran his finger gently down the kitten's back as she held it.

Deirdre glanced up into his intense gaze. "A girl. She will need a strong name, for she is a survivor."

"That she is, lass—like you."

Chapter 19

His third trip around the bailey and second time through the manor making sure everything was ready for Richard, and he still worried he'd missed something. Bryce despised all the effort that went into making Richard feel like he was worthy of his crown and more than comfortable. Truly, God's favor had left the king. He no longer sought what was right but concerned himself with filling his own coffers so he could go on yet another expedition to Ireland.

Irritation ate at Bryce as he considered how he must go through the wasted time and expense for a man he hoped soon would no longer be his king. But he must play the part lest he go the way of Arundel and Gloucester.

Spotting Deirdre strolling around with the basket on her good arm, he picked up his pace and headed her way.

"How is the kitten?" He slowed and fell in beside her.

"She is getting stronger every day and I believe her eyes will open soon." Deirdre put her finger under the kitten's chin and gently lifted it for him to see.

"'Tis good. You are a good mother."

A pink hue crept into her cheeks. "I get up all through the night to feed her. I worry she will die."

The kitten rolled to its back in the basket and stretched as it gave a big yawn. "You have done well with her. Have you given her a name?"

"Cathal." Deirdre rubbed the kitten's belly, and she kicked Deirdre's finger away with her back feet.

Bryce smiled. "Battle strong—a good name for her. She has won her battle between life and death."

"I do have hope."

"How are you feeling, Deirdre?"

"Better. Every day I wake feeling much improved." She eyed him carefully.

The distrust remained. He could understand it. He didn't

trust her either. That was why Finley watched her. And perhaps she knew the man always had her in his sights. It mattered not. The reason she ended up at Rosen Craig was cause not to trust her.

Her riot of red curls escaped the *plait* that someone had weaved for her. He'd like to push back the fugitive tendrils just like he had for Clarice in the past.

The memory made him uneasy. He didn't like that this woman made him think of his dead fiancée.

Deirdre stole a quick glance at him before setting her sights ahead of them. Uncertainty is what he witnessed in that split second. Not every woman was like Clarice, he told himself for the hundredth time. He couldn't distrust every woman who crossed his path.

A battle waged in his mind. She had lied to him about the reiving—but she feared for her life. However, she did not now, and she still had not told him who she really was.

"I asked you once your name. Would you like to change that?" The gruffness in his tone could not be helped. Why couldn't the woman just be honest?

She drew the basket and kitten into her. "Do you change your name at a whim?" She threw back defensively.

There. He'd given her a chance, and she chose not to tell him the truth. Just like Clarice. "Nay, but I do not tell a falsehood when asked my name."

"And you accuse me? What makes you bring this charge?" She swept her arm around in a grand gesture. "Is there someone here who claims a different name from what I have given?"

Her hands trembled, even as she moved both onto the handle where the kitten slept.

"Nay you have no other accusers. But I know you lie to me." He'd said it and couldn't be any more honest than that. Now she could prove to be of Brithwin's ilk or Clarice's.

"I dinna ken of what you speak."

Bryce let out a snort, angry with himself for ruining the

short conversation he had with her and angry with her for not being the kind of woman his brother had for a wife. Brithwin was a woman of honor. So much so she'd trusted Clarice even when she knew she shouldn't. She wanted to give the woman a chance.

But Clarice proved to be a woman all about herself and furthering what she wanted. Unfortunately, he seemed to draw women like that to him. How could he ever trust his own judgement with a woman when the ones who drew him were deceitful?

††††

This was why her insides quivered when he'd approached. Her instincts told her there was more to his friendly conversation. But she must stick to her story lest he find out the truth and use her as some pawn as her father wanted to.

He folded his arms in front of him. "You do know. For I saw it in your eyes when you realized you had given your true identity away."

She stared into his eyes, refusing to give in to the desire to look away. Instead, she swallowed and lifted her chin to look taller. She'd look the man directly in the eyes if she could. It was about survival.

There was always the hope that God would not count the lie against her more than once since she told it to the same person. She would hold to that hope because she had told more lies since she'd been here than she had in her lifetime. Unless living as a boy was a lie....

He sighed as though dispersing some of his anger. "So you will not admit to being a Kincaid? It makes good sense. The Kincaid clan reive my land, they burn my fields, they steal my cows. And *you* were caught with my cows."

She shrugged. "I told you they had wandered ontae Scottish land. We only took them tae care for them." Lord have mercy on her. Here she was repeating another lie. But could God expect her to tell the truth in the midst of this?

"Ack! Woman. You expect me to believe that? I am no man's fool. But I have pardoned your sin of stealing what is mine. What I want now is the truth from you."

"You have all you will get from me, milaird. You say you pardon my sin, yet who is that over yonder?" She pointed across the bailey to Finley, who had followed her for the last several days at a distance. "If I am forgiven for what you believe I did, then why am I watched?"

"I said you were forgiven, not trusted. I will not seek punishment for your crime, but as I said earlier, I am no fool either. I protect that which is mine."

She glared at the man. "If you will excuse me, milaird, I believe Cathal needs to be fed." She spun on her heel, but before her second step, the laird's angry words reached her.

"I shall see you at the evening meal, Miss Kincaid."

Back in her room, Deirdre settled on the small wooden chair and placed the kitten in her lap. Dipping the rag into the milk she let Cathal suck the liquid from it. As she considered their conversation, she justified her answer. She was not a Kincaid. Her mother had been before she married, but Deirdre was not. Her last name was Mackenzie. So she had not truly lied. Her heart was immediately heavy. Now she lied to herself.

"Be thankful you are a cat. Your only worry is where your next meal comes from. And I will take care of that." She scratched behind the animal's small ears as it suckled the cloth.

"Why did I let my guard down and start tae trust the laird? I will remind myself he is English lest I start tae forget due tae his charms—responsible for so many deaths. And Ian, sweet Ian, who will never be the same. But when it is safe for me tae leave, little one, I shall take you with me."

She was mad at herself for being the fool and letting a man charm her. Men, her father, her uncle, and her captor were all cut from the same cloth.

Cathal yawned.

"I hope you never feel unloved." She scooped the kitten off her lap and drew it to her chest. "I will love you, and mayhap you will love me. I ken no' what 'tis like tae have someone love me. At least your mother died. My family all lives, but do no' care. I wish tae ken what it feels tae have someone love you."

A tear slipped down her cheek, but she didn't care. There was no one to see and no one to care.

Cathal licked Deirdre's chin with its rough tongue, much like a sand covered rock scrubbed across her skin. She glanced down and smiled. "I see your eye is aboot tae open."

The corner of the little creature's eye had released, and she could see the faint shine of her eye.

She made her way to the bed and curled up with Cathal. The first thing she saw in her mind when she closed her eyes was the smiling face of Laird Warwick.

†††

Bryce sat at the noon meal with Michael. Alex balanced on Michael's shoulder eating the fruit that Michael handed up to him.

"Do not bring that thing to the table when the king is here."

Michael grinned, and Bryce knew he was about to hear more of Michael's rubbish.

"The king might like squirrels. You do not know. He may well consider Alex fine entertainment."

"I think not. We could have enough problems without adding a squirrel offense to the record."

Michael cut off a piece of the mutton and stuck it in his mouth, chewed, and swallowed before answering. "You still worry about the king's intentions, then?"

"I would be foolish if I did not. I cannot shake this feeling there is more to his visit than meets the eye."

"Perchance guilt causes this. 'Tis not as though we have not been discussing our displeasure with his rule."

Bryce glanced around. "Keep your voice down. I do not

want anyone to know what we discuss. Most of all that."

"I saw one of the king's riders come in. Will Richard arrive today?"

"Aye, he comes from seeing Rothburg. He will arrive late." Bryce pushed the food around on his trencher with his knife, wishing he had an appetite.

"I have not seen Deirdre. Where does the lass hide?"

Bryce welcomed Michael's change of subject. "I do not know. I believe I made her angry, and I have not seen her since."

Michael set down his knife, turned his head, and met Bryce's gaze. "What did you do to make her angry?"

Bryce shoved his trencher away. "I pushed her to admit she is a Kincaid."

"Did she?"

Bryce huffed. "Nay. She continues to deny it. But I know by her own words that she is."

"Aye, she did admit it even if it was not what she intended to do. I wish all truth would come so easy. Would make life much simpler."

Alex walked carefully down Michael's arm, then leapt to the table. Bryce lowered his brow as the animal ran down the table, stopping at trenchers as he went or was shooed away.

"Perchance, 'tis best the way it is. I would not want Richard to know such truths. Could cost me my head."

He gazed across the great hall in time to see Deirdre slip out of the kitchen with a plate of food. He didn't take his eyes off her until she disappeared out the door. He frowned. She wore the same gown every day since she had arrived. He'd not thought about her needs. He'd speak with some of the ladies and see to it she had what she needed.

"Bryce...Bryyyyce." Michael called his name getting his attention.

"Sorry. Woolgathering."

"Aye. That I could see. I hope not envisioning what that would be like."

"Deirdre in a different dress?" Bryce looked at his friend, a bit confused.

Michael chuckled. "Weel, I can see where your mind was, but not where I had worried it would be."

"What are you talking about?" Bryce tried to weed through Michael's words.

"We were discussing you losing your head by the king's order. But I can see it is actually a Scottish lass who causes you to lose your head." Michael slapped the table with his hand as he let out a howl of laughter.

Alex, who'd found Pater would share his grapes, stuck one in his mouth and ran to Michael, up his arm and perched on his shoulder.

Bryce grinned. "'Twould be much more pleasant, would you not say?"

But the truth was he didn't want to think about the redheaded lass nor the impending arrival of Richard. Neither he considered good. Both brought trouble.

The two moved to the parlor to wait for Richard's arrival. They hadn't been there long when Pater stuck his head in the doorway.

"May I enter?"

"Come in, Pater. We await the king's arrival." Bryce waved him in.

Pater found a chair and lowered himself onto it.

"What brings you out this late?" Michael asked, his legs stretched out before him and his squirrel on his lap, enjoying the strokes from his master.

"I have not had much time to speak with you. You are a busy man, I can see." Addressing Bryce, Pater folded his hands and gently placed them in his lap.

"'Tis not always as such. The king's advent has cost much of my time. I cannot say that I will be sad to see this visit end, and he has not even arrived."

"You look troubled."

"He is." Michael interjected.

Bryce frowned at Michael. Pater was an honorable man, but he'd not needed to share that with Royce's father-in-law.

Pater turned his eyes on Bryce. "And what troubles you about the king's arrival, son?"

"This could be a personal visit, as the king has suggested. He passes through and needs a place to sleep and eat. 'Twould not be the first time this manor has entertained a king. But the land is in turmoil. The throne is not stable, and no noble is safe."

Pater leaned forward, but left his hands folded in his lap. "Trust. You must trust in the Lord to look after you."

Bryce scoffed. "Aye, like He looked after my parents? Nay, I will look after myself."

At that moment, if Bryce had not known the king was coming, he'd have been worried he'd angered God and that He'd sent an army to besiege him, so great was the commotion coming from outside.

He stood. "It looks I need wonder no longer why he is here."

Once outside, the three made their way forward to view the spectacle. The king's knights and entourage filled the inner bailey. Bryce noticed the full armor they wore. A sign that Richard was well aware of the unrest with his nobles? Did he fear retaliation?

The king arrived on his white destrier. Men came to his aid as he dismounted. Bryce stepped forward and gave a deep bow. "Your Highness."

Richard flipped his hand toward him. "I am weary and wish to retire. We have much to discuss on the morn, as I have just come from Rothburg, and he gives me news that does not please me."

Chapter 20

It was before dawn and the small room in the upper portion of the stone turret provided the best privacy and least chance that the king or one of his men would stumble across Bryce and his men. He left one man outside the door as guard. He couldn't assume all was well. They needed a plan—just in case things went bad quickly.

"How much do you think the king knows?" Michael asked.

"I know not. But he made it clear he was not pleased. Methinks he wanted me squirming, and that is why he spoke of his displeasure and went off to his room."

Hugh moved into the small cluster of men. "How could he have found out?"

Geoffrey kept his voice low. "We have been very careful where and when we have met."

Roger nodded in agreement.

"Once when we talked, I thought I saw someone slinking through the great hall, but I thought it too far away for anyone to hear anything," Ranald offered.

"Aye, I saw that, too. I hoped whoever it was had heard nothing. 'Tis hard to know whether the king has any information at all." Bryce glanced toward the heavy wooden door, thinking he heard something. He'd not be able to relax until the royal entourage left. And he hoped he could then. "He did say he'd been with Rothburg, and we all know the man would like to see me dead. He could be filling the king's ears with lies."

Michael grinned. "Except they are not lies. Rothburg just thinks they are."

"'Tis not a laughing matter, Michael. I for one like to have my head attached to my body." Roger spat.

"Enough! We are not here to determine who told the

king but what our next step is."

"You are right, Bryce." Michael's serious apology drew Bryce's attention.

"We need to find out how much the king knows and whether he has the proof he needs. He cannot do anything with only suspicions. We need to learn if Rothburg has a spy in Rosen Craig. Keep alert, and if you see anything suspicious, I want to know. If you hear anything, I want to know. If I am not so lucky and the king has his evidence, then Michael you go to Royce and tell him." Bryce grinned. "Of course, if you are arrested with me, then Geoffrey, you go."

"Me? Why would I be arrested?" Michael shot back. "I am merely an unlanded knight trying to serve my king by protecting the border land,"

"And that is what you say should any of you be arrested. You know nothing. I want no heroes. You are no good to me or this country dead. Are we all in agreement?" Bryce looked at each of the men. There was much murmuring, none looked him in the eye, and all of them suddenly found their boots of great interest. "That is an order. Agreed?"

"Aye." The answer finally came from one knight and then another. None too happy they were being forced into agreement.

"We go down in pairs or alone. I do not want to draw attention to ourselves." Bryce extended his hand toward the door dismissing the group.

Geoffrey and Ranald were the first to head out. With hand on the latch, Geoffrey turned to Bryce. "What if Royce is arrested as well?"

Bryce shook his head, refusing to allow those thoughts to materialize. "Let us not consider it. He has a wife and a babe on the way."

Geoffrey nodded and he and Ranald were the first to leave the small, secluded room.

†††

Bryce had relinquished to the king his place at the cloth-covered great table on the dais. His attendants tended to his royal needs and guards stood nearby—certainly not a normal visit to one of his subjects. They had taken extra precautions with this stay. Richard knew his nobles were not happy, and he took no chances with his life.

The king appeared intrigued with the elaborate center piece. Bryce was impressed himself with the beautiful workmanship. Nog really had outdone herself on this one. The centerpiece represented a lush hilly green lawn. Violets and other sweet-smelling flowers were scattered in the lawn. Stag antlers with moss covering each point were dispersed around the lawn as trees. Deer, cows, goats, rabbits, boars, small birds, and even a peacock all sculpted from wood and covered in the appropriate fur and feathers grazed in the grassy terrain. Small birds sat in the trees, looking to fly down in search of worms. Aye, indeed, Nog *needed* to be commended for this fine piece.

The aroma of freshly cooked stag and mutton simmered in spices of cloves and cinnamon infiltrated the room as the trays of prepared meat were brought into the great hall waiting to be served.

One of the king's men sat on either side of him. Bryce sat, leaving an empty seat and Michael sat next to him, and then Geoffrey. The rest of the table was filled with the king's men of distinction.

Bryce picked up his trencher and examined it while the king continued to point and talk to the man next to him, amusing himself with the centerpiece. The wooden trenchers, meticulously made, were set around the table. A carved vine full of grapes wrapped around the edge of each trencher. Bryce ran his finger over the workmanship to find it as smooth as a piece of glass. They were stunning. Each setting had a silver spoon beside it as well as a knife.

Where had Nog come up with these and how much money had she spent? He'd told her to see that the table be fit for a king, but heavens, he'd never have spent this much on this king.

He let out a huff. Ah well, what was done was done. He'd be clearer next time he gave Nog directions. As he glanced up, the food squires wove their way toward the dais with trays of food. When the meal had been served, it truly was made for a king.

He'd have to thank Nog and do something for her, maybe give a sennight off. She obviously had worked herself to the bone. The feast that lay out before them included stuffed chicken and loin of veal, both covered in a golden sugar-plum and pomegranate seed sauce. There was roasted wild boar, roe deer, stag, mutton, and rabbit garnished with sauces. Hard boiled eggs were made in the design of an elaborate shield and covered in saffron and flavored with cloves. Sturgeon was cooked in parsley and vinegar and covered in a powdered ginger, complementing the other meats.

There were jellies, a white cream, sliced cheese, strawberries, plums stewed in rosewater, fruits and nuts heaped on platters. Sweet custards, pastries, and delicacies topped off the table.

He almost let out a sigh. This feast was grander than what he and Nog had discussed. Richard could not fault him for the food.

Once they were well into the meal, the king turned his way. "Excellent meal. Not a mediocre dish on the table."

"Thank you, my liege," Bryce replied.

"Aye, what is planned on the morrow?" Richard inquired.

"I thought perchance a boar or stag hunt might be to your liking."

Richard pulled off a piece of mutton and began to chew as he looked up thoughtfully. "'Tis been some time since I have been on a hunt. It sounds enjoyable."

"I shall make sure all is ready. How many of your men

will be going?" Bryce asked.

"Not more than ten." Richard wiped his sleeve over his mouth, removing the meat juices from his face. "Have you had much trouble on the border of late?"

Bryce couldn't help but notice how Michael gave a slight cough and immediately stuffed his mouth with stag. "We have had some. As it happens, a month ago a herd of cattle went missing. We gathered a group of men to search and bring home the animals."

"Did you find them?" Richard took another bite of food as he waited for Bryce to reply.

"We did. As well as the men guilty of the crime."

"What became of these men?"

"A few ran off, and a few died." Bryce really wanted to end this conversation.

"So, you brought none back with you?" He picked up his goblet and took a drink of water

Bryce gritted his teeth. "We brought a woman back with us."

Richard's brows shot up. "A woman, you say?"

"Aye. There was a woman reiving with the men. Most of them were nearly boys, and she disguised herself as a lad. She is spirited. She attempted escape only to fall from a window. A knife she'd hidden in her belt stabbed her abdomen."

"'Tis a shame. I would have liked to meet this woman."

Michael, overcoming his coughing and choking spells spoke up, to Bryce's displeasure. "She is still here with us, recovering."

Bryce shot Michael a warning look. "Aye, Michael speaks the truth. The lass survived the fall and stays at Rosen Craig as she mends."

"What will you do with her?" The king asked.

"Her friends have died, and she has nearly died, twice. I think the lass has suffered enough. I will allow her to go back to her people but with a stern warning that she is to take back to them."

The king swirled the liquid in his goblet as he stared into it. Bryce began to think the king didn't care for his answer.

"I would like to meet this young female reiver."

"That can be arranged, my lord." Bryce tapped his finger quietly on the table, wishing Deirdre had not come up in conversation. It was no surprise that he'd not been able to keep her a secret from the king, but he had wanted to. He'd not admit to himself why he didn't want the king to know about the Scottish lass. She'd been his prisoner, and she'd been through so much that he felt sorry for her. That was all. He could not have soft feelings for a woman who was not of the same character as his mother and sister-in-law. He'd not allow himself to. Not this time.

"I would hope, since I have traveled this great distance. But this is not what I want to talk with you about. I wish to discuss some disturbing news I heard from Rothburg."

Bryce's heart slammed in his chest, but he forced himself to keep eye contact with Richard and not steal a glance at Michael or Geoffrey. He'd not say anything to cause the king to accuse him of treason. "I am afraid I am at a disadvantage, my lord. I know not of what news you speak."

"Rothburg tells me that some of your men have been raiding the borderland. I had all I could do to keep him from storming your demesne. He has his own problems with Scottish reivers and blames your men for keeping the tension on both sides of the border."

Bryce almost laughed. Almost. The relief was so great. Rothburg didn't accuse him of treason, only reiving, which was an absurdity. The man was out of his mind to say such a thing. "I would not want to accuse Rothburg of lying to my lord, but you know the man has never liked my family. He wants Rosen Craig."

"'Tis true the man is not fond of you. He believes Rosen Craig should be restored to his family since his grandfather was eventually cleared of charges of treason, albeit too late for the man."

"My liege, your uncle, John of Gaunt gave this demesne to my father after he took it from Brighton for not supporting your coronation as a boy. This was given to the Brighton family after the Rothburgs lost it." A glint of Royce's troubles with Edmond Brighten flashed through his mind. Surely, the king had already heard of that.

Richard chuckled. "If prone to believe in such things, one might believe this castle cursed. Two families lost Rosen Craig due to treasonous acts, your parents were murdered here, and you nearly were as well. 'Tis possible this place causes the lords to lose their mind and commit treason."

Careful to keep his voice steady, Bryce wouldn't allow himself to take the much-needed deep breath. "My parents died loyal to you."

"Ah, aye, but they did die because of someone else's treason. What of you, Bryce? Are you loyal to me?"

"My lord, have I given you any reason to doubt my loyalty? I have always been available and supported you whenever you needed me. Why would you question me now?" Bryce needed to know if the king truly doubted his loyalty and why. He eyed him carefully.

"'Tis turbulent times. I wish to know if my subjects remain faithful to me." The king did not break eye contact, perhaps in challenge.

"You need not question my dedication."

"Hmmm, 'tis good to hear from your own mouth. Perhaps it is the bad blood betwixt you two, for Rothburg would like to imply I should."

Chapter 21

Finley stood before the familiar dais of Laird Rothburg's keep, rehearsing his reasons for being there. In such uncertain times, it was dangerous not to hedge one's bets. One never knew which way the die would be cast. He purposed not only to gain favor with the man but also to secure a position and prove himself loyal. Though in his heart, Finley decided long ago his loyalty rest with naught but himself.

Rothburg stepped off the platform to stand before the knight. "Don't just stand there. What do you have for me, man?"

Rothburg's gruff demeanor grated on Finley, and he fisted the hand folded behind his back as he took a deep bow before the man. Straightening, he smiled, and met the man's gaze with a caginess in his eye.

"I dinna have to help you," Finley reminded the laird.

"'Tis not you." Rothburg waved a wrinkled hand in the air, and his tone changed. "I have received unwelcome news. Have you learned anything helpful?"

Finley shrugged. "The king has arrived. I heard him tell Laird Warwick he was no' pleased with him. Something to do with reivers to the north."

Rothburg turned and made his way to a chair, signaling Finley to follow. Once settled in the chair, he leaned forward and grinned, showing a missing top and side tooth. "Then the king took my words to heart." He leaned back, pleased with himself. "Very good. Did you hear any more? Did Warwick appear troubled by the king's announcement?"

"Aye, I could tell the laird was none too pleased with the king's words."

"Is there anything else that displeased our king?"

"I dinna stay to find out. I took my leave whilst everyone was busy seeing to King Richard's needs. I must hurry back before the laird finds me missing. The man has me spying on a lass. 'Tis not a knight's job to be watching a wee woman."

Rothburg's brows rose. "Why does he have you watching a woman? Tell me about her."

Finley huffed. "She was caught reiving. The other reivers that dinna get away were killed in the skirmish. She dressed as a lad. She was injured attempting to escape and spent several sennights recovering. 'Tis not much to tell. She is a thorn in my side. I dinna wish to walk around watching her, making sure she behaves."

"You say she walks around. A reiver is free to go where she wishes on the grounds?"

"Aye. Warwick said she is no longer a prisoner. But he told me he does no' trust her and I must keep watch on her."

"Who is she?"

"A Kincaid. To me, she claims to be a Maxwell. Warwick claims she is a Kincaid or of the clan I am told."

"Interesting. I wonder what makes this girl special. How old is she?" Rothburg tapped his fingers on the arm of the wooden chair.

"'Tis hard to ken. As I said she dressed as a boy. Her hair is short."

"Give me a guess then."

"What concern is this lass to you?"

Rothburg's brows drew down. "Answer my question."

"Perchance twenty summers. 'Tis hard to ken."

Rothburg stared off. "Befriend the girl."

"Why would *I* want to befriend this lass? That I must watch her is a humiliation. I am a knight."

"She could be valuable to us. There is a reason Warwick does not punish her. Perchance he is attracted to her. If you befriend the woman, then you can gain her trust. Possibly you can get her to help us."

Finley snorted. "Why would she trust me?"

"You are both from Scotland. You have that in common. Use it to your advantage. And if Warwick is attracted to the woman, she may be able to find out information you cannot. If you can win her over, she could be the key to gaining Rosen Craig."

"I dinna think the lass likes me. And I dinna think she trusts anyone."

Rothburg stood abruptly and began to pace. "We need her. Especially now."

Finley eyed him as the laird walked to and fro. "What has happened?"

"It does not concern you."

"If you wish me to help with the lass, then I wish to ken why this is so important."

Rothburg returned to the chair and sat. "My reivers were caught by Mackenzie."

Finley's heart skipped a beat. He knew the men Rothburg had sent as reivers. "Did the Scottish laird hang them?"

"Nay, he did not. But I may. The cowards told all when Mackenzie pressed them. They claim they feared for their lives. If they were loyal to me, they would have died for me rather than give away my secrets."

A bit relieved, Finley released the breath he'd been holding. "What exactly did they tell Mackenzie? I have heard he is no' a man one wishes to cross."

Rothburg narrowed his eyes. "They told him I had sent them north to reive his land. And when pressed further, they told him why."

"That could be problematic. What did Mackenzie say to them?" If Mackenzie was going to bring his clan down to fight Rothburg, Finley had no wish to be present when they arrived.

"'Tis what concerns me. He sent them on their way with no message other than he did not want to see them on Scottish soil again."

"I think that I would put extra men on the catwalk and sleep with one eye open."

"My thoughts exactly."

†††

The raucous noise below Deirdre hadn't quieted since the king's arrival. Commotion had awakened her from dozing in the chair. She'd gone to the window to see what brought the excitement. King Richard and his grand entourage had graced Rosen Craig with their presence. Laird Bryce and his man, Michael, bowed low to the king. That was when Deirdre had decided to stay in her room. She'd asked to have her meals brought up to her rather than bow to the English king.

Hours had passed, and her food had been brought to her room as she feigned illness. She'd finished her eating and sat gazing out the window. The inner court was alive with people running to and fro—surely the demands of a spoiled king. She huffed and turned away. Surrounded by a castle full of people and yet the loneliness gnawed at her insides.

Try as she might, she couldn't block out the noise around her. It wasn't the laughter from below that piqued her curiosity, but the beautiful sound of bagpipes. After much vacillating, she gave in to the instrument of her heart. She stole out of her room and down the hall to peer into the great hall where the music originated and where the laird entertained the king.

She leaned her cheek against the cold stone wall as she peered at the man playing.

Most of the eating had finished, though the king still picked at the food left sitting near him. The center tables had been cleared from the great hall floor, and men, women and even a few children stood or sat along the walls watching a man dancing on a rope attached on opposite walls and high in the air. Below a small group of minstrels, with fiddle, lute, psaltery, flute, bagpipes, triangle, and bells played as the man spun on the rope.

The bagpipes drew her attention away from the dancer. How she loved the pipes' music. Her gaze shifted to the dais to see if the laird was drawn to it as much as she. But he sat listening to the king. He didn't seem overly interested in Richard's words. But then he wasn't too happy about the king's arrival either.

Laird Warwick's attention shifted from the king, sending a bolt of lightning through her veins the moment his eyes met hers. Her knees weakened. She took several deep breaths in an attempt to chase away the fear invading her body. She had no reason to fear the laird. To prove it to herself, she stepped into the room.

He frowned. He wasn't happy to see her. Weel, if he didn't want her there, then that was precisely where she was going to be.

She walked toward the dais, passing by the children and adults sitting along the wall enthralled with the evening's entertainment. Not wishing to speak with the laird or the king, Deirdre found the first open spot on the wall and slipped in, leaning against the cold stone exterior.

Forcing herself to watch the dancer, she refused to steal a glance to see if the laird still looked her way. The dancer lost his footing, and the crowd gasped as he caught himself before tumbling to his death or at least severe injury. Once back on his feet, he gave a sly smile and bowed, making Deirdre believe that was all part of the act to get the crowd more engaged. She smiled at his tactics.

Someone slipped in beside her during the dancer's stumble. She didn't bother to look. It would be an unfamiliar Englishman. A few moments passed and her attention remained fixed on the rope strung across the hall and the man who this time teetered as though he'd lost his balance. The crowd gasped again and the man immediately grinned and went back to dancing.

"'Methinks some just wait for him to fall."

Deirdre turned to see the man the laird called Michael standing beside her. The same man who'd insulted her when she'd first arrived and the same man who kept a pet squirrel.

"Weel, 'tisn't a surprise. The English enjoy the sufferings of others."

"Och! Lassie, you have a sharp tongue. Should I conclude that all Scotsman have a sharp tongue?"

She glared at him. "Only when they speak with an Englishman who likes tae insult them."

"I would suggest you bite that tongue of yours. The king wishes to meet the reiving lass who disguises herself as a boy."

"Weel, tell your king I dinna wish tae meet him. I am only here tae listen tae the bagpipes."

"'Twas not a yay or nay answer, lassie. The king wishes to meet you, so meet you the king shall." His grin told her he enjoyed the banter.

She did not. She wished he'd go on his way and leave her be. "I was told I am nay longer a prisoner here. I dinna wish tae speak with your king."

"'Tis true Laird Warwick gave you your freedom, but if you are on English soil, which I remind you that you are, then you are subject to our king's wishes."

"Why does he wish tae speak tae me?"

"You intrigue him with your courage. Enough talk. He is waiting." The knight pushed himself off the wall and started toward the dais.

Begrudgingly, she followed, wishing she'd not given in to her longing for the bagpipes. When they reached the raised platform, she stepped up, and he led her to a seat, the laird's seat, only now he sat where Michael had sat, putting her in between him and the king.

Laird Warwick stood, introducing her to his king before she had time to sit. "My lord the king, this is Deirdre—" He hesitated and stole a glance her way. "Kincaid. The woman I spoke to you about from the border."

Her knees weakened, though she didn't know why. Relief filled her when he didn't introduce her as the reiver. She'd not put it past the laird's good friend to have introduced her that way.

"Your Grace." Deirdre gave a curtsey.

"Be seated, Miss Kincaid." The king gestured toward her seat. Bryce pulled out her chair, and Deirdre let herself down into it.

The king smiled at her. "So my dear, what brings you to this side of the border?"

Chapter 22

Bryce told himself to breathe as he waited for the lass's response, willing her not to lie. That would not bode well for her should she think to deceive Richard.

"Weel, it seems your fine laird here found me irresistible." The lass smiled.

Richard chuckled. "Did he now?"

"Aye. There I be, helping those wee little cows who had lost their way when I was set upon by what I could only believe was brigands. T'would have been a shame had some of those cows lost their lives to wolves. Would no' you agree, Your Grace?"

"You argue a good case, Miss Kincaid. I believe I would like to hear more."

The lass was charming, to be sure—and very sly with her words.

"As I was saying, Your Grace, I had remounted my palfrey after helping a calf who had stumbled and fallen when we were surrounded by—" she glanced at Bryce, "—the Laird's men. I dinna ken what tae think, it all happened so quickly. I might add, Your Grace, that we were on Scottish soil when this occurred."

Richard turned to Bryce with brows raised.

"They had just crossed over from Rosen Craig land, and they were our cows," Bryce defended.

Deirdre avoided eye contact with Bryce as he turned his attention back to her.

"Go ahead, lass," Richard prodded.

"A sword fight followed, with one of my good friends dying. He was only a boy." Tears welled in her eyes.

Bryce drew in a breath and hoped her theatrics did not sway the king in her favor since he already questioned if he and his men were reiving.

"We put down our swords in surrender. But instead of

being taken here for trial, we were set upon horses with ropes around our necks. I dinna remember much after that due tae the slap on the horses and no' being able tae breathe. I woke tae find meself on the ground with your laird here beside me. From there I was brought here."

"But Lord Warwick claims you are not a prisoner. So why do you remain here?"

The lass thought to drop her gaze to the table. He could only imagine while she thought up a good tale to tell as to why.

"I am no' sure I will be welcomed back." Her voice held sorrow in it.

She'd never told him this. He believed she stayed because of her injuries. He'd never probed further to find out if there was another reason she didn't leave.

The king reached out and touched her hand. "And why is that, lass?"

She sighed and drew sad eyes up to meet the king's. "Because I am the one who lived. I ken that the laird will no' be pleased that he lost guid men who followed me. But we have been fighting English reivers who come tae steal, pillage, and burn our crops for years now. We only wished to compensate for that which has been lost."

"'Tis good that Lord Warwick has given you a safe place to live whilst you decide what to do."

"Aye, it was kind of the laird."

Bryce would have liked to give his account, but he didn't believe the king would welcome it at the moment.

"Where will you go if not back to your home? I am sure you do not wish to stay here forever."

"I have no' decided, Your Grace. Perchance a neighboring clan."

"And Lord Warwick tells me that you were injured. Do you improve? How are you feeling?" The king patted her hand.

Deirdre brought her splinted arm up and rested it on the

table. "It still pains me, as does my ankle. But it continues tae improve each day. Grammercy for asking, Your Grace."

Bryce couldn't believe what an enchanter this lass could be. She'd not wasted any of her efforts on him. But the king seemed quite taken with her.

"And you did this how?"

She batted her eyes at the king. Bryce couldn't believe he'd just witnessed that.

"Trying tae escape my enemy. I thought tae climb from the upper window, but that did no' go as I had planned." She smiled at the king.

Richard chuckled. "Nay, I would guess it did not. Tell me, lass, do you still think Lord Warwick is your enemy?"

"I would be a fool, my laird, tae answer that any other way than, nay, since he has given me safe refuge and I have no other place tae go."

The little vixen stole a glance his way as she spoke. If nothing else, he had learned more information about her— information that could be valuable.

"You will have my protection, Miss Kincaid, I assure you. I do not wish to have this continued border reiving— Scottish or English. I wish to know your honest opinion. Do you believe that these reivers you speak of come from Rosen Craig?"

Bryce was sure his heart stopped beating for a few seconds. Did the king really ask this Scottish reiving lass that? Would he take her word over his since Rothburg put that idea in his head? Bryce waited for Deirdre's reply. He knew the answer. She'd made it clear that she believed his men were guilty. The question was, had he convinced her otherwise? Or if she did still believe his people responsible, would she share that with the king?

"Now I am no' sure, 'tis true. The laird has told me he does no' allow such behavior from his people."

"And you believe him? Remember, you have my protection, Deirdre."

Bryce understood what the king was about, using the lass's given name. He hoped to put her on a more personal level with him as he sought answers.

Deirdre met Bryce's gaze, and he could not read what her answer would be. He could only hope.

"I dinna ken. I have no' been able tae determine if he tells me the truth or no'." She kept her sight locked on his. "What I can tell you is he does no' trust me, and I dinna trust him. 'Tis a mutual feeling we share."

The king patted her hand again and removed it as he leaned back in his chair and rested both hands on his lap.

"Remember, you have my protection."

Bryce would have liked to ask Richard from whom did she need protection. He knew the king implied it was from him and Rosen Craig. Yet hadn't he looked out for her and done everything he could to keep her alive?

Richard turned to Bryce, done with his conversation with Deirdre. Bryce had the uneasy feeling Richard had hoped the lass would confirm Rothburg's words.

"An early morning hunt, Warwick?"

"If you wish, my lord." Bryce was happy the conversation had turned away from Deirdre and reiving.

"I will look forward to it."

"I would love tae go on a hunt with you, Your Grace." Deirdre's eyes sparkled with excitement.

The king's brows shot up. "A stag hunt?"

"Aye, milord. I am a vera guid shot."

"Lass." Bryce interrupted before the king could answer. He didn't want Deirdre around the king any more than necessary. "You forget your arm is broken and your ankle sprained. The healer has said you need rest to allow your arm to heal."

Deirdre lifted her nose. "'Tis been neigh on five sennights. 'Tis nearly healed."

"I wish to have Miss Kincaid join us. Perchance she can show us Englishman a thing or two about hunting stag."

"As you wish, my lord." Bryce answered begrudgingly.

She gave him a smug smile and turned her attention to the performance.

Bryce was not in the mood for entertainment or talking—he was glad when the evening was over and the king retired to his room.

†††

Deirdre removed the wooden splint the healer had made for her. As she lifted the wood from her arm she winced. The rubbing of the splint had caused an oozing sore. Even her chemise hadn't prevented the abrasion. She went to the bowl of water that was delivered to her room daily by a servant and dipped a cloth in it, saturating it, before pulling up her sleeve and pressing the cloth to her wound. The cool water gave temporary relief to the burning flesh. She'd ask Nog for salve to apply to it before they left for the hunt.

Excitement surged through her. She was good with her bow and enjoyed using it. She quickly finished readying herself. She felt her hair with her hands. It was unruly as ever. How she wished she hadn't cut it when she was captured. It was all for naught. The laird had seen through her disguise anyway. The only good thing she could think of was her hair grew quickly and before long it would have some length.

She hurried down the stairs using the railing to keep the weight off her injured ankle. She didn't want the laird to notice it still troubled her. But that too, continued to get better with each passing day. Before long she'd be as good as... She slowed. As good as before this whole nightmare ever happened and she was living with Mairi, the old widow.

She shook herself from the threatening melancholy and headed toward the kitchen where Millicent was often seen visiting with Nog. Today would be the first day she might enjoy herself since she'd arrived. She wouldn't allow gloom to overshadow her.

She passed through the great hall where many still ate

and glanced to the dais to see that the king and the laird no longer were there.

When she entered the kitchen, Nog looked up from the dough she kneaded. The weary cooked smiled.

"You look tired, Nog." Deirdre's heart went out to the poor woman, who probably had been up half the night cooking for the king and his entourage.

"I am not as young as I once was. And I was never meant to prepare meals for a king."

"But the food has been far grander than anything I have ever tasted. You have done a wonderful job."

A pink blush filled the cook's cheeks. "'Tis thanks I give you, miss."

"You ken, I am much improved, and I could help you if you need. I dinna ken much aboot cooking, but 'tis the truth I can follow directions weel."

Nog gave a tired laugh. "I have no doubt you could help. But I do not think milord would approve of me putting you to work."

"Weel, 'tisn't as though he has treated me like a special guest since I arrived here. He should have nothing tae say in the matter."

"You do not wish to get me in trouble with milord. 'Tis best you only eat the food and not help prepare it. The lord has made sure I have much help. The kitchen is busy with people doing my bidding. 'Tis just a lot for this old cook to oversee."

Deirdre frowned. "But I wish tae help you. I can help direct people. Surely that would no' bring you his wrath."

Nog tsked. "What do you need, lass? Sure I am that you did not come down here to ask about my cooking."

Deirdre sighed, resigning herself to Nog's refusal of her help. "I came tae see if you had seen the healer. I wish tae ask if she has some salve for my arm."

Deirdre pulled up her sleeve, exposing the raw skin.

Nog walked around the table toward Deirdre and took

hold of her arm. "She went to get some herbs from the storage room. "Why did you not tell us of this sooner? This could have gotten infected and still could, miss."

"I did no' want tae trouble Millicent, but it has become vera sore and I am to go on the stag hunt."

"With what did you not wish to trouble me?" Millicent swung the door open and spoke the words before she stepped into the room.

"The child's splint has rubbed her skin raw." Nog continued to hold Deirdre's arm.

Millicent rushed over to them, setting a basket of fragrant herbs on the table as she passed. She took Deirdre's arm from Nog and started prodding around the wound. She tsked as she looked at it. Deirdre couldn't help but wonder if the two white-haired old women bent over her arm had picked up some habits from each other.

"'Tisn't vera bad. I only wished tae get some salve from you to relieve the sting it causes." Deirdre gently tugged her arm in an attempt to get it back.

Millicent held tight. "Nog, you keep salve in here for burns, do you not?"

Nog rushed over to a basket near the fireplace and plucked it from the floor.

Millicent tugged on her arm, leading her to the table. "Sit, child."

Deirdre sat, partially enjoying the fuss of the women, but worrying she would miss the hunt.

Nog placed the basket on the table and withdrew a jar as well as a long strip of rolled fabric and handed them to Millicent.

"Ladies, I dinna wish tae sound ungrateful, but I am tae go on the hunt with your king."

Nog looked up, but Millicent began applying the salve, focused on her task. "Have you eaten, miss?"

Deirdre's belly betrayed her and growled. Heat filled her cheeks. "Nay. I did no' have time."

Nog shuffled around the table and lifted a cloth to expose dried fruit and bread. She broke off a piece of bread and a handful of fruit and placed it next to Deirdre. "Eat. You'll need your strength."

Deirdre nodded and placed a piece of dried, chewy pear in her mouth. The sweet fruit tickled her tongue, and she chewed thoughtfully before taking a bite of the bread.

Millicent wrapped the strip of fabric over the salve and then tucked it under to secure it. "Come back this eventide, and I will put more salve on. You do not want this to become infected. I have seen things like this cause one to lose their limb."

That sent a chill up Deirdre's spine.

"Hurry, eat." Nog pushed the bread in her hand toward her mouth.

Deirdre quickly finished the fruit and bread and then swallowed down the cup of water Nog held before her. Both women pushed her toward the side door.

"Go." Millicent said.

"Bring us home the evening meal," Nog added.

"'Tis like having two grandmithers." Deirdre smiled at them as she left.

The two women beamed as she rushed out the door.

She stared toward the stables where only two horses stood. They'd left without her.

Chapter 23

The lass was upset. Bryce could read it in her body language. She stared off at the stables, her shoulders fallen. She reached up and wiped her eyes. His heart contracted.

"Are you ready? We are not too far behind the group."

She swung around, facing him, eyes wide. "You did no' leave me?"

"Nay, but the king waits on no man—or woman."

She smiled. "But you do?" She cocked her head in a most adorable fashion.

"Aye. I could see you wished to come. I did not want to disappoint you." He had tried to keep conversation going with Richard as he watched for the lass to come into the hall, but the king was anxious to get on the hunt. He hadn't noticed that Miss Kincaid had yet to join them until Bryce told him that he would follow shortly when the lass came down.

"'Tis sorry I am that I have held you up. I should have risen earlier. I needed tae find the healer for salve." She came toward him and then fell into step beside him as they made their way toward their mounts.

"Salve? Are you sure you can manage this hunt?"

"'Tis only for a spot the wood rubbed on my skin. 'Twill no' affect my shot."

Bryce grinned. "You are very sure of yourself."

"I am guid with a bow. I had tae be. But I dinna have one of my own here."

"There is one tied to the saddle."

They reached the horses, and she touched the bow with near reverence. "'Tis a fine weapon."

"Aye. My *atilliator* is very good at what he does." Bryce grasped her waist and lifted her up on her palfrey. The woman was too light. Hopefully, she had not lost too much weight while in his keeping.

A slight gasp escaped her lips. "I could have mounted Storm myself."

Bryce eyed the woman and determined there was no malice in her words—merely a statement. "'Tis glad I am to hear. I will remember that." He threw his leg over Tempest and settled on the horse. Her horse's name was not missed by him. He nudged the animal forward with his heels.

"Did you name the palfrey?" He threw the words over his shoulder.

"Aye. Storm seemed a fitting name." She pushed her horse up beside his, and he noticed she now straddled the horse like a man. Her gown, though covering some of her legs, exposed the lower part of her *hosen* that she'd arrived in dressed as a lad.

"And why is that?" Bryce waited for her response, fully expecting something trifling.

As the silence grew, he turned to see if she'd heard him. She stared at him and seemed to be making a decision.

"I named her Storm because—" There was another pause. "Because it was a difficult time in my life. She was a filly and her mother had died. The only reason I was given her was because they did no' believe she would live."

Bryce looked ahead, not wanting to give away any of his feelings. How alike they were in the naming of their animals. Tempest had much to do with Bryce's battles and less to do with the horse's unruly manners. "'Tis a good name you chose."

They rode on in silence as they went deeper into the woods. The howl of the hounds flushing out the deer guided them to the group. They reached the others as the dogs burst through the thicket right behind a large stag.

An arrow sliced through the air beside him, and Bryce's heart sank. He'd made clear to his men to allow the king the first shot but had failed to tell Miss Kincaid.

The king twisted in his saddle, looking their direction with eyes blazing. If the man didn't want to take his title and land before, he surely would now, if the anger on his face was any sign. Richard's gaze dropped to Bryce's hands that held only reins. He then shifted his attention to Miss Kincaid, who still held her bow.

Bryce found himself wanting to hide the lass behind him out of the king's scrutiny. She was a Scot, a reiver, and a woman. How would he accept that her speed had beat him on the draw of the bow? Bryce glanced over at Miss Kincaid, whose eyes still followed where her arrow had gone. The lass had no idea what she'd done.

"Miss Kincaid, was that your shot?" Richard asked from atop his stallion.

She turned his way, a broad grin spreading across her face. "Aye, Your Grace. I do believe I hit him!"

It had to be the excitement in her voice that caused the king's frown to turn into a smile and then a chuckle. "Aye, I do believe you did. Shall we go track him down and see if you have gotten our first meat for the evening meal?"

Bryce let out a sigh as Miss Kincaid urged her horse over to where the king sat. The group followed the alerts of the hounds to where the stag lay.

The king looked down upon the animal. "A fine trophy. I shall have to see if I can best you."

"I wish you best of luck, Your Grace."

"'Twill not be luck, lass, but skill."

"Weel, I am vera fast," Miss Kincaid shared proudly.

Bryce found himself glad that Michael had bowed out, telling him he had some personal business to take care of. He could foresee the fun the man would have had with this whole ordeal. And he could see him angering the king.

He shook off the thoughts, needing to get back to the important situation at hand. He would take the lass aside and let her know she must allow the king the next stag. He wasn't sure how long the king's charity would remain.

Bryce looked around. Where was Finley? He'd specifically requested the man be here for this reason.

"Guernon, where is Finley?" Bryce continued to search for the young knight through the men on horseback.

"I could not find him, milord. He was not at the keep."

"Clean the stag and take it back to Nog. And find Finley. I want him to report back to me. I wish to know where the man has been."

†††

Deirdre's muscles had become soft, for she'd done no riding since she'd been captured and very little else. She walked around the courtyard, attempting to work the kinks out of her body that she'd developed from the previous day's hunt.

The laird had caught her after she'd taken down the first stag of the day and let her know she needed to allow their king to take down the next. She smiled. The English were strange people. What they did to please their king. She had to wonder if the man knew that he got the second stag of the day only because no one else was allowed to shoot unless the king's arrow missed. She shook her head. What enjoyment would the king get if all was given to him on a platter? He hadn't truly earned it.

Her thoughts were interrupted by heavy footfalls behind her.

"Miss Kincaid."

She turned to the familiar voice. "Aye?"

Finley, the man whom the laird had watching her, fell into step beside her. "I hear you took down the first stag yestermorn. I laughed when I was told. I see you have nay special feelings for this English king either."

Deirdre eyed the man. "I did no' ken that the English had such strange traditions and accommodated their king in such frivolous ways. I had the opportunity, and I took it." She shrugged.

"How did the king respond tae your shooting the first stag?"

"He was vera gracious, I would say, since I was no'

supposed tae shoot it. He congratulated me on the kill."

The tall, slender man, with hair nearly as red as hers, continued to walk beside her. "Must be because you are a bonnie lass. 'Tis sure I am the king could no' miss that. Even an English king."

Deirdre stopped and faced Finley. He was young, with spotty facial hair on his chin and cheeks. "You speak as though you dinna care for King Richard."

He shrugged. "I am Scottish. Why should I like him?"

Deirdre eyed him carefully. "You have left Scotland for English soil. Why would I think anything other?"

"You are here as well. And still you did not answer my question."

"Weel, I did no' choose tae come here tae English soil, unlike you. And as tae the king, he was kind tae me. I have nothing bad tae say of him." Deirdre didn't know if she should trust the man just because he was born of Scottish blood. The man did choose to live with her enemy.

"But you are free tae leave. I heard the laird tell the king. And yet you remain." The right corner of his mouth twitched. Something she'd noticed he'd done several times since talking to her.

"And I will leave when I have healed completely." And she would. She just wasn't sure how quickly after she healed that she would leave and where she would go. She thought to ask him again why he was here rather than in Scotland but decided she really was not that interested.

"Do you no' miss your clan?" The man pushed her for answers.

She narrowed her eyes. "Why the sudden interest in me?"

"I would no' call it sudden." His mouth twitched again.

"You have watched me from afar, per the laird's orders, since I arrived. You have had many opportunities."

"Weel, you intrigue me more now. You dressed as a lad, are a cow reiver, you attempted tae climb out a window and down a turret, you were the first tae take down a stag, and you have no fear of a king. And you are a lass."

Deirdre laughed. "Which part intrigues you? That I am capable and a lass?" It was true, there were not many women like her. And most would frown on her for what she did. But growing up disguised as a lad, always fearful her father would discover her, Deirdre took special pains to make sure she acted like all the other boys.

"All but that you are a bonnie lass and able tae have the courage tae do all of it."

"We do what we must. We dinna get tae choose some things in life. We must make the best of what we are given."

He smiled. "Ah, you speak in mysteries as well. You are a woman who could blind a man with love."

"Ha! Now you speak empty words and try to *blind me* with them." She laughed.

The last two days were the best days she'd had since she'd been dragged here against her will. The laird was kind to her, she'd had a grand time at the hunt, and now she laughed with her own—a Scotsman.

"Finley!" The knight they called Guernon, yelled and motioned for the Scotsman to come.

"Och! I have tae go. The laird wishes tae speak tae me aboot something. I dinna like facing him withoot kenning what he wishes tae say tae me."

"I ken what he wants."

Finley had taken a step toward the keep and stopped, swiveling back to face her. "How is that?"

Deirdre once again eyed the man. Did she trust him? Should she trust him? It would be nice to have a friend, one from Scotland.

"He wishes tae ken why you were no' on the hunt and where you have been off tae."

Finley's brows shot up. "Then I shall have tae come up with a reason quickly, aye, lass?"

"'Twould be wise, if you dinna wish the laird's wrath."

"Could I use you as my excuse?" Finley glanced toward the man who had called him.

"I was with the laird and king. He will ken 'tis a lie. I would no' suggest you use that."

"I will tell him you requested I find you a bow for the hunt. You were no' aware he would provide one."

Deirdre really wanted to help the man. She wouldn't want to face the laird's anger, and Finley must have been doing something he didn't want to share with the laird. But she had been deceitful enough to protect herself. She didn't need to add more sins to her growing offenses. "Tell him what you wish. 'Tis no' my concern."

Finley smiled and turned, taking quick strides toward the keep and his reckoning with the laird.

Chapter 24

Bryce drummed his fingers on the table as he waited on
Finley. He looked over the accounts Ralf had handed him
earlier of what the king's visit was costing him in stores and
manpower—his mood darkening by the minute. Ralf stood
waiting for any questions Bryce had for him.

This was the third day with the king, and he was more
than ready to see the man and his entourage leave. But then,
he'd never wanted the man to come either.

At least he did gain a bit of knowledge with Richard's
visit. He now knew that Rothburg could not be trusted in
anything when it came to Rosen Craig. And he also learned
that the man would lie to the king himself to get what he
wanted. At least he hadn't put the idea of treason in the
king's head.

"Milaird." Finley strode through the manor to where
Bryce sat.

Bryce turned to Ralf. "You may go."

The steward dipped his head. "Aye, milord." Then he
made his way out of the room.

Finley stopped in front of the table where Bryce sat.
"You wished tae see me?"

What was it about the man that Bryce didn't like? It was
more than that the man was lazy and couldn't see
responsibilities without them being pointed out. He stared at
him, and Finley shifted his stance and averted his eyes.

He didn't trust him. That was what it was. He should let
the man go to find another keep to serve. But Bryce wasn't
the type of lord to get rid of someone without proof, though
his laziness was enough reason.

"How long have you been a knight?" Bryce knew the
answer.

"Two years."

"Do you feel you learned much under your tutor?"

He drew himself up. "Aye. All I needed tae."

"I have not been pleased with you since you have arrived. You argue the tasks given to you, claiming they are not the jobs of a knight. And if I do not give you a task because I feel you should know that it needs to be done, you do not do it. I am too busy to follow you around making sure you do what is expected. 'Tis your choice. You need to take on the responsibilities as my other men do without being told, or you need to move on."

Fire blazed in Finley's eyes. "I have been watching the lass you assigned me tae. I can no' keep my eye on her and do all the other tasks that others do."

"I will not argue with you. What I have said I will stand behind. You need to be a knight I can trust and rely on."

"Is that all, milaird?"

"Nay. I wish to know where you were yestermorn when we went on the hunt. Once again, I had a task for you, but you were not there."

"Miss Kincaid had said she looked forward to the hunt but had no weapon her size. I went searching for one. Is no' that what you wished me to do? Look after the lass?"

"So if I ask Miss Kincaid, she will confirm what you have told me?"

Bryce wasn't sure, but he thought he saw a flicker of fear in the man's eyes before he spoke. "Aye. She will tell you that I speak the truth."

"We shall see. You are dismissed."

Finley turned around and stormed out. Bryce sighed. He didn't need a knight like that right now. He had too many other worries to have to retrain a man to what his responsibilities were.

Bryce finished looking over the accounts the steward had given him. He pushed back his chair and reluctantly went to find Richard. The king had given him no indication of how long he'd be staying, and Bryce certainly would not inquire.

Having the king visit caused much unwanted stress.

Fortunately, he could rely on Nog to prepare meals fit for a king. And the steward had seen to the entertainment without much direction, only confirmation. Finley could take lessons from them both.

Michael joined him as he headed out into the bailey. "You do not look too well, Bryce."

"As well as a man can be who is trying to keep a king happy, I suppose."

"Aye, 'twill be none too soon for him to leave. I have avoided the man. 'Tis difficult to act loyal when all I want is him off the throne."

Bryce quickly surveyed their surroundings, making sure no one was within earshot. "Aye. I wonder if he sees through the lies of my loyalty. 'Tis hard to stomach him, knowing all the man has done—and wondering if he wishes the same for me as he has done to some of the Appellants."

"'Tis enough to put one's teeth on edge. Glad I will be when this pretense is over."

Pater walked toward them, and the two men slowed.

"My lord, Michael, how are you this fine day?"

Michael leaned around Bryce and spoke before Bryce had a chance. "'Twould be a better day if we had nay royal company."

"It does seem the king's presence has made many uneasy. 'Tis perilous times we live in. I must say, I have found much to occupy myself with since his arrival." He looked to Bryce. "I apologize for missing the meals. I find it much more comforting eating in my room whilst I pray. 'Tis hard to know what Richard truly thinks of Lollards. I wish to meet my new grandchild when it comes."

"Nay reason to apologize, Pater. Your daughter would never forgive me should something happen to you."

Pater smiled. "Brithwin worries too much."

"I appreciate your attention to Lucas since the king's arrival. I have seen you together several times." One never knew what would come from the lad's mouth. It was best for

Bryce and for Royce that the boy stay far from the king.

"Aye. I have attempted to keep the boy with me as much as possible. He does not always know when to hold his words. We do not need him getting the king stirred up. 'Tis good for the boy to learn some prayers." Pater grinned.

Bryce and Michael laughed.

"Aye, 'twould not be good. One never knows what the boy will say," Michael said.

"My thoughts as well. I do thank you, Pater, for keeping him busy during the hunt. My hands were full with a certain lass. I do not know if I could have kept up with Lucas as well." Bryce's mind went back to Deirdre taking down the first deer.

"I heard the king took Deirdre's error well," Pater responded.

"Aye, much better than I would have anticipated. I had been sure to inform all my men but did not think about the lass."

Alex, who'd been riding quietly on Michael's shoulder, scurried across his back, leapt onto Bryce, using him only to spring off and land on Pater. The squirrel settled onto the pater's shoulder before picking through the man's hair. Bryce chortled. "Looks like you have gained a friend, Pater. Michael, you may have lost your edge with women."

Pater looked up. "What is it you speak of, Bryce?"

"Nothing," Michael interjected. "He is jealous. That is all."

Bryce and Michael turned to climb the steps to the keep.

"I will leave you good men here." Pater nodded. "You may take your squirrel with you, Sir Michael."

Michael put his hand out for Alex, and then the two continued up to the keep. Michael pulled open the door and held it as Bryce stepped through.

"Time to find the king."

††††

Deirdre stepped out the side door and into the sunshine

she'd missed so much the first month she'd been at Rosen Craig. She'd spent the better part of the morning with the English king. When she had a chance to slip away, she took it. She glanced down toward the main entrance in time to see Bryce step into the keep. The man had probably been avoiding the king. At least if she were him, she would. The king thought way too much of himself and, from what she could tell, way too little of his people.

"Guid day tae you, miss."

Deirdre jumped, not expecting to have anyone approach her, as she still didn't know many here.

"Good day, Sir Finley. Are you on watch duty for me today?"

The man grinned. "Keeps me from other duties."

Deirdre shook her head. "Weel, here I am. I dinna understand why you must still keep an eye on me. I am free tae leave at any time, you ken that as well."

"Aye, 'tis true, I ken and I asked the laird why. He does no' trust you because you are Scottish."

He obviously trusted this Scottish knight, since he was the one watching her. It was more likely because she'd been caught reiving. "Weel, I dinna plan on doing anything that would get me locked back in a windowless room."

"You ken, the king does no' trust Laird Warwick. I heard he asked if he was loyal tae him."

"I dinna care of the English politics. They are no' my concern." She had learned that Finley had a propensity for gossip.

"You are a Kincaid?" He looked at her, waiting for a different response, she had no doubt.

"As I have said."

"Nay, you did no'. The laird said you were."

"So what if I am? We are enemies. I think he has determined that by my reiving."

"'Tis the point I wished tae make. I am here no' because of my loyalty tae England but my loyalty tae Scotland. The reiving on our borders must stop. I could use your help."

She stopped and waited for him to stop as well and face her. "How can I help? I dinna even have a place tae go if I were to leave."

"I dinna understand. Go back home."

He thought it so simple. No one could understand her dilemma. "My uncle—" Sweet mercy! She almost told him who she was. "I can no'. They will blame me for the loss we suffered during the reiving."

Finley stared at her. "What about your uncle? Did you live with him?"

Deirdre's mind was reeling. What did she say? She'd hoped he'd not paid that slip of hers any attention. She bit her bottom lip, trying to come up with an explanation.

Finley shifted his weight, waiting for her response.

"I dinna wish tae speak of him. 'Tis upsetting tae me."

"'Tis sorry I am, lass. Dead by an English hand I would imagine. 'Tis a reason for you tae help your country and seek justice for your uncle."

Deirdre would just let him believe her uncle was dead. It was better he thought that after her slip. "What can I do?" She wanted to steer as far away from the subject of her uncle as possible.

"You can get close tae the laird. 'Tis obvious he is taken with you or he would no' have freed you."

"And what guid is that tae do?"

"You can tell me what he says."

Deirdre wanted to laugh at the man. "What do you wish to hear? What he likes to eat, or perchance how I should no' have shot the first animal on a hunt? 'Tis all the man would ever share with me."

"Lass, you can win him over. I have nay doubt aboot that at all."

"You are a foolish man if you believe I can gain favor with this laird. He does no' like me. 'Tis all he can do tae tolerate me. 'Tis true I dinna ken why he allows me tae stay on here and eat his food when I dinna contribute tae his keep. But you did no' see him like I did. For when he found the locks of hair I had cut off and tossed them down, he glared at me with near hatred. Nay, the man is no' a man tae be trifled with."

"You underestimate your beauty and appeal, lass. I am a mon, and what I ken is that you can win this laird over."

"If I can, and I dinna believe this, what can he tell me that would be of use tae you?"

"See if he talks treason or if he tells you anything of what the king has spoken."

"Do you really believe that the laird would share information with me that the king has shared? Dinna forget he has you watching me because he does no' trust me."

"What would we lose if I am wrong and we gain nay information? You still love your homeland, dinna you, lass?"

Deirdre sighed. She did love Scotland. But something inside her appreciated what this laird had done for her. He'd forgiven her for her reiving. He'd given her a place to stay, food to eat, and expected nothing in return. She could not fault him for not trusting her. She'd given him lots of reasons not to. But she would do anything to have peace on the border of her country. Too many people had died. Too many lives were changed because of it, and too many people had lost all they had for survival. How could she turn her back on that? "Aye, I will help."

Chapter 25

The day couldn't be better. Bryce breathed in the spring air, enjoying its warmth. Although the weather certainly cheered him, that didn't make him nearly as happy as finding out that King Richard would leave on the morn. That was the best news he could have received. After a sennight of Richard's presence, under fear of slipping or saying the wrong thing, Bryce only had to get through one more evening.

Michael met him in the bailey and walked beside him and Wolfhound. "What has you grinning? I would think with just speaking to the king you would be in a poor mood."

"Weel, I would be, but the king has informed me that he needs to move on to other places. He has business to take care of."

"'Tis good news indeed." Michael slapped his chest. Alex shot out of his shirt, chattering with irritation.

Wolfhound began barking and jumping up at Alex, now on Michael's shoulder.

Michael frowned at the small thing still scolding him. "Do not bite me if you do not like the consequences."

Bryce couldn't help but laugh at his friend and his unusual pet. Wolfhound continued to bark. "Hush." Bryce put his hand out in a sign the dog understood, and she ceased barking.

"I wish I could teach Alex such things. But he does as he wishes."

"Squirrels were not meant to be pets."

"I told you, I did not choose him. He chose me. Ack! You would not understand. 'Tis not what I wished to speak with you about. I received a missive from my mother."

"Is all well?"

Michael stroked the squirrel and calmed his chatter. "I do not know. She said she is coming for a visit. 'Tis not like her to come for a social call without a reason. I do not remember if she has ever come to see me without an underlying purpose. And she has never come this far north. 'Tis what concerns me."

"When do you expect her?" Bryce turned toward his men practicing out in the field.

"Within a sennight. 'Tis glad I am that Richard will be gone. If there is a problem, I do not wish the king to be privy to it, and I am not so sure she would not share with him, should he ask."

"I do not know that I agree with you. She does not tell you what she does not wish you to know."

Aye, 'tis true. She never told me about my father other than he was not a good person. But I was young then, and I think she feared if I knew who he was, I might try to be like him."

"When did that change?" Bryce couldn't imagine growing up not knowing his father.

"When I became a squire, I served under Lord Holloway. He was a good man and taught me I did not need to know about my father. That I was my own man, and I could choose my own path in life."

"A wise lord." Bryce stopped at the practice field to watch the knights as they fought in mock battle. Yesterday he would have liked to have been out there to take out his frustrations, but with Richard leaving on the morrow, things were looking much brighter. Something his father had instilled in him—better to take your frustrations out on the practice field than carry them around with you. How he missed his father, who'd taught him so much. It was hard to not blame himself for his parent's deaths when the woman he had planned to marry was a key factor in their demise.

"Shall we join them?" Michael grinned.

"You go ahead. I must go finish my duty, seeing to the king's wants. I fear if I leave him too long, he will not be happy with me. One more evening…"

Michael put Alex on the ground, and Wolfhound moved

toward him.

"Nay, girl." Bryce's stern tone brought her back to his side.

Michael shed his tunic, picked up a practice sword, and headed out to the field. With Wolfhound by his side, Bryce turned away and headed back toward the keep and the king, wishing he could partner with his friend and enjoy the mock battle.

Miss Kincaid strolled through the bailey, apparently not in a hurry to get anywhere.

"Miss Kincaid." Bryce quickened his steps to reach her. "How are you this fine day?"

"I am well." She gave him a beautiful smile. "Enjoying the sunshine. One does no' appreciate it until they have lost it. I shall never take it for granted again. I am surprised you are no' in with your king. It seems he is spoiled."

Wolfhound sniffed the basket she carried. A paw reached out and smacked her nose. She yelped and fell back in beside Bryce.

Bryce laughed. "That will teach you to keep your nose out of things it does not belong in."

Deirdre peered around Bryce. "Poor girl."

"How is your kitten doing?"

"As you can see, she is very feisty. I think she will do well for herself. She is a fighter, as her name says."

"'Tis good to hear."

"Did you need something from me?"

Bryce cocked his head. "Why do you ask?"

"You dinna usually seek me out."

That was true, he didn't. He avoided her. He didn't like how she made him feel. Not when he feared she could be like Clarice. "Will you join us for the evening meal?"

She glanced down at her gown, and Bryce remembered he'd planned to see to that. When the king came, it was forgotten.

"I dinna ken the kingly rules—as you discovered. 'Tis

why I have avoided meals."

"Methinks you have won the king over. He was much impressed with your marksmanship. He has spoken of it many times since the hunt and enquired of you." He found himself hoping she would say aye. Her fiery soft curls now touched her shoulders. His mind shot back to when she'd cut her hair to hide her identity. He wished she'd not cut it. Did the lass not realize her beauty? How could she ever think he'd believe her a lad?

She again looked down at her dress. "I dinna ken—"

He interrupted. "I have been meaning to get another gown to you, but with the king's arrival, I fear I had forgotten."

She looked up at him with uncertainty in her eyes.

"It would please me if you would join us."

She hesitated. "Grammercy. I hope I dinna cause you more problems with your king."

"Do not worry. He leaves on the morrow. I look forward to things getting back to how they were."

They made their way up the steps to the door, and Bryce pulled it open. "I will send someone with the dress to fit to you and apply any alterations needed."

"Grammercy, milaird."

Bryce turned and headed toward the flagstone steps that led to the room he slept in while the king was at Rosen Craig. He'd had the trunk that held his mother's gowns removed and now he was glad he had.

Once in the room, he went to the trunk and lifted the lid. Pulling out a royal blue gown, he could almost see his mother busying herself around the keep, overseeing meals and other responsibilities. His heart ached. He reached in and pulled out the next gown, a red one, and set it aside before taking out a lavender dress. The color pleased him, and he put the red gown back in the trunk and closed it.

With the two other dresses in his hands, he headed toward the door to find Ella, hoping she hadn't returned to her home. Miss Kincaid would be comfortable with her. He headed to the kitchen, the last place he'd seen her.

He stepped through the door and was relieved to see she was directing servants in their duties as Nog gave others instructions on the meal. The kitchen was a flurry of activity, with bread dough being kneaded, large simmering vats being stirred, vegetables being chopped, and a centerpiece being decorated. He almost hated to take Ella from Nog.

The cook looked up from her duties. "Can I help you, milord?"

"Aye. Could you spare Ella for a bit? I need her to help Miss Kincaid."

Nog frowned, and he knew she was none too happy with him.

Millicent left her kneading. "Is it something I can help with, milord?"

Bryce smiled. "Can you sew?"

Nog snorted. "How many times has she sewed you or one of your men?"

Bryce cocked an eyebrow.

"Aye. I can sew. What do you wish sewn?"

He handed her the two gowns. "These need to be fitted to Miss Kincaid. One in time for the evening meal."

Millicent glanced down at the dresses now in her arms.

"They were my mother's. I am sure she would approve."

"As am I, son." Millicent's understanding eyes gave him the assurance he sought.

"I do not know if they will be long enough." Though his mother and the Scottish lass were much the same size, his mother was not a tall woman.

"We will make them work. I shall go find her now."

"Many thanks, Millicent."

She smiled and sailed out of the kitchen.

It was time for the evening meal before Bryce caught a glimpse of Miss Kincaid wearing his mother's purple and white gown. She stood at the far end of the hall. Bryce stood and excused himself from the king.

"I shall return. I see Miss Kincaid has arrived." He didn't give the king time to respond but stepped off the dais and headed straight for the lass.

She moved toward him, and he glanced down, pleased to see the dress fit her perfectly.

"Grammercy for the gowns. They are lovely."

"I was worried they would not be long enough." He bent his head and spoke as they walked.

"Millicent is quite competent with a needle and thread. She added a wee bit of fabric at the waist tae make the gown fit properly."

"You look beautiful, lass. Fitting a king." His gut twisted as he realized he meant every word.

Deirdre stopped. Bryce turned to see the cause.

"Am I?" She reached up and touched her hair, which had been plaited with ribbons.

"You know not your own beauty, lass? Aye, you are."

The loveliest red hue filled her cheeks, and she dropped her gaze. "Grammercy. I am used to looking like a boy."

Bryce frowned. What a strange thing to say. When she lifted her gaze, he quickly smiled. He would inquire about that later. Tonight, he wanted her to enjoy herself.

He helped her up on the dais and seated her where she had been before, between the king and himself.

"Good eventide, Miss Kincaid." The king spent a little too much time admiring her for Bryce's liking. "'Tis glad I am that you could join us on my last night."

"As am I, Your Grace."

"What has kept you from partaking the meals with us?" Richard did not take his eyes off her as he waited for her reply.

"I am limited on my clothing, Your Grace. I did no' wish to offend you by my attire. Laird Warwick was kind and found some gowns to be altered so I could attend this night."

Richard shifted his gaze to Bryce. "You could not have

done this sooner?"

Bryce reminded himself this was his king. At least for now. It was obvious the king wished to shame him for this. "Aye. 'Tis sorry I am that I did not notice sooner."

The king humphed and went back to his meal.

As the courses passed, Bryce could see that Nog had once again outdone herself with the white sauces, meats in jellies, sweet aromas of spices, and the centerpiece depicting the king's coat of arms.

The evening's entertainment started with a juggler who, Bryce had to admit, was quite good. The knives he juggled looked sharp enough to wound, if not kill, should he miss one. By the time the juggler finished his act, they had finished eating and his steward introduced the second entertainment—a puppet show that certainly was designed for the king and his high esteem of himself. The king roared with laughter as the play depicted him victor over MacMurrough and his other Irish followers.

When the entertainment ceased, Deirdre turned to the king. "If you do no' mind, Your Grace, I wish to retire. It has been a full day."

The king patted her hand. "Have a good rest, lass. 'Tis glad I am that you could join us this meal."

She smiled and stood then dipped her head. "Grammercy for the meal, milaird."

"Can I see you to your room?" Bryce would have liked to leave the presence of his king as well.

"'Tis no' necessary. Stay with your king. I can see myself to my room."

Bryce watched as she walked away. How had he missed her beauty? Was this why he had been so uncomfortable around her? Because of her beauty? Because he didn't want to repeat a mistake?

He shifted his attention back to Richard. To his pleasure, it wasn't long before Richard made his excuses and retreated to his room. Bryce was happy to find his way up to his bed as well. A lengthy sennight with royalty. One he was happy to put behind him.

Once in bed, he closed his eyes, only to find a redheaded lass in a purple gown filling his thoughts.

He awoke before dawn to commotion in the bailey. Bryce dressed and headed down to the hall, his boots clicking on the flagstone steps and echoing through the empty entrance.

Richard's people must be packing and preparing for the next leg of their journey. He did not envy the next lord who must host the king. Stepping outside he surveyed the activity.

Men hustled past him carrying trunks toward carts already loaded down. He stood and watched the progress for a moment, enjoying what it meant—his king was leaving. The horizon held a pink glow as the sun rose to start the day.

He turned on his heel and went back in the keep, heading for the great hall. When he entered, Nog had the morning meal prepared for the king and his men. Richard sat on the dais eating, and like every day since he'd been there, a knight stood guard a few feet back and on each side of him.

Bryce took his seat next to Richard, knowing if everything went as he hoped, this would be the last time he sat next to Richard as king. "Good morn, Your Grace. I trust you slept well the night before your journey."

"Aye. As well as can be expected."

Bryce reached forward and tore off a hunk of bread from a trencher and began to eat. Richard chewed his food thoughtfully before turning to Bryce.

"I wish to hear one more time that you remain faithful to your lord the king."

Chapter 26

Finley approached Deirdre, as he had every day since he'd first asked her to help Scotland by spying on the laird. Eleven days of him pestering her. Something inside her told her not to trust Finley, but the other part of her said he was a Scotsman. Her instinct said the laird was a man to be trusted, yet she argued with herself that he was English and her enemy.

Deirdre sighed as Finley reached her.

"Is something wrong, lass?"

"Nay. But I dinna have anything for you. The laird has been busy since the king left, and I have no' talked with him much."

Finley frowned. "'Tis the same thing every day. Dinna you want revenge for your people?"

Deirdre shook her head slowly. "I did once, and look what it got me? More death. I lost two friends and have nay place tae call home now. Revenge does no' always work how you think it will."

"You are becoming soft tae these English."

Deirdre glared at him. She didn't wish to say something she should not or something she would regret. "If you will excuse me, I must go."

Finley grabbed her arm. "Wait."

Deirdre looked down where his hand clasped her upper arm, and he let go.

"'Tis sorry I am. I dinna mean tae speak poorly of you. 'Tis only I tire of the way the English take advantage of my fellow Scotsman—and you. You lost two friends and were a prisoner here. 'Tis no' right."

"But I am no' a prisoner now."

"Nay, but you were. And now you can help me oot."

"If I discover news, I will let you ken. But as I said, since the king left, the laird has been vera busy and has no' had time for me."

Cathal meowed from the basket, and she made her excuse that she needed to tend to her kitten. She reached in and stroked the grey and white ball of fur. If ever there was a blessing, this wee one had been one to her. She needed to be needed, and Cathal required her attention all the time.

She crawled out of the basket, clinging to Deirdre's sleeve. Deirdre pulled her off and snuggled her against her chest, laying her cheek against her silky fur. "'Tis thankful I am for you."

Deirdre looked up as she walked and just before she ran into Laird Warwick.

He grinned down on her. "Weel, lass, I am humbled."

Deirdre's first thought was to correct him for his misguided humor but decided against it. "Oh, aye. Methinks this little kitten was a grand trade-off for a few cows."

His grin grew into a smile that caused his eyes to twinkle. "Glad I am that you have her, and she has you. 'Tis a good match. Do you have time to stroll and talk?"

Cathal meowed again, and she was reminded the kitten wanted to eat. "Aye, Cathal can wait a wee bit for her milk." She put the kitten back in the basket and walked beside the laird.

"'Tis a beautiful spring day."

"Aye, but sure I am that you did no' ask me tae walk with you tae speak of the weather." She liked to get straight to the point. Especially if it was not good news.

"How long do you think to stay at Rosen Craig?"

Deirdre's heart danced in her chest, almost taking her breath away. "I dinna ken. I have nay—" She stopped herself before she gave too much away.

"'Tis only curiosity, lass. I am not wishing you gone. I may be riding to Hawkwood in a fortnight and did not want to come back and find you gone."

"And why would this matter tae you?" Deirdre searched his face.

He stopped and placed his hand on her shoulder. Not like Finley had done moments earlier. He'd grasped her arm with force. This laird gently laid his hand on her, beckoning her to stop. She turned to face him.

"Lass, I know I have not been kind to you, and I ask for your forgiveness. I am no *caitiff*. I wish peace on my border, and treating you unkindly was not a way to achieve that."

"I would no' accuse you of acting like a caitiff." She grinned. "Weel, perchance when you first arrived after I was captured from helping those wee lost cows. You were no' vera kind tae me then."

The laird chuckled. "Aye, helping them. Helping my cows find their way to your clan." His smile faded and his features grew serious. "When you wish to return to your home, I will personally see to your safety and take you there."

"Grammercy. I dinna ken when I will wish tae return. I dinna believe I will be welcomed at the moment. Men died, and I did no'. I ken I have wished many times to switch places with them."

"'Tis very glad I am that you did not. You are a welcome guest as long as you wish to stay. Michael's mother will be visiting soon. Perchance you will find common interests with her." The laird returned to strolling and guided her with his hand.

"You ken her well?" Deirdre glanced up at him as they walked.

"Nay. I have met her only once, mayhap twice. But she is a kind lady."

"I shall look forward tae meeting her, then."

"It is sure I am that Michael will be pleased knowing his mother will have someone to visit with whilst she is here."

"Even a Scotswoman?"

Bryce laughed. "I do not think that is of any matter to him."

"Reiver?" She prodded. Although the people from Rosen

Craig had all been kind, not all people would be as gracious.

"Aye. Michael does not hold grudges."

"Weel, 'tis good to ken. And your king, does he hold grudges?" She would test the goodness in this man.

"The man holds long grudges. Have not you heard of what he did to the Lord Appellants?"

"Aye, I had heard rumors. But I did no' ken what was truth."

"Over ten years had passed, and Richard sought revenge for the loss of his friends and what the Appellants had done. One does not wish to cross our king. He has a long-reaching memory."

"Why did your king come tae Rosen Craig? 'Tis strange from how I think. The man does no' seem tae trust you." Deirdre stole a quick glance to see his reaction.

"Nay, he does not. The man has much reason to distrust my loyalty to him." The laird didn't hesitate in his answer to her.

"Oh? And why is that? Are you no' devoted tae your king?" Perhaps Finley was correct. Perhaps the laird did have secrets.

He chuckled. "'Tis not my loyalty that is the problem. 'Tis Richard's friend, Rothburg, that is the problem. The man wishes to have possession of Rosen Craig and feeds lies to the king."

"He does no' like you, this Rothburg?"

"Nay. He has a fierce hatred for me and mine."

"I hope you dinna mind me asking so many questions, but this is curious tae me."

"Not at all, lass."

"Why does he hate you and want what you have?"

"'Tis a long story."

Deirdre grinned. "Methinks I have nothing but time."

The laird smiled back. "I will attempt to shorten the story. It goes back many, many years when Edward was king. Rothburg's father, Hugo Rothburg, lost the land due to acts of treason. Peter Cuthbrid was given Rosen Craig. Many years after Hugo Rothburg's death, more evidence was brought forth and the accusations were deemed false. But Rosen Craig was now under a new overseer, Lord Cuthbrid. So, the son of Hugo Rothburg was given Wolves Forest Castle to help settle his grievance of the loss of Rosen Craig."

"Heaven above! I think I am befuddled."

The corner of the laird's lip twitched. "What has you befuddled?"

"Two other men, no' family that have been laird of Rosen Craig?"

"Three, if you would like to count my father. Hugo Rothburg lost it, and it was given to Peter Cuthbrid."

"This Rothburg, the son of Hugo Rothburg, he is the man who speaks lies aboot you tae your king?" The whole thing was very confusing.

"Aye, that is he. He is not loyal to Richard as much as he is loyal to himself."

"Then how did you end up laird?"

"Peter Cuthbrid was found guilty of treason and put to death. My father was given Rosen Craig in his stead."

"Your father died, and the title passed tae you?"

"Aye, recently."

"'Tis sorry I am. I hear the sorrow in your voice. Was his death unexpected?"

"He and my mother were murdered. I was believed dead, and my brother, Royce, served as lord until I recovered and came back to Rosen Craig. But that is another story for another time, lass. I am afraid duty awaits me, and I must leave you." The sadness in his voice she understood. She felt that same way when she thought about her mother and having to grow up without her. In her heart she knew her mother no longer lived. She just hoped that she wasn't the cause of her death. Her uncle never came out and said her father killed her mother, but things he'd said left her to conclude that.

She tried not to give too much thought to it and attempted to believe that her mother just stayed away because she protected her from her father. Could a mother, who loved her child so much never come back to see her? One thing would certainly prevent her, and that was death.

†††

Bryce sat across from Michael and his mother, Catherine Iannetta, in his solar. The lady had just arrived with some traveling minstrels.

"Do you know these people you traveled with? And do you plan to leave when they do?" Michael asked his mother.

"They are very nice, Michael. I met them whilst I stayed down in Wiltshire. They allowed me to travel along with them for safety."

"And use of your horse, I am sure," Michael grumbled.

Michael's mother sighed. "Would you rather I traveled alone, son?"

"Nay, but I do not wish you to travel such a great distance."

"How else can I see my son? You have not been back to see me in years. A mother misses her only child. Life gets lonely."

"Why are you here? Surely not to visit. I was much closer when I served in Essex."

"Well, Michael, since your preference is to get right to the point, I wish you to come back with me. I do not like living so far from my son. I am gaining in age, and I would like you nearby."

Michael paused. Bryce didn't believe he'd ever seen his friend at a loss for words. He smiled inwardly. He needed to learn the magic this woman had over her son.

"I am here to help Bryce. And I have determined that I like the north. I do not know if I shall return to Essex."

Bryce had never heard his friend proclaim his loyalty this way. It both surprised and pleased him.

A slight gasp escaped the woman and Bryce shifted his attention from his friend to his mother. Alarm filled her eyes. Her hand flew to her neck. "Stay here? No, you must come home with me."

Michael frowned. "Mother, is there something you wish to tell me? Are you in trouble and need my help?"

His mother regained her composure. "Not at all, Michael. I just wish to have you near."

"Do you need money? Is that what this visit is for?"

She shook her head. "You need not concern yourself with that, son. I only wish you to come back where you belong."

The woman was troubled. Perhaps she didn't feel she could talk to her son openly whilst he was in the room. Bryce stood. "I will give you some time alone."

"You need not leave, my lord. If my son trusts you, what I have to say, I can say in front of you."

Chapter 27

"Prithee sit, my lord. My mother is right. Anything she can say in front of me, she can say in front of you." Michael gestured with his hand for him to sit back down.

"Is there a woman in your life, Michael?" Michael's mother gave him a smile.

"A woman?" Michael's expression looked so shocked it was almost humorous.

"Aye, you understand. A woman you wish to marry?"

"Nay." His answer was abrupt.

Bryce knew his friend and that response meant Michael wanted that to be the end of the discussion.

"I am not getting any younger son. I wish to see my grandchildren before I die." The woman blinked innocently, apparently not concerned that her son didn't want to continue the conversation.

Michael sat up and leaned forward. "Are you ill, Mother?" Concern now covered Michael's face.

"I am well. We are only promised so many days on this earth. We do not know when the good Lord will call us home." She shrugged. "I wish to see my son married and meet my grandchildren before I go."

"If you are having issues with your health, Bryce has a very good healer. Perchance she could help you."

"I am not sick, Michael. I am of age that most women have grandchildren. Do you have a woman here who catches your eye?"

"You do not need to concern yourself with a wife for me, Mother."

"There are two young ladies I think you would find most desirable if you would return with me. I would be pleased to introduce you."

"Mother, you are not listening to me." Michael's frustration continued to grow.

Bryce enjoyed watching his good friend squirm under his mother's questioning.

"They are both very beautiful, and young."

Michael didn't respond this time. Instead, he just looked at his mother.

Mistress Iannetta turned to Bryce. A creamy headdress covered her black hair, the same hair color as her son's. But that was about as far as the resemblance went. Michael did not look like his mother. "I do not wish to trouble you, my lord, but I am tired from the trip."

"Say no more." Bryce, who'd never retaken his seat, moved to the door. "We have a room ready for you."

The woman rose with so much grace, Bryce pondered her background. Michael didn't seem to know much about his parents.

She smiled. "Thank you. It will be nice to clean up and sleep in a bed this night."

Bryce took her to her room and returned to his solar where Michael still sat, frowning, his fingers tented in front of him.

"She has not come here to visit. I tell you the truth. I know my mother. Something is amiss." Michael huffed and sat back in the chair.

"From her pleas, I would say she wishes her son to marry and give her grandchildren. Perchance she is lonely living so far from her only child."

"Then she can live here. I do not wish to move to Wiltshire, where she lives, and I find that Cumberland agrees with me. I should never have sent her the missive telling her I left Essex and came to serve under you."

"I do not know what to tell you, my friend, but what I do know is that I would give the land I own to have my mother back."

"I do not mean to sound ungrateful. I am indeed blessed. I wish she had married after my father died to help with her loneliness. Even though she is my mother, I can still see that she is beautiful."

"Aye. Perchance the memories of her married life have kept her from wanting to marry again."

"I would agree with that. They are dark enough that she does not wish to speak of my father."

"You are all she has. So she desires for you to be near her. I remember when we lost my sister. I was very young, and she was only a babe, toddling about the house. My mother's wails seared through me so, I can still hear them today. She was never the same after that day. It was as though a part of her had died with my sister. A mother's love runs deep, Michael. I think your mother needs to have you near. She said the words herself. She worries she will never get to see her grandchildren. One does not know what has made your mother think about her mortality."

"Do you think she tells me an untruth when she said she is not ill?"

Bryce wanted to assuage his friend's worry. "She looks healthy."

None of the mischief or love of life that Bryce was used to seeing danced in Michael's eyes.

"I am not ready to bury my mother."

Bryce hurt for his friend. "There will never be a time when you are."

†††

Bryce sat across from his friend, once again in the solar. Only this time it was the two of them. His mother had settled into a routine the past sennight and had struck up a friendship with Miss Kincaid.

"Did I hear the king mention convening Parliament?" Michael stretched out his legs in front of him.

"Aye. He mentioned we were in need of convening. It has been a while since Parliament has been held. The last time we convened was in September of ninety-seven."

"Over a year and a half. Did Richard say for what matters he wished to convene?"

"We can be sure the king wants more money. And I shudder to think what else he wishes to discuss, remembering the previous Parliament."

"I did not even need to be present to know what the other lords must have felt as they witnessed the revenge Richard meted out on the Appellants."

"My father spoke vividly of what took place over that time. It was a very dark time and is why we are concerned for our safety even now. Many feared the king's revenge knew no end and was far reaching to his own benefit."

Michael shook his head. "I heard stories when down in Essex of Thomas de Beauchamp throwing himself before the king and begging for mercy. 'Tis said that his plea brought many to tears—even the king."

"Richard showed mercy in that he was not hanged, drawn, and quartered. But exiled for life to the Isle of Man. But Richard cannot be trusted in his promises and dealings. Not all of his pardons ended up true pardons. And let us not forget that if anyone should request freedom for those exiled, their pardon is rescinded. Richard has done so much to give the nobility a reason to doubt his ability to rule England and its people fairly."

"I would say that these are nearly as treacherous times as when Richard turned on the Appellants. Your father would not have wanted to walk this road again. No noble or knight can be sure of his safety. Richard has no reason to question your loyalty, yet 'tis true that he does. He has made that clear with his visit."

"If ever I had doubt that Richard needs to be replaced by Henry, it is gone. I am a bit relieved that I have had none of the king's men knocking down my door, and he has been gone more than a sennight now. We must either find a way to silence Rothburg or get Henry on the throne before Rothburg can feed the king more of his lies."

"Silence Rothburg?" Michael raised his brows. "That does not sound like you."

Bryce chuckled. "There is no way to do that legally or morally, so getting Henry on the throne to replace Richard is the only answer if we wish to be free of looking over our shoulders all our days."

Deirdre stuck her head in the cracked door. "I have a message for Sir Michael from his mother."

Michael's gaze latched on to Bryce's, and Bryce knew his friend wondered the same thing as he did. Had the lass heard their talk of deposing the king?

Chapter 28

Bryce couldn't take his eyes off the woman standing in the doorway holding the kitten he'd given her. His heart raced, and he wasn't sure if it was from concern of what she'd heard or what he was beginning to feel for the woman. It didn't seem to matter how much he told himself she was not the woman for him, his heart had its own desires, and staying as far from Miss Kincaid as possible was not what his heart wanted.

Michael stood and turned his attention on Miss Kincaid. "Where might I find her?"

"She was in the kitchen speaking with Nog."

Michael stopped and reached out, scratching the kitten's head. Purring ensued. Alex popped his head out of Michael's shirt and scurried down his arm, chattering as he went. The kitten swung her paw, and Alex flew up his sleeve and onto Michael's shoulder.

Bryce chuckled. "Your squirrel seems to have a hard time making friends."

Michael stroked the squirrel's bushy tail and headed out the door. "They misinterpret his intentions."

The lass giggled as she turned to follow. Bryce rose from his chair, not wishing to look too anxious. "Would you like to go for a stroll?"

She stopped, and her lips lifted to a smile. "I would enjoy that."

No basket adorned her arm for Cathal. Instead, she cuddled the small creature against her chest. When the kitten let out a cry, she kissed its head. "Shh. You are no' hungry, so dinna fash yourself aboot food, little one."

"Do you need to feed her?" Bryce didn't want to take her from her duties of caring for the animal.

"Nay. She would eat all day if I would feed her." She scratched behind Cathal's ear, and the cat began to purr again.

Bryce smiled. The lass would make a good mother. He found himself wondering if she'd thought about children. His eyes went to her lips that had just kissed the downy fur, and he wished to know if her lips would be as soft.

"Is something wrong?"

Bryce shook himself from his unwanted thoughts. "Nay. Woolgathering."

"I do that as well. Where would you like to stroll?"

"I see you walking in the inner bailey each day. Would you enjoy going someplace else?"

"You watch me? I thought you had your man, Finley, watching me."

He hadn't realized how much his words would reveal. He did watch her. More than he should. Not because he was concerned, but because whenever he saw her, something inside of him drew him to her. "Perchance I should have said I have noticed. Would you care to stroll outside of the outer bailey?"

"Aye. A change would be lovely. I believe I have made a path in here."

Cathal gave a tired meow and snuggled into her arm, closing its eyes. Bryce guided Deirdre through both the inner and the outer bailey before they went through the portcullis and onto the road leading to the small village.

"I see the kitten is doing well and is content with you."

"She has been a comfort tae me. I thank you again for thinking of me. She has made my time here much more bearable."

"'Tis glad I am that she has helped. I know this has been difficult for you, living among strangers and people you considered your enemies."

She slowly lifted her eyes and met his gaze. "I am sorry. You and your people have been vera kind tae me. 'Tis difficult letting the past go and trusting."

"I understand about betrayals. A broken trust is a

difficult thing to mend." As he said the words, Clarice's lifeless body lying at his feet flashed through his mind, her death a result of her treacherous deeds done to him and his family.

"You sound as though your betrayal was no' by your enemy, but perchance someone close tae you. Those are the most painful."

"And you speak as though you have encountered the same." There was no question what he saw in her eyes—no, her soul. She'd been hurt deeply by someone she loved.

"Have not we all?"

He recognized the veil she tried to put up to keep him from seeing the truth. But the sadness told it all. His gut wrenched. He longed to see the smile return to her delicate face. "I see you wear the blue dress. 'Tis most becoming on you."

The slightest pink hue rose into her cheeks before the smile appeared. "Thank you. 'Tis nice tae have a choice of dresses. I dinna believe I asked you where you found such lovely gowns."

"They were my mother's."

"I hope it is no' difficult seeing me wear them."

"Nay. Quite the contrary. And I could not think of anyone I would rather see in them. I know my mother would want that as well. She was a generous woman. I think you would have liked her."

"She made vera guid choices. I have enjoyed wearing both of her gowns. 'Tis a wee bit difficult tae get familiar with all this cloth surrounding my body."

Bryce chuckled. "Would you rather have your men's clothing back?"

Again her cheeks flushed. One thing he knew for sure about Deirdre. She didn't know her own beauty and, if she did, she had no pride in it. Deirdre...he liked to think of her like that instead of Miss Kincaid.

"Nay. 'Tis only I have worn breeches for a vera long

time. 'Tis most difficult tae change what one is used tae wearing."

"I do not wish to pry into your affairs, but why have you worn boy's clothing?"

"If you please, my lord, I dinna wish tae answer that. No' now. Perchance, in time I will share that with you. 'Tis a hard part of my life that I have no' wished tae think aboot since I have arrived here."

"I can respect those wishes. I hope you will be able to share that part of your life with me some day."

"'Tis no' pleasant memories."

They kicked up dust from the dry road as they walked, and the stout breeze dispersed it. Avoiding the cart ruts, they continued on as the village came into view. Shoots of greenery poked up through the ground on either side of the road, promising the continuation of warm weather. He prayed there would not be a drought this year. The sun beat down, but the cool air sent a chill. The acrid scent of smoke from one of the houses blew their way.

Deirdre drew her arms closer to her body, still cuddling the kitten.

"Let's turn back. You are cold."

"Just a wee bit. 'Tis the wind. Cuts through my clothes."

Bryce shed his tunic and draped it across her shoulders.

"But what of you? Will you no' be cold?"

"I am fine. This shirt is enough for warmth."

Deirdre picked up her pace, the wind at her back, pushing her along. When they stepped through the portcullis, she rushed over to the protection of the *curtain wall*. She shivered and began to remove his tunic.

Bryce put his hand on hers. "Nay, lass, you keep it until you get inside."

She hesitated, glancing at the tunic. "Grammercy."

Deirdre's words gnawed at Bryce. He had wanted to know why she wore boy's clothing for such a long time.

She was reiving when he caught her. Perhaps they

couldn't afford gowns, and she wore boy's clothes from a neighbor. Or perchance she lived in disguise even in her home burgh. He glanced over at her, admiring her heart-shaped face, surrounded by red curls—nothing boyish about her.

†††

Deirdre sat in a chair in the great hall, facing the fireplace as she admired the large picture hanging above it. A family—a husband and wife, two young boys, and a wee babe. She could only imagine it was Bryce's parents, as he had his mother's eyes and his father's cheekbones and square jaw. Husband and wife sat on the ground while the boys picked flowers. A turret could be seen in the distance through the leafy green trees. The husband handed his love a piece of fruit.

She'd often had dreams like this. Dreams that she had a family, a loving mother and father, a sister and brother. But more often than not, that dream would turn to terror as she ran for her life.

"You look lost in thought, lass." Finley sauntered up.

How she wished he'd lose interest in her. "Enjoying the beauty of this hanging."

He took a seat in the other chair. "'Tis glad I am tae see you assisting me. I could no' help but notice you spent a guid bit of time with the laird yesterday. Did you glean any information that I can use?"

"I believe you are mistaken, sir. As you said, I have spent much time with the laird, but what I have found in these sennights of getting tae ken him and the time yesterday is that he is an honorable man. He is no' the person I first believed him tae be on my arrival. I was vera wrong. He has nay ill will for our people but seeks peace as we do."

Finley leaned forward abruptly. "You are wrong. He has hoodwinked you. You are no' seeing the truth of his deception."

"Nay, I dinna think you ken him. He has no malice in

him. You run a dangerous game, and I dinna wish tae play."

"Dinna be a fool!" He raised his voice, and the knuckles gripping the chair arms turned white.

"I think we have finished this discussion." Deirdre got up to leave.

"Wait. 'Tis sorry I am. Remember, I have been here much longer than you. I dinna want tae see him take advantage of you, 'tis all. I have seen things you have no'. Things I hope you never have tae see. Dinna forget your friends who lost their lives at his command."

Deirdre didn't sit back down. Her stomach twisted as she listened to Finley's words. "I will think on what you have said. If you will excuse me." She dipped her head and glided toward the flagstone steps that would take her to her room. Never bothering to look back at Finley, Deirdre made it to the top of the stairs and turned toward her room.

"Deirdre." A kind voice called to her as she passed Michael's mother's room.

She stopped and took a step backward, peering inside. "Guid day to you, Mistress Iannetta."

"Come in, come in." She gestured for her to enter. "And prithee, call me Catherine."

Deirdre stepped into the room and moved toward the gold and red tapestry chair next to the woman, who continued to pat the seat until she sat. "Thank you vera much."

"How are you, dear?"

"I am well, grammercy, and I hope you are as well."

"I would be better if my son would agree to return to Wiltshire with me. The man will not listen to me no matter how many times I ask. I can only pray that his heart will eventually soften for his mother."

Deirdre smiled at the lady who had become as close to a friend there as anyone. No one spent much time with her other than the laird and Finley. And Finley always wanted something from her. "'Tis sorry I am. I do wish I could help you, but your son and I have no' ken each other long. I dinna think he would take any advice from me."

"I do agree with you. Michael is a man who is hard to move if he has made up his mind. He has been that way since he was a young child."

From what Deirdre had witnessed of Michael, she would agree. "Is no' that the way of most men?" Her treacherous mind shot back to the death of Walter. A friend who did not want to go reiving that fateful night she was captured, and he lost his life. But he came because of her.

"I do suppose that is the way of it. Do you have a special man in your life? One you will marry?" Catherine brushed at the umber gown with gold thread, sending dust sparkling in the sun's rays.

"Nay. I dinna wish tae think of marriage."

"Oh? A beautiful young woman like yourself, why ever would you not wish to?"

Deirdre ran her finger along the arm of the chair, following the thread design and trying to come up with an answer.

"You do not need to answer, my dear. There is one thing I understand, and that is a lady with deep secrets."

Chapter 29

The day couldn't be more beautiful, and Deirdre walked with an extra spring in her step. Her ankle was finally feeling like she'd never injured it, and the aching in her arm had all but subsided. The wound in her gut from her knife had closed nicely, for Millicent and Nog had done fine work stitching her up and caring for the area. The laird asked her daily how she fared, and she was glad she'd finally be able to tell him he need not ask anymore because all had healed.

Cathal scampered behind her, swatting at her gown. As she often did, she sent out a screech as her nails entangled in the fabric and sent her sailing along with her. She squatted and gently removed the claws hung from the cloth. "You foolish kitten. Dinna you tire of this?"

"Do you go anywhere withoot that cat?"

Deirdre almost moaned when she heard Finley's voice. "She needs me."

"Cats can take care of themselves." He folded his arms in front of himself.

"Cathal is a kitten." Still squatting, Deirdre glanced up from her charge at the commotion near the portcullis.

"Riders from the north!" A knight yelled down from the gate tower.

"How many?" Another yelled up from the ground.

"Six."

Deirdre scooped up Cathal and stood. "Why the interest in riders? People come and go."

"They must come with weapons and armed. Those are always announced. And these are coming from the north— the borderland."

"This is unusual?" Deirdre's heart skipped a beat.

Finley eyed her and shrugged. Turning he stood and watched the portcullis. Men from the inner bailey hustled toward the outer bailey. She sent up a silent prayer, something she'd not done in a very long time. *Lord, You have watched oot for me when I doubted You. You gave me refuge in the house of my enemy, tae be cared for and freed. So I ken You care for me. I ask this is no' my uncle searching for me or come to retrieve me.*

She wasn't sure that, if it was her uncle, he would arrive with concern for her or anger. The clip clop of many horses' hooves hitting the packed dirt road sent shivers through her body. Her heart pounded in her ears, and her throat went dry.

"I must go. Cathal needs tae eat."

Finley glanced from the gate, where knights stood at the ready, and back to her. His brows rose.

She needed to leave before he suspected she did not want to see who the riders were or, more, that she did not want them to see her.

"If you will indulge me one question."

"I really must go."

He ignored her. "Do you have any information I might find useful?"

She turned as the pounding of hooves and jangling of metal grew louder. "Nay, I have no'."

She nearly ran toward the keep. Her heart pounded so loudly in her ears she couldn't hear her own footfalls. The kitchen side door was her closest escape, and she slipped through it, glancing back to see Finley watching her. She passed the *larder* and slipped into the kitchen.

Nog glanced up from her work. "What is wrong, child?" She rushed around the table and grasped Deirdre's hand. "You are white as the whitewashed walls."

Deirdre gave her what she knew was a weak smile, but it was the best she could do with her insides shaking so. "Nothing is wrong." She certainly hoped there wasn't. "Cathal is hungry. Could I get some milk and a wee bit of meat tae feed her?"

Nog patted the hand she held. "Certainly. We have some milk right over here." She pulled Deirdre along with her. She gave her the milk and then wrapped up a small piece of venison in a cloth and placed it on her palm, closing her fingers around it. She leaned in. "I will say a prayer for you, child. I am here if you wish to talk. I keep secrets well." She gave her hand a squeeze. "Go take care of your charge." She smiled and went back to kneading her bread.

Deirdre slipped out. The ruckus in the bailey had not quieted. Wishing to know whether it was her uncle who had arrived, Deirdre slipped back to the side door and cracked it enough to see out.

Her knees nearly buckled. Instead of the patchy auburn hair of her balding uncle, her eyes fell on the wild red hair and piercing green eyes of the man from her earliest memories, and her heart shrank in terror.

How had her father found her, and here, of all places?

†††

Bryce strode out of the great hall in time to see Deirdre run up the stairs. Cathal, in the same hand she clutched her gown with, meowed. He stopped, not taking his eyes from her. She reached the top, turned and rushed toward her room, never noticing him watching her.

He continued out the keep and to the bailey where six men stood next to their horses and surrounded by his men. He'd been happy when Michael pulled him away from his duties with his steward. He left him there to answer Ralf's questions.

One man stepped forward and reached out his hand. "Colin Mackenzie."

Bryce accepted it and gave it a firm pump. "Good to meet you, Bryce Warwick. I hope it is peace that brings you to us."

"Aye, 'tis peace. I dislike the reiving and border wars as much as you. I have come with news and wish tae speak in private with you." The man's curly red hair matched half of the men with him.

"We can speak in my solar. Give me one moment. I must

speak with one of my men. I will return anon." Bryce turned and headed back from where he'd come. Michael stepped into the bailey, saving Bryce some time.

"Michael," Bryce called to his friend.

Michael strode him. "Interesting visit, would not you agree?"

"Aye, I do. I need you to find Lucas and send him to Deirdre. I do not wish for him to be around these men. 'Tis hard to know what the boy would say. And I do not want Deirdre's name spoken. Make sure the men are aware of that as well."

Michael smiled. "As you wish, my lord."

Bryce returned to Mackenzie, and the man fell in step beside him.

"You come quite a distance, and in uncertain territory, considering the distrust between our borders. Your news must be important."

"'Tis vera important what I must speak tae you aboot."

Bryce guided him up and into his solar and gestured for him to take a seat while he shut the door. "'Tis private here. We can speak without being heard or interrupted."

He joined Mackenzie and sat in the chair across from him. "What is this news you speak of?"

"Reivers from the south of our border have been stealing cattle, sheep, and crops. We have had crops burned, houses burned, and innocent lives lost for nay reason."

Bryce searched the man's face for truth. "We too, have suffered loss due to reivers coming south. Not many months ago, I captured Scottish men taking my cows. It is a problem we both have. But I give you my word, my people do not reive. I am very clear on that and the punishment of it should I discover such behavior."

Mackenzie's eyes never left Bryce as he spoke. "What happened to the men you caught?"

"Several escaped and two men died before I got there. I did not want bloodshed, but a few of my men let their anger outweigh their good judgement."

"Do you ken what clan they hailed from?"

"I believe the Kincaid clan. But I cannot know this with certainty. The ones who escaped may not have told truths and the ones who died never spoke before their deaths."

"Kincaid is an evil man. I dinna like tae speak poorly of my own countrymen, but I will tell you he is oot for only himself."

Bryce studied Mackenzie for truth to his words. Living so close to Scotland, he had heard many stories of the clan leaders. The stories of Kincaid didn't seem any worse than others, and Bryce understood how rumors were just that and not truths. If Mackenzie was wanting something from him, it would behoove the man to make Bryce believe they were in agreement. But what Mackenzie didn't know was that Bryce had also heard stories of how hard and clever a chieftain he was. Bryce wasn't going to let down his guard. "I do not wish to offend you, but forgive me if I choose to wait before passing judgement."

Mackenzie gave a quick nod. "'Tis a fair statement. If you have no' had dealings with the man, 'tis only my word."

Bryce attempted to decipher what he implied. "You have had dealings with the man? Are your clans at war with one another?"

Mackenzie snorted, sending his long red curls bouncing. "Aye, I have had dealings with the man. He is my brother-in-law."

Bryce sank back into the chair. Interesting. So this man very well may be Deirdre's uncle. That would explain the way she ran up the stairs when he arrived. "Your sister's husband or your wife's brother?" It didn't really matter but he wanted to understand more about Deirdre's family.

"My wife's brother. I dinna try tae turn you against him. I only warn you tae be vera careful with trusting him."

Bryce smiled. "I am careful with trusting any Scot living on or near my border." Finley's image shot through his mind.

He needed to be careful of him as well.

Mackenzie roared with laughter. "Well said, well said."

Bryce let down some of the shields he'd raised when they first rode in on Rosen Craig soil. "You said you have news?"

Mackenzie's smile disappeared quicker than it had appeared on his face. "Aye, I do. It is the reivers."

"And do you know where they hailed from?"

"Their colors were Rosen Craig."

Bryce frowned, but would not show any emotion. He still didn't know what this man really wanted. "As I have said, neither my men nor my people reive. I can assure you."

"They claim to be your men," he shot back.

"Claim or not, they do not belong to my demesne, and if they did, they would not for long."

"My clan has lost much tae these reivers. We tired of it and laid in wait. When they came, as we knew they would, we captured them."

"Do you still have them? I will ride up with you and tell you if they belong to my demesne."

"I interrogated them and sent them on with a strong warning they were tae take back with them."

Bryce leaned forward, tenting his fingers together. "And you wish to know if I have received a message? I have not."

"Nay. I ken you have no'. Rather, I expect you have no'. I ken the men lied to me. Their stories were identical. Nay variance at all. Nay two men see everything the same—unless they memorized it. Aye, they said they came from Rosen Craig, but after some interrogation, they changed their minds and saw the truth would be better told. 'Tis when I discovered your neighbor, Rothburg, has been sending reivers in your name and colors."

Bryce slammed his fist onto the chair arm. "Devil's ransom! That man is a thorn in my flesh. What is his plan? Does he wish for your clan and my people to be at war?" Or did his plan go deeper and darker than he could imagine?

"That I dinna ken. I could no' get that information oot of them nay matter how hard I tried. Perchance they did no' ken the answer. But I do ken that Rothburg wants us enemies, and that is why I came down here tae meet with you. I wanted tae talk tae you face tae face. I did no' wish tae allow Rothburg tae cause unjustified war between us."

Chapter 30

The ruckus in the great hall while the men ate kept Deirdre on edge. Would the laird tell her father she was here? Laird Warwick had no way of knowing that Laird Mackenzie was her father, and why would her father suspect it was her, even if he was told they had caught a female reiving? She had to calm her fears. And hadn't the laird sent her food up to her? And sent Lucas as well, she assumed for comfort. He most assuredly knew she did not wish to be found.

Lucas stopped eating and looked up at her. "You are quiet, milady."

"Am I? I did no' realize that."

"Aye, you are. Do you have lots on your mind? That is what my lord tells me when he is quiet."

"Is it now? And which laird are we talking of?"

"Laird Warwick."

Deirdre turned to see if the lad made fun with her and discovered him back to eating. She grinned.

"Laird Warwick, you say?" Deirdre wanted to see if he'd realized what he'd done.

"Aye, that is what I said. Are you sad, milady?"

"Nay, I am no' sad."

"I suppose not. I saw you sad when you first had come. But I know something is wrong, milady. I can tell."

"'Tis nothing for you to fash yourself aboot, Lucas."

"Are you scared? You look scared. I will protect you, milady."

Deirdre smiled and ruffled his hair. He twisted his head and slipped off from her attentions. "I am no' frightened, Lucas. Dinna let your imagination go tae far."

"I calls it as I sees it, milady."

"Weel, you see it wrong, sir."

Lucas scraped up the last bit of his food with his bread and ate it. "Are you going to eat up all your meat? I forgot to save some for Cathal."

"Aye, you can give this to her. I am no' vera hungry today."

He took the chunks of chicken in his fingers and let the cat pull it apart and eat it. "Are you going to marry the laird?"

Deirdre's gaze shot to him, but he continued to feed the kitten without looking up.

"Nay. What would make you ask such a question, Lucas?"

He shrugged. "You spend much time with him. And I do not want tae steal another man's lady, especially the laird's. He would not be happy with me."

"You dinna need to fash yourself about the laird and myself. We will never marry." At that moment, there was a check in her spirit. She brushed it off and thought to take advantage of Lucas's presence. "Will you watch Cathal for a few minutes? I will be back anon."

His eyes brightened. "Aye, milady. I would do anything for you. I will make sure she is safe and has a full belly."

Deirdre smiled. "Thank you, Lucas." She turned and made her way out the door. Aware of all the help below scurrying here and there, Deirdre crept down the stairs and moved along the wall to catch a glimpse of her father and Bryce.

She peeked around the corner of the entranceway into the great hall. Laird Warwick and her father sat beside each other. The laird's good friend sat beside him with the little squirrel perched on the knight's shoulder. Catherine sat beside her son, seemingly unaware that Alex looked to be contemplating jumping to her shoulder. Deirdre stood motionless for several minutes, wanting to make sure she didn't draw their attention. The three men laughed and ate like long ago friends.

Deirdre leaned in a bit further to see her father better. How much had he changed in the seventeen or so years since she'd seen him? She watched—curious about him. Would he tell the laird about her mother? Would she be able to find out if her mother still lived?

The hairs on the back of her neck rose. She scanned the great hall to find what caused her senses to be on alert. Her gaze locked with Laird Warwick. She jerked back. Heart pounding, she lowered her gaze and darted for the stairs.

Hands grasped her arms before she collided with the person in front of her. She looked up into the eyes of Finley. "Where are you off tae in such a hurry?"

"I-I need tae get back tae my room."

"Come sit with me in the great hall. We have countrymen in there we can visit." He had a slight smirk on his face.

A chill coursed down her spine. What did he know? "I left Lucas in my room. Please release me so I may return tae him."

"He is a boy. You dinna need tae go. 'Tis sure I am that our countrymen will welcome you. Dinna you want tae meet them?"

She tugged her arms, but he didn't release her.

Footfalls rushed down the stairs and relief flooded her. She turned to see her rescuer. The relief that she'd felt moments earlier, fled when Lucas appeared beside her.

"Let go of her, sir." Lucas glared at the man.

Finley snickered. "Go away, lad, you are bothering us."

"Nay. Milady does not wish your company. You must leave her be." Lucas stomped his foot.

Finley released one of her arms and shoved Lucas backward.

"Dinna push the child, sir." Deirdre yanked to free her other arm, but his fingers dug into her skin.

"Let her go, or I will tell my lord." Lucas took off running toward the hall.

Finley released her arm and spun on his heel.

"Lucas." Deirdre called to the lad. "Come with me." She

rushed toward the steps, her room, and safety.

Lucas ran to her. "Did he hurt you, milady?"

"Nay." Her feet hit the flagstone as fast as she could move them. She slipped into her room with Lucas behind her and locked the door, sagging against it.

"Milady, he is a bad man. I thought I might have to fight for you. But I did not want to hurt the man."

Deirdre reached out and pulled Lucas into her arms, giving him a hug. "Grammercy, my protector. Sure I am that you scared the man away. But I dinna believe Finley is a bad man. He wanted me tae come intae the great hall with the others, and I did no' wish tae. You rescued me from being dragged in there." And perhaps being discovered by her father. A shudder overcame her at the realization of how close she'd come. She mustn't allow her curiosity to get the best of her again while her father was near.

†††

Finley strutted through Wolves Forest Castle on his way to speak with Rothburg in hopes the laird would add some coin to his coffers with the new information he'd obtained.

He found him in the atilliator's workshop, looking over a new design of longbow. It irritated him that the laird didn't even acknowledge him when he entered. But he mustn't let that show if he wished for coin. He stood just inside the door opening, waiting for the two men to finish speaking.

By the time Rothburg finally acknowledged his presence with barely a nod of his head, Finley wished he'd not bothered to come.

"I have news." Finley folded his arms in front of his chest. He'd make him pull the information out now.

"It had better be good. I begin to wonder for which lord your loyalties lie." Rothburg handed the five-foot longbow back to his atilliator and headed out the door, passing Finley by.

"As long as you continue to pay well, my loyalties remain here." Small windows not much bigger than the size of his head shed light in on the east side of the stone wall as Finley followed Rothburg down the spiraling stairs of the turret.

"If I find otherwise, you will not need the coin." Rothburg's voice echoed in the turret stairwell.

And if he thought this laird threatened him, he could easily dispose of him right now and no one would be the wiser for hours. Not until the atilliator left for the evening. "You will find this of interest."

Rothburg came out of the armourer's tower and into the middle ward. "Have you finally gotten me proof of Warwick's treason against the crown?"

Finley drew himself up. "No' per se, but you may—"

"Get on with it, man. What do you have for me?" Rothburg's cross tone only angered Finley more.

"Bryce had a visitor yesterday. Mackenzie himself came."

"Interesting. Is he still there?"

"Aye, he was there when I left tae come here."

"Were you privy to their conversations?"

Finley sniffed. "Nay. Warwick does no' invite me on the dais for meals."

Rothburg frowned at Finley. "So, you have no real information to give me."

"I thought you would want tae ken that your little secret of border reivers was most likely oot."

"Aye. 'Tis no' good news. Warwick will be watching more carefully now. 'Tis glad I am that Richard has gone. That would have been some uncomfortable explaining on my part. Is there any more news?"

Finley thought for a moment. "The lass must have some knowledge of Mackenzie, for she is vera fearful of the laird."

Rothburg let out a sigh. "What lass, Finley?"

"The one Warwick caught reiving on his land. I saw her spying on the lairds from the hall entrance."

"Have you spoken with her about gaining information

we could use?"

"Aye, I have."

Rothburg shrugged. "Perhaps she hoped to glean from the men's talk."

"She did no' seem tae interested in helping me when I mentioned it. And as I said, the lass is scared. I have no' seen her so afraid since she arrived. No' even when Warwick first captured her. There is something aboot Mackenzie that causes terror in the lass."

Rothburg scratched this bearded chin. "How old do you say she is?"

"She passed for a young boy, but if she tells the truth, she has told me she is one and twenty."

Rothburg drummed his fingers on his chin. "And you say Warwick claims she is from Kincaid's clan?"

"Aye. That is his belief."

"Hmmm. If rumors are true…"

"What rumors are those?"

"None that concern you. What is the woman's name?"

"Deirdre Kincaid." Finley got the feeling that these were much more than questions from curiosity.

"Interesting. And she hid herself as a boy, you say?"

"Aye. 'Tis what I told you."

"I have to think about this. I cannot make an error here. It could be costly…deadly."

Finley frowned. What was wrong with the man? "I need more coin if you wish me tae continue tae risk me neck."

"I need treason. The king drains my coffers. Bring me proof of such, and you will have all you need."

Finley balled his hands into fists. Rothburg thought himself so high and mighty because his friendship with the king. But it wasn't his own neck he risked. If the laird caught him gathering information for Rothburg—he could feel the noose tightening on that gallows.

"Have you befriended this Deirdre?" Rothburg pushed his booted toe down on a purple flower pushing its way up through the grass.

"As much as possible." He didn't want to tell Rothburg that the lass didn't seem too taken with him.

"Have you urged her to help you in this quest? Surely you can convince her that it is in her best interests as well as her clan's to rid themselves of Bryce Warwick."

"I have, but she claims she has learned nothing." He wouldn't tell him that he sought her out nearly every day to ask and the lass seemed annoyed of late when he did.

"I need you to bring me Warwick's signet ring. If you cannot find me proof of treason, I will make my proof."

Finley stared at the man. Did this hatred he have for the laird of Rosen Craig addle his mind? "How can I do that? Cut off the man's finger?" Truth be told, he'd never seen the laird wear his signet ring. But Rothburg needn't know that, for either way it would not be easy to gain access to it.

"'Tis for you to figure out. I tire of waiting. Trust me, you do not wish to have both Bryce Warwick and me as your enemies. You are best to stay loyal to me and get me what I want."

"You ask too much," Finley protested.

"Away with you. Return only when you have what I wish." Rothburg turned his back to him and strolled away.

Chapter 31

Heat from the noonday sun warmed Bryce as he headed to the practice field, wondering if he'd need to shed his shirt. Wolfhound trotted ahead of him, oblivious to the activity around them as she chased a grasshopper that managed to stay a few hops in front of her. May usually brought less rain and warmer temperatures, something he welcomed every year, and this year was no different.

Catherine and Deirdre slowed as he strode across the bailey, intercepting his progress on his way to the field.

"Beautiful day today, my lord." Michael's mother stopped and shaded her eyes with her hand as she gazed up at him.

"Aye. I admired the weather as I walked," Bryce responded as he stole a quick glance at Deirdre, who stroked Cathal lovingly. Her red hair had grown since he'd brought her to Rosen Craig near four months ago. Those tight curls now fell loosely past her shoulder from their weight. She seemed to grow more beautiful with each passing day.

"Seems not the only thing you admire these days."

Bryce jerked his gaze back to Catherine to find a knowing grin on her face.

Deirdre glanced up from her attention of Cathal. "And what is that?" she asked innocently.

The last thing Bryce wanted was to try to explain himself to either of the women. He smiled and reached out to pet the cat. "I see you have done a fine job with Cathal. I believe she is nearly as large as the other cats running around here."

Deirdre smiled. "She will be a big girl when she has finished growing."

"What sort of mischief have you two been up to?"

Catherine answered. "We return from a walk to the village. We brought Widow Townsend more food."

"Is she any better?" The sweet widow from the village had been sick with what Millicent thought to be the sweating sickness at first but decided not since no one else had come down with it. Catherine and Deirdre had been faithful in taking food and medicine since most of the village was worried about getting sick as well.

"She is no' worse, but I am no' sure she is better."

"'Tis better news than it could be."

Wolfhound returned to Bryce's side and gave a bark. Cathal reached over Deirdre's arm and gave the dog a swat. The dog lunged up sending Deirdre back a step. Bryce reached out to steady her, and Cathal sprang from her arms and sprinted across the bailey with Wolfhound on her trail.

"Cathal!" Deirdre yelled to the cat.

"Wolfhound will not hurt her. I would worry more for my dog if she corners her."

"Are you certain?" she asked, worry in her voice.

"Aye. She only plays. There is not a mean bone in the dog's body."

Her eyes followed the duo. "Excuse me." She darted after the pair.

With Deirdre gone, Bryce wanted to be on his way. "I have men waiting for me."

"If I could have a moment of your time, my lord." Catherine's smile was unsettling.

"What can I do for you?"

"Michael... I wish to have him return to Essex with me. I do not wish to overstay my welcome here."

"You do not have to worry yourself about that, madam. You are welcome here as long as you wish to remain."

"Let me speak plainly. I have been gone longer than I had anticipated and need to return, but I wish to return with my son."

Bryce looked his friend's mother in the eyes, searching for truth. "Why is this so important to you? Why do you want Michael with you now? I know from Michael he has not lived near you since his years of squiring."

She glanced off behind him. "I need him to come with me."

Bryce frowned. "Are you afraid to return alone? Do you need protection?"

"I need you to convince him to return with me." She glanced back to him.

"Michael is a grown man. I cannot tell him what to do."

"But you can use your influence—persuade him."

"Nay. Michael is my friend. I will not use that friendship to influence him. Not when you will not tell me why."

She smiled at him. The same kind of smile his mother gave him when he was a young boy. "We all have our secrets, Bryce."

"Aye, we do. But I will not jeopardize that friendship for someone else's secret."

"Michael is fortunate to have you as a friend. He had no brothers but you. You are as much of a brother to him as blood could be. I trust you will always protect him."

"You have my word. And you have my protection as well. If you would only tell me why you cannot return alone."

A faraway looked filled her eyes as she again looked past him. "I fear all will learn of my secret before long."

"The Lord will watch over you." The words slipped so easily from his mouth. Perhaps Pater's sermons were starting to sink in.

She blinked and drew her gaze back to him, the faraway look gone. "But you, what will you do with your secret?"

Bryce's mind raced. Did Michael tell his mother about their conspiracy? Did she know he supported Henry and not the king? "Secrets?"

She laughed. "I am sure you have many secrets, my lord, but I am talking about the beautiful Scottish lass for which you have fallen."

"She is a woman who has my protection and home,

madam, just as you do. Now I must get to my men. I do not wish to have them saying I delayed to avoid battle with them."

Michael held his sword to one of Rosen Craig's knights until he cried mercy, then strode over to Bryce as he shed his tunic. "What did my mother want? She can be very persuasive."

"And I can be equally as stubborn." Bryce tossed his tunic to the ground.

"Ah, so she is now attempting to enlist your help." Sweat dripped from Michael's brow, and he wiped it away with the back of his hand.

"'Tis of no consequence. She needs to tell you what troubles her."

Michael nodded. "Shall we?" He swung his sword out in invitation to the practice *melee*.

They had stepped up their battle practice, and Bryce had made sure his armorer's tower's provisions were full. They could very well be facing battle soon. "Aye. Time to sharpen our skills."

†††

Not wanting to raise the laird's suspicion, Deirdre hadn't mentioned her father since he'd left nearly two sennights ago. But she could wait no longer. Their strolls outside of Rosen Craig had become almost a regular occurrence. But today they'd walked out to a grassy area with dried apples for Tempest and Storm who grazed there.

Deirdre held out the apple slice in the palm of her hand. Storm gently wrapped her mouth around it and munched.

"Would you like to ride, lass?" Bryce held out an apple to Tempest.

A ride? She'd not ridden Storm since she'd gone on the hunt. "I would love to."

The laird walked over to a tree branch where two bridles hung and grabbed them. She smiled to herself. Bryce had planned this, anticipating her answer would be aye. When had she started thinking of him as Bryce? A better question was when did she stop thinking of him as her enemy? This feeling she had nearly controlled her. She planned her daily strolls and slipped away from Catherine when she knew the laird was out in the bailey in hopes he'd walk with her. She looked forward to each meal, knowing she'd sit with him. What was happening to her?

He had the bridles on both horses before she realized he stood before her handing her the reins. She took them and walked over to Storm's side. Glancing down at her gown, she sighed before grasping the horse's mane and swinging up on him.

"I had planned on lifting you up, lass." Bryce stood there grinning. "Or are you still not wishing to be touched by an Englishman?"

Deirdre's face heated as she yanked at her gown in an attempt to cover her legs. She huffed and gave up. So he remembered their first encounter quite well. "I guess old habits die hard." She smiled, hoping that her face was not as red as her hair.

He chuckled and swung up on Tempest. "Do you have any place you would like to ride to?"

She wanted to remind him the only direction she really knew was north, and she didn't want to go that way. "Nay, 'tis just nice tae be on Storm once again."

"Then we will ride to the village. I know where we can get a pear torte like none other."

"It sounds wonderful." She wouldn't tell him she'd never had a pear tarte. The sweet old woman she'd lived with had never made them. She supposed that was a luxury that need not be afforded.

The horses sauntered along, Storm frequently going off track to the green grass coming up along the sides of the road. The horse seemed to be as happy as she was to be seeing different pastures.

"So tell me, lass, have you made any decisions on what

you will do?"

"Nay. Do you wish me to leave?" Her stomach did a small flip.

"I only ask your plans. 'Tis no more than that."

But there was so much more she just couldn't tell him. She couldn't share all that was at stake for her.

"The laird who came several sennights ago, what did he want?" Deirdre groaned inwardly. So much for casually easing into the conversation of her father so as not to make him suspicious.

"I did wonder why you had not asked about him since he hailed from Scotland. I understand why you did not come around whilst he visited, but I expected you to inquire of him."

"Until I have decided what I must do, I wish nay one tae ken my whereaboots."

"And why is that? Do you still not trust me?"

Deirdre glanced at the tall, muscular man beside her. She supposed she did. At least she thought she did. But there was still something inside her that couldn't let go and trust with her whole heart. "Nay. I dinna think you are oot tae do me harm."

They rode along in silence, and she feared she'd offended him somehow. Her feelings were so jumbled, she was glad she sat upon her palfrey, for her knees were weak thinking of this handsome laird. Never had she felt like this. Was this what love felt like? It addled a person's thoughts and unsettled their stomach? If so, she wanted nothing to do with it. Yet the desire to be around him grew each time she was with him.

They entered the small village that was a part of Rosen Craig's demesne. Villeins peered out small windows and children ran into the narrow street as the horses walked along.

"Guid day, milord." A young woman in soiled clothing curtseyed.

"Good aftermete, to you," Bryce replied. "How is your family?"

She smiled. "'Tis well we are, milord. Much thanks for asking."

"Where is your son?"

"He went with his da' to work the field." The woman looked to be ten years older than Deirdre. The dirt smudges on her face couldn't hide the beauty in her fine features and blue eyes.

Bryce opened a pouch tied to his belt and pulled out a sweet. He leaned down and handed it to her. "Give this to Roger. Tell him it is from his lord for a hard day of work."

Her smile grew. "Aye, milord. Thank you."

As they continued down the dusty track of a road, children ran from their small homes, arms stretched out. Not a hand was left empty. The contents of the purse appeared endless, much like the widow's jar of oil in Elisha's day.

"You must do this often." Deirdre broke the silence between her and Bryce.

He shrugged, appearing uncomfortable. "They do not have much. 'Tis a small thing I can do to bring them joy. And Nog loves to make them for the children."

"'Tis vera kind of you. I dinna ken another laird who has such kindness in his heart."

"You know other lords? Methinks there is much about you that I do not know."

Several more children ran out to him before he stopped at a small wattle and daub home and swung from his horse. He came around and plucked her off Storm before she could slide off.

A middle-aged woman came out of the home with a cloth package. "Ye are jist in time, milord. I jist took 'em off the fire." She eyed Deirdre, and she felt the woman had handed down judgement. She hoped she passed. "I made 'em extra sweet for yer lady." She smiled at Deirdre.

Deirdre smiled back, a bit relieved she'd passed the

woman's inspection. "'Tis vera kind of you. What is your name?"

The woman's eyes grew large. "Cora, milady."

"'Tis nice tae meet you, Cora. It is sure I am that we will enjoy these tartes. Laird Warwick has spoken so highly of them they have made my mouth water."

Bryce took the cloth-covered pastries and pressed a coin in her palm. "Thank you, Cora."

She beamed at him.

"Grammercy." The aroma of the pear tartes reached Deirdre's nose, and her mouth truly started to water.

Bryce opened the cloth and handed one to Deirdre, then grabbed Tempest's reins and began walking. She tossed Storm's reins over Storm's neck so the mare wouldn't step on them and so she could use both hands to hold the small pie. She walked beside the laird, and Storm followed her obediently. She took a bite and moaned.

The laird grinned. "I did not lie, eh?"

"They are heavenly." She savored the sweet pears as they tantalized her tongue. "You should have her bake these for your home."

"I fear Nog would worry for her position."

Deirdre brightened. "Have Nog make them." She took another bite and sighed.

"Nog would do anything for you, lass. Ask her."

They walked beyond the villein's homes and into a small field, stopping as they reached a tree line. Bryce let go of his horse's reins and the stallion began to graze. Storm joined him, munching on the new spring grass.

The laird removed his tunic and spread it on the ground motioning for her to sit. Deirdre lowered herself onto the tunic and the laird sat near her, their arms nearly touching. She wrapped her arms close to her body.

"You did not answer me, lass. Do you know many lords?"

Her heart sped up. "Nay."

"Do you know Lord Mackenzie?" He shifted a bit and looked at her.

She had to answer his questions with as much honesty as she could without telling him who she was. "Nay. He is a vera important laird, I understand."

"He is to Rosen Craig. You avoided coming around whilst he was here. Have you met him?" He hadn't taken his eyes off her.

She swallowed. She must be careful. "Aye. When I was but a bairn. The memory is faint. But I remember he frightened me. I have since heard he is a harsh mon."

Bryce gave a slow nod. "'Tis hard to be a lord. There are difficult decisions that must be made. Someone will not like them, to be sure."

This worked well for her. She was glad he'd asked. She was honest in all her answers, but now she could find out why he came. "'Tis strange that a Scotsman would come tae an Englishman. One where the borders are nearly at war. Do you no' fash he has come for nay guid?"

"'Tis possible. But I do not think he came for anything evil. He came with a warning."

Deirdre attempted to show little concern. "And how is that, my lord?"

"Would you be comfortable calling me Bryce?"

"It is no' done, my lord. People will talk."

He grinned. "I have never given much to gossip. But you could when we are alone."

Her gut did a somersault, betraying her again. She tightened her arms around herself. "Thank you, Bryce."

"And may I call you Deirdre?"

Her throat went dry. "A-Aye."

"So, Deirdre, tell me your secret."

Chapter 32

May 1399

With the way she'd avoided Mackenzie, Bryce was sure she'd known the man. But he watched her closely when he'd asked her, and other than her slight hesitation, he saw no signs that she lied to him. Her fear of the man most likely caused that. Bryce had met many lords while working for his father, some reputed to be harsh men, showing no mercy. But just as his father had to hand out punishments and decide between right and wrong when cases were brought before him, so did these other lords. Decisions were not always popular. Many times, lords were not liked because one man didn't agree with a ruling. Rumors of an oppressive lord were much more believed than that of a kind lord.

And now he would have to make those hard decisions. But he wanted to be different. That's why he went to the village and bought from his villeins. That's why he gave sweets to the children. He wanted them to see he was no different from them. All were children of God. He was blessed with Rosen Craig, but he was also responsible for these people and, in some respects, held to a higher account to his country and king.

Deirdre pulled her gown around her feet. "'Tis true, I have a secret, but don't most?"

"Aye, to be true." And his secret, if discovered by the wrong person, could get him drawn and quartered.

"Many at Rosen Craig keep secrets. I can see it in them. It seems the life of the nobles is no' an easy one."

She still fussed with the fabric of her skirt and never looked up at him. Did she realize what she'd just told him? She came from noble blood? A wee bit of her secret revealed. That would explain why she'd met Mackenzie. The two lords had probably met at one time, and her father had taken his family with him or Mackenzie had come to them. He'd like to ask Mackenzie, but what was the chance he'd remember a small child. And she was hiding from someone, and he wouldn't betray that trust.

"At Rosen Craig?" Bryce chuckled. "I hope they do not keep them from me."

She tipped her head sideways, nearly laying her cheek on her drawn up knees. "You and Sir Michael have a secret. And so does Catherine."

How much did she know and how much could he trust her? "And how is it you think Michael and I have a secret?"

She pushed the tendrils of red hair way from her face and gave him a knowing smile. "I would be blind no' tae see it. You two seclude yourselves away often, making sure no one is near."

"Michael came at my beckoning when I was thrust into my father's position. He is my confidant, 'tis all."

"So you say. What happened to your father?"

"We were all betrayed by…my fiancé and my uncle."

"We? You and your father?" She wrapped her arms around her legs and drew them closer to her body.

"My mother and father were murdered. I was thought dead as well, but Millicent and Neil, her husband, found me and took me away until my injuries healed."

"But your brother, he was not injured?"

"We had been told he died in battle." Bryce didn't want to go into more detail about that. Royce had already fought his demons.

"So you only had one brother?"

She asked a lot of questions, but if he could answer them, perhaps it would help her trust him more. "I had a sister who died young. Royce is all I have left."

"'Tis sorry I am. Your sister, how old was she?"

"Four. Kinna was a sennight from her birthday." He hadn't thought of that tragic day for many years. Perhaps since he'd become a knight. It took him a long time to move past it. When he was a child, the pain had been unbearable.

"Kinna, 'tis a beautiful name. I dinna mean tae pry, but how did she die?"

The sobbing of his mother came back to him, reliving the moment. His father's groans of agony. The only time he'd ever seen his father's eyes misty. He could see it all in his mind's eye. "She was killed by a wolf. I learned much later in life she'd been mauled. To a wild animal like that, she was no more than an easy meal."

A gentle touch brought Bryce's gaze to Deirdre's hand resting on his arm. "Oh, Bryce, sorry I am. Please forgive me for asking so many questions. What a horrible thing for your parents tae endure. And you and your brother tae lose your sister at such a young age."

"'Tis fine, lass. Much time has passed. The hurt lessens. When I was a boy, I did not want to go to bed because I dreamed of it over and over. I feared dusk. Feared that same wolf would find me."

"How did the animal get in the castle walls?"

"It did not. Malle, the maidservant who tended to Kinna, Royce, and me, had taken Kinna to the village with her. The tailor was to make my sister new apparel for her birthday. Kinna begged Mother to allow Malle to take her. She wanted Mother to be surprised when she got her new clothes. I am unclear on why they were delayed, but darkness had fallen before they returned. They never made it back to the safety of Rosen Craig."

†††

Michael rode into the bailey and jumped off his horse as Deirdre strolled with Bryce. Much like her sweet Storm, Michael's horse followed along behind him without being led by reins.

"What did you find out?" Bryce asked Michael when he reached them.

"'Tis true Richard has left for Ireland to campaign. We can breathe easier now." Michael grinned broadly.

"Tis good news then. Looks like we keep our heads this

time," Bryce quipped.

"Keep your heads?" What did the man speak of? Deirdre looked to Bryce for an answer.

"King Richard questioned my fidelity to him."

"And this king of yours could have your head for that?"

"'Tis more than that. Rothburg would like to see me gone. I have no doubt he is the reason that Richard questioned my loyalty. I have given the king no reason to doubt that."

Michael and Bryce gave each other what she could only call a knowing look. Secrets. The two shared a secret, and it had to do with their king, she would surmise. Was Bryce's faithfulness to his king really to be questioned?

"I dinna understand. Why would you believe your king questioned your fidelity if you have done nay wrong?" She frowned.

"Richard himself asked."

"Oh, my. But you have convinced him you are trustworthy?"

Bryce smiled. "Apparently I have. Rothburg loses this round. But I have nay doubt he will try again. He has been unhappy about the decision of Rosen Craig for a very long time. He has begun to take things into his own hands. But with Richard gone, I do not have to watch my back at all times. I have a reprieve for the moment."

Michael reached into the neckline of his tunic and pulled out a missive, handing it to Bryce, but not before his pet squirrel Alex stuck his head out of the shirt. "I met one of Mackenzie's men riding into the village as I came through. He asked me to deliver this to you."

Bryce took the missive and frowned. "Devil's ransom, man! You need to do something about your squirrel."

Deirdre tipped up on her toes and leaned over to see what had frustrated Bryce.

Michael chuckled. "He did not eat much, Bryce."

The end portion of the missive was chewed. She eyed

Bryce as he broke the wax seal and opened the letter.

His eyebrows rose.

"What is it? Not more trouble with reivers is it?" Michael asked.

"Nay." Bryce shook his head. "He says he wishes to speak again and will return."

A bolt of fire rushed through Deirdre's veins, her stomach knotted, and her legs weakened. Why was her father returning? Had he somehow found out she was here? She wanted to ask questions, but she feared the words would not come out, as dry as her throat had become.

"Interesting. I do wonder what he returns for, as he did not give me a reason." Bryce glanced back down to the letter in his hand.

"Does he say when he will return?"

Deirdre was thankful Michael asked the questions that she wanted to.

"Nay, or perhaps I should say aye, but some aggravating varmint has chewed that part of the paper, and I do not have a day."

Michael chuckled again, and Deirdre wondered how he could not be bothered by the laird's frowns.

"Do you wish for Alex and me to return to the village and find Mackenzie's rider? Perhaps he can answer that question?"

"'Tis not necessary. 'Tis doubtful he *kent* the contents of the missive. When he comes, he comes. I can always send *you* to Mackenzie's demesne if I need to ken. You can explain to the lord how your pet squirrel chewed his missive." Bryce chuckled.

Michael stroked the squirrel's head, which still peeked out from the tunic. "Did you hear that, Alex. We may take a trip."

"If you will excuse me, my laird, I will leave you two ta your business. This talk of Alex reminds me I need tae feed Cathal."

Bryce gave a bow and smiled. "I will see you anon then, at the evening meal."

Deirdre returned his smile, knowing if her stomach did not calm, she would not be able to eat a bite. "Aye, anon." She nodded to Michael and headed back toward the inner bailey.

She understood Bryce's relief that the king had left for Ireland. For she had felt the same way when nearly a fortnight had passed and the laird hadn't asked her any more about her secret. She'd done well in circumventing that question of his by asking him about his secrets. Little did she know that it would lead to a sad story of family loss. She found that the vulnerability she saw in him at that moment only softened her heart more to the man who always showed such a tough exterior. But now, with her father's imminent return, it stirred up the apprehension she'd felt when he was here. She could not risk being discovered.

Yet if she continued to avoid the meals during her father's stay, Bryce or even Michael could become suspicious.

She'd barely walked through the portcullis when a hand reached out and grabbed her, pulling her aside. She let out a startled yell.

"Hush, lass. It's me."

She turned to see Finley. She did not want to deal with the man today. "What do you want that you pull me aside?" She sounded annoyed even to herself.

"Calm yourself. I saw you looked troubled."

"I fash of nothing."

"I can see it in your walk and the unease on your face."

Deirdre took a long blink, holding in the sigh. "'Tis none of your concern." The trepidation that built within her dissolved the annoyance she'd felt moments earlier like water on fire.

"Nay, lass." His voice softened. "I dinna like tae see you upset. What troubles you so?"

If she told someone, perhaps it would make her feel better. "Laird Mackenzie will return tae Rosen Craig. I dinna wish tae see him. I hear he is an evil man."

Sir Finley stared off. "I have heard the same."

"There is nothing you can do." Deirdre sighed.

"Perhaps there is." He ran his hand down his beard, smoothing it.

She could only wish that he could help. She certainly wouldn't go away with the man, if that was what he suggested.

"Can you get me the laird's signet ring?" Finley asked. "I can send a missive telling him Warwick does no' wish for him tae come. Of course, tae do this, Mackenzie would need tae believe the letter came from the laird."

"Are you daft? What do you wish me tae do? Go ask the laird? 'Tis sure I am he is no' going tae fulfill that request."

"Dinna call me daft." He spat the words out with venom. "I ken he is no' going tae hand you his ring, but if you wish for me tae make sure Laird Mackenzie does no' return, I will need the signet ring tae send a missive. You will have tae *borrow* it from where he keeps it, for the mon does no' wear his ring."

"Even if I can locate the ring, if he discovered I took it— my neck would return tae a noose from whence he rescued it. And he will discover the ring missing."

"I will no' keep the ring. You will need tae return it quickly so he does no' ken it was ever gone. The choice is yours, lass, but 'tis the only way I ken tae keep Laird Mackenzie away."

Deirdre stared thoughtfully at this fellow countryman. His wish to help her did seem genuine. And if her father discovered her here, she would be forced back to his home, under his cruel and possibly murderous whims. But to steal the laird's ring—her throat went dry again, just as it had when she learned of her father's return. Nay, it would not be stealing, it would be borrowing. She would return it as soon as she secured her safety. Surely, the Lord of heaven would understand.

She swallowed, attempting to bring moisture to her now parched throat. "Aye, I will do this which you ask."

Chapter 33

Bryce, Michael, Catherine, and Deirdre lounged around the large fireplace in the great hall where a fire burned, warding off the chill. For a fortnight the weather had remained favorable and only a few logs were needed this evening as the daytime sun had warmed the castle.

Bryce smiled as Catherine continued her barrage to persuade Michael to return with her. Michael changed the subject as many times as his mother returned it to him to coming home with her.

He tore his eyes from Michael and his mother and fixed his gaze on the woman occupying so much of his thoughts these days. Deirdre stroked her sleeping kitten in her lap. She hadn't been the same since she'd learned of Mackenzie's return visit. The lass had been nervous for days. If only he could put her mind to ease. He'd questioned her some, but the subject upset her. He wished she could trust him, believe that he would not let any harm come to her.

The more he got to know Deirdre, the more he saw the beauty in her. She had gained in physical beauty as she healed from her bruises. Her red locks had grown out of the boyish style she'd cut. But more than anything, she'd gained in inner beauty as she became comfortable at Rosen Craig, and her fear had left.

He didn't want to see her distressed again. He didn't want to lose the Deirdre he'd come to know. More than anything, he wished she'd not learned of Mackenzie's return. He could not overlook her intense fear of the Scottish laird. She knew the man much more personally than she was willing to admit. He had his suspicions. He would learn the truth. Even now as they sat around and Catherine prodded Michael and it became a game of wits, Deirdre had drawn into herself and spoke little.

Her heart was large. Tender. She valued the villeins, the

people who worked in the castle as well as the children. There was no haughtiness in her such as he had seen in Clarice. There was something in him that just wanted to draw her into his arms and tell her he would protect her—she had nothing to fear.

Lucas and Pater sauntered over. Pater seemed to enjoy the lad's company. Lucas sat down on the floor at Deirdre's feet.

"Pater." Catherine sought the man's attention.

"Aye, my lady?"

"Do you not agree that my son should return with me to Wiltshire. Does not the Bible say one should honor his mother?"

Patter choked and adjusted his stance. "Aye, the Bible does say that."

"There you have it, Michael. Even the pater agrees you should return with me."

Pater placed his hand on the back of Deirdre's chair, appearing to ready himself for a battle. "'Tis true the Bible tells us to honor our father and mother, but I am not sure that Michael remaining here and earning a living would constitute not honoring."

Michael threw his head back and laughed. Alex scampered down his leg and perched on the floor, looking at him. "Mother, I am afraid this good man and the Bible are on my side. It does say a man should leave his mother and father."

Catherine frowned.

Pater cleared his throat. "Again, 'tis a true statement, Michael. However, that is when one marries. The man is told to leave his father and mother and cleave to his wife. Are you soon to marry son?"

Michael grinned. "Marriage is not for me, I am afraid. Not now. Perhaps never."

Catherine let out a moan. "You will never give me grandchildren? It is a woman's desire to hold the child of her child in her arms. Would you deny me that?"

Cathal opened her eyes and instantly sprung from Deirdre's lap landing nearly on top of Alex. Alex let out a loud chatter and ran up Michael's leg, followed closely by Cathal. Before Bryce could stop Wolfhound, she lunged for Cathal. She hissed and swatted the dog many times her size. Wolfhound lunged again, this time ending half in Michael's lap. Alex moved to higher ground on Michael's head as Cathal moved up to Michael's shoulder.

Michael flew from the chair with both animals still on him and Wolfhound barking at his feet.

A melodious sound came from his right. Bryce turned to see Deirdre holding her stomach in laughter. She stood, still laughing, and moved toward Michael. Bryce joined her, grabbed the scruff of Wolfhound's neck, and pulled her away.

Deirdre plucked Cathal off Michael's shoulder, but not before the cat took another swipe at the squirrel, hitting Michael in the head instead when Alex jumped to his other shoulder. Wolfhound continued to bark.

"Lucas." Bryce called to the child. "Take Wolfhound outside and walk her around the bailey until she gets her energy out."

"But, milord, I wanna watch," Lucas protested.

"Nay, Wolfhound is perpetuating the situation. Take her now."

Lucas pushed himself up from the floor and pulled the dog along with him.

Deirdre wiped tears from laughter from her face. "I have no' laughed so hard in a vera long time."

"Laughter is good for the soul," Pater announced.

"Aye, I believe it is." Bryce went back to his chair and sat.

"I was attacked by two animals, and you laugh at my expense." Michael made a poor attempt of sounding offended.

"'Tis sure I am that you have received far worse on the practice field." Bryce stretched out his legs as he settled in.

"Ack." Michael reached into his tunic and pulled out a missive, handing it to Bryce. "I forgot to give you this. It's from Mackenzie. I caught the messenger who delivered your letter and explained to him that parts of the letter were damaged and unreadable. He sent you another. It arrived today."

Bryce broke the seal and scanned the words penned. "It would seem we will have the pleasure of his company once again."

"Aye. We knew that. When will he come and why?"

"In a fortnight. He is vague, but it seems 'tis something important to him."

A gasp sounded beside him. Bryce swung his gaze to Deirdre as the color drained from her face.

†††

Deirdre paced the floor of her room. Her imagination ran away with her as she attempted to guess why her father would return to Rosen Craig after only one month. From what she learned from Bryce, her father's last visit was the first time they'd met, so why would he want to return in such a short period of time? She would hope and pray it had nothing to do with her. Aye, she must pray.

Deirdre bowed her head.

Lord, I dinna ken why You allowed my life tae be as it is. Why I dinna grow up with a mother and father. But You have protected me and looked after me with Mairi and since I have come tae English soil. I ask a favor of You. Please dinna allow my father tae come tae Rosen Craig while I am here. Please protect me and keep me safe. She whispered, "Amen."

As much as she didn't wish to borrow the laird's ring, she would have to in order to keep her father away from Rosen Craig and her. Perhaps this was how the Lord would keep her safe.

Deirdre made it a point to stay close to Bryce, attempting

to learn his routine. The more time she spent with him, the more she came to see he had a very kind heart. Why hadn't she seen that when he'd spared her life when he caught her reiving? Or when he spared nothing to save her when she was injured? Guilt crept in as she thought about how she would borrow his ring. But she continued to tell herself she was not stealing it and she would return it.

But it seemed the Lord smiled down on her this day. For the laird had informed them as she sat in his solar with Catherine, Michael, and Pater that he and Michael would be gone the following day to attend to some problems on the border land. She didn't ask any questions. She just prayed that it had nothing to do with her father or his people.

"Will you be gone long?" Catherine looked to her son for an answer.

"Nay, we will leave before dawn if we hope to return at eventide. That is, if the weather cooperates and we are not slowed down." Bryce answered her before Michael had a chance.

"And why must Michael go? Can you not take one of your other knights?" Lines of strain showed between Catherine's eyes.

Michael didn't give Bryce enough time to answer. He smiled at his mother, but the smile held a warning that even Deirdre could see. "Mother, I am my lord's friend as well as his knight, and you have no place to question what he asks of me. You forget yourself. I am a grown man."

Catherine lifted her chin. "And you forget yourself, son. I am your mother. It is my right to concern myself with you. Must I remind you again that you are my only living blood?"

Bryce cut in. "Madam, I am not in the habit of putting my life, nor the lives of others, in harm's way foolishly."

"Of course, my lord. Please forgive my impudence." She didn't sound the least bit contrite.

Deirdre continued to scrutinize Catherine's behavior. The woman surely had a secret as deep as hers. She had a fear just like Deirdre had. She obviously didn't want to be without her son. His presence seemed to give her some sort of security.

She wished they could share their secrets with each other. Surely, having someone else who knew the demons she battled would lessen the fear.

†††

Deirdre barely slept, wanting to hear when Bryce left. Every sound woke her. But this time it was Bryce and Michael, as well as a couple of other knights, she'd heard talking. She'd stuck her head out the door in an attempt to see. She couldn't make a mistake about his departure. They stood down by the entrance talking, their features difficult to make out in the dim light of torches on the castle wall.

When they went out, Deirdre hurried to her window, which looked over the inner bailey. She pulled back the curtain and peered out. It was still dark, and she couldn't see them but could hear their voices. She waited there with the curtain drawn back until the sound of horses' hooves beat against the ground and faded as they rode away.

She let the fabric fall from her fingers and made her way back to the bed. She would lie there and rest until dawn, then she'd steal away to the laird's room and retrieve the ring.

That was the last thing she remembered as she stretched in her bed. She sat up abruptly and swung her feet to the floor. Heavens! The sun was high in the sky. She must have overslept.

After she splashed water on her face from the bowl in her room, she slipped into her gown and plaited the little bit of hair she had, pleased it was long enough to braid.

She stole out of her room and down the hall, heading for the laird's solar and bedroom. Her gut twisted as she thought of what she was about to do. But he'd be none the wiser and it wouldn't harm him. It would just secure her safety.

Noise from the kitchen resonated up and through the empty halls. She had to hurry. She'd slept too late, and everyone was sure to be up by now. She turned the corner and stood steps from Bryce's door.

As she pulled on the door, it let out a loud moan of protest. Streams of sunlight streaked in through the windows, allowing her to see around the spacious solar. She went directly to the table. She glanced around, picked up a small wooden box and looked in it. She set it back down and quickly moved around the room, searching for the ring.

Nothing. With a few steps, she stood in the middle of the room and made a slow perusal. There didn't seem to be a place she'd missed. Perhaps he carried it around his neck on a chain.

She drew in a deep breath to give herself courage. Entering his bedroom truly felt like a violation of his privacy. But if the ring wasn't in the solar, and if he did not take it with him, then his bedroom would be the next likely place.

The tips of her fingers pressed against the cold wooden door. It opened silently. She moved in, her heartbeat increasing with each step. This felt so very wrong.

She glanced around the room. No fire burned in the fireplace. A large wooden bed had been placed against the far wall, its posts, bigger around than Wolfhound's girth, were intricately carved. A small cloth-covered stool sat at the foot of the bed. Two carved wooden chairs and a matching table were placed in the center of the room and in front of the fireplace. Benches were placed beneath both windows. Beside the bed, on each side, was a slim wooden table pushed close to the wall and bed.

Beautiful tapestries of castles and woodland animals hung on the walls. But the thing that drew her attention most was a painting of a young couple. The two looked like they belonged together—like they loved each other. As she examined the painting, she recognized the couple as the painting with the two boys and babe that hung above the hearth in the great hall.

Deirdre drew in another deep breath for fortitude and

began her search. She worked her way around the room. She checked every box and every item sitting out to no avail. Her heart sank. She had to find the ring if she hoped to keep her father from returning. Moving back to the middle of the room, she surveyed the room again, noting every place she'd looked. As her gaze reached the fireplace, it rose to the mantle and to the items resting on the stone. Without thought, she glided over, searching for the elusive ring.

She reached up and lifted a small cloth bag made of blue silk. She loosened the strings and peered inside. Her heart hiccupped. The ring. She'd found the signet ring. Curling her fingers over the cloth and ring, she started for the door, then stopped. Perhaps she should leave the cloth bag where she'd found it. The laird might not notice the ring missing if the bag remained.

Hurrying back, she placed it on the mantle, turned and nearly ran to the door. She'd be so glad when she was back in her own room, or better yet, when she no longer had possession of the ring.

She cracked the door leading into the solar and peered in. It was empty. Her heart thudded so loudly in her ears that if someone had been in the room making noise, she didn't think she'd have heard them. She slipped through the opening and rushed to the door leading to the hall. Again, she opened the door and peered out. When she saw no one, she stepped out and closed the door behind her.

She'd made it. She glided down the hall as quickly as she could, wanting to get out of the laird's wing. She turned the corner to find Lucas sitting on the floor. He jumped up, and she let out a slight shriek.

"'Tis sorry, I am to scare you, milady. I did not mean to." Lucas looked at her with concern.

"Nay harm done, Lucas. I was no' expecting tae see anyone is all."

He looked up at her with consternation. "What were you doing in milord's room?"

Chapter 34

Deirdre's knees nearly buckled. She forced a smile that was weaker than her knees. Her mind raced for an answer. "I-I lost my knife last night whilst we visited in the solar. I went to see if I could find it."

How did the lad know she was there? She thought she'd been so careful.

Lucas's gaze followed the cord that hung from Deirdre's waist and to which her knife was tied. "'Tis good you found it."

Deirdre reached down without thinking and grasped the knife, but in doing so she nearly dropped the ring. "Aye, I would no' want tae be withoot my eating utensil." She let go of the knife, allowing it to fall into the folds of her gown.

But Lucas's eyes were on her hand. The hand that held the laird's ring. She folded her arms in front of her to hide her hands.

"And what are you doing up here? Were you looking for me?" Deirdre tried to get his mind off what he'd just witnessed.

"I was looking for you, milady. 'Tis a beauteous day and methought perchance you would walk with me since the lord is not here to walk with you."

"I would be honored, kind sir." Deirdre gave Lucas a small curtsey. "But I must first speak with someone. Wait for me in the great hall by the fireplace, and I will find you anon."

Lucas grinned. "Ack! Is milord going to be jealous?"

"And, Lucas, can we keep losing my knife between you and me? It would be a wee bit embarrassing tae me if the laird ken I lost it in his solar."

"Aye, milady. I will be waiting." He took off running down the hall.

Lucas descended to the main level, headed for the great

hall, before she made it to the stairs.

Finley needed to be her focus at the moment. The sooner she could get the signet ring into his hands, the sooner she could get it back in the laird's chamber. Putting it back might prove harder than getting it when he was away.

The bailey bustled with people since it was the day when people brought their wares to sell. Finding Finley would be harder than she'd anticipated. She stood on the top of the steps leading to the entrance and tried to spot the lanky, redheaded knight.

So many people were milling around, she gave up and decided to head for the practice field. If she were lucky, she'd find him there. She passed a merchant selling fine silk fabric and gave in to the temptation to stop and run her hand over the soft fabric. She'd glanced up at the man and his wife. She'd never noticed them at Rosen Craig before.

The woman rushed over and took the fabric and rubbed it against her cheek. "Soft." The woman said with a strong accent she didn't recognize.

"Aye, 'tis beautiful." Deirdre had never owned a dress of such fine fabric. But she'd owned very few dresses in her lifetime.

"You buy?" The woman pushed the fabric toward her.

"Nay, but grammercy. I have nay money."

The woman's shoulders dropped.

A hand grabbed hold of her arm and pulled her away. She turned to see Finley. Deirdre jerked her arm away from him, noticing the woman she'd just been speaking with frowning at Finley.

"Dinna put your hands on me, sir."

He ignored what she said. "Did you get the ring?"

"Aye. And I dinna ken how I will put it back. You need tae return it tae me anon. 'Twill no' be easy tae get back in the laird's room." She held out the ring and dropped it into his hand.

"That is your problem, lass." He closed his fingers

around the ring.

Deirdre glared at the man as her body turned cold and nausea consumed her. She'd made a grave error. "Perhaps I should return the ring." She reached out to retrieve it from his fingers.

He jerked his hand away. "Dinna be so hasty. I will return the ring anon."

He spun on his heel and walked away, disappearing into the crowd.

†††

Finley stood before Rothburg, not really sure the man would stand behind his word to him. The man cared little for others unless they could do something for him. Like procuring this ring.

He had no choice if he wanted to move up to a better position than watching a lass. He was sure Warwick didn't like him. And he really didn't care if Rothburg did or not, as long as he got what was promised to him.

"I have the ring." Finley held it up for Rothburg to see.

A smile that sent a jolt up Finley's back spread over Rothburg's lips. He'd seen a lot of hard men, even evil men, but none of them caused the discomfort Rothburg did right now.

"Give it to me." Rothburg grabbed the ring from his hand. "Now tell me how you came upon this."

"Weel, from what the lass tells me, Mackenzie is returning tae Rosen Craig, and she is vera fearful. I told her if she could get me Lord Rosen Craig's signet ring, I could send a message that would keep him from coming."

"And so, she retrieved the ring?" Rothburg inquired.

"Aye."

"Hmmm. Interesting that her fear of Mackenzie is greater than her fear of being caught stealing." Rothburg cupped his chin and rubbed a finger against his unshaven skin. "And when will Mackenzie return?"

Finley shrugged. "I dinna ken. Seems there is some sort

of confusion there."

"I may need to act quicker than I had expected. Does the lass leave Rosen Craig much?"

"I have noticed of late that she and another woman go tae the village more frequently tae bring food tae a sickly widow."

"Do they have guards?" Rothburg held the signet ring closer to look at it.

"Nay, just the two lasses."

Rothburg gave him a wry smile. "Very good. Wait here."

He disappeared out of his solar. Finley walked around the room, running his hand over the darkly stained wood walls. The tall walls drew his attention to the decorative arches made of the same wood that graced the ceiling. The man certainly knew how to live.

He'd never understand why he wanted Rosen Craig when he was laird of Wolves Forest. He fingered a wall hanging of the finest quality. It portrayed a bloody battle. Finley shuddered. He didn't like the idea of war. It wasn't for him. He'd be happy if he never had to raise his sword in battle. Why should he fight for someone else? If he was going to put his life in danger, it would be for his gain, not some laird.

Rothburg's favorite chair, he was sure by the wearing, called to him. He sat in it. Aye, he could get used to the life of a laird. He stretched out his legs and leaned his head back, closing his eyes to imagine what life would be like.

He woke to the creaking of the door and jumped up. Rothburg came in glowering at him.

"Enjoy your rest?"

Finley decided not to answer, since the man was now in an ill mood. "Did you get done what you needed tae?"

"Aye. 'Tis done. Bryce Warwick will nay longer be a thorn in my flesh." He handed the ring back to Finley.

††††

The men accompanying Bryce rode hard to return to Rosen Craig so they could sleep in their own beds and not on the damp ground. Bryce would never tell Michael, but it was much more than a soft bed that he looked forward to in coming home. It was a green-eyed, redheaded lass.

The woman was never far from his thoughts the whole trip. Wasted trip, he might add. They'd been told there was a skirmish on his land bordering the Scots, but when they rode along, they saw nothing, and when they asked the tenants, none had had any problems of late.

The shadows of dusk had long faded as the faint outline of Rosen Craig came into view. The place had never looked so inviting.

Michael pulled his horse up next to him. "Tis good to see the castle walls still stand. I feared why we were sent on this wild chase."

"Aye, the thought had entered my mind as well. But I am glad to be home nonetheless."

They rode through the portcullis to find all quiet, as it should be. Bryce cared for his horse as the others did but rushed through the job in hopes of seeing Deirdre before she retired for the evening.

As he strode up the steps and pulled open the door, Michael ran up to him. "You seem to be in a hurry this evening. Any reason I might be interested in?"

Once inside, Bryce centered his gaze on his friend. "None that I care to share with you."

Michael gave him a knowing grin. "I believe I will turn in. Alex has been complaining the last half of this ride. I will be happy for him to sleep so I can get some peace."

"I do not know why you take that animal with you." Bryce threw the remark over his shoulder as he headed into the great hall without Michael.

The hall was empty and dark except for two torches burning on either sides of the hearth...and Deirdre. She sat in the chair, her legs tucked up under her. He smiled. Deirdre did not conform to the tenets of other women. And he admired that about her.

"Guid eventide, Bryce." She stretched her arms over her head and swung her legs down, straightening her gown as she did.

"Good eventide to you, lass. You have stayed up late."

She rewarded him with a timid smile. "Would you believe I could no' sleep?"

"I could not either, as I was on my horse. Although one time I did fall asleep whilst on my horse, and the results were not good."

She giggled. "I dinna believe you tell me the truth."

"Oh, 'tis true I am afraid. We rode for two days and only stopped…for necessities. I am afraid my mind thought I could ride, but my body did not agree."

"Guidness, did you get hurt?"

"Only my pride. I was young, and my father told me it was a good lesson for me to learn."

"They do say pride cometh before a fall."

Bryce chuckled. "Aye. That could have been the problem. Did you have a good day today?"

"Aye. It was much as every day. Catherine and I walked down tae the village to bring Widow Townsend food. I was pleased to see she was up today and moving around, though she is still weak."

"'Tis a good sign that she no longer lays abed."

Deirdre yawned.

"You need sleep, lass. Let me walk you to your room."

She nodded and stood. "I do believe I can sleep now."

Bryce took her arm, and she glanced up at him. He smiled, and she returned the smile.

"I am humbled you waited for my return, lass." Her concern for his safe return did something to his heart. It made him long for her to always be waiting at home for him.

"One never kens what they will run intae at night. I thought you could use my prayers."

They reached the top of the stairs, and he wanted to slow the pace. He didn't want this moment to end. Dare he believe she cared for him? "I thank you for them. The good Lord listened, for here I am."

"And I must thank Him for His answer." She yawned again, and he realized what a sacrifice it had been for her to wait up for him.

They reached her room, and he put his hand on the knob to open it but paused. She looked up at him when he didn't open the door. Those large green eyes sparkling in the torch light was his undoing. He brushed a tendril of hair away from her face and tucked it behind her ear.

She continued to gaze up at him but not with offense over his touch.

Did he dare kiss her? The echo of her words when they first met still haunted him. *I will no' touch an Englishman. I would walk first.* But the desire overcame the worry of rejection, and he lowered his head and gently brushed his lips over hers. When she didn't pull away, he leaned in for a second taste of her sweet lips as he wrapped his arms around her.

He pulled back reluctantly, not wanting to overwhelm her. He wished he could see her features more clearly.

"I have never been kissed before." Her voice was husky with emotion.

He smiled, feeling so much happiness. "And I have not desired to kiss a lass in a very long time."

Chapter 35

The morning meal was well underway, and Deirdre now replaited her hair for what seemed like the tenth time. How could she face the laird after allowing him to kiss her—not once but twice? Could she even look him in the eye? She sighed as she put the final touches on her hair.

A knock sounded on the door. Her heart stopped for a second or two, she was sure. This very well could be the death of her. "Aye." She expected to hear the laird reply.

"Milord asked me to check on you, milady. He wants to know if you are well." Lucas cracked the door, and she could only see his mouth and nose.

She smiled. "Aye, tell the laird I will be down anon. I overslept."

And well she had. Every time she woke, she could not get up to face the laird. But now—now she had no choice.

"Aye, milady." The door closed, and Lucas's footfalls grew faint.

She waited a short while, pacing the floor, then sat on the bed, looked out the window, and finally decided she must face the laird.

When she stepped into the great hall, he looked up. Sir Michael and his mother sat at the dais with him. There was no sneaking in now. She swallowed, marched forward with her head up, and sat next to Bryce.

He smiled at her. "Good morn. You slept well, I trust?"

She flashed a peek under her brow. "Perchance too well, I fear."

Deirdre focused on the bread and fish on her plate to avoid talking. Both Catherine and Sir Michael kept glancing her way, but she gave them no notice. Something bumped her, and she glanced down to see Cathal had followed her down and now rubbed against her leg.

"Deirdre." Catherine got her attention. "I thought we

could take Widow Townsend her food early today. Would you like to go when you finish eating?"

She glanced up and gave Catherine her full attention. "Aye, I will be ready anon."

"Then I shall go gather the food from Nog." Catherine pushed back her chair and rose.

Michael stood as well before addressing Bryce. "I will see you on the field then."

The lord nodded and watched as the two walked away.

When they were far enough away not to hear, he turned toward her. "You do not have to be embarrassed, lass."

His warm hand suddenly covered hers. She swallowed. Angry with herself that her throat always went dry when she got nervous, she took a drink from her cup.

"I am no' embarrassed, milord."

"Bryce," He corrected her and squeezed her hand.

She looked him in the eye this time. "I am no' embarrassed, Bryce." And as the words left her lips, a telling heat shot up her neck and into her cheeks and ears.

"Do you regret *yesternight*?"

She broke the eye contact and looked at her plate. "Nay. I dinna regret it. But I dinna ken if ..."

What exactly did she say to him? Her heart didn't regret it. Her heart would like for him to kiss her every night before she went to bed. But her head told her this desire was wrong. They were not married or even betrothed.

"You do not know what, lass?" His thumb began to trace a circle on her hand.

"I dinna ken if I should have. We are enemies."

Bryce chuckled. "Oh, lass, if only all my enemies were as sweet as you, I would live a good life."

Deirdre swallowed her last bite of food. "What will you be doing today?"

Bryce grimaced. "Today is one I dread. I must sit before the villeins and be judge for them in their disagreements. So many petty grievances that should be settled among themselves are brought to me to pass judgement on. And as much as I would like to delay this, I must see to my duties."

Her stomach knotted. She needed to come forth with the truth. Bryce deserved no less. "Perhaps this eventide we could talk...alone. I wish tae share with you some things aboot Laird Mackenzie." And tell you what a fool I have been.

Bryce gently laid his hand over hers. "Do not let this trouble you. I suspect I know more of Mackenzie than you realize. All will work out, lass. And seeing you when I finish my duties gives me another reason to look forward to this eventide." He smiled at her.

She hoped he would still feel this way about her once she told him all her secrets and what she had done. "I must go as well. 'Tis sure I am that Catherine is waiting on me—somewhere." She looked around but didn't see the older woman.

"Let us go face our day, lass." Bryce pushed his chair back and stood, then turned and drew Deirdre's chair back for her.

"Grammercy. Enjoy your day." She returned his smile.

"I am sure I will have a grand time." He gave her a rueful grin.

Deirdre found Catherine visiting with Nog, who had sent boys to gather firewood and servants to clean up.

Lifting up a cloth covering a basket filled with food, Deirdre peered in. "Is this the food for Widow Townsend?"

Cathal leapt to the table and nosed the cloth. Deirdre scooped her up and placed her back on the floor.

"Aye, it is," Catherine answered and then turned to Nog. "And I suppose we should be on our way. I told her yesterday we would be by early since we did not have much bread for her."

After saying their goodbyes, Deirdre grasped the handle and hefted it off the table.

The two made their way out to the bailey where a throng

of people had gathered to see Bryce. Merchants had returned to peddle their wares to that crowd. She and Catherine scooted around the cluster of people coming and going out of the first and the second bailey.

The road also bustled with those heading in the direction they were leaving.

"The laird will be very lucky if he finishes with his rulings before nightfall," Catherine observed.

"Aye. I think you are right. I would no' want that job. In each case, there will be one who is no' happy with him."

Catherine gave her a meaningful smile. "Some lords are so cruel that neither person leaves happy. But I have a feeling Bryce Warwick is one of the fairer lords and few will be able to fault him."

"He does seem tae be a fair laird. Something I dinna see growing up." Her uncle was always open to bribes, and she could only imagine what her father was like.

"I have experienced much the same in my years. You are a fortunate young lady to have caught the eye of this lord."

"You are mistaken, Catherine. The laird has nay more interest in me than any other." His kiss flashed through her mind.

"Do not fool yourself, child. Lord Warwick has much interest in you."

By the time they got to the village, the stream of villagers and merchants had thinned, and the street was quiet. They went to Widow Townsend's hut and tapped on the door.

"Come in." The widow sat in the only chair in the house.

Deirdre took the basket to the table and set it down. "Are you hungry?"

She turned to the widow, anticipating her response.

She smiled, showing only one missing tooth. "Bread would be nice."

Deirdre quickly pulled a hunk of bread from the loaf and took it to her.

"Thank you, deary. Can you stay and visit today?"

"We would not have it any other way," Catherine responded.

Deirdre rolled in two logs, and she and Catherine each sat on one. They visited until the widow finished her bread and seemed to tire and then excused themselves.

They took their time strolling out of town and then continued to follow the narrow road. They'd not gotten too far when hoofbeats thundered from the west.

Deirdre stopped and glanced around to find out who was forcing their horses in a mad run.

Catherine grabbed her arm. "Hurry."

Deirdre glanced at her new friend. "Why? We are on friendly soil."

Catherine looked out toward the incoming horses and riders. "We must run!"

Fear welled up inside Deirdre. She looked back toward where they'd just come. "The village is closer."

"The village is not safe. We must make the castle." Terror now filled Catherine's voice.

Deirdre dropped the basket she'd brought back with her, grabbed Catherine's hand, and ran. She was fast. She'd raced boys growing up, but Catherine was much slower. She glanced back toward what she could only assume was an enemy. They were closing the distance between them. Rosen Craig was not in view. They would never make it in time.

"We canno' make it. We must hide in the woods." Deirdre pulled her friend with her into the cover of the trees. Branches seemed to reach out and grab their clothing, impeding their progress.

"We must still run toward the castle. The trees will slow the riders down." The words came out choppy as she ran.

"A-aye." Catherine gasped.

Deirdre's heart pounded as dark memories flooded her of the last time she ran for her life in the woods. And she'd lost two friends that day.

"How do...you ken...they are...after us?" She gasped out. "We have...done nothing... wrong." This was probably foolhardiness. They were tearing their gowns on branches and briars for no reason. The men on horseback would probably continue on toward Rosen Craig. They probably had news for Bryce. She slowed, realizing the folly of it all.

Catherine now pulled her. "Do not...stop." She gasped.

Just then the horse's hooves crashed over the dry litter of forest leaves. Her knees weakened. They *were* after them. She picked up speed. Lord have mercy on them. She could not go through being caught and taken away again. These men might not be as kind as Bryce.

And how did Catherine know they wanted them?

What if it was her father? What if he'd learned she was at Rosen Craig? They had to get to the castle. To Bryce. He would save her. The fear nearly swallowed her, and her head began to spin she worried she might swoon.

"I am slowing...you down. Run...get help." Catherine pleaded.

Deirdre shook her head. "I canno'."

Tears filled Catherine's eyes. "It is our...only chance."

Deirdre let go of Catherine's hand, lifted her gown and ran like she had never run before. Though she could not see people, she must be getting closer to Rosen Craig, for she could hear voices again on the road parallel to her path.

If this was her father, she prayed he would not bother with Catherine but come for her. She didn't want her friend to suffer at her father's hand.

A scream rent the air, tempting her to turn, but she didn't. She kept running. She had to get to Bryce. She had to get his help. She could not do anything for Catherine by herself. The men on horses didn't stop. She could almost feel them upon her. She wasn't going to make it. Out of the corner of her eye she could see a sorrel horse.

Suddenly, pain split through her head as the man reached down and grasped her plaited hair. "Got her!" one rider yelled, and she was surrounded by men and horses.

Chapter 36

Deirdre peered beyond the horses to see Catherine running for the road. So they were after her. But they were not Scottish. They were not her father's men. The one knight still tugged on her plait. She closed her eyes and sent up a prayer. *Lord help us, please.*

"Get the other woman." The man spat. She opened her eyes to see a man who looked faintly familiar. He was dressed in fine raiment and light armor, and had a destrier that wore nicer equipment than her clan's clothes.

One of the knights broke from the circle they'd formed and raced toward Catherine.

"Leave her be. You have me." Deirdre still gasped as she tried to catch her breath.

The one man who seemed to be the leader snorted derisively. "And you are going to do what?"

The other men chuckled.

Catherine screamed again. Deirdre's heart sank. There was no hope for it now. Bryce would not know what happened to them.

Deirdre studied the leader. How did she know him? Was it a childhood memory? A friend of her father's? Or even her uncle's?

The knight who had gone after Catherine caught her attention. He had ahold of Catherine's thin wrists in one hand and dragged her along as he rode on his horse.

Catherine twisted and pulled. Branches hit her in the face, tearing her skin. Deirdre's heart ached for her friend.

The knight stopped and tossed Catherine into the circle of horses with her. The older woman fell to the ground. Deirdre placed her hand high on her plaited hair and jerked it from the man's handgrip and ran to Catherine. The men laughed.

She helped her friend up, but Catherine kept her head

down. Deirdre frowned. She must not show fear to these men. It emboldened them.

The leader of the group jumped off his horse and walked over to Deirdre. He ran the back side of his hand on her cheek. She lifted her chin. He'd not intimidate her.

"What is your name?"

She glared at him. "Deirdre."

"Your surname," he demanded.

Stick with your lie. "Kincaid. Deirdre Kincaid."

"Methinks not."

Could he know the truth? She'd not told anyone. Not even Catherine. She didn't respond. It was best to say as little as possible.

He put his hand under her chin and locked eyes with her. She hoped he couldn't see the fear he invoked.

Another man jumped off his horse, his feet crunching leaves and sticks as he hit the ground. "Can I have the other one?"

The knight pulled Catherine's plait, causing her head to lift. The leader glanced over at her, and his eyes grew wide. He dropped his hand from Deirdre and stepped over to Catherine.

"Can I milord?" the man begged.

So he was a laird. That was even more frightening.

The laird shoved the knight away. "Keep your hands off her."

He stared at Catherine. "Well, well, well. What do we have here? Seems the lost dog has come home."

He knew Catherine? What was going on here? Her friend remained silent.

"Are you so happy to see me you are speechless?"

"Who is she milord?" the knight who'd ask for Catherine inquired.

"This is Catherine Rothburg, my long-lost wife."

Silence fell among the knights, and Deirdre realized things did not bode well for Catherine.

Catherine glared at him. "Unhand me."

Rothburg gave her no warning. His hand slammed into her face so hard she lost her footing, landing on the ground.

"You forget to whom you speak, madam," Rothburg spat.

"Trust me, Osbertus Rothburg, I forget nothing." Catherine said the words as she pulled herself off the leaf-covered ground.

†††

Too much time had passed. Deirdre and Catherine should have returned. They'd missed the nooning meal, and with today being the day he had to sit and listen to complaints, he hadn't thought much about it. And now he didn't have that much more time before the sun would set.

With long strides he went to the kitchen. "Nog, have you seen Deirdre or Catherine?"

"Nay, milord. Not since morning when they gathered food for the widow."

"If you see either of them, tell them to find me."

"Aye, milord."

Bryce went to the stairs and climbed them two at a time. He'd checked their rooms several times already, but he'd check again. He knocked on Deirdre's door. No answer. He opened and stepped in. Nothing looked amiss. She'd not returned here. He went to Catherine's room to find the same.

His gut roiled. Something was wrong, he could feel it. He went to find Michael. His friend's mother was missing as well.

Michael was in the blacksmith shop sharpening his sword.

"Michael," Bryce called to him.

The knight made a final sweep on his sword and stood. Alex, who sat beside him as he sharpened his knife, leapt to his shoulder as he stood. He walked over to Bryce. "You look troubled."

"Your mother and Deirdre are missing."

"What do you mean, 'missing'?"

"No one has seen them since they left for Widow Townsend's place." Bryce scanned the bailey in hopes they'd returned.

"They most likely lost track of time. Or perhaps the widow has taken a turn for the worse and they stayed to care for her." Michael slid his sword in its scabbard.

"Nay. Something is telling me they are in harm's way. We ride to the village." He headed to Tempest, who grazed with Michael's destrier.

Michael fell in beside him.

Bryce stopped. "The squirrel stays."

Michael let out a low whistle. "You are worried. Is anyone else riding with us?"

"I'll gather the horses. If you see Hugh, Ranald, and Roger, I want them to ride along."

Michael sprang to action, and Bryce went to gather the mounts and equipment. The men met in the bailey and rode out.

"Is this why my mother wanted me with her? I wonder if she fears someone. And perhaps this person she fears has followed her here and taken the opportunity when presented to abduct her, and Deirdre, because she was with her."

"'Tis hard to say what has happened. There are so many possibilities it frightens me."

"Her uncle could have discovered Deirdre was here, and Catherine was taken to keep her quiet." Or if his suspicions were right, Mackenzie may have discovered his "dead" daughter lived and she lived at Rosen Craig. He'd done a little bit of investigating to discover Mackenzie once had a daughter near Deirdre's age.

"Aye. None of the possibilities sound good." Michael kicked his horse into a trot and the rest followed suit.

Once in the village, they rode to the widow's home. Bryce and Michael both dismounted, and the other three waited.

Bryce knocked.

"Who is there?" A shaky voice asked.

"'Tis Laird Warwick."

"Come in."

Bryce opened the door. The pale woman started to rise from her chair.

"Nay. Stay seated. Did you have visitors here today bringing you food?"

The woman sunk back into her chair. She hesitated.

"We cannot find them." Bryce hoped to put her mind to ease.

She nodded. "Those angels bring me food every day since I got sick."

"Did they stay long?"

"Nay. They talked for a short bit and then went on their way."

"Did they say where they were going when they left?" Bryce knew what the answer would be.

"Nay, milord. They just wished me well and left. I thought they were headed back to Rosen Craig."

Bryce and Michael walked over to where the others sat on their horses. "We need to go to each home and speak with everyone inside. Find out if they saw Deirdre or Michael's mother today."

The men split up. By the time they had talked to everyone in the village, darkness had fallen. Several had seen them leave, some said they heard a scream but that was all. Bryce wanted to continue searching but he had no idea where to look. His gut twisted as his heart tightened. What was happening to her? He didn't want to imagine what life would be like without Deirdre.

†††

Deirdre jumped from the bed as Catherine was shoved through the opening and fell on the floor. The door slammed behind her.

Deirdre rushed over, helping her friend up. "Are you

hurt?"

A large lump had risen on her cheekbone, and her eye had a rosy hue to it. She touched it, and Catherine winced. "He did this to you?" Her lip was already torn and bleeding from when he hit her in the woods.

"I will be fine. 'Tis nothing I have not faced before." With Deirdre's help, she hobbled to the bed and sat.

"This is terrible that he would do such a thing. I thought he looked familiar." Deirdre paced the floor in front of Catherine.

"Shhh." Catherine motioned for her to come near. "The walls have ears," she whispered.

Deirdre glanced around the room in search of someone listening. "I dinna see anyone," she whispered back.

"Trust me. I know. They are out there listening." She kept her voice so low Deirdre had to lean in closer to hear. "What you were about to say? Osbertus looked familiar?"

"Aye." Deirdre nodded, keeping her voice a whisper. "Michael looks very much like him. I am surprised Bryce— er, Laird Warwick has no' seen the resemblance."

Catherine smiled. "You do not have to hide your attraction for him from me. I have seen it blooming. I do not believe Bryce has seen Osbertus much. Perhaps at Parliament a few times."

"How long ago...did you run away?" Their stories were different but very much the same.

She glanced around. "I had just suspected I carried Michael. I could not risk my baby's life in the hands of such a cruel man." She kept her voice to a whisper. "You must never tell him he has a son."

"Do you no' think he will find oot now?" Surely Bryce and Michael would come looking for them.

"I can only pray he does not. He will never let me go now that he has found me."

"This is your secret?" She didn't really need to ask. It was a secret like hers that instilled fear at being discovered.

And now Catherine had to face that fear.

"Aye. As I told Bryce, we all have our secrets. Even you, lass. I can see you want to tell someone. Does your secret have something to do with why my husband wanted you?"

"I fear so, but I dinna ken how he would ken. I have no' told anyone. 'Tis been my secret alone."

"Who are you," Catherine asked, "that Rothburg would risk so much to capture you. And for what?"

Deirdre glanced around at the walls that Catherine said had ears, and she shivered. No one must hear. She continued to keep her voice down. "'Tis a vera long story. And I am fearful tae say tae much. If he kens who I am, I dinna ken what will happen tae me. For I am the daughter of Laird Mackenzie."

Catherine's brows rose, and her eyes grew wide. "The Laird Mackenzie who visited Rosen Craig?"

"Aye. 'Tis why I did no' come around. I was a young child the last time I saw him, but I dinna ken if I look like him or my mother. I could no' take a chance."

"And he is cruel? He seemed like a nice man, but then many who meet Rothburg think the same. Men like that know how to charm people and hide who they really are."

"'Tis true." Deirdre shivered. "And tae think I believed that was how Bryce was when I met him. But he is no' like any of the lairds in my life."

"We will pray Rothburg does not know your real identity and that he does not discover it. Is there any other reason he might have to bring you here?"

Deirdre shook her head. "Nay. I dinna believe so."

The door swung open and banged against the wall, causing Deirdre and Catherine both to jump.

Rothburg stood in the doorway sneering. "What are you two whispering about?"

Chapter 37

One sennight had passed. Bryce, Michael and half his men had been out searching. There were many people in and out of Rosen Craig the day the ladies went missing and many of them peddlers. They'd gone to the village and spoke with every person who'd come to see him with a complaint. No one had any new information.

Bryce and Michael were the last ones back to Rosen Craig this day. The men were in the great hall eating when they arrived.

Bryce walked into the room and stood on the dais to get their attention. The room slowly quieted.

He asked the same question he had asked every day. "Do any of you have any news?"

A lot of heads shook, some rumblings of nay, but no one spoke up.

Bryce took his seat, his heart heavy.

"Milord." Lucas walked up to the dais.

"Nay, Lucas. We have not found her, yet."

The lad shook his head. "Milord, I know you told me not to leave, but I could not stay here when milady might be in danger. I went to the village."

Bryce was tired. He had not the inclination to deal with the boy. "'Tis understandable, Lucas. We are all worried. In the future, you need to obey orders—especially if you want to be a knight someday. Obeying orders is important. Your lord needs to know he can trust you to do what he tells you. Do you understand?"

"Aye, milord."

"You can go eat now, Lucas."

"But, milord, I want to tell you I talked to someone who saw milady."

Bryce's heart hiccupped and then reality set in. They had knocked on every door in the village. They had talked to every person in every household, going back several days in a row to accomplish that. They questioned every merchant who came through Rosen Craig's gate, and not one had seen anything.

Bryce sighed and motioned for Lucas to come up on the dais. "Who did you talk to?"

"I talked to Crowder, milord."

Crowder was an odd man who lived in the forest. He often talked to himself. A man didn't find Crowder if he didn't want to be found. He was unusual, to be sure, but he was harmless and kept to himself. Occasionally when he didn't have food, he came to Rosen Craig and begged for something to eat. Nog was always generous with him. One year the weather was extremely cold, and he came to ask for a blanket. Nog gave him a blanket and let him sleep in by the kitchen fire. The man would not hurt anyone.

"How did you happen to talk to Crowder? Did you find him, or did he find you?"

A deep blush covered the boy's face. He dropped his head. "I was sitting on the side of the trail on the fallen tree where it crosses over the road leading to the village." He looked up at Bryce.

"Go ahead, lad." Bryce knew where the path crossed the road and where the tree had fallen.

"There may have been some moisture in my eyes. He heard me, and he came out of the woods and asked me why—what was wrong."

So the lad had been crying. Bryce hadn't thought about how Lucas would take her disappearance. But he should have. The lad was fond of her and very protective.

"What did he say about Deirdre, lad?"

"I told him I was searching for milady. That she has been missing for a sennight. I told him how you and your knights have gone through the village several times asking everyone if they'd seen her." Lucas's eyes became misty.

"What did he say, Lucas? Did he see something?"

"Aye, milord. He said he was sleeping in the woods when he heard horses come crashing through. He hid. But he saw several men on horses, and they captured Milady and Lady Catherine and rode off with them."

"Did he know which way they went when they left?"

"He said they went out of the woods the same way they came."

"Did he say anything else?"

"One of the men hit Lady Catherine."

"Thank you, Lucas. You can go eat."

Lucas stepped down off the dais.

"And Lucas."

He turned. "Aye, milord."

"You are not to disobey me again. I appreciate your help, but I will not allow you to risk your life. We do not know who these men are and what they want or what they are capable of doing."

"Aye, milord."

Bryce sat back down at the table, thankful nothing had happened to the boy. "What are your thoughts?" he asked Michael.

"Do you think the boy tells the truth?"

Bryce nodded. "Aye. I do. But what of Crowder? Did he see your mother and Deirdre or tell the boy this to stop his crying?"

"But if he only tried to appease the boy, would he have told him they were taken against their will?"

"You have a good point. I have not known Crowder to spread untruths, but the man is peculiar. He remains detached from society and other people. 'Tis surprised I am that he spoke with Lucas. He does not care to be around others."

"This news helps us not." Michael stabbed a piece of venison a bit harder than needed.

"It does confirm our suspicions. The ladies did not go willingly. Now we must figure out who would want them and why."

"Perchance they have been taken for ransom."

"A sennight has passed. If they were taken for ransom, I would expect we would have heard from them by now."

"Unless things did not go as they had planned, and injury or death befell them. You know as well as I that Deirdre and my mother both can be determined." Michael's jaw flexed. "When I find this person who struck my mother, he will pay for his crime against her."

"We will not think that way, Michael. We will continue to search until we find them. In the morn, I will send out men to ride to the neighboring lords and ask questions."

"Borderland as well?"

"If they are not found here, then aye. We will go north. But we have no reason to believe that any of Deirdre's people even know she is still alive, let alone at Rosen Craig."

"Perchance this has to do with my mother. She has been persistent wanting me to return with her. I do believe she felt threatened."

"I have thought that as well."

"Will you go to Rothburg? He is your adversary."

"Would he be foolish enough to jeopardize all he has by capturing two women from here?"

Michael shrugged. "One would think not."

"I cannot believe the man would be so foolish. But I will not leave a stone unturned."

"On the morrow we will find Crowder and see if he can tell us more."

†††

The door swung open and Rothburg stepped inside without warning. "You will come with me, wife."

Catherine glared at him. "Your wife is dead."

Rothburg lashed out so quickly Deirdre never saw it coming or she'd have tried to stop him. The back of his hand hit Catherine so hard she came off her feet and landed on the floor.

"You need to learn your manners," Rothburg spat. "I can

see being away from me has done you no good."

Catherine pulled herself off the bedroom floor.

He grabbed her arm and pulled her out. Once again Deirdre was left alone. Rothburg had spoken very little to her since their arrival. But rarely a day passed when Catherine wasn't taken from their room.

Deirdre fell asleep sitting in the sunshine. They were treated much like prisoners, and well they were. They could not leave the room in which they were locked. The food that was brought was the food of peasants—pottage made from peas, beans, and onions. Something she had grown accustomed to growing up. But she had been spoiled since living at Rosen Craig. They were given nothing for their comfort. No water to wash in, no change of clothes.

She and Catherine were able to talk very little due to the spies listening to their conversations. 'Twas hard to believe her friend was the wife of such a wicked man.

Later that day, the door opened, and Catherine was shoved through the doorway. Deirdre jumped up and rushed toward her.

"Did he hurt you?" The ruddy handprint on her check told her he had.

"Do not worry yourself, Deirdre. 'Tis something I had grown accustom to before I left."

"But you have been gone a vera long time. 'Tis not right that he does this tae you. What did he want this day?"

Catherine gave her a sad smile. "He believes I keep something from him. He thinks I left him because of a man. He wants me to tell him his name."

"But you did no' leave him because—" the warning in Catherine's eyes reminded her to watch her words. "—of another man. Does he no' ken that a woman tires of being treated nay better than a dog?"

Catherine touched the handprint on her face. "He does not think a woman is much better than a dog, I am afraid. He wishes to know where I have been and everything I have done since I walked out the doors of Wolves Forest twenty some years ago."

"And you have told him where you were?"

"I told him I do not recall. I have been like a gypsy traveling around. I have had no place to call home."

Deirdre frowned. No wonder he continued to have her brought to him. Rothburg could see through her friend's lie. Catherine's dress was what an upper-class woman would wear. She held herself as an aristocrat, and she spoke to people as though she was not used to being told no.

Deirdre walked to the window, resting her arms on the stone sill, as they'd agreed to do if they wanted to talk.

Shortly, Catherine came to stand beside her, and she too, looked out the window.

"Perchance you should tell him where you have been tae stop these beatings," Deirdre suggested.

"Never," she whispered back. "If he knew where I resided, it would not take much to learn everything. I will not lose that which I have protected my whole life."

"Do you no' think that Michael can look oot for himself? He is a grown man, a knight, and from what I have seen on the practice field, one of Bryce's best. You should no' put your life at risk when Michael can see tae his own."

"Osbertus has many men. He does not fight fair. You have heard how much he hates Bryce and his family. Michael is Bryce's closest friend. How do you think he will feel about that?"

Deirdre gazed out the window that was several floors up. She'd not try to climb down this one as she had Rosen Craig. But she must form a plan of escape because no one knew where they were.

"But Michael is his son. His only son. You canno' tell me that even a man like Rothburg does no' wish for a son tae carry on his legacy."

Catherine let out a half-snort, half-laugh. "He will say Michael is not his. He will never believe that I was with child when I ran from here. And if he did believe Michael is his, he may consider him a threat, that his heir might try to overthrow him."

Deirdre turned to look at Catherine. "He canno' deny him. Michael looks vera much like him."

"It is of no concern. I do not wish for him to ever know he has a son."

"You will keep subjecting yourself tae your husband's cruelty tae protect a grown man who does no' need protecting? One time, Rothburg may go tae far."

"I will try to befriend one of the servants. Perhaps they will be able to get word to Bryce that we are here."

"Does Rothburg ken who I am?"

"Oh, child." Catherine covered Deirdre's hand with hers. "He not only knows who you are, you are the reason we are both here."

Chapter 38

Crowder proved to be harder to find than Bryce had thought. The man was not to be found if he didn't want to be. As the days turned to nights and then to days again with still no sign of Crowder and no news from surrounding lords questioned, Bryce's hope began to fade. He wouldn't ever give up, but unless God intervened, he feared he'd spend his life searching and still never see Deirdre again.

Bryce stepped out of Rosen Craig to begin another day he hoped would be more fruitful. Michael hastened his way and, by the concerned look on his face, he came with bad news. He didn't need any more of that. It seemed ever since that fateful day he lost his parents, only evil tiding had filled his life. He stood at the top of the steps, waiting for Michael.

"Go back inside," Michael ordered.

Bryce frowned. "What is this about?"

Michael grabbed his arm as he passed him and tugged him back through the door. "The king's men are here at the portcullis, and they have come to arrest you for treason. They say they have a letter proving the charges. Hugh and Ranald stand at the gate impeding their entry."

"What? I have not been foolish enough to put anything in a missive. And the king is in Ireland. What is this foolishness?"

"King or not, I saw your seal on the missive. They are on their way in now to arrest you. You must go out through the bolt hole. Go to Hawkwood."

Bryce shook his head. "Nay. The first place they would look is there. I will not bring disaster down on my brother and his family."

"Are you not hearing me, Bryce? You need to go *now*."

"Nay. Rosen Craig belongs to me. I will not leave my people to the king's men. If I am not here, they will try to force my whereabouts out of my people. I will not endanger their lives to save mine."

"What will happen to your people if you are hanged for treason? The king will install one of his favorites here. And we both know what kind of men they are."

The pounding of hooves and commotion in the bailey drew his attention. He turned toward the large wooden door separating him from his fate. He gave Michael an apologetic smile. His gut twisted, and his heart pounded like the stomping horses outside. Would he ever see Rosen Craig again? Would he ever see Deirdre? "I fear my time has come."

The doors flew open and a dozen or more of the king's men rushed in like ants to a fallen morsel of bread. They stood in front of him.

One man came forward holding a paper. "Bryce Warwick?"

"Aye." Bryce answered.

The man held up the paper. "Bryce Warwick of Rosen Craig, you are being arrested for treason against the crown and our king."

Bryce folded his arms in front of him. "May I see this evidence that you have?"

The man reached into a leather pouch he carried and pulled out a missive. Bryce recognized the broken seal. It was his. The man didn't hand him the document, but instead he held it for him to see. The words were incriminating for sure, but they were not penned by him.

"Surrender your sword, sir."

Bryce gave his sword to Michael.

"You may gather items you will need." The leader nodded to one of the other men, and he came and stood by Bryce.

He needed to go over many things with Michael but had no time. He'd faced death before, and he feared that he would face it again.

"Michael, come with me," Bryce ordered.

"You will leave your weapon as well, sir." The man in charge spoke to Michael.

Michael took both of their swords and handed them to one of Bryce's knights before he and Bryce walked toward the stairs that led to Bryce's room.

Bryce inclined his head to give Michael a discrete message. "Go to Royce. Inform him of what has taken place. Do not stop searching for your mother and Deirdre. You must not give up. When we get to my room, I will see if my signet ring is there. Someone must have taken it and used it. I did not write that missive, as well you know. I will leave you in charge of Rosen Craig until you get to Royce and he makes that decision."

"Aye, my friend, you know I will do as you ask. We will find out who has betrayed you as well. And woe is that man."

When they reached his room, Bryce quickly gathered a few items. He made his way to the mantle where he kept his signet ring. The cloth bag was there. He scooped it up, surprised by the lightness of it. He squeezed his hand around it. Empty. He tossed the bag to Michael. "Find out who has been in my room, and you will find my betrayer."

Michael caught the empty bag and gave him a somber nod. "Aye. I will find him, my friend."

As he rode out through the gates of Rosen Craig, Bryce turned back to take a last look. Perchance the king was right. Perhaps Rosen Craig was cursed.

†††

How could her life go from one calamity to another? It seemed she was doomed to repeated misfortunes. Catherine had been taken from their room early in the day and, with darkness upon them, still hadn't returned.

She'd given up on Bryce or Michael finding them. A fortnight or longer had passed, and there was no sign of anyone searching for them at Wolves Forest. Michael, not knowing that Rothburg was his father, would not know to search here. She pushed up from the chair and strolled to the window. The days were long with nothing to do and much of the time no one to talk to.

The clear moonlit sky allowed her to see shadows of people in the courtyard. Knights walked the catwalk, guarding the castle. Someone like Rothburg probably never felt safe. He certainly didn't seem to mind making enemies.

Hard as she tried, she'd still not come up with an escape plan. Never leaving the room in which she was confined left her few options. She'd talked to Catherine about what she might do, but she was never left alone when allowed out of her room.

She wasn't sure why Rothburg hadn't already made a deal with her father, but she was sure it was because it did not fit in his plan…yet. If he'd gone to the trouble of capturing her, then it would happen when it would best benefit him.

Deirdre went to the bed and lay on it. The room was dark. They gave her nothing for light. She closed her eyes and started to drift off to sleep, remembering Bryce's kiss. If only she could feel his strong arms around her again.

The creak of the door woke her, and she sat up. "Catherine?" Her heart galloped in her chest.

"Aye. 'Tis me," Catherine answered, sounding exhausted.

She swung her feet to the floor. Rothburg stood beside her holding a candle. Deirdre searched her friend's face for signs of abuse. But no new physical marks were there. What she could see was a woman who looked defeated. Her heart ached for her friend as well as herself.

"I'm glad to see you are awake, Deirdre." Rothburg's voice boomed into the once silent room.

She stood, not wanting to show any signs of weakness. "And why would that be?"

"I wanted to come and thank you myself." He chuckled.

"Thank me?" The man had to be daft. Or perhaps he wanted to thank her for having his wife along when he captured her.

"Aye. I want to thank you for insuring Warwick's hanging."

"What do you speak aboot?" A knot formed in her gut.

"Why, the signet ring, my dear. I could not have done it without you. That tiny matter of a seal had me perplexed, but when you provided that means you *sealed* his fate." He snickered at his joke.

Deirdre thought she might be sick. "Th—that ring was—" She stopped herself.

"To stop your father from coming?" He laughed again. "Oh, my dear, how trusting you are. There was never a missive sent to your father. I needed that ring to create a treasonous act performed by Warwick."

Catherine rushed over and engulfed her with a hug.

"Well, I shall leave you ladies to yourselves. I see you have much to discuss." With that he closed the door and the lock clicked into place.

Tears flowed down her face as she tried to breathe. What had she done?

"Shh." Catherine rocked back and forth as she crooned to her. "You did not know, child."

"What Bryce must think of me, if he kens. I deserve whatever fate is bestowed upon me." Deirdre sobbed.

"Nay. You are innocent. Rothburg is the one who has turned this to evil."

Deirdre leaned back. "Finley! Finley must work for Rothburg. He is the one who told me if I got Bryce's signet ring, he could stop my father from coming."

"Aye. I have seen him here talking to Osbertus. He is an evil man as well."

"May God have mercy on my soul for what I have done."

"Your only fault was trusting your countryman. Come to bed. We will figure something out, but we need clear heads to do so."

Deirdre climbed onto the bed, and Catherine wrapped her arms around her, just like so many times she'd wished she had a mother who could. Catherine was the closest thing to a mother she could remember.

"I dinna see how we can escape or help Bryce," Deirdre whispered. She'd lost all hope.

"We must spend time in thought and prayer. And I may have to tell Osbertus he has a son."

Chapter 39

The irony of conspiracy. He'd been ever so careful not to write one missive so there could be no proof of his loyalty to Henry and not Richard. And yet a treasonous letter not penned by him was used against him as though he had written it.

And then to be held at Dunstanburgh Castle, one of the reasons he'd turned his back on his king. Here he bided the time he had left at the very castle that would still belong to Henry, had not Richard seized all Gaunt's lands.

A fine castle to be sure. One he'd visited on many occasions. Happier occasions. Only a three-day ride from Rosen Craig. Word would travel fast. Michael would deliver news to him of Deirdre and of Royce all the more swiftly.

Bryce could not complain of the treatment he'd received thus far. But then, he was nobility, and though he might die by hanging or beheading, he would be treated well until that day. Truly he could get no answers from any of the men who brought him here or from any he'd seen up until now.

The letter that was discovered seemed to be written to no certain person or have no true purpose other than to have him arrested for treason. But proving his innocence of writing the missive could be difficult, especially considering that he had committed what the king would call treason.

As the days passed, Bryce was given several rooms in the western most tower. What good were rooms when there was naught to do? These days of no activity were sure to cause him to go daft.

He paced the floor worrying about Deirdre. How could God do this to him? He needed to be out looking for her and Catherine, and instead he was imprisoned for something he had not done. Perchance he should try to overpower his guard. If he managed to do so, he could get back to Rosen Craig and their search, and if not, he might be lucky enough to die before he became a raving lunatic.

Why hadn't Michael come to give him news? Or had he, and he wasn't allowed to see him? Michael would have gone to Royce by now. And he wouldn't have given up the search for his mother and Deirdre.

Bryce was allowed to come down to the hall and eat with the men. He sat beside Peter Gatelond, the master-at-arms, as he had every day since he'd arrived. "Any news on when Richard returns?" Bryce asked the man before stabbing a piece of meat and eating it.

"Nay. We do not hear much. I am usually one of the last to get any information." The man seemed much of the same nature as himself.

"I am in no hurry for his return." Bryce grinned.

The master-at-arms chuckled. "I do not imagine you wish to ever see our king return."

Something in the man spoke of his honor. When the men around them had finished and left the table, Bryce thought to get information. "What have you heard about me?"

Gatelond shrugged. "Your brother inherited your title at the untimely death of your father. You were thought to be dead as well. You returned a year after your father's death to claim the title from your brother."

Bryce frowned. "'Tis not what I ask, and well you know."

The corner of Gatelond's mouth twitched. "What is it you ask?"

"Have you heard who accuses me of writing this treasonous missive?" People talk. There had to be more than one person involved in the treachery. He suspected Rothburg was behind it. But he wouldn't offer a name.

"'Tis always best to keep your head down. Keeps you out of trouble. But I will ask around."

"'Tis much appreciated. I am sure all say they are innocent. I have done many things in my life, but of penning this letter of treason I am innocent."

The master-at-arms leveled an intense gaze on Bryce. "I believe I am a good judge of a man's honor. I believe that you did not send it." He took a few more bites of his food and then took a drink from his mug. He set it down with a thud. "I will ask around and see who this person is who has accused you and has no honor."

"Again, many thanks," Bryce replied. "Am I allowed visitors?"

Gatelond nodded. "Aye. As long as they come unarmed." He smiled.

Bryce wasn't sure if that was good news or not. He'd have to wait to find out what held Michael from coming.

†††

One of the knights whose duty was to stand guard knocked on his door and opened it, stepping in. "Someone to see you."

He stood aside, and Michael strode in. The grave look on his friend's face did not bode well.

Bryce turned to the guard. "You can leave."

The guard closed the door, and Michael came over to him. "How do you hold up?"

"I am going mad with worry. Any news of your mother and Deirdre? Come, sit down." He led Michael over to the only two chairs in the room.

"Nay, we still search. We found Crowder, but he can tell us little other than they were taken by force."

"That we had already surmised. Did you tell Royce I have been imprisoned for treason?"

"Aye. He is asking around and meeting with trustworthy lords in an attempt to find who wrote this treasonous letter in your name." Worry lines etched the skin around Michael's eyes.

Bryce leaned back. "Then that is all we can do. You must keep searching. I have had much time to think. Rothburg went to the trouble of raiding Scottish land in my name to anger the king. He hoped to have the king's ear, but

Richard did nothing. Methinks he could be behind this missive and perhaps Deirdre's and your mother's disappearance."

Michael leveled his gaze on Bryce. "I think you are right. I have news that I wish I did not have to share."

Bryce's gut knotted. Not more bad news. Not when he could do nothing to fix it.

Michael leaned forward and rested his forearms on his thighs. He clasped his hands and stared at his fists but said nothing.

"What is it, man?"

Michael looked up with somber eyes. "It's Rosen Craig. Rothburg has seized the demesne."

Bryce flew from his chair. "What say you?"

"Aye. I gathered over a dozen men. We rode to villages and keeps inquiring about my mother and Deirdre. When we returned, we were stopped by Ranald before we reached the keep. He told us Rosen Craig was now under Rothburg's rule."

Bryce paced the floor. "How can this be? The audacity of the man. No king will allow this. We are not an uncivilized nation."

Michael cleared his throat. "Richard is in Ireland. Rothburg has Richard's ear. You have been accused of treason. I believe Rothburg may have figured out a way to get what he wants without the king's wrath."

"I must leave. I cannot stay here when Rosen Craig is in jeopardy."

"You cannot leave, Bryce. Listen to yourself. Do you think they would not know where you go? That would give Rothburg an opportunity to kill you without a trial."

"Does Royce know of Rosen Craig's fall?" How could all this be happening to him? It made him question whether God had suddenly turned his back on him that fateful day a year ago when he nearly died.

"I sent Ranald and Hugh to Hawkwood to inform Royce.

I came here to find out what you wish me to do." Concern etched Michael's brow.

Bryce sat down to gather his thoughts, feeling he might jump out of his skin. He got up and began to pace again. He had lost control of his life. How had this happened? He must make sure Catherine and Deirdre were safe before…he swallowed. Before he faced his trial. And he must see to the people of Rosen Craig's safety.

Bryce turned to Michael. "'Tis not a good feeling to be facing death again and to have so many lives in peril."

"Do not give up hope, my friend. I do not believe God is finished with you."

The words did help his spirit. "I hope not."

"What do you wish me to do, Bryce?"

"Where are the men who were not in Rosen Craig when it was sieged?"

"They continue to search for the women."

Bryce nodded. "Very good. Have one man slip in through the bolt hole and see how things fair at Rosen Craig. Have him find any weaknesses. Speak with Nog and Millicent. They can be valuable if we need a sleeping draught. Then have him take this news to Royce." Bryce took in a deep breath trying to clear his mind of anything but what he needed to apprise his friend of. "And Michael, have him see how my people are treated by Rothburg's men."

"Aye, I will do all that you ask. Do not give up hope. We will find and prove the truth of who is behind this, my friend."

"The more I have time to think, the more I am inclined to believe I am right and that everything that has befallen us has to do with Rothburg. But how to stop a man who has the king's ear?"

Chapter 40

July 1399

Though Catherine spent every day attempting to lift her spirits, Deirdre could not forgive herself for the misfortune she'd brought upon Bryce. Every time she saw Rothburg, he was a happy man. He seemed to delight in the fate of Bryce.

And his pleasure continued to be a reminder of what she'd done. He even allowed her and Catherine out of their room on occasion. But much like Bryce had done when she'd first been captured, they were followed closely by one of his men.

"Catherine, is there no' a way of escape from here?" She asked as her friend plaited her hair for her. "I thought perchance, since you have lived here before, you might remember an opening that one could slip through."

"I was young when I lived here, and it has been many years, nigh on to twenty-eight. I do not remember much of this place. I spent many years trying to forget my life here. I eventually was able to put this place behind me."

"Now that you are here, has it caused you tae remember anything we might find helpful? If I could get tae the king, I might tell him I took the ring, and I gave it tae Finley. Maybe the king would release Bryce."

On a day when Rothburg allowed them freedom, their room was left unlocked. They departed the confines of their room. Walking in the sunshine helped Deirdre. Her mind had no rest from what she had done to the man who'd only been kind to her.

They'd not walked halfway around the inner baily when Deirdre spotted Finley. Anger she'd held pent up for a fortnight boiled inside her. She hiked her gown, the only gown she'd worn since she arrived, and ran toward the man.

He continued to walk, ignoring her as she reached him. "You!" She yelled at him. "You are nay better than a dog.

Nay, you are no' even as guid as a dog. They are loyal."

He stopped and turned. "Careful, lassie, you are nay longer under Warwick's protection."

Protection. Perhaps she could use the king's words to free her and Catherine. "King Richard gave me his word I would be under his protection."

Finley laughed. "Do you see the king here? He is in Ireland. I dinna think he will be helping you, lass."

"I will still speak the truth. You lied tae me, and you betrayed me as well as your laird. You are a snake."

His hand flew out so quickly she felt it before she realized what was about to happen. Her feet went out from beneath her, and she landed on her backside. Pain shot through her jaw and into her temple. The metallic taste of blood filled her mouth. She pushed herself to her knees and a searing bolt laced up her back from her hip. She'd not let him see any weakness. She stood.

Gathering herself together, she spit the blood from her mouth and looked him in the eye. "Och, you are a braw man, hitting a defenseless woman. You didno' deserve to serve under the laird of Rosen Craig."

Finley glared at her. "Dinna be foolish, lass. Shut your mouth before you anger me."

Her words troubled him, or he'd not have hit her. Perhaps she could reach him—make him see the truth of what he'd done. So great was her ire and her desire to make him understand, she'd risk it again.

"I will speak the truth of you. 'Tis ashamed I am tae call you a fellow Scotsman. You are a blight tae our people..."

Before she could finish all she wanted to say to him, Catherine grabbed her arm and tugged her away, causing her to stumble.

"Has the devil stolen your mind? We do not need more enemies here than we already have." Catherine continued to pull her along as she scolded her.

"Listen to the woman, Deirdre. Otherwise, I may tell her

secret as well." Finley snickered.

Catherine went pale. "My secret?"

"Aye, your son." He grinned. "'Tis our little secret, eh? That is, until it benefits me to tell Rothburg."

Catherine pulled her away and toward the keep.

"He is the reason we are here. He is the reason Bryce could die. He is the reason you may have to tell your husband he has a son." A lump rose in her throat as she swallowed back the tears. She could blame Finley all she wanted, but had she not been so naïve, he'd never have gotten the laird's signet ring from her. And if she had trusted the Lord to protect her from her father, she'd never had felt the need to steal the ring.

"Come. 'Tis time to get back to our room. I do not wish to give the man a reason to tell Rothburg of Michael. If he is to find out, I wish it to be from me." Catherine continued to tug her along.

"Nay. We have no' been oot in the sunshine long. I am no' wishing tae go back in and sit in that room. I will no' speak to Finley again." She was not ready to give up the breeze, fresh air, and sunshine and go back into their stuffy room.

"'Tis best. Rothburg will hear of what you've done. Many of the men watched. He knows all that goes on in his keep."

Deirdre followed along, feeling much like a chastised child. She did not wish to bring more problems on Catherine. She would pray that Rothburg wouldn't hold his wife accountable for Deirdre's actions.

Once back in the room, Deirdre curled up on the bed. Her jaw throbbed, and her hip ached where she'd fallen on it. She closed her eyes, trying to form a plan of escape. If only Rothburg would allow them out on days that the merchants came to Wolves Forest, she could attempt escape then or have one of the vendors go to Rosen Craig.

But Rothburg chose the days they could leave their room

carefully.

When Deirdre opened her eyes, the room was dark. She put her arm out, feeling the bed for Catherine, but it was empty. "Catherine?" Deirdre called out into the darkness as she sat up. "Catherine? Are you there?"

Only silence answered her question. She climbed under the thin blanket given to them and curled back up waiting for her friend.

In the wee hours of the morning when the sun had just broken over the horizon, giving a red glow to the sky, Deirdre rubbed her eyes and rolled to her side. Catherine sat in a chair.

"Have you been up all night?" Deirdre pushed herself up and swung her feet to the floor before stretching her arms over her head.

"Aye. I could not sleep. I lay there 'til the sun began to rise. 'Tis sorry I am I woke you." Catherine's feet were tucked up under her in the chair.

Deirdre walked over and sat down. "Where did you go *yestereve*? I woke, and you were no' here."

Catherine snorted. "Is there any place I can go? Rothburg requested my presence at the evening meal and then wanted to reminisce about old times."

"Is this why you could no' sleep?"

"Nay, 'tis what I heard whilst I was at the meal. I do not know if it was Rothburg's intention for me to hear or not. But truly it is troubling."

Deirdre's stomach roiled. "What did you hear?"

"Henry has landed in Ravenspur and marches south, garnering support from his nobles."

"That is important, why?"

"From what I heard, some believe he has come to do more that reclaim his rights as Duke of Lancaster."

"I dinna understand." She remembered Bryce speaking of Henry, but she couldn't recall what he'd said.

"Richard banished Henry. 'Tis a long story but I will tell

you that was Richard's downfall. He took all of what was John of Gaunt's and should have been Henry's. Now that Richard is in Ireland, Henry has come to reclaim all that was taken from him."

"And why does this trouble you, Catherine?" The English could be hard to understand at times.

"Henry is garnering much support. More than is needed to reclaim his rights."

"Aye, and this could bring battles tae your people?"

Catherine snorted. "Let me say it this way. From what the men spoke of last night, Henry may be here to take the throne from King Richard."

"And who do you wish tae see as your king?" Richard seemed like a good enough king to her. But she didn't know how good and fair he was to his people.

"I wish it were only about who I would like as king. I am afraid it is much more than that."

Deirdre yawned and stretched, again. "Oh? And how is that?"

Catherine leaned over and took Deirdre's hand. "I overheard one of the knights saying that Osbertus was trying to push for Bryce's immediate execution."

Deirdre gasped.

Catherine squeezed her hand. "With Bryce being considered a traitor, I fear that some men loyal to King Richard very well may be convinced to move forward since the king himself is not here."

Chapter 41

Royce Warwick pushed his horse and his men to reach Henry Bolingbroke before he pressed farther south. Michael rode along with him, as well as Royce's men and the handful of Rosen Craig's knights not held by Rothburg.

"I pray Henry will settle this quickly," Royce yelled out as they rode. "If not, we could be fighting our fellow countrymen."

"Aye," Michael answered as he urged his destrier up beside Royce. "Perchance with Richard still in Ireland, Henry will garner enough support that Richard will relinquish the throne."

"'Tis my hope as well."

They rode on for another hour until the horses needed water and he and his men needed a rest. But Bryce's life hung in the balance. They crested a hill. The view below him gave him pause—hundreds of mounted men.

"I believe we have found them." Michael grinned as he kicked his horse into a canter.

"Aye, I believe we have." Royce replied to no one but himself, for Michael was four horse lengths ahead.

Bolingbroke broke off from his men and came their way.

As they neared each other, Royce raised his hand in acknowledgement of the duke. "Bolingbroke, what brings you back to England's shores?"

Henry grinned. "To reclaim what has been wrongfully taken from me."

"Just your duchy and lands?"

"Seems I have much support to move this country forward as well. We shall see as we continue to move across the land where loyalties lie."

"You know you have mine as well as Bryce's."

Henry glanced past him. "Where is that brother of yours? I heard he entertained Richard for a sennight."

"Aye, he did. Richard questioned Bryce's loyalty but nothing more. Rothburg told Richard that Rosen Craig reived the borderland. As you know, Rothburg has Richard's ear, and the greedy nobleman still wants Rosen Craig."

"And you have not come all this way just to wish me well. Do you have news for me?" Henry asked.

"Bryce is held at Dunstanburgh Castle on treason."

"Treason? What has transpired of which I am not aware?"

"His signet ring was stolen. We believe Rothburg was behind it. A treasonous missive created with Bryce's seal. Word has it Rothburg has gone to Dunstanburgh and is pushing to have Bryce hanged without trial due to your return, and even now he fears you garner support against Richard."

"Then we ride to Dunstanburgh. 'Tis rightfully mine as part of the Duchy. Father may have lost interest in the place when he gave up his role as Lieutenant of the Marches, but 'tis a good place to let Rothburg understand I am not my father."

†††

Royce and a small portion of his men rode on ahead and entered Dunstanburgh Castle with no resistance. Had Michael not been there to see Bryce before and been able to freely leave, and if Henry and his men hadn't been right behind him, he'd have been nervous at how easily they entered. With Brithwin due to deliver any day, he did not need to be held on treason as well.

Royce and the twenty men with him dismounted. Rothburg strutted over to him.

"I assume you are here to say parting words to your brother." Rothburg sneered.

"You know as well as I, he is innocent."

"So you say. But then you are blood."

Royce glared at the man. "I would guess you are the one who confiscated his seal and forged the treasonous missive."

"Ha! If that is your defense, I am afraid your brother will hang."

A call rang from the catwalk. "Close the gate! Close the gate!"

Rothburg's gaze swung to the portcullis. Royce grabbed him and pulled out his knife, holding it to his neck. "Do not move if you value your life."

Royce's men swung into action, covering all the men in the bailey and keeping the gate up for Henry and his men. Within minutes, Dunstanburgh was filled with Henry's knights, as well as Royce's and Bryce's men.

"Where do you keep my brother?" Royce still held Rothburg, though he'd removed the knife from the man's throat.

He spat at Royce, missing him and hitting one of the soldiers. Royce shoved him to the soldier and strode away. He'd find Bryce on his own.

He glanced back. Henry dismounted and walked toward Rothburg. Royce entered the keep. What kind of lies would Rothburg spew to Bolingbroke to keep his freedom?

Royce took the steps two at a time, his boots clinking on the flagstone. "Bryce! Bryce Warwick!" He yelled as he ran down the hall, throwing open one door after another.

He stopped when he came to one that was locked from the outside. "Bryce." He called in as he threw up the thick board and pushed open the heavy wooden door.

Bryce stood at the window looking out—a grin on his face. He strode over to Royce and embraced him. "What took you so long?"

Royce shook his head. "A few hundred miles. Are you well?"

"Aye. I am, and it seems I will remain so." He pulled Royce to the window that overlooked the commotion in the bailey and pointed to the left. "That was to be my fate had you shown up any later."

Royce glanced to where Bryce indicated, and a chill

coursed through him. Wooden gallows towered over the green, casting a hideous shadow that stretched across the curtain wall, pointing a crooked finger toward them.

†††

Bryce had never been so happy to see his brother. He'd stood in the window most of the morning watching them build the gallows and had made up his mind this was his last day. He knew Rothburg rushed the execution for a reason but thought no one beside himself knew it was today.

As they had finished securing the last piece of wood, Bryce had looked toward heaven. *Lord, if this is my fate, I accept it. But if you can see a way past this, Lord, I will spend my life serving you rather than myself. Either way, Lord, I ask forgiveness, and I put my life and my trust in you.*

He'd seen a difference in Royce when he'd stopped living for himself and started living for God. He saw a peace in his brother that he'd never seen before, and he didn't understand it. But now, now that he had trusted God with his life, even though he'd believed he was about to die, he knew true peace—the same peace Royce had experienced and tried to explain to him. A peace that passed all understanding. No matter what happened, God was in control.

Now his life would never be the same. He'd made a promise, and he would fulfill it. He'd serve God rather than himself.

"God's timing is always perfect." Bryce smiled. Even though he had peace, he had to admit knowing he'd live to see another day felt good.

"God?" Royce stared at him with a look of uncertainty.

"Aye. There is something about knowing you are about to face the Almighty that causes a man to want to get his life right."

Royce grinned and embraced his brother again. "You will find your life is much more peaceful."

"I believe you. I am ready to get on my way and claim Rosen Craig back for the Warwick family."

The two left the room and headed down the steps to the lower level. Dunstanburgh was a magnificent castle with its long, arched ceiling, large tapestries and oil paintings hanging on the walls, and its impressive stronghold ability. Thomas of Lancaster had made the imposing bastion by taking advantage of the site's natural defenses. His insight to use the existing earthworks from an ancient fort was clever.

Noise of a commotion in the direction of the bailey reached them. Royce pulled his sword and ran down the stairs. Bryce went to pull his but came up empty handed. He followed close behind his brother without a weapon.

Much to his relief, when they reached the courtyard, Henry still stood and seemed in good health. But at his feet, lay Rothburg with blood pooling around him from a wound in his belly. Michael leaned over him.

They rushed over. Michael looked up. Bryce glanced from Michael to Rothburg. Both possessed black hair with a hint of wave, a square jaw, and deep-set eyes. He turned to Royce, who quite obviously saw the same thing. How could he have not seen the resemblance between the two men before? Perhaps because he'd never seen them together. The two could not deny one another. That certainly explained a lot about Catherine.

"What?" Michael frowned. "The blackguard drew a sword on Henry. I could not let him kill the future king." He turned back to the dying man. "Where is my mother? Where is Catherine Iannetta? Did you take her?"

Rothburg's mouth opened and closed several times before any words escaped. "Your mother?" He gasped the words out.

"Aye, Catherine Iannetta and her friend Deirdre Kincaid. Did you take them?" He grasped Rothburg by his shirt, the words coming out in near desperation.

Bryce found himself wanting to breathe for Rothburg so he could answer the question. They needed to find the women. But instead of an answer, Rothburg's eyes grew round, he grabbed his chest, let out a gasp and went limp.

Rothburg would cause them no more grief, but Bryce had to question what it would do to his good friend when he learned that Rothburg was his father.

Chapter 42

Bryce walked with Henry, stepping away from Rothburg and the others. "Did Michael or Royce inform you of Rosen Craig's capture?"

Henry nodded. "Aye, they did. I fear I cannot help you regain your demense. I must continue, seeking the loyalty and support of other nobles. But I surmise you will find little resistance once they learn Rothburg has died."

"'Twould be a blessing, indeed. And what of Wolves Forest now that Rothburg is gone?"

Henry met Bryce's gaze. "Iannetta does not know?"

"Nay, he is not aware. I did not know until I saw them side by side. But I see Rothburg only when I must and that is at Parliament." How many other people had noticed the resemblance?

"Will you tell him?"

"Nay, Catherine needs to tell her son. He will have many questions."

"I'd imagine so. Well, I can leave now, knowing that Wolves Forest will be in good hands and loyal to my cause."

"Aye, milord, you can be assured of that."

"Godspeed, and I wish to hear that you are restored to Rosen Craig." Henry turned and they walked toward his mount.

"May the Lord be with you. I thank you. I owe you my life."

Henry smiled as he swung up on his destrier. "Do not think it was all unselfish, my friend. I need strong lords in place keeping peace on the borderland."

Bryce gave a slight bow to the man who was sure to be his new king and watched him and his procession continue on their journey.

He strode back toward his brother and friend, as the line of mounted horses rode past him. He prayed they would avoid war with his fellow countrymen.

"Are we ready to take back that which is mine?"

†††

Word reached Deirdre that Rothburg was dead and at the hands of Henry Bolingbroke. The keep was in turmoil. They'd only heard snippets of conversation about what had happened, but one thing was for certain. Everyone believed their lord was dead. She and Catherine had been kept in their room, and no one had come or spoken to them. They would not have known if they hadn't heard the gossip in the hall as servants passed.

Deirdre went to the window and peered out as many a knight left through the portcullis. "The knights must fear Henry coming."

Catherine strolled over to the window. "Osbertus was an evil man. I have lived in fear all of Michael's life that he would find out the truth of his father. But I will not have to fear any longer. Look at his men leaving him. They have no loyalty to Osbertus, and they know Henry will not be pleased with any of them"

"Look!" Deirdre pointed to a mounted knight heading toward the portcullis. "'Tis Finley. The coward. He runs away now that Rothburg is dead."

"My husband has no one who will grieve him. I am not sure how I feel. His death certainly will change my life."

"You will not have tae live in fear. And he will never summon you from this room again. You are free tae do as you wish now, Catherine. You dinna have tae return tae Wiltshire. You can stay here with Michael."

She smiled and turned away from the window. "You are so right. Osbertus will never again dictate where I must go."

"I am happy for you. And if it were no' for Bryce, I would be happy for me as well. I dinna need tae fash myself aboot being sent tae my father's either, because if Rothburg told nay others, then my secret has died with him."

"I feel guilty that I am not sad he is gone."

"You have nay reason tae feel guilty for no' grieving his death. And you now have your chance tae live withoot a shadow of fear over you. I do fash aboot Bryce. Did someone rescue him in time? Or did my foolish actions cause an innocent man his life?"

"You must trust the Lord, Deirdre. He has seen you through thus far."

She gave Catherine as much of a smile as she could rally. "Even if he does live, I dinna think he can ever forgive me. And there is still Finley. I dinna ken if Rothburg revealed the truth tae him about my father."

"Where do you think Finley went?"

"He headed north. Perhaps back tae Scotland. One can easily disappear in the highlands. He'd be a fool tae return tae England."

A knock at the door drew her attention. She hurried over to it. "Aye?"

"Miladies, the lord has died." A female servant spoke from the other side.

"Can you let us out?"

"I must first find a key, milady. I will be back. Wait right there."

Deirdre grinned. "I dinna think she has tae fash herself aboot us going anywhere."

Catherine giggled. It was good to hear the lightheartedness in her friend. "Nay, I do not believe so."

About fifteen minutes later, the door swung open. The young servant who'd brought them their food since they'd been at Dunstanburgh stepped in the room. She'd always hurried in and out when delivering their food.

"You are free to go, miladies. But take care, as I do not know what the soldiers would do, should they see you."

"Do you have some cloaks we might use? We would return them when it is safe."

"Aye, milady. I will find you some." The young woman hurried from the room.

"I do hope we will not be questioned because of wearing cloaks in warmer weather." Catherine's brow furrowed with concern.

"I dinna believe so. These men are tae concerned aboot their own necks tae be checking women in cloaks."

"You are most likely correct." Catherine shivered. "I will be glad to be out of these walls. The memories are not good."

Deirdre stood at the window observing the exodus of knights. Perhaps by the time they left, all the men would be long on their way elsewhere. She went to the chair and sat down. She might as well rest her feet before her journey.

Nearly a half hour had passed. "Do you think she has plans to return?" Catherine asked Deirdre.

"She seemed sincere. Perhaps she was stopped and ordered tae do something."

Catherine gave an unladylike snort. "Is there anyone left to order her about?"

The door swung open a few moments later. "I have yer cloaks, miladies." The young woman's arms were full, and perspiration dripped down her face.

"Where did you go tae get these?" Deirdre asked as she took them from the girl.

"To me family's home, down the road and into the village." She smiled, showing a perfect set of straight teeth.

"What is your name, lass?" Deirdre admired the young woman's now cheerful disposition. She couldn't help but wonder how bad her life had been under Rothburg.

"'Tis Aleysia." She gave a curtsey.

"Thank you for your help, Aleysia. 'Tis my promise that these will be returned."

They donned the cloaks. The garments were old and worn, and Catherine's dragged on the floor, so they were a good disguise. No one should look twice at them. Her thoughts went to the last time she had worn a disguise and tried to escape. So much had occurred in the months since.

"I will take you to the servants' door. Methinks fewer people will notice you leaving."

Aleysia guided them down the wide staircase to the lower level. Deirdre kept her head down. They walked down a long passageway and into the great hall. A good bit of activity went on as they hurried through the large room. Upon exiting the hall, they entered the kitchen.

A woman stopped her. "Who do you have with you, Aleysia?"

Deirdre flashed a peek beneath her hood.

"Hush, Beatrix. Do ye not know this be the lord's wife and her friend?"

Deirdre smiled beneath her cloak.

"You keep this to yerself, now, ye hear?" The young woman suddenly sounded like she carried authority.

Deirdre took another quick glimpse to see the woman watching round-eyed. Catherine and Aleysia slipped out the door ahead of her.

"Do ye want me to take you outside the walls?"

Catherine answered before Deirdre could. "Nay, you stay here. We do not want to put you in any danger. Thank you for the cloaks and for helping us. We will not forget your kindness."

"Godspeed." Aleysia smiled and waved as they left.

The two headed for the portcullis. The activity seemed to be slowing down. Deirdre lifted her head and glanced around the grounds. A few remaining knights stood talking in the bailey, and servants and other laborers milled about, all giving the appearance that nothing had changed. And perhaps it hadn't for them—yet.

"Put your head down, lass. We do not want to draw attention to ourselves by looking curious."

Chapter 43

Deirdre kept her eyes focused on the road ahead of her. "Where will you go? Surely not to Rosen Craig."

"With Osbertus dead, there is no reason not to return. I wish to find Michael, and that is the best place I have of finding him."

"But what if Rosen Craig remains under Rothburg's men's rule? Will you stay in the village?"

"I do not believe they will remain there. Look at the knights here. Do you not think they have gone to Rosen Craig to tell the others what has happened?"

"Aye, 'tis true. They will see Wolves Forest men on the run and will not want to wait to face an uncertain fate." Once they passed through the gate and to freedom, Deirdre glanced behind them.

The two walked along with no one questioning them and the farther along they traveled, the fewer people they saw. It wasn't safe for two women to travel over a sennight alone, but they had no other choice. She worried that Catherine would not fare as well over such a long distance.

She glanced over her shoulder to see the walls of Wolves Forest distancing. They needed a horse. And didn't everything Rothburg owned really belong to Catherine? A plan started to form in her head. "It is tae late tae start traveling this night. Let us go tae the village and find where Aleysia lives. We can spend the night there and leave early for Rosen Craig."

"I would like to be on our way. As you say, 'tis a very long trip. We *need* to be on our way," Catherine replied.

"A guid night's sleep will do us well. We can perhaps find some food for the trip."

"I do suppose that it would be wise to have something to eat for such a long journey. Perhaps we should do as you suggest."

Once they found the home of Aleysia, they waited for her to return from her work at the keep. Once she arrived, Deirdre saw that Catherine settled in.

With her friend resting, Deirdre left under the ruse of gathering food. If Catherine knew she would head back to Wolves Forest, she either wouldn't allow her to go or she would insist on returning with her. Neither of those did Deirdre want. But she must find a horse for them to ride.

How hard could it be to sneak back into a near empty castle, borrow a horse, leave, and not be seen? It sounded like a good idea considering the distance for two women traveling alone. But as she walked out of the village, the task in ahead of her seemed daunting.

"Milady! Milady!"

Deirdre turned to see Aleysia running after her with her gown hiked. "Is something amiss?"

"You will not find food this way, milady. 'Tis the other direction."

She waited for the girl to reach her. "I only told Catherine this so she would rest. I am returning tae Wolves Forest tae get a horse. The trek to Rosen Craig is tae far for Catherine and tae dangerous for two women."

"Oh, milady. 'Tis not safe for you to do this thing. Stealing a horse could cost you your head."

"I am no' stealing the horse. Who owns the horses at Wolves Forest?" Deirdre continued toward the castle.

Aleysia walked beside her. "Lord Rothburg."

"Aye, but he has died. So who now owns them?"

"I do not know, milady. He had no children."

"But he has a wife."

Her eyes grew large. "Aye, he does. And they would be hers now."

They reached the gate and saw the exodus of knights had stopped. It would be convenient if only servants remained. They walked through a strangely quiet outer and inner bailey. That was good.

Aleysia put her hand out, clutching Deirdre's arm and stopping her as they reached the stables. "Wait here."

From where she stood, Aleysia could be heard speaking with a man. She assumed it was the man responsible for the horses. A few minutes later the lass returned with two horses in tow.

"Two horses? How did you manage that, Aleysia?"

The girl's grin nearly went from one ear to the other. "I told him with the lord dead, he should think about who would be overseeing the place since the mistress is back. Then I told him this act of kindness would go a long way with her. And if he made her walk, she might question his loyalty."

Deirdre laughed. "You are very wise. What is his name, that he might be rewarded when the time comes?"

"Guy be his name." She took the reins of one horse and turned to go head back toward the village. "Let me get food for your journey."

The horses had been easy enough to acquire. Food should be even easier. "Should I wait here?"

"Nay, follow me. The cook is kind." They fastened the horses to a small bush near the side kitchen entrance and went in the door.

They left with two bags of food that would surely go bad before they could eat it all. The cook was old and had been at Wolves Forest prior to Rothburg's arrival. And well she remembered Catherine and thought highly of her.

After tying the bags to the horses, the two of them started out.

Deirdre's heart was full. She'd get Catherine back to Rosen Craig safely before being on her own way. "God has watched over your mistress. I dinna ken how all of this will end, but she is a guid woman and will be fair tae her people."

Aleysia smiled.

"Halt! Who steals horses from the king?" A deep voice yelled to them from behind.

Deirdre's heart skipped a beat, and she dared not look

behind her.

†††

Before Deirdre could speak a word, Aleysia stepped in front of her. "Ellis, say you these are not Lord Rothburg's horses? I was unawares the king left his horses here. 'Tis sorry I am. We will return them."

"Have you not heard? Lord Rothburg is dead by the hands of Henry of Bolingbroke."

"Aye, I have heard. Are these milord's horses?"

Aleysia almost had Deirdre convinced that she didn't know who the horses belonged to.

Ellis, a young man not old enough to be a knight, stopped when he reached them. "Because the lord is dead, they are the king's now, with Lord Rothburg having no children. I must protect what is our king's."

Aleysia raised her chin with an air of authority. "He may not have children, but he has a wife, and well you know it."

He shrugged. "If she has not disappeared again."

Aleysia's eyes narrowed. "She has not, and she has requested the horses for her travels."

"She left our lord long ago. Why should she be allowed to have anything of his, let alone his horses now that he is gone?" The beardless youth replied.

"Because she is still his wife, and she will be the one who runs this keep. Do you want her to find out that you have denied her comfortable travels?" Aleysia shot the words at him, sounding less like a peasant.

He glared at her. "Do as you please. But if King Richard wants an accounting, I shall tell him you stole the horses."

Aleysia rolled her eyes, turned her attention back to Deirdre, and smiled. "We must hurry."

By the time they returned to the small cottage, Catherine had fallen asleep. Deirdre curled up on rushes and covered herself with the borrowed cloak. Tomorrow would be here before she knew it.

Deirdre yawned and stretched. The sun had broken the horizon and light streamed in through the window. She glanced around. Catherine was nowhere to be seen. Deirdre pushed herself off the floor and stretched, placing her hands in the small of her aching back. She'd not slept well.

Stepping outside, she found Catherine. "Good morn. I hope you have no' waited tae long for me."

"Nay, not long at all. I see you were busy yestereve whilst I slept."

Deirdre yawned again. "Much grammercy must go tae Aleysia, as I dinna believe I would have gotten these beasts withoot her." Deirdre looked around. "Is she gone?"

"Aye, she is back up to Wolves Forest helping to feed whoever stayed. Are you ready to be on our way? I am anxious to find Michael."

The two mounted the horses, both much larger than her sweet palfrey, and rode out of the village with their sacks of provisions.

They rode until the sun was high in the sky and hunger pangs burned at her belly. "Are you ready to stop and eat?"

"Aye. I could use a rest." Catherine slowed her mount and slid off its back. "'Tis been a long day. I fear I am not accustomed to riding for long periods anymore."

Deirdre dismounted with a moan at her aching backside. "I tae. I dinna ken if the pain of moving is worse than riding."

Deirdre pulled off a sack and took out some bread and dried meat, handing a portion to Catherine. Neither of them chose to sit.

"We need tae ride in the wooded area and off the roads and trails. The later in the day, the less safe 'twill be for two lasses."

Catherine nodded her agreement.

They rode on, stopping before darkness fell and rising with the first rays of the sun. Two days of riding passed before they reached Rosen Craig's demesne. They rode until

the village came in sight.

Chapter 44

Rosen Craig Demesne,
July 15, 1399 Morningtide

Deirdre wiped her brow. The village road had few trees to give much relief from the morn sun. "This is as far as I ride."

Catherine swung her head to look at her. "We are here. The castle is not far beyond this village."

"Aye. Well I ken. I can no' return. Nay one will welcome me. If Bryce is d-dead." She choked out the words. "I fear his people would rightfully seek my death. And if God has shown mercy on him and he lives, he will no' welcome me. I am no' willing tae give up my freedom again. It seems it has come and gone much of late."

"You must come. I will see to your safety."

"You are kind, but I will no' put you in that position. I will ask one favor of you. I ask you to keep my secret. I dinna wish for Bryce tae ken of my foolishness."

"Deirdre, you know not what you say, child. *This* you ask is foolishness. You do not wish for the lord to believe you intentionally betrayed him."

"It matters not. He will no' believe me, and I dinna blame him." She laughed. "'Tis hard for me tae believe I trusted Finley in such a foolish way."

"I cannot promise you this."

"I have no' asked much of you, and I kept your secret with no hesitation. My last request, as your friend, do this for me."

Catherine gave a slow nod. "I will, but 'tis fear speaking in you, child. You need to tell Bryce the truth of things. He will understand.

"I wish you well, Catherine. It has been guid tae have a friend." Deirdre kicked her horse into a trot. She'd known this day would come and had tried not to think about it. Her heart ached at the thought of never seeing Bryce again. And of him believing she wanted to see him dead. Rosen Craig had become more of a home to her than anything she could remember. A home. She snorted. Where would she go? She had no place to welcome her, no place to call home, no one to love her.

†††

Rosen Craig Castle,
July 15, 1399 Eventide

The Lord was with them. Laird Mackenzie met them as they rode toward Rosen Craig. He'd been denied entry and was returning home. He agreed to join forces and reestablish Bryce as lord of Rosen Craig.

Now as they waited in the forest, there was no moon and Bryce could barely see his own hand—surely a gift from the Almighty.

"I will go slip in through the *bolt-hole* and find one of my men. I will have him get word to the others that we are here waiting to move in." Bryce shared his plan with his brother and a few of his top men.

"Nay, Bryce, you are not entering Rosen Craig. 'Tis not safe. Too many of the men could recognize you." Royce argued.

"I can go," Michael interjected.

"Nay." Bryce and Royce answered at the same time. They couldn't take a chance that someone would see the resemblance between him and their now dead, lord.

"And why is that?" Irritation could be heard in Michael's voice.

"'You have been seen with me too much. The risk is just as high for you as 'tis for me," Bryce answered.

"I agree," Royce added. "Hugh, that leaves you."

"Slip in, inform one or two men, and have them spread the word." Hugh turned back to his horse and, pulling his sword from its sheath, rent the air with a metallic ring.

"We will wait here for your return, unless you send out a call." Royce leaned against a tree, following the knight's faint outline against the curtain wall.

"I am not staying here," Bryce announced. "I will accompany Hugh in case there is a problem."

"Nay. 'Tis not a good idea," Royce argued. "I do not trust you to stay out of Rosen Craig."

"I will go along," Michael said.

"'Tis settled then," Bryce answered.

"Michael, do not allow Bryce in the bolt-hole."

Though Bryce could hardly see his brother's outline, he knew there was a frown on his face.

"Do not worry, Royce. I will see he behaves." Michael chuckled.

"I do not like sending my man into unknown danger that should be mine."

"I will not be in danger, Bryce. I will be careful, and they will not know me from the other men. You are someone they may recognize."

Bryce left Royce while he, Michael, and Hugh made their way to the west wall of Rosen Craig under the cover of darkness. His father had made sure that the walls were open and away from the forest should there be an attack, an unfortunate situation for them at the moment. Not a word was spoken among the three. When they reached the wall, they flattened themselves to it as they edged toward the bolt-hole.

Bryce pulled the branches and leaves aside, allowing Hugh to step down to the hidden sliding door. As Hugh disappeared behind it, Bryce let the bushes fall back in place.

Not a word could be said until they were back to the safety of the trees where their voices could not be heard. Too much time had passed. Hugh should have been back out by now. He only had to inform a few men and have them pass the word throughout Bryce's knights. He didn't like this. He wanted to go in, but Michael, standing by his side, would not let that happen.

The door slid open.

Bryce placed his hand on his sword handle as the dark figure stepped out. His heart thudded in his chest. Friend or foe?

"'Tis done." Hugh's whispered words met Bryce's ears.

He let out a sigh and let go of his sword. "Let us head back."

They hurried to the heavier cover of the woods. As soon as they reached Royce, Bryce turned to Hugh. "What are the conditions inside?"

"I spoke with Guernon. Rothburg's men are in confusion. Word has reached them that Rothburg is dead and Wolves Forest knights have fled. They fear Henry's wrath, should he be crowned king."

"And fear they should. No king will turn his head when a demesne is attacked by another English lord. 'Tis not done or acceptable." Bryce calmed the anger in his voice. "And what of my men? Have they lost their weapons?"

"Aye, they have, but Guernon believes these men will not fight. They will lay their arms down if we storm the castle. He will get men in position to open the portcullis when we arrive."

"We will come from the front and the back," Royce said. "Bryce, I will take my men and go in through the bolt-hole. We will try to disarm all with whom we come in contact and give their weapons to your men still inside. I would like to see as little bloodshed as possible this night."

"Mackenzie's men and my men will wait to be let in from the gate," Bryce said.

They remained there an hour to give Bryce's men in the castle time to spread the word and get into position. As they moved out, Hugh pulled Bryce aside.

"I need to speak with you."

Bryce stepped out of the near silent procession. "What is it?"

"There is news from inside Rosen Craig."

Bryce glanced at the shadows passing them. "Out with

it." He needed to be with his men.

"Guernon found out who your traitor is."

Bryce directed his attention to Hugh instead of the men. "Who is he?"

"'Tis Finley."

"Ack! The Scot. I never cared for him. Did he do it to continue the unrest at the border?"

"He had an accomplice—Deirdre."

The ground beneath Bryce's feet seemed to give way, and he swayed. He reached out for Hugh's shoulder to steady himself lest he stager. Deirdre had betrayed him after all, just like Clarice? Another woman he'd grown to love had almost cost him his life?

"So our finding her reiving was not by accident."

"That I do not know, Bryce. Only that she is the one who stole the ring and gave it to Finley, who in turn gave the ring to Rothburg."

Bryce's chest squeezed so tight he could barely breathe. And to think he considered her an honorable lady like his mother or Brithwin.

He was a terrible judge of a woman's character. In a moment, his shock evaporated like mist beneath the scorching sun of his anger.

He'd never marry. He couldn't live his life wondering if he could trust the woman beside him.

"Bryce?" Guernon reached out and clasped Bryce's shoulder. "Are you unwell?"

"I am well." Bryce choked out the words. He wasn't though. His heart compressed and his head spun. But he had a home to rescue from the hands of his enemy and the traitor he loved.

†††

They'd left their horses in the woods and all stood close to the castle walls waiting for the portcullis to be raised. Their wait wasn't long. The squeaking metal and rattling of chain rang on the night air.

Yells from within and the clanging of swords caused Bryce's blood to rush through his veins in anticipation of what lay within the walls of Rosen Craig. The men slipped under the half-raised gate with swords drawn.

The order had been given to disarm Rothburg's men if possible. Bryce wanted no useless deaths. The battle was short. They were outnumbered, and well they knew it. Most gave up without a fight.

Bryce scanned the bailey. A few injured, but none dead. His gaze stopped on a man. Those ice-cold eyes locked with Bryce's. He recognized the man as the one whom he'd fought in the woods—the one who had escaped. So it had been Rothburg's men that day.

Royce strolled up to Bryce and slapped him on the back. "Welcome home."

"'Tis good to be back. Shall we go in and see what has occurred in my absence?"

The knights, still in the bailey, were boisterous in celebration of their triumph. Bryce made his way into the keep, leaving the business of Rothburg's men in the hands of his master-at-arms, Ranald. Michael, Mackenzie, and Royce followed him to his solar.

"One might expect you would find more happiness in having your home back, brother," Royce goaded him.

"My mind wanders. I am pleased to be home and with no loss of life." He just wished things were different. That he could choose a woman as well as his brother had. "Mackenzie, what brings you back to England? Are you changing your allegiance?"

Mackenzie chuckled. "Nay, I have no' lost my senses. I return because I have heard of Henry's arrival. I wish tae ken if he will support peace if he is crowned king."

"I do not like this border reiving any more than you, Mackenzie. And with Rothburg gone, we will not have to contend with the likes of him stirring up trouble." Bryce was glad to get his mind off Deirdre.

"How do you ken that the new laird of Wolves Forest will be better?" Mackenzie asked.

"I can assure you that you will not have to concern yourself with that," Bryce replied.

Michael leaned forward. "Has Henry mentioned who he plans to replace Rothburg?"

"Not directly." Bryce sought to change the direction of their conversation. "Have you spoken with anyone about the women? Have they been found?"

"Nay. You may not have noticed, but we were a bit busy reclaiming Rosen Craig."

Mackenzie's brows shot up. "Your women are missing?"

"Aye. They went missing over a fortnight ago, before Bryce was charged with treason." Michael sat back in his chair and rubbed his neck.

"A fortnight is a long time for lasses to be missing. You must be vera worried aboot them." Mackenzie shook his head slowly, staring at the floor in front of him. "'Tis dangerous for women tae be oot alone."

"Aye, my mother is one of the ladies who disappeared."

"Catherine?" Mackenzie turned to Michael. "I met her last I was here. A fine lady."

Michael smiled. "I would have to agree with you."

"And have I met the other woman?" the Scottish laird inquired.

Bryce hoped to catch Michael's attention, but his friend didn't look his way. He didn't want him mentioning Deirdre. Even after what she'd done to him, he wanted to protect her.

"She is a lass we caught reiving on Rosen Craig last winter," Michael answered.

"Reiving? Is she Scottish? And you say winter? Is she a prisoner?" Mackenzie frowned.

Bryce shook his head. He had better step in. Hopefully he could answer the questions without giving the laird too much information. "Nay. She was, but she nearly killed herself trying to escape. I decided she had punished herself enough."

Mackenzie cocked his head, and Bryce wasn't sure the laird believed him.

"If you freed the lass, then why did she stay on?"

Bryce glanced at Michael, wondering how much he should tell Mackenzie. Deirdre seemed frightened of the man, the man Bryce suspected was her father. But then she was gone, and chances were she'd taken Catherine. Now that he knew she was the traitor, he had to question if she was truly taken or if she conspired with the ones who took Catherine. "She chose to stay here because she feared returning home. Several of the men reiving with her were killed. She had attempted to disguise herself as a boy, but 'twas not hard to see through the ruse."

Mackenzie's interest seemed to be piqued. "A lad, you say. What is her name? Her clan?"

"She's a Kincaid." A part of Bryce felt he'd betrayed Deirdre.

Mackenzie now sat forward. "Tell me aboot her? What do you ken? Did she dress as a lad only to reive?"

Bryce had asked himself that same question. But the way she had trouble with wearing a dress and little things she'd said made him believe she lived her life like that. "'Tis a strange question. Why do you ask?"

"There were rumors aboot a lass that Kincaid hid as a lad. I had made several attempts tae find oot if there was truth tae the story. But I could find no such lass."

The hairs on the back of Bryce's neck stood up. The man had about confirmed his suspicions. He would not let this man harm Deirdre, father or not. "And why are you interested in a lass who dresses as a lad?"

A knock sounded at the door. "Who is it?" Bryce's words came out harsher than he intended, so eager was he to hear Mackenzie's answer.

"Catherine."

Chapter 45

Michael sprang from his seat and pulled the door open before Bryce could grant her entrance.

"Mother! Where have you been? We have been looking everywhere for you." Michael drew her into his arms.

"It is a long story, son." Catherine patted her son on the shoulder.

"Come sit, Catherine. We have time." Bryce gestured to one of the seats. Did the woman not know how worried they'd been about her?

She sat across from him. "Osbertus, excuse me, Rothburg captured us whilst on the road between Rosen Craig and the village. He took us to Wolves Forest. He kept us locked in a room most of the time. On occasion, we were allowed to walk out around the baileys. But when news reached the castle that their lord was dead by Henry's sword, many fled in fear of their lives. It was during the confusion that one of the servant girls who had brought us our food helped us to escape. I came straight here, believing that Rosen Craig would no longer be under Rothburg's men. That was until I had entered. I am relieved to see it back in your hands, Bryce. It was not a good feeling when I realized I walked back into Rothburg's control, even if he had died."

So Rothburg was responsible for their disappearance. He sent up a prayer that no harm had come to Deirdre. "Where is Deirdre, now?" He glanced toward the door almost expecting her to enter. And realized his mistake in speaking her name.

"I do not know. When we reached the far side of the village, she would come no further. She would not tell me where she went. Only that she could not return to Rosen Craig."

Of course she wouldn't return here. She only stayed here to use him, to gain his trust and get close to him so she could betray him with his own seal. "How long have you been here?"

"I arrived earlier today."

"May I interrupt?" Laird Mackenzie leaned forward in his chair.

Catherine glanced between the men before answering. "Certainly."

"Can you tell me aboot Deirdre?"

"What...would you like to know?" Catherine asked hesitantly.

"Anything. Everything." He clasped his fingers together in front of him.

"She is a beautiful young lady. She is very resourceful." Catherine smiled. "Fearless would be a good way to describe her. She went back to Wolves Forest to retrieve horses, fully aware we'd just escaped from there and she could end up locked in a room again."

"Did she mention her family at all?" the laird asked.

"She has no family—at least that she claims. They were not good to her. She grew up with an uncle."

"What was her uncle's name?"

Bryce had to stop the interrogation. Catherine appeared to be getting agitated. "What makes you ask so many questions about a young lady you have yet to meet?" He would make the man explain his intentions.

Mackenzie sat back with a deep sigh. "Because seventeen years ago I lost my daughter. She was said tae have been stolen away whilst my wife visited her brother. I've never stopped searching for her. But Scotland and England have much land to cover. Something aboot the story never sat well with me. Years later, I began hearing rumors of a lass in Kincaid's clan who dressed as a lad. I went there, trying tae find oot the truth, but every time I went, Kincaid and I would end up shouting at each other, and I would leave kenning nay more than before I got there. If he had no' been my wife's brother...but he is, and she has been through much. My dear wife blames herself tae this day for the loss of our daughter."

"I am sorry for your loss. But why would you think Deirdre might be your daughter?" The man must have good reason for bringing it up.

"You told me she was a Kincaid. And the head of that clan is my wife's brother. There was something in my spirit that kept drawing me back here. I believe now, God has brought me here because of this young lass. And did I mention our daughter's name was *Deredere*?"

A few weeks ago, Bryce would have laughed at the thought that God had guided Mackenzie here much like the star had guided the wise men. But not today. Not anymore. Still, he must approach the subject of Deirdre with caution. "'Tis sure I am that many young women are called Deirdre."

"Aye, that is true. But one who dressed as a boy and lived with the Kincaid clan does narrow down the likelihood."

Bryce looked Mackenzie square in the eye. "Deirdre feared you. 'Tis why she did not come to eat when you last visited. She did not wish for you to know she was here."

"Tell me, does she have a scar that goes from just below her right ear down into her neck?"

The question sent cold water through Bryce's veins. The faint scar on Deirdre's neck had faded with the years, but it was still visible. Could she really be the daughter of this mighty Scottish warrior? "You did not answer me. Why would Deirdre fear you if you are her father?"

"I canno' answer that because I lost her when she was a bairn. She had nay reason tae fear me. I loved her vera much and still do."

"Perhaps I can help." Catherine spoke, drawing all eyes.

"Please do." Bryce gave her a nod. Deirdre had spent much of her time with Michael's mother.

"Deirdre lived with an old woman growing up. Her uncle told her stories of what a cruel man you were, that you beat your wife and were harsh to your people. He instilled in her to fear you. If what you say is true, and Lord Kincaid stole your daughter from you, making you believe someone else had taken her, then he would want to keep her from ever wishing to return home."

"I would never hurt my child. I never gave up on her—never stopped searching." This braw warrior's voice, who many feared in battle, now wavered with emotion. "My heart would no' let go of my daughter. Even when my sons were born and my other daughter, I continued to search. Is it true, the rumor? Was she raised as a boy?"

"I fear so, milord." Catherine answered with sympathy in her tone.

"I will kill the man!" Mackenzie's fist came down, slamming onto the arm of his chair.

"Do not fear, Mackenzie, your daughter is very much a woman now." The words came out of Bryce's mouth before he put much thought into what he said.

Michael grinned.

"I hope you have treated my daughter with respect."

"Do not insult me, Mackenzie." Bryce glared at the man. Deirdre was his only concern.

"'Forgive me, Bryce. You canno' ken the anguish of losing my daughter—of kenning I have never been there tae protect her."

Bryce turned back to Catherine. "Where do you believe Deirdre has gone?"

"I truly do not know, Bryce. She will not return to her uncle. And we both know the fear she had of Laird Mackenzie. She said she could not return here. I do not know where she will go." She turned to Deirdre's father. "Is there perhaps a clan she would go to for safety?"

Mackenzie shook his head. "I wish I ken, but I dinna. I dinna ken my own daughter."

Bryce's heart constricted for the warrior. He'd lost all those years with Deirdre. He knew more about the lass than her own father did. "On the morrow we will rise and look for her with all of our men. We are many. Just as you never abandoned your search for her, neither will we. Now you know she lives, and you do not chase a ghost. We will find her." The words came from Bryce's mouth and he believed them. They would find her. "Rest my friend. Today was good news for you. Your daughter is alive."

Bryce called a servant and had Laird Mackenzie shown to a room. When he returned to his solar, Michael, Catherine, and Royce remained.

Royce stood. "I believe I will get some rest as well. Tomorrow will be a full day and, I hope, fruitful."

As Royce left the solar, Michael yawned and stood. "I believe I will head that way as well."

Catherine shifted in her chair. "I wish to speak with you, Michael."

"What is it, mother?" He continued to stand.

"Prithee sit." Catherine looked up at her son from the chair, and he sat back down.

Bryce started to get up.

"Bryce, prithee stay."

He sat back in his chair, sure of what she was about to say. It was a private affair, and he wished she'd not requested his presence. But perhaps Michael would need him.

"Did you meet Osbertus…excuse me, Lord Rothburg, before he died, Michael?"

Michael cocked his head. "One could say that, aye."

"Had you ever met him before?"

"Nay. I had no reason to. He is not a person I care to have much to do with. Why do you ask?"

Catherine shifted in her seat again. "I wondered if you had a chance to talk with him. Did you find anything… familiar about him?"

"Mother, what is it you wish to say? Nay, I did not speak with the man. I killed him as he raised his sword to kill our future king." Michael not only sounded annoyed, but he looked it as well.

Catherine gasped. "*Y-you* killed Osbertus? I thought Henry did."

Michael's brow drew down. "Osbertus? Why do you keep calling him that?"

"You did not answer me. You killed him?"

"Aye, I did. And you, Mother, did not answer me. Why do you continue to call him by his given name?"

"Because that is what I knew him by. He was my husband." Catherine's words came out strangled.

"Your husband? Did you marry him after my father died? Or did you never marry my father?

"He is my only husband, son." Her eyes pleaded with him to understand.

If only Michael could have seen the resemblance when he was side by side with his father, he would have known then.

"So you are telling me I am misbegotten." He snorted. "'Tis of no concern to me. 'Twas asked of me plenty growing up, but I always denied it. But as I grew older, I suspected." He laughed. "'Tis glad I am that I did not know this as a child."

Catherine looked him in the eyes. "Nay, Michael, you are not misbegotten."

"What are you saying?" Michael's mind seemed to be searching for a different answer.

"Osbertus is your father, Michael."

"Nay. 'Tis not so." He shook his head, but then looked at Bryce. "Tis ludicrous. And yet, you do not look surprised. Did you know this as well?"

Bryce nodded. "I realized he was your father when you leaned over him as he died. The resemblance was unmistakable."

"You said nothing."

"'Twas not my place. When I saw you together, everything with your mother started falling into place." He turned to Catherine. "Your urgency to have Michael move with you away from here. Your fear of him staying. Your protectiveness of him. It all came together."

"Why? Why did you not tell me, Mother?"

Tears welled in her eyes. "I did not want you influenced by him growing up. He was such an evil man. I wanted you to be better than your father."

"But I have been a grown man for many years. Why did you continue the pretense?"

"I cannot say other than the fear he caused in me. Can you forgive me, Michael?"

"I hold no ill will against you. But I need time. I have lived my whole life thinking I had no father, and now to discover he was my enemy—'tis much to digest."

Chapter 46

It was still dark when Bryce woke with Deirdre on his mind. She'd spent the night out there alone. He was thankful it wasn't cold, but there were animals and men who would take advantage of her. Thoughts of her situation badgered him. And the more he tried to remind himself of what she'd done, and he shouldn't care, the worse it got.

And he didn't really know why he cared. She'd planned to see him hang. And very well might think he was dead. What a disappointment that would be for her. But even so, he could not wish bad things for her. Somewhere during the time she'd spent here, he'd fallen in love. How could he love her, knowing what she'd done? She'd stolen from him, again. And this time used it for his death.

He rolled to his side and punched down his pillow. He could almost feel the soft red curls between his fingers. He wasn't sure he could live without her now, but he didn't know if he could live with her either—living in constant doubt that he could trust her. Trust—it was a powerful thing.

Cathal. He sat up. He'd forgotten about the kitten. How brokenhearted Deirdre would be if something happened to that cat. He'd not seen it since the two of them disappeared. He lay back down. He'd check her room when the sun came up. If she'd planned this whole thing, then she'd have seen that the kitten was looked after.

Bryce continued to toss and turn, fighting the visions of a beautiful redheaded lass, until the sun finally broke over the horizon. He jumped out of bed, pulled on his clothes, and headed down the hall to Deirdre's room.

He pulled the door open and drew a deep breath in as he entered. Nothing smelled like it had died in the room. That was a good sign. He walked over to the window and pulled the coverings back, then turned to the room. Cathal meowed from her spot on Deirdre's bed.

Bryce walked to the bed and scratched the soft grey and white kitten. "You have grown. 'Tis almost time you start earning your keep with the mice."

He looked around the room and spotted two bowls. One with water and one with crumbs. "Who is your protector, Cathal? I see someone is caring for you." He'd like to know who cared for the cat and if Deirdre had asked the person to. It would tell him if she'd planned everything. He must speak with Lucas.

He met Mackenzie heading down the stairs to break his fast. "I trust you slept well yesternight."

Mackenzie nodded. His face was etched with concern. "I would guess nay worse than you."

"Let us break our fast and then head out."

Michael showed up with Alex on his shoulder and sat down. A servant brought a plate of food and set it before him. He took the squirrel and placed him near the plate to eat. But Alex ran back up his shoulder.

"Looks like your pet does not want to get left again."

"I could not keep the animal out of my bed yesternight. He climbed all over me. Made for a miserable night's sleep."

Mackenzie looked at Michael. "You English choose vera odd pets."

"I did not choose him. He chose me." Michael defended himself.

Bryce let out a chortle. "Methinks that is not the whole truth."

The men finished eating, keeping the conversation light, before they headed into the bailey to mount up and begin their search.

Mackenzie stood on his horse's back, putting him where all the men could see him. He let out a shrill whistle. Silence fell in the bailey. "I want every door knocked on in the village and questions asked. I want every person you pass questioned. Deirdre spent the night somewhere, so if you see a place in the woods that looks like someone has rested there, search it oot. She is alive, and I want tae be sure she stays that way."

The men rode out, and Bryce sent up a prayer that God would direct them to where Deirdre had gone. As much as she had hurt him by her betrayal, he could not wish ill on her. He wanted to see her reunited with her father. They'd lost many years. Perhaps if she'd been raised by an honorable man instead of Kincaid, she'd have turned out more like his mother.

Bryce rode north through the woods, the same direction in which he'd found her the first time. He didn't go to the village. She wouldn't have gone there, and he knew it. Nay, she would go to what she knew, and that was the forest.

On and off throughout the day, he passed some of the other men searching. If she was out there, they would find her.

The nooning hour passed, and he reached in his satchel and pulled out some dried meat and a hunk of bread. He hoped Deirdre had food to quell the pangs of hunger. He thought to ask Catherine this morn if she'd had any provisions, but the woman had not risen by the time they'd left. He imagined she was exhausted after her talk with Michael last night. He'd wanted to ask her about the lass last night after the others left but never got a chance before she confessed to Michael who his father was. He just needed to find Deirdre and see that she was returned to her family.

Mackenzie came crashing through the woods on his mount. "I give it tae the lass, she is guid at keeping herself hidden when she wants."

"Aye. That she is." They rode side by side.

"'Tis sorry I am that Deirdre betrayed you, Bryce. And after you showed her kindness despite her reiving. 'Tis difficult tae believe she would do such a thing. But I did no' raise her, and I do ken what kind of man her uncle is."

"I thought she was different." Bryce laughed. "I am a poor judge of women. Maybe if she had grown up with you and her mother, she would have been different. I trusted her."

"If I dinna ken you were hurting, Bryce, I would knock you off your horse for speaking of my daughter in such a way."

Bryce shrugged. "And what makes you think I am hurting, Mackenzie?"

"Because no man who has been betrayed by a woman seeks tae find her for anything less than punishment."

"Perchance I do this for you. I owe you a debt. I do not think Rothburg's men would have surrendered so easily if we had not had such a force of men."

"Are you saying I should knock you off your horse?"

Bryce leaned forward. What did he just see? He kicked his horse forward and caught a glimpse of brown fabric disappear into the brush. "Crowder? That you? It is Lord Warwick." Bryce stopped, put up his hand for Mackenzie to stop, and waited.

"Crowder, I need to speak with you."

Silence.

"Crowder, do not make me come find you."

Rustling. More silence.

Crowder stepped out from thick underbrush. "Milord."

Bryce swung down off his horse. "Have you seen Deirdre, the lass from above the border? Red hair?"

Crowder stuck out his chin. "Why you want her? She do somethin' wrong?"

Bryce tipped his head toward Mackenzie. "That is her father. He is looking for her."

"Nay. Deirdre wishes not to see him."

"He is not bad, Crowder. Where is Deirdre?"

"Methinks it best not to tell you. Deirdre is my friend."

"Have I ever done anything to harm you?"

"Nay." Crowder glanced around. "She said you are angry with her."

"Have I ever done anything to harm Deirdre?"

Crowder slowly shook his head. "Nay."

"Tell me where she is. You know I will not allow harm to come to her."

His gaze fell to the ground. "You promise?"

"Aye, I promise."

Crowder led them through the woods for near an hour. And Bryce began to think the man hoodwinked him.

Bryce was about to turn back.

"Deirdre!" Crowder called out.

Deirdre stepped out into the open. Her gaze met Bryce's, and he could see the uncertainty in her eyes. But then she shifted her gaze behind him. She let out a gasp and turned and ran.

Bryce expected as much from her. He urged Tempest into a gallop, coming up beside her before she could disappear into the thicket. He leaned down and grasped under her arm, pulling her up onto his horse.

"Stop squirming before you fall and get trampled by this beast."

"You promised you would not hurt her," Crowder yelled.

Bryce shook his head. "I am not hurting her. If she doesn't stop flailing, she will hurt herself." He said it for both Crowder and Deirdre.

Deirdre tried to pull his arms from around her as she twisted her body. "Let me go."

"Stop fighting me, Deirdre. You are not going anywhere." He tightened his grip on her.

She turned to him. "Please."

His heart constricted. The pleading in her voice nearly did him in. "It is not as it seems, lass. Trust me."

Mackenzie rode forward, stopping when he was less than a horse's length from them.

"Deirdre, I am your father." Mackenzie spoke the words softly.

"I ken who you are. I ken what you are." Deirdre spat the words out at her father.

Bryce loosened his hold. "Nay, lass, you do not know the truth of who your father is. You only know the lies that have been told you. Come back to Rosen Craig and talk to him. If you do not wish to stay, I will assure your safety to leave—alone."

Mackenzie stared at his daughter. She glanced at him briefly, then looked away. She nodded. "I will hear him oot."

Chapter 47

Deirdre sat in the solar with the others, listening to her father explain what had happened all those years ago.

"Your mother was distraught when her brother told her you had been captured. That night she fell into an exhausted sleep. The following morning, Kincaid claimed they had searched all through the night and well intae the morning and there was nay sign of you."

"But why? Why would he do that?" She wanted to believe him, wanted to believe her father was a good man.

"He hated me. Enough to where he would cause his sister immeasurable pain as well if that meant I would suffer. I think originally he had planned to marry you off and gain an alliance with one of the clans. But because I never gave up searching for you, there was nay clan member who would marry you, knowing who you were. They would not cross me there. And I believe that because I continued to search for you, he knew he caused ongoing pain for me."

"If you believed all these years he was behind this, why did you not look for me there?"

"I did lass, many times. And every time, your uncle and I would have words. When I never saw you there, I determined he would have sent you far away."

"And Mama? Does she still live? Uncle said he thought you might have killed her." She held her breath, waiting for a reaction and an answer.

Mackenzie laughed. "Killed her? Nay, lass. But she could vera well be the death of me. Your mother is a vera strong woman. Your brothers, nearly grown, dinna question her. She misses you every day. She has no' allowed one thing tae be moved in your room. Your brothers and sister were no' allowed in, lest they touch something."

"I have brothers and a sister?" She'd never thought about family beyond her parents.

"Aye, you have three brothers and one sister. And your sister will be vera happy tae have another lass in the home."

"And Mama has no' forgotten me? She has missed me all these years?" Even with four other children her mother still missed her and wanted her. Tears prickled the rims of her eyes until she had to swipe them away.

"Aye, 'tis true." He paused and gazed at her, his eyes full of compassion. "And I missed you, Dearie."

Dearie—the name and memories came rushing back. The special name he'd called her, riding on his back, he was her trusted steed, him throwing her in the air and catching her, her mother making a crown of flowers and him placing it on her head, telling her she was his princess and always would be.

She had a family—real family with brothers and a sister and a mother and a father. A father who was not cruel and who loved her. Her heart was so full. God had indeed given her the desires of her heart. Again, tears welled in her eyes, only this time she didn't worry herself, should they fall.

She could not contain the joy within her. Never in all her years had she been so happy. She was so full she didn't know what to do.

Her father smiled at her. "I still love you, lass. Nay less than the day I lost you."

Deirdre jumped from her chair, nearly toppling it over, and rushed to her father. He pushed out of his chair and stood, opening his arms and she landed between them. They curled around her, giving her the security she'd always longed for.

†††

Deirdre had hardly slept. She was going home. Home. What a beautiful word. She had a home—a place to go and feel safe and loved. And she would meet her brothers and sister. And her mother—the dream that helped her get through all these years—the love that she'd clung to. She would meet her again.

There were no belongings to gather since she came with nothing. She had no clothes, only the two gowns Bryce had given her. The one had been ruined that fateful day in the woods with Catherine, and the other she wore.

She glanced at Cathal sleeping on the bed. She wouldn't ask Bryce if she could take her. Lucas would continue to care for the cat. She walked to the door and turned back. This had been her room for six months. Living here had been the closest she'd ever had to belonging. Bryce had welcomed her more than she deserved. How many men would have forgiven her reiving? And then given her a place to live, never expecting anything in return?

She walked out and pulled the door shut behind her. She'd severed that relationship. Though Bryce searched for her and spoke to her, there was a coolness in his voice. Much like when they'd first met. The warm and caring Bryce she'd grown to love was gone to her. And she couldn't blame him. She'd nearly cost him his life.

When she'd seen him in the woods, relief flooded her to know he still lived. She wanted to tell him how sorry she was, explain to him she didn't mean things to turn out like they had. But then she'd seen her father and that relief had turned to fear and getting away.

She met her father at the bottom of the stairs. He waited for her, a smile on his face as she walked down to him. Bryce stood near the door speaking with Michael.

"Are you ready, Dearie?" Her father's special name filled her with so much joy.

How could she be so happy yet be so sad? She longed to go home and meet the rest of her family, but her heart ached for the way things had ended with Bryce. She'd had her first kiss with him, and that kiss would be her last from him as well. She likely would never see him again.

"Could I have a moment tae speak with Bryce, Da?"

He nodded and gave her a knowing smile. "I shall go see that our horses are ready. I will wait for you there."

Catherine's words filled her thoughts. *'Tis fear speaking in you, child. You need to tell Bryce the truth of things. He will understand."*

Deirdre waited for Michael to leave. Bryce turned and met her gaze. She took a step toward him. "'Tis sorry I am for all the pain I have caused you. I dinna mean for things tae turn oot as they did. I hope you will find forgiveness for me some day. I am sorry, Bryce. I never meant tae hurt you."

†††

His gut twisted. If only that were true. But how do you steal a signet ring, write a treasonous letter, and not mean that for evil? "Why did you do it, Deirdre? I just cannot understand why you would turn against me."

"I dinna turn on you, Bryce. When Finley saw I feared Mackenzie, he told me if I got the signet ring, he could have a missive sent tae my father tae keep him from returning tae Rosen Craig. I was so fearful of my father discovering I was there that I went in and took it. Finley assured me he would give it back tae me and you would never ken 'twas gone. But he lied tae me. He stole your ring and gave it tae Rothburg tae write that treasonous missive with your seal."

Bryce's head spun. She didn't write the letter that nearly cost him his life? "Did you not suspect Finley's untrustworthiness?" And even if she didn't write the letter, she stole from him, and she lied to him again. A lie of omission perhaps but still a lie. Something he couldn't live with, not after his fiancée's betrayal.

She stared at him with a look of consternation. "Nay, I dinna think aboot anything except what my father finding me meant." She sniffed. "And then tae find out he is a guid and loving man. I allowed fear tae guide my every action and every thought. I am fortunate that the Lord is forgiving and understands when I fail tae trust Him. Can you forgive me, Bryce?"

"Aye, lass, I forgive you. 'Tis glad I am that you were not the one who wrote the letter or hoped for my demise."

She seemed suddenly captivated by her hands. "Is there a chance for us…has this changed how you feel aboot me?"

He wished he could tell her otherwise. But he wouldn't lie to her.

†††

His eyes held pain. "Some things take time. I wish you well with your family. 'Tis glad I am that you have found them."

"Thank you. The Lord knew the desire of my heart, and he has given it to me."

Bryce nodded. "Aye, the desire of your heart. I trust you will have safe travels. Godspeed, Deirdre."

She swallowed the lump in her throat. How could leaving hurt so much when she was so anxious to meet her family? "Grammercy for all you have done for me. I shall never forget it." *Or you,* she whispered under her breath.

Deirdre walked out of Rosen Craig and to Storm. Her father lifted her to her palfrey much as he had when she was still his little lass. "Grammercy, Da." She glanced back to the entrance where Bryce now stood with arms folded in front of him. It seemed the desires of her heart had changed.

"Dinna fash yourself, Dearie. You are going home at last."

†††

Bryce sat on the dais breaking his morning fast. How empty his keep felt without the presence of Deirdre. He chastised himself for feeling anything for her. She would cause him no trouble where she went. A Scottish lass and an English lord were worlds apart. She had her loyalty, and he had his, and living on the border only widened the chasm between them.

Royce gave Bryce a nudge, drawing his attention. "Where are you?"

"Reliving all that has transpired."

"I will ride home to Hawkwood today and bring Pater and Lucas. I pray all is well with Brithwin and the babe. I

370

always hesitate to leave her since she lost the first babe."

"You will need to send word on how she fared without you. And again, when that momentous occasion happens. I wish to know if you have a son or a daughter."

Royce grinned. "Indeed. I look forward to the day I can. I do find comfort in that Penelope and Thomas arrived for a visit before I left. Thomas assured me he would remain and keep Brithwin from overdoing until I could return."

"Thomas is a good man." Bryce had met him a few times. The man had honor.

Bryce went in search of Lucas and found him sitting against the stone wall. "What say you, Lucas?"

The boy looked up. "I do not want to return to Hawkwood. Milady needs me."

"Nay, lad, Brithwin needs you now. Deirdre has her father and brothers to look after her. They will care for her."

His head drooped, and his bottom lip quivered. "But I will miss her."

Bryce squatted down on one knee and rested his forearm on his thigh. "I will as well, lad. 'Tis part of growing into a man. But she is where she needs to be."

He raised his head, and tears pooled in his eyes. "I do not like growing up, milord. It hurts too much."

Bryce reached out and drew the lad to him, enveloping him in his arms. He understood the ache the boy felt. And there was nothing that would help it except for time and staying too busy to think about it.

"Will I ever see her again?"

"I cannot answer that, Lucas. Only the good Lord knows. But I do know that Lady Brithwin and Lord Royce will need your help with the babe coming. And whether it is a boy or a girl, it will need a champion like you. You will be able to look after the child and keep it from harm's way. It will be your duty."

He pushed back and sniffed. Then wiped his eyes with the heels of his hands. "Milady is a good person just like

Lady Brithwin."

Bryce patted his head. "But Lady Brithwin is the one who needs you now, Lucas." He didn't have the heart to tell the lad that the two women were worlds apart.

Michael and Bryce saw off Royce, Pater, and Lucas. As much as he hated to admit it, he would miss the boy.

"Mother and I will depart in the morning. Are you sure you do not want to come with us?" Michael asked.

"Aye, I need to stay at Rosen Craig until Henry is crowned. I have lost it once. I do not plan to make it easy for someone to come in and take over again."

"I cannot believe I am about to become Lord of Wolves Forest. I did not think I would ever be more than a knight in the service of a lord. How quickly my life has changed."

"Aye, as did mine. You will do well, Michael. 'Twill be good to have a friend to the east of me and not a foe."

"'Tis still difficult to believe my father was Rothburg. Had I known that, I am not sure I could have killed him to save Henry. 'Tis probably best I was unaware."

Bryce smiled. "You would have done whatever you had to do. Do not doubt yourself, my friend." He slapped him on the back. "I am always here if you need me."

Bryce stared off toward Royce and his companions, who were fading from view. Royce rode home to a woman with unfailing loyalty and love, something Bryce began to think he would never have.

Chapter 48

October 1399

News came in the way of a missive. Richard abdicated the throne on September 30, and Henry's reign began. Bryce could breathe a sigh of relief for himself as well as for his brother and Michael.

Henry had ridden south, garnering support as he went. By the time Richard had sailed back to England from Ireland, it was too late. Henry had the backing he needed, and Richard gave up his throne.

With Richard no longer a threat, Bryce hoped he could live a peaceful life. Kincaid still sent reivers to his land. He'd sent his men up north to try to quell the trouble but had yet to make that ride himself. He had enough memories that troubled him without going to the borderland and stirring more.

He supposed he never really knew what love was with Clarice. That had been an arranged marriage. He'd grown to care for her. And he thought she had for him. They'd got along well. Her betrayal had been a lesion—a cut that had eventually healed. Today he felt nothing for her other than anger at himself for not seeing her for who she really was.

But Deirdre, he loved her. He loved her laugh, her smile, her walk, her delightful, spirited mind. And her betrayal still felt like a raw wound. She was all he could think about. He had to get her out of his mind.

Perhaps a trip to see his new nephew would do him some good. Now that Henry was securely on the throne, he could leave Rosen Craig and not concern himself about an attack from one of Richard's favorites.

From Royce's latest missive, Brithwin had the babe, though it had come early they were fine. The boy was small but Royce put his trust in the Lord that he would grow to be a strong warrior.

It was hard to believe everyone had been gone that long. Michael had made a couple of visits since he took over Wolves Forest. His mother's early experience with the place had been a blessing for him.

Bryce went to his solar and gathered things for the trip down to his brother's keep. Just the thought of getting out of Rosen Craig and away from the memories lightened his mood.

A knock at the door drew his attention. "Come in."

It was Ranald. "You have a visitor in the great hall."

Bryce followed his master-at-arms out of the room and headed to the great hall. It wasn't until his visitor turned around that Bryce recognized the man.

"Guid day tae you, Warwick." Laird Mackenzie strode toward him, extending his hand in friendship.

Bryce glanced around looking to see if he'd brought anyone with him. "Good day to you. What has brought you all this way?"

"I come tae you because my daughter is sick."

His heart stuttered. For him to come this far for help, she must be gravely ill. "My healer is very good. I can send her with you."

"I wish for you tae come as well." Mackenzie's gaze pleaded with him to say aye.

"Do you know what ails her?" He'd already begun gathering his things, but the travel was to get his mind off this lass, not to go visit her.

"She loses weight, does no' eat well, and is somewhat listless. She grows pale, and I worry she fades now that she has returned to me."

His chest constricted, stealing his breath. "When did you wish to leave?" His voice sounded weak even to himself.

"As soon as you and your healer can gather your things."

Bryce sent one of the servants to get Millicent while he went back upstairs to collect a few things for the trip. He would go see Royce upon his return. He had a feeling he would need to.

Millicent met them in the great hall, ready to travel. He was pleased to see her back to herself and no longer looking tired. They traveled to the northeast, away from where he'd first met Deirdre.

"Have you spoken with Kincaid since Deirdre has returned to you?"

"Nay. Me wife insists it will accomplish nothing. However, I know it will accomplish much." He grinned at Bryce. "But I am showing great restraint for the benefit of my wife and my daughter."

"What will you do? Surely you will not allow him no consequences."

"He will have charges brought against him, and 'tis possible that Deirdre will need tae testify."

"I would not tell her that until she is stronger."

"Nay, I have nay intention of doing that now."

They continued, Mackenzie quieter than Bryce remembered him.

"What does your healer say about Deirdre?"

"She has tried all that she kens tae do. That was when she sent me down tae Rosen Craig." He turned to Millicent. "Are you doing well?"

Millicent shifted on her horse. "Aye, I am still sitting upright, so all is well."

Mackenzie chuckled. "We are no' tae far now."

Bryce heard Millicent murmur something about thanks be to her Heavenly Father.

They'd been riding the whole day, pushing their horses to make good time. Millicent never complained.

Dusk was upon them. They crested a rise, and what lay before them was rolling hills of purple heather. The view was magnificent. And on the adjacent hill sat Mackenzie's keep. The lass would never want for anything living there.

They rode on the ridge overlooking the blankets of heather. Bryce determined he could wake every morning to this view.

Mackenzie stopped his horse at the wall gate. "Welcome to Ermine Castle." He flicked his horse's reins and rode in. "My youngest children." He motioned to a young lass chasing after her brother. Both had hair as red as Deirdre's. "And my older boys." He pointed to two young men with auburn hair examining the blade of a sword.

The laird took Millicent in to see Deirdre while Bryce cared for his horse. He finished and was met by Mackenzie as he headed toward the manor. "Come meet my wife."

Bryce had barely stepped in the house when a woman came toward them.

"Ah, there she is." A woman stopped before them. "My dear, I would like you to meet Laird Warwick. He is the one who rescued our little Dearie."

Rescued? Had Deirdre told her father that?

"'Tis guid tae finally meet you."

"Good eventide, Lady Mackenzie. 'Tis good to meet Deirdre's mother." He could see where Deirdre got her bright red hair as well as her two youngest siblings.

"I understand you saved my daughter's life on many occasions. I must thank you for that."

"I really did nay more than anyone would do."

"'Tis no' what our daughter has told us. She speaks vera well of you, sir."

"She is very kind."

"Are you hungry?"

"Aye, we could use food." Mackenzie answered for him. "And when Millicent finishes with Dearie, the healer will need food, too."

Soon after they finished, Millicent returned.

"How is she? Can you help her?" Bryce stood and helped Millicent with her chair.

She gave him that knowing smile she had given him since she took him in and brought him back from the brink of death. "Aye, I believe she will soon recover."

"'Tis wonderful news," Lady Mackenzie exclaimed. "We had hoped this was the answer."

Bryce turned to Deirdre's father. "May I go see her?"

"I will take him, *dearling*." Lady Mackenzie stood and guided Bryce down the same hall Millicent had just come from, stopping by a door.

Bryce entered the solar to find Deirdre sitting in a gold tapestry chair, her legs tucked up under her. He smiled to himself, seeing the familiar way she always sat.

She lifted heavy eyes and blinked. "Bryce?"

He strode into the room. "Aye, 'tis me."

"What are you doing here?"

"I heard you were unwell. I came with Millicent. You did not think I would let her come here without me." She *had* lost weight, and her face was pale. She'd looked so healthy when she'd been at Rosen Craig.

"You came here for me?" She swallowed. "After all the pain and grief I have caused you?"

"I do not wish any ill against you, lass." He wished her anything but that.

"I have missed you vera much. Will you be staying long?"

"Lass, I forgive you, and I am trying to understand, but on the morrow I must leave. Millicent tells me you should recover, and I am pleased to hear this. Perchance you will feel well enough to break your fast with us before we head on our way."

He hoped he'd put it to her in the gentlest of ways, that there was no hope for them. That the kiss he'd given her no longer meant anything to him.

She glanced up at him, tears pooling in her eyes. "You are vera kind, Bryce. May God be with you and bless you."

There seemed finality in her words. But wasn't that what he'd just told her? There was no chance of anything more than what they had this very moment?

His chest constricted, as though he'd fallen from his

horse and every ounce of air had been knocked from him. He wanted to tell her nothing had changed, but it had. He couldn't get out of his mind the betrayals of the women he'd cared for and what they had nearly cost him. "It has been a pleasure getting to know you, lass."

Chapter 49

With that, he walked out and shut her door, but not before he saw the glimmer of a tear slide down her cheek.

When Bryce returned to the great hall, he found everyone gathered there. He discovered he was just as uncomfortable as he'd been with Deirdre. He sat down, and everyone looked his way, saying not a thing. He smiled.

"She has lost much weight." Bryce stated what was obvious to all and part of what had brought him here.

"Aye." Deirdre's mother responded. "She has no' had much of an appetite."

Bryce nodded in understanding.

Mackenzie leaned forward. "How did she seem?"

Bryce frowned. If they were concerned enough to have him come and bring Millicent, hadn't they gone in to see their daughter today? "She seemed well, I believe."

"Did she seem in guid spirits?" Mackenzie inquired.

"I would not say so."

"Was she no' happy tae see you, Bryce?"

"She seemed pleased, aye."

"What did she say?" Mackenzie shot another question at him.

Bryce was becoming annoyed with his host's questions. "She asked for my forgiveness."

"And you gave it tae her, aye?" Mackenzie reminded him of Lucas when the lad wanted something.

"Aye, I did. I do not wish to see the lass suffering like she is."

An uncomfortable silence ensued. Bryce broke it. "I will leave on the morrow. If you feel it necessary, I can leave Millicent with you for a sennight."

"Leaving?" Deirdre's mother spoke up. "Why would you leave Millicent here?"

Bryce cocked his head. Was there something going on

that he was not aware? "For Deirdre? If you feel she still needs a healer, I can leave her."

"Oh." Deirdre's mother almost seemed surprised by his answer.

Bryce stood. "If you will excuse me, I believe I could use some rest. Where would you have me sleep?"

Mackenzie guided him toward the room he would be sleeping in. Bryce followed, feeling like they knew something he did not. He would pray for Deirdre, that her illness was not more serious than he believed.

Bryce lay on the bed, with his hands folded behind his neck, wishing sleep would take him. But it eluded him. His gut felt like it did much before battle, tumultuous. He punched down the pillow and threw his body to his side. He would never get to sleep if he couldn't get Deirdre off his mind. She was like the aroma of baking sweets that drew him to the kitchen to see, and once he laid eyes on them, he could not get his mind off them until their satisfaction was his to taste, to enjoy. Like he had her sweet kiss....

Seeing Deirdre only increased the agony he'd been in since she moved back to Scotland to be with her family. He loved her, his heart ached for her, but he couldn't be with her.

He climbed out of bed and paced the floor to pass the time and hoped to tire himself enough for sleep to come calling. However, the only thing that came calling was a vision of a redheaded Scottish lass.

Lord, I did as You have commanded us to do. I forgave Deirdre. Now please ease my heart and mind.

But in his spirit, he knew the truth.

He had said the words *I forgive you,* but no more. The words were just that, words. They didn't come from his heart.

Truly forgiving her meant reconciliation and opening himself to vulnerability...again—and that frightened him. He believed she was sorry and that she regretted what she'd done. He'd seen the fear that lived in Deirdre when he'd met her. She'd never known security. She had always had to look out for herself. Fear could cause a person to do a lot of things. And he'd witnessed the terror in her eyes when she'd seen Mackenzie.

He spun on his heel and walked back across the room. *Trust.*

The word could not have been clearer had Michael spoken in the room. But he was alone, and it wasn't Michael. *Trust Me.*

Trust God? For Deirdre? Releasing everything into the Lord's hands and trusting Him to take care of things was more frightening than going into battle. At least in battle he had some control over his destiny and outcome. It was a frightening thing to leave everything in God's hands.

But hadn't he given his life to the Lord? And trusting Him was part of it. He took a deep breath and knew what he had to do. He had to forgive as he was forgiven, and he had to trust the Lord to guide him through this labyrinth.

With his decision to trust and forgive made, each step he took exchanged the emptiness and turmoil inside him for calm.

He went to the bed and stretched out. On the morrow he would speak with Deirdre. And the next thing he heard was the chirping of birds.

Streams of light sliced across the room. Bryce swung his feet to the floor, slipped into his clothes, and went to the bowl to splash water on his face.

Dressed and ready to head down for the day, he took a deep breath. First thing he needed to do was speak to Mackenzie. Then he would go see Deirdre before he did any other thing. See if she would forgive him for being a fool.

Bryce hustled down the steps. He turned to go into the great hall where a good many men were already breaking their fast. Bryce glanced toward the dais, saw Mackenzie, and strode toward him.

Mackenzie gestured to a chair beside him, and Bryce sat. "You look tae be in a hurry this morn. I hope tis no' my hospitality."

"Nay, Mackenzie. I wish to speak with you about an urgent matter." Bryce's heart pounded in his chest. He was more nervous now than when he faced ten men in battle.

Bryce swallowed.

The laird's brow drew down into a *V*. "What is this urgent matter? Is there more trouble on the borderland that I dinna ken aboot?"

"Nay, nay. Nothing of that nature. I wish to speak with you about your daughter. I wish to ask for her hand in marriage."

"Ah, is that so? You have had a change of heart, aye? As I recall last night, you were heading home this morn."

Bryce ignored his goading. "You know I will treat her well, and she will have a happy home with all she needs and wants. That is, if she will have me."

"And I will agree tae the union," Mackenzie added.

"Aye, I would prefer your blessing on the marriage." Bryce would not be intimidated by Deirdre's father.

Mackenzie raised a brow. "Perhaps we could have peace on the border then, eh?"

Bryce grinned. "If I can keep your daughter from reiving your land."

"Methinks you mean if you can keep *your wife* from reiving my land."

"I will take that as an aye." A sense of relief filled Bryce.

"I dinna think I really have a choice in the matter. That daughter of mine is vera headstrong. She will do what she has set her mind tae do."

"You are not telling me anything I have not learned firsthand. And now if you will excuse me, I have a lass I would like to speak to."

Bryce left without breaking his fast and walked toward

Deirdre's room, his heart hammering in his chest. How could a wee redheaded lass cause him so much angst?

When he reached her room, he knocked on the door. Lady Mackenzie opened it. "Bryce, 'tis guid tae see you come by this morning. I fashed you had gone on your way."

"Good morn. May I speak with your daughter?"

She glanced behind her where Deirdre sat. "Come in."

Bryce nodded and stepped in the room. Deirdre smiled, but it didn't reach her eyes. Bryce's gut twisted.

"Are you well enough to go for a stroll, Deirdre?"

"Aye. It sounds lovely." Deirdre stood, and Bryce's heart squeezed. She'd lost so much weigh her dress looked several sizes too large.

He gave her his arm, and they strolled out and down the hall. "Have you broken your fast this morn?"

"Aye, Mother nearly sat on me until I ate some of what she brought. Father is right aboot her. She is a vera strong woman."

Bryce laughed. "Your father says the same of you." It was good to hear her talk about her family. He waited until they got outside. The air was warm, the sky blue, and the sun shone. A beautiful day. God smiled on it.

"He does, does he? 'Tis sure I am he has nay room tae talk."

"I think I would agree with you."

She cocked her head and looked up at him as they strolled. "I thought you may have left for Rosen Craig. 'Tis glad I am that you came tae see me before you left."

"I must ask you to forgive me, Deirdre. I have been a fool to not see what has been before me. Can you forgive me?"

A tinkling of laughter came from her. "Bryce, I dinna ken of what you speak. I am the one who needed tae seek forgiveness. You have been nothing but kind tae me."

Bryce stopped and turned toward her, grasping both her hands in his. "Deirdre, I would like to put the past behind us and start anew. Could we do that?"

She swallowed. "I would be vera happy tae."

"That makes me happy as well."

"I shall never forget the mercy you have bestowed on me, Bryce."

"I would be happy to remind you of it every morn if you would marry me."

Deirdre stared at him. "You are asking *me*?"

"Aye, lass, will you do me the honor and marry me?"

†††

Deirdre's knees nearly gave way beneath her and would have if Bryce hadn't tightened his grip on her hands, giving her support. Marry him? Had she really heard him right? Bryce Warwick wanted her to be his wife. God truly did give the desires of one's heart.

She smiled up at him. "Aye, I will. I am the one who is honored."

Bryce picked her up and swung her around before letting her feet come back to the grass. He lowered his head and brushed his lips against hers. He was gentle, and his lips lingered on hers until whistles sounded in the bailey. Bryce pulled back and grinned.

"That was not very chivalrous of me."

Deirdre's faced burned. She peeked up at Bryce, who did not seem the least bit troubled by all the hooting and whistling going on. "Shall we tell my parents before they hear about this?"

"'Tis not a bad idea, lass. I fear your father would not approve of my behavior."

"Nor mine." Deirdre giggled. Within the space of a minute, her heart had gone from broken to near bursting with joy.

As they walked in to speak with her parents, Bryce turned to her. "I would marry you as soon as the banns are read. Truth be told, I would purchase a license to marry you now, but since you have recently found your parents, I do not wish to take you away before you are ready."

She would miss her parents, to be sure, and her brothers and sister who she'd only begun to get to know. But one thing the death of her friends, and even the loss of her family at a young age had taught her was that no day was promised. She would miss her parents and the siblings she hardly knew. But their lives would continue, and she would come back to see them. And they could visit her at Rosen Craig. She would marry Bryce now and enjoy every day they had with each other. She would not take one day for granted, for she had never believed she would have the privilege of marrying for love.

"I am ready tae marry. I dinna need tae wait. I have missed you, Bryce." Her heart swelled as she confessed her feelings.

Bryce pulled the large wooden door open and gestured for her to enter, and he followed. "Then we will tell your father."

"Tell me what?" her father asked.

Deirdre hadn't seen her father standing in the entrance.

"That your daughter has agreed to marry me."

Her father stepped forward and stuck out his hand. "Congratulations, Bryce. You could no' have found a better bride."

"Aye, I agree with you, sir."

"Remember, you are taking something from me that is vera precious and I have lost once. I ken you will be guid tae her. I had better no' hear anything other." Her father threatened. And she had no doubt he meant every word of it.

"You do not have to concern yourself with that. I will treat Deirdre with the respect she deserves."

Her father turned to her and wrapped his arms around her. "'Tis happy I am for you, daughter. But 'tis sad for me and your mother. We just got you back after all those years. I wish you had fallen in love with a Scot and no' an Englishman." He pulled back and winked at her. "You need tae return for visits."

"I will, I promise."

†††

Six months later

Deirdre grinned at Brithwin. Between feeling well, the beautiful day, and Brithwin's babe of six months being fussed over by Nog and Millicent, Deirdre was determined to get her and Brithwin away for the day. "He forgets who his wife is. I will gain his attention."

She snatched her bow and a single arrow off the wall and dashed for the stairs that would lead her to the castle wall-walk. How dare he tell her to stay put and then ignore her protests. And how dare he not believe her when she told him she felt well enough to hunt.

She slipped out the door and over to the steps leading to the castle wall-walk. Three steps up, and the cumbersome gown nearly sent her back down from whence she came. She grasped the gown in her free hand and hiked up the fabric, showing her snowy white calves. She glanced around, making sure no men could see her dress pulled so high.

Once on the wall-walk, Deirdre made her way to the spot she needed. Dropping her gown back over her bare legs, she reached for the arrow and nocked it to the bowstring. Spreading her feet to shoulder-width, she turned toward her target. Her husband stood near the stables, and all his men stood to his left. Her three fingers lightly held the arrow on the string. She raised the bow and drew back the string as she took her aim.

Holding the string taut, her fingers gently touched her face as Bryce gave orders, and she willed herself not to tremble. She took an account once again of where each man was, including her husband. She'd take no chances. She relaxed her fingers as she released the arrow from her grasp. The arrow soared and hit its target, the black knot in the stable wall. Bryce's head jerked up as his men on reflex surrounded him. Metal scraping metal met her ears as the men drew their swords while searching for the enemy.

Bryce's gaze moved up to the wall and latched on to Deirdre. "Woman, you trying to kill me?" he bellowed.

Deirdre rolled her eyes and drew herself up to her full height before lifting her chin. The cool breeze blew through her red locks, sending her hair into disarray. "If I had wanted to kill you, Bryce Warwick, I assure you that arrow would not be ten feet away and in the center of that knot."

He walked over and plucked the arrow from the building. Oh, how she wanted to lean forward to get a better look at the expression on his face as he ran his fingers down the arrow. But she would not move, for he had not taken his eyes off her since he pulled it out, and she would not chance him thinking she wavered.

His fingers reached the tip of the arrow and still his gaze did not shift from hers. "You have made your point, wife." He tossed the arrow to one of his men. "And the answer is still the same. You will stay."

He turned and strode to Tempest as the men sheathed their swords. Royce was laughing, and she'd have given anything to hear what he had said to his brother.

Bryce stopped and turned toward the wall stairs and what she could only assume was her. She rushed off the walk to meet him, not sure of how this new husband of hers would react to her method of objection.

She reached the bottom of the stairs and nearly ran into him. His hands grasped her shoulders, not as a man showing his strength, but gently. He looked down and their gazes met.

"My sweet and stubborn wife, the answer is still nay."

"But I have told you, Bryce, I am well. I wish tae go on the hunt."

"I am sure Brithwin would prefer your company."

"Brithwin will come as well. You have kept me from doing anything since we married."

"You have barely increased in weight. And need I remind you that you have not felt well for the past month.

You need to gain your strength."

Deirdre folded her arms in front of her, dangling the bow off her finger. "I am strong and in guid health. We will have a shooting contest tae prove it. And if I win, you must let Brithwin and me go with you."

Bryce laughed. "And what do I get if I win?"

Deirdre thought for a minute. "I will tell you my secret."

Bryce cocked an eyebrow at her. "You keep secrets from me?"

"Aye, I have one."

He nodded. "I will play your game, Deirdre."

Brithwin peeked out the door and Deirdre motioned for her to follow. She could use an ally.

Bryce gave some orders to his men and went to retrieve his bow.

"Do you think you can beat him, Deirdre?" Brithwin asked.

"I have no' seen him shoot, but I am vera guid with a bow. I do no' miss where I aim." She grinned at Brithwin. "And I have nothing tae lose. He was no' going tae allow us tae go, anyway. And I had planned on telling him my secret this very night."

Brithwin giggled. "I do like the way you think."

Bryce returned with his bow. "Where is our object?"

Royce walked over to the stable and pointed to a small white dot of wax pressed into wood.

"Let us get this over quickly." Bryce strode a great distance from the stable, where the wax could not be easily seen. "Would you like to go first?"

Deirdre cocked her head. "Do you fash yourself that I am better?"

"Nay, I do not. I know you are good with the bow. I have seen you take down a deer, and I pulled the arrow from the knot in the wood. But you underestimate your husband, wife. I only do this to appease you."

He would not beat her. She took her stance with feet

apart, drew the line back until her hand touched her cheek. She steadied herself as she took aim on the small piece of wax. She let go of the string, and the arrow whizzed through the air.

"She hit it!" Royce yelled. "And near the center."

Deirdre smirked at Bryce.

He chuckled. "'Twas a very good shot. One to be proud of, but you have not won yet."

Bryce took his stance, and silence fell as he pulled back the string, taking aim. He released the arrow.

Hooting broke the quiet.

Bryce bowed slightly and put out his arm for Deirdre. "Shall we see who won this match?"

Royce stood in front of the arrow that still remained. "Before I reveal who won, do either of you wish to withdraw? Once I step aside, the loser must fulfill thy promise."

Deirdre giggled. "I have naught tae lose. I believe I shall wait tae see who won."

Bryce folded his arms and shook his head. "I do not quit."

Royce grinned. He seemed to be enjoying dragging out announcing the winner. "Do either of you wish to guess?"

The truth was even the wind could have caused an arrow to go a little high or a little low if it blew at the right time. But a good marksman took that into account as best he could.

"Enough, Royce. Let us see who the victor is. I wish to get on with this hunt."

"Ah, but the question is, will your lovely wife be accompanying you?"

"Royce." Bryce used a warning tone.

Royce laughed and stepped aside.

Deirdre's excitement fell. Bryce's arrow could not have been any closer to the center. He had won.

"Well, my dear wife, methinks you will be making a confession to me," Bryce prodded.

"Aye, when you return from your hunt, I will tell you." She took a step toward Brithwin and looked back over her shoulder at her husband. "You are vera guid with the bow."

Bryce grinned. "I have never lost a competition with a bow."

Brithwin spoke up. "That was not fair. You should have told her that."

"But I did not choose bows. My wife did that."

"Come, Brithwin, I will show you Cathal, if I can find her. She has become quite the hunter." She slipped her arm around Brithwin's as they began their walk back to the keep.

Bryce let out a heavy sigh behind her. "If I allow you to come, Deirdre, you must promise you will not exert yourself or go chasing after the prey. You will let my men do that."

Deirdre squealed and ran to Bryce, throwing her arms around him. "Thank you! I promise I will do as you wish."

Bryce yelled to the stableman. "Ready a horse for my wife and Lady Brithwin."

"You still owe me a secret." Bryce smiled before quickly stealing a kiss.

†††

Bryce entered his solar. The hunt had gone well, and they returned with two stags and a boar. To Bryce's surprise, Deirdre didn't bring her bow. She and Brithwin had followed along at a leisurely pace, talking and watching the hunt.

Sometimes he did not understand this wife of his. Bryce took a seat next to Deirdre, putting his arm around her shoulders.

"You have a secret you wish to tell me?" Bryce asked.

"Aye, I do. But I should inform you that I had planned tae tell you even if I had won today."

"Is that so? And what is this secret you have kept from me?" As he waited for Deirdre to tell him her secret, he had no concerns, only curiosity.

Deirdre tucked her feet beneath her and snuggled under his arm. "I spoke with Millicent today."

"Does this have anything to do with your secret, or do you delay telling me?"

"It does. The healer said I am no' sick, but given a few months, I will be much improved."

"'Tis good news. What is this that ails you, love?"

"I am tae have a babe. 'Twill be a Christmas babe."

"A babe? We will have a child? This is why you have not felt well?"

She nodded. "Aye, 'tis the wee one."

Bryce wrapped his other arm around her and drew her to him. His heart was full. God had indeed given him all the desires of his heart. He looked into the eyes of the woman he loved. The woman he trusted. He leaned down and kissed her, savoring the response from her. He pulled back and looked into her eyes. "I hope the babe is a girl and just like you, sweet, stubborn, and full of mischief. But if it is a boy methinks we should name him Gavin."

Thank you for reading SWORD OF TRUST! I hope you enjoyed Bryce and Deirdre and the supporting characters. If you haven't read book one in the **Winds of Change Series**, pick up **SWORD OF FORGIVENESS**, and find out how Brithwin is forced to marry Royce, a man who thinks she is responsible for his parents' murders!

There are two novellas in the **Winds of Change Series.** Each give a minor character his own story. Discover how Thomas finds his happily-ever-after in **SWORD OF THE MATCHMAKER** and Phillip in **THE PERFECT BRIDE.**

If nineteenth century is a time period you like, try BRIDE BY BLACKMAIL set in Charleston, SC with a quick witted Scot and a strong willed southern belle. Also, **SHATTERED MEMORIES** is set during the 1886 Charleston Earthquake where having amnesia could get one killed.

One of the best ways to let me know you enjoyed *Sword of Trust* and say "thank you" is to write a favorable review on Amazon, Bookbub, Goodreads as well as other sites! Thank you so much!

I love hearing from my readers. If you have any comments or questions please feel free to contact me at debbielynnecostello@hotmail.com.

Catch me online at:
My website: DebbieLynneCostello.com
Facebook: https://www.facebook.com/debbielynnecostello
Amazon Author: Amazon.com: Debbie Lynne Costello: Books, Biography, Blog, Audiobooks, Kindle

IF YOU'D LIKE TO KNOW WHEN I HAVE A NEW BOOK OUT SIGN UP FOR MY NEWSLETTER:
https://mailchi.mp/276616916748/debbielynnecostello

Debbie Lynne Costello has been writing since the young age of eight. She went to college for journalism. She enjoys medieval settings and stories set in nineteenth century Charleston, South Carolina. She loves the Lord and hopes to touch people's lives through her stories. Debbie Lynne lives in the beautiful state of South Carolina with her husband of 35 years, their four children, Tennessee Walking horses, Arabians, miniature donkey, four dogs, and a cat.